THE
DESTINY MEDALLION
CONSPIRACY

A Jonah Blackstone Novel by
JOHN DARR
BOOK FOUR

A special thanks Lisa Styles, a wonderful youth counselor and friend, who read the first drafts and provided timely advice and feedback.

Thank you to my friends, who's constant inquiries about the status of the novel kept me motivated during this long journey.

Last, I dedicate this fourth novel of the series to all those who've held back, afraid show the world their unique gifts. Walk in your power!

– John Darr

Table of Contents

"Choice is a burden, one you can't escape," Deyanira cautioned. "You're going to uncover more hard truths about the people around you, young Blackstone."

CHAPTER ONE
DARK RITUALS

Dark clouds blotted out the evening sky and a light rain fell on the abandoned brick and stone building stretching across the hillside. The structure's windows were shattered, with only jagged pieces of glass hanging from rusted metal mesh coverings.

Faded paint chipped away from weathered bricks and the rotted, wooden front doors gave the building the aura of a haunted house. The property's weathered sign read *Central Georgia Mental Hospital*. The evening was eerily quiet until…

The air stirred, and a split formed over the pockmarked street. The rip in the very fabric of reality expanded in length, swelling into a circular vortex that repelled the rain. Finally, the bright circle stabilized, revealing a lone figure in a dark green traveling cloak.

Jennifer Motombu stepped through the vortex. After a quick wave of her slender hand to close the magical opening, she pulled the cloak's hood forward and approached the old hospital's high gate. She removed a talisman from a pocket. It was a crude metal circle with an all-seeing eye at the center.

Holding the talisman high, she waved it near the gate, which unlocked and swung open. Jennifer entered before the gate finished moving, and ignoring the cracked concrete sidewalk, she angled toward a weather-beaten statue of an angel instead.

Less than half a dozen steps inside the compound, Grim Hounds padded into view, growling and exposing double rows of razor-sharp teeth.

The doglike creatures were from the Underworld and vicious, yet the beasts kept their distance when she waved the talisman at them.

"I'm expected," she hissed.

As the creatures backed away, Jennifer turned back to the statue of the angel. Stowing the talisman beneath her cloak again, she took a breath and stepped through the statue's base—a mirage.

All at once, a set of steps to a tunnel appeared. Peering into the dim opening, Jennifer shivered, wondering why the Rasmussens had summoned her here?

Was it about her cousin? She feared that was the case as she descended into the passageway. At the end of the tunnel, rough-hewn steps led up into the building's old lobby. That's when an echoing scream reached her ears. *Antwan!*

Hurrying through the decayed lobby, she nearly tripped while running along the debris-strewn hallway. Years of dirt, dust, discarded files, rotted wood, and other things clogged the floors.

Another piercing scream caused Jennifer to wince as she reached the doorway to an old operating theater. She shoved the door open, ignoring the squeak of rusted metal hinges, and rushed inside.

Antwan lay on a bare table, bound at his wrists and ankles with thick straps. Sweat coated her cousin's face and head, and deep spots stained his pale orange shirt at the armpits and chest. Tremors gripped his body and he groaned.

Beside him, floating inches above a second table, was the energy-wrapped body of Fabian Rasmussen, a KIN. The beefy, dark-complexioned Reaper had a head of thick, curly black hair. He wore a black tunic and pants, much like the blue tunics the Alliance Mages wore. The sorcerer's levitated body trembled and strange ripples played along his arms and legs.

Antwan sucked in a ragged breath before he screamed again. Every time his body writhed in pain, awful, bruised skin showed beneath the restraints. He must have been here for some time, she decided. Finally, Antwan slumped into relative quiet. His chest heaved up and down, and his breaths were labored.

As she took a step toward the table, a cold voice called out.

"Ah, there you are, Apprentice." Thera Rasmussen stood on the observation balcony. Like her twin brother Fabian, she too wore the black tunic and pants, but she had on her red Reaper's cloak with the hood thrown back, exposing her face and unruly maroon curls.

Faint scars crisscrossed her face from the ritualistic cuts all KIN sported in the Afterworld. The crossing-over process could never fully hide evidence of the practice.

With a start, Jennifer realized Thera wasn't alone. A ghostly visitor stood nearby. Though the form wavered from the spell used to bring him here, Jennifer recognized the Alliance Mole by his short stature.

"Your cousin is resisting Fabian and causing himself unbearable pain," Thera said to Jennifer, slipping into her Eastern European accent, a sign of her agitation. "Speak to him."

At that moment, Antwan's body jerked again and he lifted his head to look at her, but it wasn't Antwan's face. Fabian's ghost marred her cousin's features. "Talk to him, girl, before he ruins the test!" The voice came out with a strange mix of European and African accents.

With everyone's eyes on her, she moved to the table. "Let me speak to my cousin," she said in a steady voice, thankful the travel cloak hid her shudders.

Fabian's features dissolved, leaving Antwan's familiar face visible. Her cousin's deep brown eyes stared at her. "Help me."

Gripping his hand, she squeezed it and leaned close. "I will, but for now, stop resisting. It'll be over soon." She tried to whisper this but also knew the others could hear everything. "Please, try to relax, cousin."

Brave words, Jennifer thought to herself. She wasn't the one under a forced possession. At least not yet.

"Why are you worried about possessing the boy?" the Alliance Mole asked Thera. "The Wraiths don't have this much trouble."

"It's not about the possession," Thera said with strained patience. "And we are not Wraiths."

The mole made an impatient sound, but another wail from Antwan cut his comment short. This one sounded less intense to Jennifer, as if her cousin was trying to give in.

"When we cross over," Thera said into the sudden silence, "the process wraps our spirit in a mortal body." She gestured to Fabian's floating body. "My spell allows us to maintain that temporary body while our spirit possesses a willing mortal."

"Yes, yes." The mole sounded testy at her chiding tone. "If the spell doesn't work, you're trapped here, in the mortal's body."

"No. Our souls are lost," Thera hissed.

Jennifer suppressed a gasp. She had never known this and wondered that Thera would reveal such a weakness to the devious mole. He was a fallen one, a former supernatural who gave up Afterworld duties in exchange for a permanent mortal existence again. Thera and Fabian were real Reapers and as KIN, members of the Grim Reaper's inner circle, they hated mortals and would never give up their station.

But they served their master, and he required them to interact with mortals from time to time, hence the need to cross over, gaining a temporary mortal body. What Jennifer couldn't understand was why Thera sought a way to prolong the time she could remain in the mortal realm.

Glancing at Fabian's floating body, Jennifer's eyes widened because she finally recognized the significance of the strange waves rolling across it. Without his soul inside, Fabian's temporary mortal body would decay and dissolve the same way a dead Grim Hound's body dissolved into ectoplasm and disappeared. Thera's spell delayed that process.

"I don't understand why you bother at all," the mole said.

The man's nagging question mirrored Jennifer's doubts. She gazed at the observation area while stroking her cousin's trembling hand.

The Alliance traitor had moved toward the balcony railing. "It seems the spell is a waste of time, considering you'll have to cross back anyway."

"There are some objects we can't touch, even in a temporary mortal body. But if I possessed a true mortal with an affinity to touch and use an object like a Protector's Ring," Thera stated, her voice full of confidence as she turned to look at Jennifer, "I could overcome that ancient restriction."

"You mean the Destiny Medallion?" The mole's voice betrayed his shock. "I warned you the medallion on display in the museum is a fake," he said. "It's an Alliance trap."

"We are aware of the risk, traitor," Thera responded, "and have prepared." Her right hand had curled into a fist, like she wanted to hex the mole. "Having the fake medallion and the Tales will ensure we find the real Destiny Medallion."

The mole stirred. "The Tales are locked away. The Council's afraid I'll find a way to steal them. It's actually delicious to see the confusion and distrust I'm creating."

"That may be," Thera answered. "But no matter the distrust you've produced, even I know the Alliance Council wants to decipher the ancient book. That means they'll make it available to the boy. Unless your intel was flawed."

"My information is accurate. The Alliance can't fathom how I obtain my information from the primary sources," the mole answered, sounding smug yet offended at the suggestion. "They'll give the brat a copy."

"You had better be right," Thera warned, "because I'll bring the Alliance to their knees when my plan works. The Grim Reaper will honor my brother and me above all other KIN."

"But..." the mole stuttered. "You have someone?"

Thera turned her possessive gaze from Jennifer and merely grinned at the mole before moving to the rail. "Leave him, brother," she called out. "I've seen enough."

Fabian's spirit detached from Antwan and returned to his own shuddering body. The sorcerer's eyes fluttered open, and he sucked in deep breaths as the spell holding him aloft dissipated, lowering him to the table. An attendant rushed forward from the doorway and helped the sorcerer to stand. Fabian snarled at Antwan as he staggered from the room.

Thera and the mole disappeared, leaving Jennifer alone with Antwan. She began opening her cousin's restraints. When she finished, she pulled out a small bottle of deep green liquid from a hidden pouch. Removing the stopper, Jennifer poured a little bit on her fingertips while muttering under her breath. Antwan let out a sigh of relief when she touched her fingertips to his skin.

Working on one bruised wrist at a time, she applied the thick liquid in tight, circular motions. The concoction glowed for a few seconds and a faint scent of jasmine wafted through the air.

Once she completed the last ankle, she helped Antwan off the table. He almost collapsed, but she managed to lay him down on a discarded, dirty pad. She sat on one end, ignoring the filthiness around them, and cradled his head in her lap.

"It's okay," she whispered to her cousin in a soothing tone. "I won't let her do this to you again."

Deep inside, Jennifer knew she could never stop Thera. Maybe one day, when she became a full sorceress, she'd have the power to protect her cousin and herself. In truth, her actions in Mount Vernon had come under fierce scrutiny. Although the mole had heeded her warning about Jonah's power and had saved his butt, the odious man had also moved to shield himself from the Grim Reaper's fury. She'd been sacrificed instead, and shunned, like Deyanira, until Thera had summoned her.

Jennifer didn't know why the twins needed her; certainly not for her powers. Hers seemed so meager when compared to theirs. So why did Thera place so much value on her? Was it an insult to her former mentor, Deyanira? Or was it because of Jonah Blackstone? Did they expect her to persuade the boy to change sides?

Yet Jonah Blackstone had helped her.

"You did it to save your cousins," Jennifer whispered, hating her moment of doubt.

Antwan groaned and opened his eyes, thinking she spoke to him.

"Relax," she said. Her hate for Jonah overshadowed any doubts about his motives. Deyanira's failure and imprisonment were his fault. Now, Jennifer served the

Rasmussen twins and her cousin suffered. Didn't she have the right to protect her family? Of course she did.

Jennifer realized she'd have to make a name for herself first. What better way than to defeat Jonah Blackstone and show that he wasn't so special after all?

THE
DESTINY MEDALLION
CONSPIRACY

BOOK FOUR

CHAPTER TWO

THE MOUNT VERNON SOCIAL CLUB

The Wraith was pissed. That's the only word Jonah had to describe the way the disembodied spirit smashed against the bedroom walls. Thanks to his best friend, Mike Littleton, glowing sigils covered every surface, preventing the enraged spirit from escaping.

As a result, when not hitting the walls, the Wraith buzzed around the room's ceiling. Jonah's clients, an older couple, huddled on the large bed. The wife's arms wrapped protectively around her bedridden husband whose body jerked in the throes of a fevered delirium.

The room reeked of sweat, vomit, and other smells Jonah tried to shut out. It's one reason he had stationed the other members of the Mount Vernon Social Club outside the bedroom. There was no need to sicken them. But he could sympathize with the couple because he had suffered the same ordeal.

When he was just seven, his deranged aunt had subjected him to the horror of forced Wraith possession. Even at seven, he had been more powerful than anyone expected and resisted until his mom could save him.

Sure, his current client had chosen possession, but Jonah's chest burned with righteous anger toward the Wraith. If not for their plan to catch the spirit, he would have banished it back to the Underworld.

"We're ready," Wick's voice said over Jonah's earbud.

Here goes. Jonah flung open the sigil-covered bedroom door. The powerful Wraith let out a screech of ethereal rage, roared out the bedroom door, and careened down the darkened hallway. It banged against the walls, leaving old portraits dangling askew or sending them crashing to the floor.

"Stay here, ma'am." Jonah warned the shocked woman and fled after the spirit. Up ahead, the apparition rounded a corner, followed by a shriek of surprise.

Jonah hurried to the bend in the hallway in time to see his cousin, Robert Hightower, swiping at the spirit with iron blades. Despite his cousin's resistance to learning to use the weapons, Robert sliced the Wraith, forcing it to veer away.

On the second-floor landing, the Wraith shot toward a large window, only to slam into a blue magical barrier. The thwarted spirit changed directions and swooped down toward the first floor next. Jonah reached the railing and started for the stairs.

Lynn Hightower, Robert's twin sister, waited below in the atrium, appearing defenseless as planned. The Wraith shot straight for her, trying to scare Jonah's cousin into dodging aside. But Lynn stood her ground and raised a pair of pure iron blades at the last minute. She cut the Wraith twice, causing the spirit to roar in pain and roll sideways to avoid more strikes.

Jonah reached the atrium and activated real Reaper blades. The Wraith reacted with fear and fled down the main hallway toward the rear exit. That wouldn't work either, because Wick had placed himself in the middle of the hall. Jonah watched with anticipation and a little trepidation. *This better work.*

Wick held a bottle decorated with Angelic symbols. He had called it a Spirit Bottle, but with the shapes cut out of the rounded surface, it reminded Jonah of a jack-o'-lantern. If you put a candle inside, the light would flicker through the designs. Wick's shaking arm betrayed his fear, but he proved brave in facing a dangerous spirit.

"Die mortal! *Dieeeee!*" The Wraith roared. Jonah knew Wick, as a young mage and part supernatural, could hear the spirit's words.

As the Wraith's essence affected the magical barrier generated by the bottle, something strange happened. Like water spiraling down a drain, the bottle sucked the spirit inside and the sigils flared with bright, orange light.

Jonah skidded to a stop in front of Wick, who struggled to hold on to the bucking Spirit Bottle. When Lynn and Robert caught up, the boy's smooth confidence returned and he stood taller.

"Good work!" Lynn said, slapping her brother on the shoulder.

Robert jerked and turned wide eyes on Wick. "Yeah." His voice was a little hoarse. "What do we do now?"

Wick took the bottle. "Jonah and I will handle it."

"You're not gonna release it, are you?" Robert asked.

"Sort of." Wick winked at his friend. That caused Lynn to frown.

"We'll meet up with you at the clubhouse," Jonah cut in. "Go on." He signaled to Lynn who had argued for a more permanent solution. Once his cousins left the house, he turned and jabbed Wick in the arm. "See? Even Robert was scared. I'm glad I didn't have the whole Club here."

"Really?" Wick hefted the bottle and slid it into an ornate iron box. "You can't hold their hands forever, Jonah."

"I know," Jonah said, turning to face the stairs and avoiding Wick's gaze. He never felt the time was right to tell the others he was Half-Reaper. That could wait, Jonah decided, at least until after the Florida vacation. "Let's just get this over with."

Wick eyed him a moment before plastering his trademark lopsided grin on his face and marching up the stairs to let the clients know the case was closed.

—

The air shimmered when Jonah and Wick appeared in the woods behind the Teen Center half an hour later. At once, Wick shift the iron box to his left hand, raised his right hand, and produced a pale blue flame in his palm.

Jonah gazed up through the trees. The sun had already set, leaving the area dark and eerie. While other kids might have been nervous in this situation, Jonah had always been comfortable with the night. Except, this time, the muted bump of the Spirit Bottle was unnerving.

Worse, he could still feel the client's clammy hands as she clutched his, thanking him repeatedly. The heartfelt praise embarrassed Jonah, and he was glad to get away.

"No one's at the spot," Wick said, nodding toward the open patch of riverbank several yards away. He started downhill.

Jonah followed while reaching out with his powers. As a Half-Reaper, he could sense the living aura and spirit of human beings. Aside from Wick, whose aura nearly blinded him, the closest people were uphill inside the Teen Center.

"We'll be okay," Jonah said.

Wick glanced back at him, grinning. "You sound so sure, Padawan. I think it's time you became a full Jedi."

Jonah laughed. Wick's sci-fi puns still relaxed him, and he needed that tonight.

"On a serious note, dude," Wick continued, "I think it's time you stopped working jobs with me."

"We did good," Jonah objected.

"Yeah, you did, but you have a crew now. It's time to take charge."

Stumped, Jonah didn't say anything. The boys continued in silence for several moments. "I kind of did that tonight," Jonah finally said. "It was my plan. I told everyone where to stand and I had Mike put up the sigils."

To Jonah's surprise, Wick laughed. "You're scared of responsibility because it puts you out front." He pointed at himself. "Me, I like the spotlight. You earned it." He nudged Jonah's shoulder.

"I don't know."

"Without taking that next step," Wick said and adopted a perfect Yoda voice, "obtain the rank of full Jedi, you will not."

Jonah grinned. "Thanks, Master Jedi." Despite his mocking tone, he took Wick's comment to heart because his friend was right on the mark. The spotlight wasn't something he sought out.

As soon as they reached the clearing, Wick placed an iron box on the ground. The Spirit Bottle inside bucked and wobbled the enclosure, taking their full attention.

Pulling the client's talisman from his pocket, Jonah held it up.

"Ever see one like this?" He waited as Wick held the blue flame closer and inspected the crude metal circle with an all-seeing eye at the center.

"No." Wick shook his head, causing his dreads to bob. "It's more like a symbol than a talisman." He knelt beside the iron box and placed his free hand on the clasp. "You ready?"

When Jonah nodded, Wick snuffed out the blue flame and released the clasp. He used both hands to lift the jerking Spirit Bottle from the box.

Closing his eyes, Jonah stretched out his hand as he thought about the Underworld. He'd developed a more reliable connection to the realm after fighting for his life against the Wraiths. Sure enough, as soon as he imagined opening a passageway, he felt the slight pull of the other side.

As always happened when he used his powers, the energy surged through his body and lowered his voice's timbre. Jonah opened his eyes and shouted, "Open!"

A rip formed in midair and light erupted from the rough opening to the Underworld, bathing the boys and the clearing in an undulating, unearthly light.

Jonah glanced at his friend. "Let it out."

Wick muttered a spell under his breath. The bottle jerked violently as the Wraith broke free, only to recoil from the Underworld's opening.

Reaching out with his power, Jonah commanded, "I send you back to your realm!"

The Wraith let out an inhuman shriek as its ethereal body oddly elongated, extending toward the rip.

"You'll get yours soon, brat!"

Jonah hesitated because Mount Vernon had experienced an uptick in Wraith activity, something he hadn't seen since the incident last Halloween. Could this spirit know why?

"What do you mean? What's going on?"

Instead of answering, the Wraith surged forward, grabbed Jonah by the shoulders with ice-cold hands, and knocked him to the ground. Jonah somehow stopped the mad spirit from ripping out his throat by bracing his arms underneath the spirit's chin. He marveled at how solid a Wraith could make itself when it wanted.

"Jonah!" Wick called out in concern.

"I'm fine," Jonah spat out.

With its face just inches from his, the Wraith grinned wickedly at him. *"You have no clue what's coming."*

"Then tell me."

"You'll see, brat!"

When the Wraith started laughing, Jonah's anger flashed. Pulling on his power, he felt sureness flood his body. "Then go, now!" he shouted.

Shoving the Wraith away, he was satisfied when the spirit tumbled into the rip and its furious screams and protests died away. Jonah slumped back, letting out a relieved breath.

Wick hurried over and helped him stand. "You had me worried."

"It was nothing." With an almost casual wave of his hand, Jonah closed the opening and plunged the clearing into a virtual pitch black after the light show. The buzzing of the evening wildlife, which had ceased, slowly returned.

"Dude, you're getting good at that." Wick placed the Spirit Bottle in the iron box and lifted it. "What's wrong? You aren't thinking about the Wraith's comments, are you?"

Jonah shook his head while gazing at the spot where the rip between the realms had been. "Do you think it hurts when I send them back?" He met Wick's gaze. "They always scream."

"Well," Wick said, ruffling his full dreads, "I hope it does. These Wraiths are bad business. Don't feel sorry for them."

"I don't." That was true. Jonah's doubt resulted from a brief sensation that something was about to happen. But the momentary unease was gone now.

Wick shook the iron case, causing the empty Spirit Bottle to rattle around inside and get Jonah's attention. "Time to celebrate."

"Yeah," Jonah agreed, reminding himself that Mount Vernon was free of overt supernatural problems. The Club made a difference, on their own and without the Alliance. Jonah's chest swelled with anticipation as he thought about the rest of their friends waiting for them.

The Mount Vernon Teen Center was a renovated Southern plantation house that Twiggs County had turned into a community center. Robert and Lynn maintained the center's social media in exchange for the unused attic space. They had dubbed it the Summit and the attic became the location to hang out and have Club meetings.

Jonah's face stretched into a wide grin as he and Wick bounded up the steps and into the mayhem of a full attic. This evening, his cousins were in the Summit section, huddled around a computer. Rico, Lynn's boyfriend, and Tamara, who was dating Wick, stood on the opposite side of the computer desk, laughing with the twins.

Wick handed the iron box to Jonah and hurried over to slip an arm around his girlfriend. Jonah waved to the group before crossing to his friends on the clubhouse side.

Mike sprang from an armchair and plucked the iron box from Jonah's hands. He pulled out the bottle to examine it. "How'd it go?"

"Easy," Jonah said, sinking into Mike's armchair. The reclaimed furniture was old and ratty, but it felt wonderful to Jonah after a stressful job.

Danita and Anthony sat together on the sunken sofa while Rodney and Lorraine shared a second armchair with wide arms, perfect for perching on. They halted their conversation to watch as Mike set the iron box and Spirit Bottle on the rickety card table that served as a makeshift conference table.

Anthony pointed at the bottle. "Is it gone?"

Jonah nodded. "Yep."

"Ha!" Anthony raised a fist in salute.

Danita hugged herself. "Well, until I saw it with my own eyes, I never would have believed it."

"Seriously?" Lorraine asked her friend. "You've seen what the Club had to face the past few months."

"I know. I just wish there was…"

"…a practical explanation for everything," Rodney finished. "We know, Danita."

Everyone laughed, including Anthony, who smothered his grin when Danita glared at him. Jonah had explained all the things that his godfather hadn't told the group when they took the oath of silence regarding the supernatural world. Every person in the clubhouse also knew about Robert's drawing ability, that Wick could do magic, and Lynn had a strong intuition.

So, Jonah wondered, why hadn't he told them he was a Half-Reaper? It struck him like coming out, something else he hadn't done. Who knew? Maybe he had nothing to fear. The group had accepted the supernatural as real and became the most incredible Club in Mount Vernon, in Jonah's opinion.

Helping Wick with his business of hunting down spirits and other things seemed like the logical next step. In the process, Jonah had let the truth about his dual nature slip into the background. Was that so bad at the moment? The way he saw it, protecting the people of Mount Vernon and the surrounding county from the supernatural world mattered more.

Deep inside, he knew that was just an excuse. If he was brave enough to face the rulers of the Afterworld, why was he afraid of being himself around the others?

As if to emphasize the point, Mike perched on the chair's arm while leaning on Jonah's shoulder. Though Mike hadn't officially come out either, Jonah noted his best friend acted freer around the others. And Jonah was sure Danita knew Mike was gay since they had been neighbors as well as friends for a long time.

Mike tweaked Jonah's ear. "Are you listening?" He waved at the full-color theme park map spread on top of the Club's old steamer trunk, also used as a coffee table.

"Yeah, I am," Jonah lied and leaned forward to focus on the map.

"We've decided on a schedule," Anthony announced.

Danita playfully bumped her leg against Anthony's. "He has a proposal."

Anthony shrugged and assumed his cocky tone while outlining his plan. Jonah found it odd that everyone waited for his opinion. While he hated being the center of attention, he realized he didn't mind it so much now. Having his own group of friends, instead of tagging along behind his more popular cousins, was amazing. As he glanced at the map, his eagerness for their weeklong vacation began to push the couple's ordeal, and his indecisive thoughts, out of his mind.

"I like your plan," Jonah offered.

Danita hugged Anthony and nudged Jonah's foot. "This has to be the best birthday gift, right?"

Jonah stroked his chin in mock thought. "I don't know…"

"Jonah!" Mike grabbed him into a headlock. Though he was still slender, Mike was part of the Practice Club and learning self-defense techniques. And, if Jonah wasn't mistaken, his friend's change into a Seeker also made Mike physically stronger.

"Okay! It's the best thing ever!" Jonah tapped Mike's arm until his friend released him. "Happy?"

Everyone laughed and broke into conversations about where they would stay and what they would see.

Jonah watched it all, feeling happier than he had in a long time. The trip was four days away, just after his fifteenth birthday. And, with Mount Vernon quiet, now was the perfect time for a break.

CHAPTER THREE
ART THEFT

As if a good omen for the upcoming trip, Mount Vernon had nice weather the next few days. A cloudless, cobalt sky stretched over the Teen Center pool as Jonah stepped onto the diving board.

Springing off the board, he sliced gracefully into the water and swam the pool's length, avoiding numerous kids as he went. Many of the others were there to splash around and socialize, but he liked to think as he swam.

After weaving through the laughing groups for several minutes, he pulled himself out of the pool near his stuff. As he toweled off, he spotted a group of girls from his high school staring at him. When they saw him looking, they started whispering furiously to each other.

"I'm surprised they haven't asked you out yet," Mike said, coming over. He grabbed Jonah's shirt off the chair and sat. Like Jonah, Mike wore long swim trunks, but he hadn't been in the pool yet.

And considering the countless hours Mike spent inside the attic clubhouse working on the Deliverer's Tales, Jonah was surprised Mike's light complexion had tanned. Perhaps it resulted from time spent in the sun on secret missions for the Alliance.

A giggle from the group of girls drew Jonah's attention. He turned and found them staring at him with appraising expressions. Gulping, he asked, "Uh, why would they ask me out?"

Mike sighed. "There's a reason Robert and Lynn are popular." He raised an eyebrow. "You have the same Hightower look."

"I know that," Jonah countered, absently rubbing his stomach. "They've never been so"—he glanced at the girls—"aggressive before."

"Well, you've been working out, right? And you've grown a few inches." A smirk tugged at the corners of Mike's mouth. "And you keep rubbing your stomach like you're showing off."

Acutely aware now that he was touching his stomach, Jonah forced himself to stop. "I'm not showing off. I'm just not used to them."

"What do you mean?" Mike sat forward. "I thought Kevin had you working out with him."

Pulling over an empty chair, Jonah sat. "Mike, I barely get a chance to see Kevin!" That was true enough, and the situation bothered Jonah. Since taking their relationship to the next level, the boys had little time together. Kevin, a Fallen Reaper, was also a full member of the Alliance and worked on assignments far away from Mount Vernon.

The older boy had speculated that Mandara, the Lead Fallen Reaper on the Alliance Council, purposely kept them apart. "They think Kevin lacks the maturity to keep me out of trouble," Jonah explained to Mike.

Except for his godfather and Trueblood, a Native American mage, Jonah had grown to dislike the entire Alliance Council.

"Okay," Mike answered. "So you're working out on your own?"

"I'm not working out. The muscles just happened." He gestured at himself, suddenly aware that Mike was right. People were looking at him. He snatched his shirt from his friend and slipped it on.

"It must be your Reaper metabolism," Mike observed.

Jonah had never thought about that. "I guess so. Maybe. I mean, my dad was big. I think Marcus is too." Considering the other Fallen Reapers, he realized they all appeared muscular.

"Well, you were born Half-Reaper," Mike pointed out. "I guess you're growing into it. According to the Alliance, this hasn't happened in a long time."

Mike's words ignited a feeling of alienness in Jonah. He glanced around the pool and at the other kids, feeling the gulf between himself and the others. "What should I do?"

"That's easy." Mike shoved him. "Stop walking around without your shirt!"

"Funny." Jonah relaxed a bit and finally noticed the section of a folded newspaper clutched in his friend's hand. "What's that?"

"I have something to show you." Mike unfolded the newspaper but hesitated before offering it to Jonah. It was a D-section article from the *Atlanta Journal-Constitution.*

Jonah took the paper. "You mean this update about someone stealing Native American Oral Histories from a museum?"

Mike arched an eyebrow at Jonah and glanced over the top of the paper to look. "No, I mean this one about a gallery robbery." He tapped the page and sat back.

Jonah read the article.

MYSTERIOUS ART THEFT BAFFLES MUSEUM

Patrons of the Atlanta Cobb Gallery of Art were in for a shock on Sunday when the prestigious gallery closed its doors because of a police investigation. Reports are that a valuable piece of art was stolen from the museum on Saturday night.

Frowning, Jonah started to ask Mike what was up when the next paragraph caught his attention.

Although the gallery tried to keep the exact details secret, sources revealed the theft of the Destiny Medallion. It is the method of the break-in that has the police baffled. The alarm was triggered, but there appeared to be no visible evidence of entry or exit. Many believe it was an inside job.

"We don't blame nor hold the gallery responsible for the theft," said Attorney Marcus Armstrong, a partner with Monarch Associates, an international law firm headquartered in Atlanta, Georgia, and the owner of the Destiny Medallion.

By the time he finished, Jonah's mouth hung open. "Marcus?"

"Yeah." Mike watched him with a steady gaze. "You said your godfather borrowed the paperweight medallion."

"Yeah, and I wondered why he wanted it."

"Isn't it obvious?" Mike said in his knowing way. "That paperweight was a replica of the real medallion."

Given the intricate details, Jonah had suspected that about the paperweight. What caused his hands to tremble was Mike's obvious conclusion. "You think they put it on display so someone would steal it?"

"Exactly." Mike swallowed, looking earnest. "This has to be part of a secret Alliance Council operation."

Jonah didn't know what to say. Mike had spent a lot of time at Alliance HQ, and his conclusions were often right. But something else troubled Jonah. That paperweight, whether it was a replica or not, had belonged to his dad. The thought that Marcus and the Alliance had allowed someone to steal it ignited a burning anger inside him.

"Thanks," Jonah said, letting the sarcasm into his voice.

"I don't want to do anything to spoil your birthday or the trip to Florida." Mike wrapped his arms around his thin frame as if cold. "But you hate it when the Alliance refuses to tell you what's going on, so"—Mike gestured at the paper—"I thought you should see that. And with Mage Trueblood refusing to tell me anything, I'm starting to understand how you feel."

Mike's frustration with the Alliance adults reassured Jonah while also causing him guilt for being sour with his best friend. "You're right. I'm sorry."

Mike waved off the apology.

Talk about the paperweight reminded Jonah of another missing object that had belonged to his parents. He eyed Mike. "You still have my mom's triptych, right?"

"Yes, I do." Mike shifted his gaze to the pool and the other teens. "I'd never let them take that."

Jonah sensed more in the answer, but he trusted Mike with the three-paneled piece of art. "Okay."

Mike looked at Jonah while cocking his head to the side. "Have you talked to your godfather lately?"

—

"This is Marcus Armstrong of Monarch Associates. Please—"

Jonah disconnected the call and dropped his phone on the bed beside him. The previous first two attempts had also gone to voice mail. Was his godfather avoiding his calls? As the anger built, Jonah composed a snide message for his godfather.

But when he called again, Marcus answered. "I got your calls and I'm sorry I couldn't respond. Things are busy here."

Jonah blinked in surprise as his prepared message slipped from his mind. "Marcus?"

"You did call." There was a tired amusement in his godfather's voice. "What's happened?"

Hearing the question, Jonah's frustration boiled over, and he blurted out, "I saw the story in the *AJC* about the medallion."

There was a shocked silence on the other end. "How did you… of course. Your uncle has a subscription to the paper."

"Yeah, he does," Jonah agreed, even though that wasn't how he found out. "You lied to me."

"Jonah…"

"You said the Alliance wanted to study my dad's paperweight, not use it in a display."

"I'm sorry to have misled you."

"Is it really gone?"

"For the moment, yes," Marcus admitted. "I can understand your anger, Jonah, but we'll get it back. I'm sorry."

"I don't want to hear that you're sorry," Jonah snapped. "Tell me what's going on."

"No."

The response was flat and carried a lot of weight, even over the phone.

Perhaps Marcus realized that. His voice was milder when he continued. "You're old enough and experienced enough with the Council to know how this works."

Jonah did. But he wasn't dealing with the Council right now. Marcus was his godfather, and for once, he wished they were face-to-face. As a Fallen Reaper, his godfather could sense emotions.

"I don't have a lot of my parents' things, not after the fire." Jonah let the silence lengthen as he stared at his memento shelf. On it was a photo of his mom and dad; a large, preserved black eagle feather; and a jeweler's magnifying glass.

The most recent additions were his dad's Alliance Council Badge and his mom's triptych, which Mike had borrowed. While his mementos had grown in number, it was a small collection given the extensive library and display cases they used to have. But that library was gone, destroyed when Grim Hounds started a fire in their house.

Marcus broke the quiet. "I'll recover the medallion. I promise."

Jonah's breath hitched when the promise produced a rush of goose bumps along his arms.

"Dwell on happier things," Marcus advised. "You turn fifteen in two days."

Given the conversation about his parents, he was reminded of the sadder fact that his birthday was also the same day he honored his parents' death. "It's been nearly two years since… you know."

"Yes, I do, but…" Marcus paused.

Jonah heard voices in the background on his godfather's end.

"I have to go, Jonah. Take care, and don't worry about the medallion."

Jonah wondered how he could feel worse than when he had first called. And the reminder of Alliance politics solidified his resolve to spend the rest of the summer with his friends.

Two days and counting, Jonah thought, when he rose on the morning of his birthday and dressed. Before he would allow himself to celebrate, he'd take the time to remember his parents. This year, he decided to visit the hideaway. It had been a special place for them, after all.

After dressing, he rode his bike to the little florist shop in the same strip mall as the salon where Aunt Imma worked. It had been her suggestion for the floral arrangement when Jonah had asked her opinion. So he'd chosen a half-dozen beautiful white roses, his mom's favorite.

With the wrapped flowers in hand, he set out for the Teen Center. Braving the hills leading to the popular location, Jonah didn't go inside when he arrived. His goal was the creek behind the center.

He considered using his backyard to phase, but carrying a half-dozen white roses would draw attention from his family. So, he decided the dense tree coverage of the creek would be perfect.

He chained the bike to the racks out front and hurried around to the Teen Center's back lawn. Crossing to the tree line, he descended the well-worn path downhill to the creek. Ever mindful of phasing's practical considerations, he paused to use his Reaper sense and make sure no one was around. Then Jonah nudged himself into phase.

One drawback of phasing was the weather. In his determination to honor his parents, Jonah had forgotten to check the forecast. Given the raindrops along the branches and plants when he arrived at the hideaway, it was clear he had just missed a rain shower.

A breeze stirred the branches, pelting him with raindrops as he mounted the old brick steps to the garden. Crossing to the alcove bench, he knelt and placed the bunch of white roses just below his parents' carved initials.

With a twinge of sadness, Jonah pulled his thirteenth birthday message out of a pocket, unrolled it, and read. Seeing his parents' well-wishes, Jonah was surprised he didn't cry. But the pain was still fresh, and he resisted retreating into his Reaper side to hide.

"I miss you, Mom and Dad," he muttered and bowed his head.

A light breeze rustled the branches again, hitting him with droplets of water. Jonah imagined it was his parents' signal that they'd heard him. Sitting on the wet cobblestone ground and leaning against the bench, Jonah pulled out his phone and earbuds.

The day of his parents' memorial service, he had fled the gathering and gone to the neighborhood park to listen to music and be alone. He chose the same piece of music today, pressed play, and reclined there, letting the morning pass.

Sometime later, he stirred and had started to rise when he noticed the baby handprint on the alcove's wall. The angle of the late-afternoon sunlight on the weathered bricks made the print more visible. Jonah placed his hand over the handprint just as he had on the first visit to this hideaway. He was struck by how much he had learned and changed in less than three years.

Again, the loss welled up inside because he could never get his parents back. Without warning, his memorial comments popped into his mind.

"What happened to my parents taught me that no one knows what will happen tomorrow. I think that we should appreciate what we have today."

Wiping his eyes, he thought about his words. What did he have today? Well, the answer was easy. He had his aunt, uncle, cousins, friends, and a new club. Plus, he had a boyfriend. Just thinking about all the people who cared about him lessened the sadness.

When he rose, he had a new determination to enjoy his birthday party and the vacation with his friends and family. After collecting his things, he lingered, regarding the white roses one last time before phasing away.

CHAPTER FOUR
UNWELCOMED VISITOR

Because of two epic failures at the Teen Center on his last birthday and Wick's magic show, everyone agreed to have Jonah's birthday party at the Hightowers'. The gathering would take place in the family room but would also spill out into the backyard. Uncle James had cleaned out the grill for the evening, and Aunt Imma stayed home from work to prepare all kinds of things for the guests to eat.

She paused in wrapping a platter of baked snacks. "Jonah, why don't you go hang out with Mike until later. We'll handle the setup."

"Yes, ma'am." He shuffled into the den, not wanting to leave everything to his family. Lynn wasn't about to let him do that anyway. She promptly put him to work, moving furniture around and hanging up limited but tasteful decorations. Jonah was glad they didn't go overboard with banners and balloons. He was fifteen, not nine.

Soon the late afternoon turned to early evening, and Jonah went off to get ready. Picking through the clothes in his closet after his shower, he spotted his forest green shirt and took it out. He held the shirt in front of his bare chest, scrutinizing his reflection in the mirror. It would do. Selecting a pair of dark blue jeans, Jonah lay the pants and shirt on the bed's corner. He still had a little time before the first guests arrived. Crossing to the memento shelf, he picked up a framed painting of the Underworld. It sat behind the empty spot where his mom's triptych normally rested.

Jonah lay on his bed, holding the picture. It was a copy of Omar's original painting of seven areas from the Underworld. When he had the triptych, he'd connect the pieces and gaze at the different terrains depicted on the image while trying to imagine his mom, Omar, and Mage Trueblood's dangerous adventures in the Wraith realm.

The names also ignited his imagination. Phantom's Passage, Spector Ridge, Haunted Forest, and Soothsayer Marsh. The locations sounded like places from a fantasy game, but these were real. He wondered if he'd ever visit these places, though he couldn't see how or why.

He continued to gaze at the painting until the doorbell rang. Hearing Danita's and Mike's voices, Jonah returned the painting to the shelf and started dressing. All the while, the noise level outside his room grew louder.

By the time he made his grand appearance, not only had Mike and Danita arrived, but so had several other kids. The side table, just inside the family room, contained an impressive pile of gifts. Mike noticed Jonah first, grinned, and gave him a thumbs-up on the shirt.

Music started, and that got everyone going. A girl Jonah knew from school pulled him into the first few dances. He enjoyed himself so much he didn't notice as the place grew crowded with most of the Practice Club members. He wasn't surprised the group of girls from the pool showed up. After greeting them, Jonah edged away before Mike's prediction came true.

Soon the older Club members shifted outside to the backyard while most of the younger kids remained inside. Uncle James acted like a short-order cook, taking requests for the grill from both groups. When the doorbell sounded almost two hours into the party, Jonah volunteered to answer it.

He opened the door to find Kevin standing outside in a light blue, short-sleeved, button-down shirt that fit his upper body well and showed off his charcoal skin. He wore a pair of comfortable, fitted dark blue jeans, and he had on an immaculate pair of white tennis shoes.

And, Jonah noted, Kevin smelled nice. The young Fallen Reaper held up a small gift-wrapped box and an expensive-looking envelope. "Happy birthday."

Jonah wanted to hug Kevin, but at the same time, he didn't appreciate his boyfriend's bogus claim that an assignment would interfere with attending the party. When Kevin moved to enter the house, Jonah crossed his arms, blocking the way. "What are you doing here?"

Flashing an incredulous look, Kevin said, "I wouldn't miss your party." Yet Jonah didn't budge. "I made arrangements, okay?"

Jonah suspected Marcus or some of the other Council members had stepped in to help. "Arrangements. I bet."

Kevin shrugged, and Jonah was on the verge of letting go of the fake irritation and hugging his boyfriend anyway when Aunt Imma stepped out of the dining room, ruining the moment.

"Jonah, that's no way to treat a guest. Come in." His aunt waved Kevin into the house before going back into the dining room.

Kevin smiled and tugged one of Jonah's fingers as he entered. "You missed your chance," he whispered and continued down the hall.

Uncle James placed a platter full of freshly grilled vegan and regular hamburgers and hot dogs on the counter. He stepped aside to avoid the rush of kids attacking the food.

For his part, Kevin blended easily into the clubhouse group. Not only did he know the others, but Kevin was a teen just like everyone else. Danita was quick to corner the Fallen Reaper and ask him all kinds of questions about his work for the Alliance. Jonah enjoyed watching his boyfriend squirm and avoid telling her too much.

"Who are those from?" Mike asked, eyeing the small box and expensive envelope still in Jonah's hands.

"Kevin."

"Just the envelope," Kevin said. "I found the box on the doorstep."

Jonah held the box away from his body and waved his hand over the silvery blue wrapping paper and bow, trying to sense any magic.

Kevin laughed. "Will you geeks just open it?"

With the other kids taking a sudden interest, Jonah

opened the attached card first. It wasn't a card, but a note, on cream paper, on which someone had written *Happy Birthday* and nothing else. Jonah thought the handwriting was like his dad's. However, he had already found his parents' gift at the hideaway last year. Why would his dad arrange for this to arrive a year later and not even sign it?

"Is it from an old friend?" Mike asked.

"I don't recognize the handwriting."

Mike took the gift, tapped it, then jiggled it. He shrugged while handing it back to Jonah. "Kevin's right. Just open it."

Jonah removed the wrapping paper to reveal an off-white, sturdy jeweler's box, the kind with a hinge on one side, allowing the top to flip open like a lid. The store name, Green Valley Jewelers, was engraved in the cover. Beneath the title was another inscription: *Fine Timepieces*. He had never heard of the place.

Opening the box with a trembling hand, Jonah discovered a sparkling gold watch resting on a deep velvet cushion. The guests nearest him uttered comments of appreciation. Jonah felt the same way as he lifted the timepiece to examine the multiple dials on its face and the curly numbers etched into its surface.

To his surprise, he recognized Angel script around the outer dial. And the little hands spun at rates different from the regular second hand. Jonah had no clue what they measured. For a second, he wondered if the second pair of dials displayed a different time rate, the way digital watches showed different time zones. While the idea was cool, it made no sense without a reference point.

"Wow. That looks expensive," Lynn observed.

Her comment forced Jonah back to the present. At first glance, he agreed with Lynn but didn't think the gold was real. It looked like the same metal as the Seeker's Compass.

With everyone watching his reaction, Jonah slid the watch on and fastened the clasp. At once, he felt the tingle of subtle magic as the watchband adjusted to fit his wrist.

So this meant the watch came from someone on the supernatural side of things. Jonah narrowed his eyes, concentrating and trying to sense anything dangerous, but his Death Sense remained quiet. The gift was genuine, even though the giver wanted to stay anonymous.

The craftsmanship drew others forward for closer looks. Jonah consented to the poking and prodding. What intrigued him was the feeling that the watch had always been his.

When he opened the other presents, Jonah's mind remained on the watch. By far, it was the best present, but Kevin's gift had been the most unexpected. Jonah removed a card holder from the expensive envelope. Opening that, he found a royal blue plastic card with the Monarch Associates logo on it in gold lettering. For a second, he thought his godfather had sent him a credit card.

"It's a key card to access the offices," Kevin explained.

Jonah caught the boy's glance and sensed longing and something else. Confusion.

"Well," Aunt Imma said after he had opened all the gifts, "maybe I should put them in your room."

"That's okay," Jonah said, coming to his senses and stopping her. "I'll do it." It did not surprise him when Kevin jumped to help him by holding most of the boxes.

Inside his bedroom, Kevin pushed the door partially closed and set the gifts on the bed. Then he pulled Jonah into a literal warm hug since the Fallen Reaper had an above-normal body temperature. Jonah felt safe with Kevin as they swayed back and forth a few moments.

Voices grew louder in the hallway outside, and Kevin released him. Turning to put the presents away, Jonah sensed confusion from his boyfriend again as if a veil had lifted.

He turned to face Kevin. "What's wrong?"

"I'm heading back to Atlanta." Kevin glanced out the partially open door. "I wanted to ask you about the trip to Florida."

"What about it? It's gonna be safe. No one's coming after me right now."

"Not that, Jonah. I mean, about *you* going."

Now Jonah was confused. "Why shouldn't I go?"

Kevin hunched his shoulders and stuffed his hands in his pockets. "You don't know, do you?"

"Know what?" Jonah demanded. Kevin didn't explain, causing Jonah to fear his boyfriend was acting like the Alliance adults. "Kevin…"

The Fallen Reaper raised his hands. "I need to check with Marcus before I say anything else."

"Are you kidding me?" Jonah peeked out the door and moved right up to Kevin. "That's what they do to me all the time," he whispered.

The wash of guilt from Kevin was fresh and mollified Jonah. *Of course he wouldn't lie to me.*

As if sensing his thoughts, Kevin leaned forward and kissed him.

All the anger Jonah had just experienced vanished for a few glorious moments. Leaning his forehead against Kevin's chin, he said, "You'd better call and tell me what's going on."

"I will," Kevin whispered in response. He moved for the door, but Jonah slid an arm around the boy's waist. "Jonah. I have to go."

"I know." Jonah held on to Kevin's hand instead until they stepped fully out of the room. If anyone noticed their delay in the bedroom, Jonah didn't care.

Kevin paused at the open front door. Peeking back into the busy house, he gently tugged Jonah's hand. "See ya."

Jonah nodded and watched his boyfriend get into a car and drive off instead of phasing to Atlanta. Returning to the party, he was determined to put Kevin's secret out of his mind for as long as he could; otherwise, all the unanswered questions would drive him up a wall.

Brilliant stars stretched across the cloudless night sky, reminding Jonah of limitless possibilities. He stood outside on the sidewalk, alternating between gazing upward and saying goodbye to all the guests.

Danita, who stood beside him, whirled on the spot, full of energy from the party. "That was fantastic, Jonah." She, too, gazed at the sky. "And to think, by this time, day after tomorrow, we'll be in Florida."

"Oh yeah," Anthony said, hugging her as they rocked back and forth.

Jonah was about to agree when Mike poked at his new watch, surprising him. "I think the dials glow a bit in the dark."

Glancing at the watch, Jonah saw the dials did glow enough to read the symbols. He eyed Mike. "You aren't jealous, are you?"

"No, I like my compass." Mike tapped the impression of the Seeker's Compass underneath his shirt. He never went anywhere without the device.

"Mike, are you coming with us?" Danita asked. She and Anthony had started down the sidewalk.

"Yeah." He bumped fists with Jonah. "See you tomorrow." Hesitating, he added, "I may have another gift for you."

"Really? Where is it?"

"I needed a little help in making it." He grinned. "You'll love it."

That intrigued Jonah because Mike was a Seeker, and the things he made worked with the supernatural world.

Watching his friends walk down the sidewalk, Jonah remained outside, enjoying the relative quiet of the night while reflecting on the party. For once, the occasion had been free of trouble. Well, except for Kevin's odd behavior and promise. Jonah took out his phone as he turned for the house. *Come on, Kevin. You promised to call.*

That's when something flashed out of the corner of his eye. He turned toward the backyard gate and his heart leaped into his throat because the Alliance Symbol floated in midair. The three interlocked circles with wings spread above them wavered in the air a few moments before disappearing.

Oh no. Can't I have one decent birthday?

A black SUV rolled to a quiet stop on his side of the street. A large Alliance Guard got out and motioned him toward the back gate instead of the front door.

Curious, Jonah headed for the backyard while noting the guard must have been watching his house all evening. That could only mean trouble. Why else send a guard and flash the Alliance Symbol?

As Jonah entered the yard, he relaxed a bit because Uncle James had finished cleaning and gone inside. His relatives didn't need to see whatever the Alliance would do next. Given that he didn't know what would happen either, Jonah wondered why he wasn't more afraid. Instead, he was irritated that his plan to ignore the Alliance had failed.

All too soon, he sensed a magical spike as a vortex blossomed into view beside the backyard shed. Jonah stepped back and waited, eager to see who would exit. An Alliance Guard Captain, the one he met in the fall, exited the vortex.

The large man wore a military-style vest with the Alliance Symbol on the left breast pocket. Below the symbol were two short, horizontal gold bars, and he cradled a dark helmet in his left hand. After a nod of recognition to Jonah, he stood to the side and waited.

A young mage emerged next. Jonah knew the guy. His name was Thomas, and he worked with Mage Trueblood. The young mage wore a short blue tunic with the Alliance Symbol on the left chest. Beneath it, he had on a pair of dark blue slacks. The overall effect was neat and impressive.

Unlike the Guard Captain, Thomas didn't nod to Jonah or wave as he stood on the opposite side of the opening right before a tall Fallen Reaper swept out of the vortex last.

Vapors clung to the long Reaper's coat, giving the man a menacing presence. Jonah noted the Alliance Council Badge pinned to his coat. The newcomer took in Jonah with a glance; then his eyes settled on the Hightowers' house. A frown creased his deep brown face as if he was not impressed.

Then the man spoke in a baritone voice that caused Jonah to gawk because it reminded him of his dad. "So, this is where Isaiah and Janice decided to send their son?" The newcomer shook his head like he couldn't believe it.

Jonah's stomach burned—he knew there were only three Fallen Reapers on the Alliance Council. Marcus was one, and through various overheard comments, he discovered a second Fallen Reaper was a woman. That left only one more person, someone he had grown to hate from a distance.

"Ah, who are you?" he asked the intimidating Fallen Reaper, though he knew the answer.

The man loomed closer and stared down at Jonah for a long moment. Then he said, "I'm Fallen Reaper Mandara of the Alliance Council."

CHAPTER FIVE
UNHAPPY NEWS

*M*andara.

The ominous name caused a flood of emotions to course through Jonah. Mandara was the person who kept Kevin and him apart and gave his godfather so much trouble. Now, the Fallen Reaper stood before Jonah, intimidating and yet familiar in a disturbing way Jonah couldn't identify.

"Why are you here?" Jonah demanded, letting all his frustration with the Alliance come through. As expected, the Fallen Reaper sensed his emotions.

Mandara squared his shoulders. "Careful, Mr. Blackstone. I am a member of the Alliance Council."

Jonah was on the verge of saying So when he caught the slight shake of the Guard Captain's head. Even so, he couldn't stop himself from being surly.

"Yeah. And I'm the Deliverer." He crossed his arms, glaring back. "You didn't answer my question."

The play of emotions on Mandara's face was satisfying to see up close. But the surge of anger from the adult concerned Jonah. Perhaps Mandara realized Jonah was scanning him because a moment later, an emotional shield came down, shutting off the man's feelings.

"You're so much like Isaiah, it's frightening," the man finally said, shaking his head.

Mention of his father took the wind out of Jonah's mounting irritation. His shoulders slumped a little. "Just… what's happening now?" He met the adult's gaze and added, "Sir?"

Mandara grunted and glanced at the Hightower house again. "It's come to my attention that you and your legal guardians did not receive the notice about Camp Alliance." He nodded at Jonah's confused look. "I'm here to secure your aunt and uncle's permission for you to attend camp. It's a necessary formality."

"Camp?" Jonah was shocked. "What camp?" As soon as he said it, his brain caught up with the situation. "Wait, when does it start?"

"This Sunday," Mandara answered.

The world shifted beneath Jonah. That was the same day as the trip to Florida! Suddenly, Kevin's apprehension at the party made sense. "I can't. No… I mean… no."

Mandara frowned at him and raised a skeptical eyebrow. "I'm afraid it's not open for discussion."

"I'm going to Florida!"

"To waste time playing around when you should be training yourself for the fight?" Mandara's voice rose.

Fearing his aunt and uncle would hear and come out to investigate, Jonah searched for a way to keep that from happening. To his horror, Mandara stepped toward the house. Jonah moved to position himself in the way, even though he suspected it was a dangerous thing to do.

"Move aside, young Blackstone."

Jonah didn't need his Reaper sense to recognize the danger in the man's voice. Before he could respond, another vortex blossomed into view behind them. The Guard Captain turned, but his posture remained relaxed when Symon Trueblood stepped through the magical opening.

The mage wore the more traditional blue tunic that came down to midthigh. Jonah let out a relieved breath as Trueblood hurried over to them. "Cedric, I told you I would come and talk to Jonah's relatives."

"You have duties at HQ, Councilor Trueblood." Mandara faced the house again. "I can take care of this."

"No," Jonah said again. "What about my plans?"

Mandara snorted. "You can go to Florida after camp. Now, let's go."

Trueblood interposed himself between Mandara and the Hightowers' home. "This has to be handled delicately. Jonah's relatives…"

"Need to sign the form," Mandara finished.

"All my friends are going to Florida!" Jonah countered, growing more anxious.

Mage Trueblood squeezed Jonah's shoulder in a sign of support. "We understand, Jonah." He paused to glare at

Mandara. "But your parents had you registered for camp since you were seven. We're sorry the letter was lost in the mail."

Turning back to Mandara, Trueblood gestured at the Reaper's black coat. "You should take that off. It looks intimidating." As if to impress the point, Trueblood took off his tunic, revealing a fitted tan shirt underneath and dark blue slacks, much like Thomas's. He handed his tunic to the Guard Captain.

Mandara balled his hands into fists until the knuckles cracked. But the man relented and, with a sigh, removed the coat and handed it to the Guard Captain. Turning back to Trueblood, he spread his arms wide, showing off his regular black dress shirt and pants. "Am I less scary to the mortals now?"

"Not really," Trueblood muttered. He nodded to Jonah, who didn't want to enter the house but couldn't find a way to stop the inevitable.

Aunt Imma seemed to swell with anger as she listened to Mandara. "That's outrageous," she finally exploded. "Jonah's going to Florida with us." She wagged her finger at the Fallen Reaper. "He can attend your camp some other time. It's your fault."

Uncle James was strangely quiet. Now he placed an arm around his wife's shoulders. "This isn't fair to Jonah."

"Exactly!" Aunt Imma agreed.

Mandara stared at his hands, but he didn't seem cowed. "Yes, it is unfortunate, but Jonah's *parents* decided this long ago."

Jonah winced as Aunt Imma gave Mandara a look that Jonah and his cousins feared. She was about to show the Fallen Reaper real righteous fury.

"What he means," Trueblood cut in, "is that we understand—"

"You said that, Symon," Uncle James replied while gently stroking Aunt Imma's arms. "The problem is you're putting Jonah in an impossible situation. You wave around his departed parents' wishes against spending time with his friends." Uncle James took off his glasses and tossed them on the kitchen table. "I expected more from you. Janice was your close friend."

Jonah had never seen Symon Trueblood at a loss for words. The mage avoided Uncle James's gaze.

"Jonah should have time to make his decision," Uncle James continued. "We won't sign anything until he does."

While Jonah appreciated his relatives' support, Uncle James was putting it all on him too. Plus, Jonah noted the resigned expression on his uncle's face and began to worry. Robert and Lynn entered the kitchen at that moment, drawing Mandara's scrutiny. Lynn stared back while she and her brother stood on either side of Jonah.

With his cousins there, a sudden thought occurred to him. "If I attend camp, can my cousins come?"

Mandara started to shake his head, but Lynn spoke first.

"We can't, Jonah. Mom and Dad spent a lot on the Florida trip. And what about everyone else who's planned to go?"

"Yeah, I know."

"Well?" Mandara asked.

Trueblood stepped forward. "Why don't you wait in the car?"

Mandara narrowed his eyes and peered back at Trueblood. After a long pause, he nodded to Jonah's relatives and headed for the front door. Mage Trueblood waited until it closed before facing Jonah and the others.

"I regret this happened, James."

Uncle James kissed Aunt Imma on the cheek and motioned the mage toward the front door.

Once the men stepped outside, Aunt Imma let out an irritated huff. "This is unbelievable." She gripped Jonah's hands. "You don't have to go, understand? I know your parents wanted this, but why not next summer?"

Jonah didn't trust himself to answer and nodded instead.

Aunt Imma surveyed the spotless kitchen as if looking for something to do. With another huff of displeasure, she stormed off to her room.

Robert gripped Jonah's shoulder and nodded toward his bedroom.

—

"Tell that Mandara guy to shove it," Robert said for the second time, standing with his back against the closed door.

Lynn leaned against Jonah's dresser, turning his Alliance security key card over in her hands. "Robert, I don't think that would be wise. He's dangerous."

Jonah, recovered from his initial shock, lay on his bed, listening to his cousins while weighing all the camp's pros and cons. Frankly, he had forgotten Marcus's promise that he could train when he turned fifteen. That had been two years ago and what felt like a million miles away.

Rolling over, he watched the twins, who normally mirrored each other's anger. Strangely, Robert was the only one to voice his opinion. Lynn had a guarded look on her face.

Sensing something was off, Jonah sat up, staring at her. "What do you think?"

Lynn shook her head, putting the key card aside. "This is your decision."

"I want my cousins to help me."

Robert laughed. "You heard my advice. Go to Florida and forget the Alliance." He glanced at his sister. "Just tell him, Lynn."

A quick frown crossed Lynn's face before she smoothed out her features. If this had been anyone else, Jonah could have used his Reaper Stare, but he never did it to his family or friends. It felt too much like an invasion of their privacy.

"Lynn, please."

She tapped her fists against the side of the dresser while avoiding his stare. "You should go to Camp Alliance."

"What?" Robert yelled then clamped a hand over his mouth. "You saw that in a vision?" When Lynn glared at him, Robert gulped and relented. "That's jacked up."

"I don't know what'll happen," Lynn quickly added. "I just get the feeling Jonah should go."

"Yeah," Jonah muttered and flopped back on the bed, staring at his ceiling. "Your dad felt the same way."

"True," Lynn agreed, watching him. "I'm guessing you'll train to use your powers at this camp."

Jonah nodded. "Kevin showed it to me once."

Robert nudged Jonah's bed with a foot. "When did this happen, little cousin?"

"It was the first time I had a phasing lesson." Jonah sat up again, embarrassed. "I just forgot to mention it."

"It doesn't matter," Lynn said before her brother could disagree. "This camp will change him."

"You mean he won't be our little cousin anymore?" Robert asked, glancing between Jonah and Lynn. "You saw that too?"

Lynn frowned as she nodded to Jonah. "When we met all those Alliance people, it finally hit me that they expect so much from you."

Jonah understood because Marcus had made a similar point after the events with their Aunt Ruby. His godfather had warned him that he'd have to take his place in the Alliance's politics.

Did that include taking his dad's paperweight and not telling him why, Jonah wondered? If so, he didn't want any part of Alliance politics.

He toyed with following Robert's idea and refusing to go. When he caught Lynn's serious expression, Jonah rejected that idea.

"Get some sleep, hero," Lynn said and hustled her brother out of the room.

Jonah stared at the closed door for a moment before getting up and undressing. He debated about his decision as he slipped under the covers. Honor his parents' plan and his godfather's promise, or stay with his friends and family? Jonah pictured all the Mount Vernon Social Club members' reactions if he chose to abandon them and attend Camp Alliance. Of them all, Mike would be the only one to understand the true implications.

Danita and Lorraine would probably say it was good to honor his parents' wishes. Rodney was a toss-up, and Anthony would agree with Robert. Just hearing their voices in his head sent a wave of anger through Jonah. He wanted to tour the theme park with them, have fun in the hotels, and enjoy the sightseeing adventures.

They were his crew. How could he leave them and go off to spend four weeks with a group of strangers? He glanced at the shelf of mementos and the picture of his parents. Camp Alliance was a part of their world and they had wanted him to attend.

Jonah rolled over and pulled his cover up to his cheek. "I hate this," he whispered. When the frustration and indecision became too much, he retreated into the quiet of his Reaper side and remained there, immune to the raw emotions, until he finally slept.

CHAPTER SIX

ENEMY OF MY ENEMY

Packing day should have been an exciting time for Jonah, yet it wasn't because of the Camp Alliance decision weighing on him. Aunt Imma dealt with her frustration over Mandara's visit by going into full-on cleaning mode. Robert and Lynn washed clothes while Jonah helped his aunt clean the house, top to bottom. He didn't argue because the work kept his mind occupied.

Best of all, no one pestered him with questions about his decision, not even Aunt Imma when she gave him a stack of clothes to fold and pack. Around noon, Robert and Lynn escaped the house to visit their friends. Jonah decided to do the same, but once he stood outside on the sidewalk, he stared down Morningside Drive, thinking.

Mike's phone went to voice mail, so hanging out with him was out. Jonah considered going by Anthony's house. While it was a sure bet Anthony would talk about their plans for Florida, Jonah could play along. He had taken his first steps in that direction when Kevin's pimped-out car cruised by him, braked, and backed up. Heavy bass shook the dark vehicle, but the sound cut off when Kevin opened the door and got out.

"'Sup?"

Jonah hurried around to the driver's side of the car to peek inside. The interior was dark because of the shaded windows. In the dimness, the glowing lights and readouts of Kevin's killer audio system winked at him.

"This yours?"

"Yep. And no, you can't drive it." Kevin playfully pushed him.

Jonah sobered, remembering his looming decision. Right now, all he wanted to do was get away with Kevin. "Let's go to my parents' hideaway."

Kevin closed the car door and leaned against it. "We can't."

"Why?" Jonah protested. "We haven't been alone in a while."

The instant surge of deep attraction from Kevin bowled Jonah over. His boyfriend felt the same way, but the Fallen Reaper shook his head.

"Everyone's watching you today. We'd never explain disappearing for so long. I have a better idea." He motioned Jonah around to the other side. "Get in."

Jonah discovered Kevin's plan didn't involve hugging or making out or anything that exciting. Instead, he drove to the Teen Center basketball courts.

"Seriously?" Jonah asked.

Kevin fetched a basketball from the trunk. "Yep. It'll take your mind off things."

"So will the hideaway," Jonah muttered. Then he snapped his fingers. "What about the stream behind the center?"

Kevin hustled him to the court. "Nope."

Jonah's irritation lasted for the first ten minutes or so, but eventually, he relaxed and enjoyed their time together. All too soon, the afternoon turned into the early evening and Kevin finally gave in to temptation. They climbed into his car and made good use of the tinted windows.

"Do you have to go?" Jonah asked sometime later.

Kevin sat back in the driver's seat. "I need to get back to Atlanta. I'll see you tomorrow, either way." He raised an eyebrow.

"I haven't decided," Jonah said and wiped the fogged window to see out.

"Well?" Kevin slid his hand into Jonah's. "Let me know."

When he started the car, Jonah tapped his arm. "I wanna walk home."

"You sure? It's just a few minutes away."

"Yeah. I want some time to think."

Kevin nodded and leaned over to give him a last kiss.

When Jonah got out, Kevin flicked on his music and pulled away. Jonah watched the car speed down the street and out of sight. He stuffed his hands into his pockets and glanced at the Teen Center, considering going inside. Nah, he decided. The weight of his indecision hung heavy in the air and he needed to focus on that, not avoid it.

So he strolled along the sidewalk, taking his time and trying to rein in his thoughts, but he sensed someone watching him. He froze, testing the sensation. That's when he heard the quiet thump of footfalls behind him. Not sensing immediate danger, Jonah took his time facing the last person he wanted to see. Brandon Warner III.

Like Jonah, Brandon had gone through a growth spurt and was as tall as Mr. Warner now. Jonah recalled the bully wanted to play basketball, but his father refused to let him. That conversation had revealed a side of Brandon he had never expected to see.

Now, Brandon gazed over Jonah's shoulder, watching the direction that Kevin had gone. He snorted. "You two were in that car for a long time."

The revealing remark made Jonah nervous until he remembered he didn't care what Brandon thought. "We were talking." Jonah lied anyway, hating himself.

"Yeah, right." Brandon crossed his arms, watching Jonah. "You being gay is the least weird thing about you."

"Okay. Well, I have things to do." Jonah turned and started down the sidewalk. His attempts to ignore Brandon didn't work because the boy hurried to stroll along beside him. Something was wrong, Jonah decided. Brandon remained quiet, like he debated saying anything else.

Unable to fathom the bully's unusual behavior today, Jonah peeked sideways at him. "Can I help you with something?"

Brandon worked his jaw for a moment before asking, "What do you know about Antwan's cousin?"

Jonah stopped in his tracks. "Nothing," he blurted out.

"You're lying."

"If anyone knows about lying, you'd be it," Jonah accused and prepared himself to fight, but, again, his Death Sense remained quiet.

Brandon just shrugged. "That's why I know you're lying." He stepped closer. "Tell me the truth."

Up close, Jonah saw the worry in the boy's eyes, and that made him nervous. "Did something happen to Antwan?"

"I don't know. He started acting weird after his cousin disappeared the night of the Halloween bonfire," Brandon said. "And then he left town as soon as school ended and hasn't returned my calls." He paused for a breath. "I went to his uncle's house in DC, but they wouldn't let me see him."

Jonah couldn't believe the concern in Brandon's voice, nor that the bully cared for his friend. Antwan was related to an ambassador, and his family was probably wealthier than Brandon's, but this was strange. "I… um." He let out a breath. "His cousin is into magic."

"Black magic? Witchcraft?" Brandon asked eagerly.

Had the world turned upside down? Jonah gulped. "Yeah, something like that."

"I knew it!" Brandon snapped. "His cousin's family is strange. I met the aunt once, and she was"—he shuddered—"she was weird." His spooked expression cleared. "She's weird like you."

"I'm not…" Jonah didn't bother to argue. "I bet Antwan's fine," he added, never imagining consoling Brandon. Frankly, the whole situation was unnerving.

Taking a deep breath, Brandon peered at Jonah. "Tell me everything." When Jonah hesitated, the bully screwed up his mouth and muttered, "Please."

Before Jonah could get over his shock at the request, he heard the whine of a large engine approaching. Looking past Brandon, he saw the black SUV roaring up the street and rapidly braking to a stop beside them. His Death Sense throbbed.

At the same time, Brandon whirled around, as if fearing someone had caught him. The back passenger door opened, and a dark-featured, slender woman in a black coat and matching pants stepped out. Even her high-heeled shoes were jet black.

In contrast, her curly hair was magenta. The wild style reminded Jonah of his Aunt Ruby's unruly Medusa locks. Adding to her menace, his Death Sense spiked when her eyes surveyed him.

A man stepped from around the SUV. Like the woman, he wore all black, and his features matched hers. They were brother and sister. Or, Jonah realized with a shock, twins.

The woman moved closer to Brandon. "Your father sent us to bring you home," she said with a slight accent.

"Really? It takes two people?" Brandon didn't act afraid of the newcomers.

The man snarled. "He's worried about you, son."

"Don't call me that. You're not my dad," Brandon snarled back.

The man's face twisted into anger, and his hand glowed, but his sister gripped the arm. "Careful, Fabian."

Even though she stopped her brother, Jonah felt the buildup of magic. On instinct, he moved forward to stand beside Brandon.

"Who are you?" Jonah asked.

The woman smiled at him and took in his appearance from head to toe. "The great Jonah Blackstone. I'm not impressed," she hissed.

"Yeah, well, you don't impress me either," Jonah shot back. He tapped Brandon's arm. "Don't go anywhere with them."

Brandon stood his ground and glared at the siblings. The tense stand-off ended when the driver hopped out, rocking the vehicle. A well-muscled man stepped into view, and Jonah could sense the Wraith inside. Yet the man's eyes remained normal as he held out a phone to the brother.

Fabian turned the phone toward Brandon. Jonah grimaced when he saw an angry Mr. Warner glaring out of the screen. The man's cold eyes shifted to Jonah and back to his son.

"Get in the vehicle now." Mr. Warner's voice carried real authority and anger. "I don't like the company you keep." Mr. Warner glared at Jonah.

Brandon's shoulders slumped. "Think about what I asked," he said to Jonah and moved toward the open back passenger door.

Fabian and his sister didn't move, but they watched Jonah. He could sense their eagerness to attack him, but not in the open and with people milling around the Teen Center. Then something behind him drew their attention.

Jonah didn't dare turn to look as he heard another vehicle pull up. Wondering if it was more enemies, he prepared to phase when an Alliance Guard stood beside him, baton activated.

It was the Guard Captain who'd shown up with Mandara. "You okay, Blackstone?"

"Yeah." Jonah relaxed, having the guard with him.

The woman gazed past Jonah and the Guard Captain.

Curious now, he turned and saw the SUV's back passenger window down. A guy with Asian features stared out.

"I grow tired of you interfering, Fallen One," the woman called out.

The guy merely smiled. "Care to give up, Thera?"

Thera scowled and focused on Jonah again. "Another time, Mr. Blackstone." She backed up to her SUV's open door and got in while her brother hurried around to the opposite side. The SUV gunned its engine, made a tight turn in the middle of the street, and roared off at high speed.

"That was foolish to face them alone," the guard said. He motioned Jonah toward the Alliance vehicle.

"I didn't do anything. I was just walking home, and everything sort of happened," Jonah finished in a daze.

The Guard Captain opened the rear door for Jonah, making him feel foolish. He wasn't important enough for that. "Thanks." He climbed in.

The Fallen Reaper was the thinnest Jonah had ever seen, and he had a nerdish quality. As the guy continued to scrutinize him, Jonah wondered if the man was an Alliance researcher or scientist.

Finally, the Fallen Reaper smiled, sticking out a slender hand. "My name's Mitchell."

"I'm…" Jonah's voice trailed off. Of course, the guy knew him. "Why are you watching me?"

Mitchell waited as the Guard Captain started the vehicle and drove away from the Teen Center. "Kevin called when he left you to walk alone. I decided to join the Guard Captain's escort so I could finally meet you in person."

The Fallen Reaper's reaction to meeting him was totally the opposite of what he'd experienced with those strange twins. To avoid the man's intense gaze, Jonah peered out the window.

Everything had happened so fast, and his mind only now began to piece it together. Could Mandara have people watching him to make sure he went to Camp Alliance? Or did it have something to do with that brother and sister? With more time to process his impressions, Jonah concluded they were sorcerers or worked for the Grim Reaper! "They're KIN, aren't they?"

Mitchell grimaced. "Yes, they were. Thera and Fabian, the Rasmussen twins."

"What are they doing in town and with Brandon's dad?" Jonah sucked in a breath. "Brandon's dad works with a security company owned by a Wraith-possessed guy."

"The Grand Oracle obviously controls the company." Mitchell's tone was neutral.

Jonah could sense the man measuring the details he revealed and decided to nudge him. "The Rasmussens are KIN. They don't work with Hunters or the Grand Oracle's mortal minions."

"Also correct." Mitchell absently touched a pin on his coat's collar. It was a Japanese symbol, and the man wore a flat-top ring on his right index finger with the same symbol on it.

Jonah had never seen other Fallen Reapers add anything to their coats except a Council Badge. When Mitchell remained quiet, Jonah grew irritated. "And?"

Mitchell drew in a deep breath. "Because of my specialty, I—or someone else in my department—try to track their movements."

"I didn't know Alliance people had specialties."

"Oh, yes. I'm an Occult Objects Specialist." Mitchell paused. "I imagine you understand about the occult?"

Jonah nodded. "Yeah, I do."

The Fallen Reaper's expression brightened. "I saw your dad's paperweight medallion. He did excellent work. The details on the object helped me understand the medallions." His eyes sparkled with enthusiasm now.

Watching the Fallen Reaper's reaction, Jonah realized he had been right about the man being a researcher. Jonah also recognized that look in the man's eyes because he'd seen it with his mom. She would come home from a trip with a new object and obsess over it for days. "So what does that have to do with the KIN?"

"Oh," Mitchell said as if he had forgotten the original subject. "Thera's into occult objects too. So the Alliance has me trail her whenever she crosses into the mortal realm."

Jonah sensed a long history between the Fallen Reaper and the twins. "Did you ever fight her?"

"Once. I prefer to avoid duels with KIN members."

"The brother's a hothead," Jonah thought to add, while wondering if Mitchell was a good fighter. "He wanted to hex Brandon in public."

"That's not surprising, but don't be fooled. Thera's worse because she's more calculating," Mitchell said. They reached Jonah's neighborhood. "Anyway, until they leave town, or you do, I'll keep an eye on things."

Jonah nodded. "You got an operation going?"

Mitchell refused to answer that, but Jonah didn't care. This conversation revealed far more than he usually found out. Spotting the Morningside Drive street sign, he tapped the back of the driver's seat. "Let me out here."

"I don't know," Mitchell began.

"My house is just down the street. I want to walk." In truth, Jonah still needed to make his decision, and so far, events had prevented that. At least the short walk was a chance to do a little quick thinking.

When Mitchell nodded, the Guard Captain pulled over. Jonah opened the door.

Mitchell gripped Jonah's forearm to stop him from getting out. "Mr. Blackstone, I heard about the mix-up with your camp invitation. That was regrettable, but surely you can see the importance of attending camp?"

"I haven't decided yet," Jonah hedged.

"Of course." Mitchell hesitated. "Please don't let your anger at the Alliance stop you from fulfilling your destiny. It's a responsibility, really, when you think about it."

"Thanks," Jonah said, keeping his voice even. Not wanting Mitchell to keep prodding him, he hopped out and closed the door.

When the Alliance people didn't drive off, he knew they would watch him walk the rest of the way home. Setting off, he tried to settle his mind on his decision, but everything he'd just learned crowded in.

One thing became clear: Brandon suspected the supernatural world existed and Mr. Warner wanted to keep him clueless. That reminded Jonah so much of his godfather's attitude, and he didn't want to have anything in common with Brandon and the boy's dad.

Still, the strange encounter wouldn't let him rest. What had happened to Antwan and his cousin, for that matter? He knew the girl had fled town after the fight at the Center Point site. Jonah had freed her so he could save himself and his cousins. But he couldn't tell Brandon any of that.

Again, Jonah shook his head at the boy's odd behavior. In a bizarre twist of fate, he was the only person Brandon could ask. That saddened him. Although he didn't envy the bully and wouldn't forgive him, Jonah found himself wishing the boy luck.

CHAPTER SEVEN
A SEEKER'S GIFT

At 1338 Morningside Drive, the Hightowers' address, stood a modest house that didn't look any different from all the others in the neighborhood. But no other home on the street had a Half-Reaper living inside nor did it have all kinds of sigils and symbols to protect those inside from supernatural attacks.

Standing at the end of the front walk and staring at his home, Jonah reflected that when he arrived two years ago, he could never have imagined his cousins already knew about the supernatural world. Hadn't Marcus sent him here to forget about everything weird and be a normal kid?

With all the adventures he'd already had, Jonah wondered if he wanted the training now. As he lingered on the front walk, his uncle arrived home and pulled his car, an old Volvo station wagon, onto the driveway.

Uncle James paused when he got out of the car. "Did you make a decision?"

Jonah stuffed his hands in his pockets and nodded.

"Well," Uncle James said, "why don't you let us all know at dinner tonight? Okay?"

"Yes, sir."

After patting Jonah on the shoulder, Uncle James went inside. Jonah heard an engine rev and turned in time to see Mitchell and the Guard Captain drive away. Despite what he had told his uncle, Jonah didn't want to go inside yet.

"Jonah?" Mike's soft voice called out from the entrance to the backyard.

"Where have you been all day?" Jonah asked as he hurried over. He was about to tell Mike about his strange encounter with Brandon when he spotted the wrapped object in Mike's hand. "Is that my gift?"

Instead of answering, Mike motioned Jonah into the yard. They stood beside the shed where Jonah or others typically phased from, or, in Mandara's case, used a vortex. Not only was the location outside the protections around the house, the shed and the mature oak tree also hid this sliver of the Hightowers' backyard from the view of the neighbors.

With the high fence blocking the line of sight from the street, the only real consideration was someone inside the Hightowers' house. Unlike this morning, when his family was out and about, Jonah relaxed now because the blinds were closed. No one would see them leave.

Mike pulled the Seeker's Compass from under his shirt. Jonah stepped close, eager because he hadn't seen the compass in months. The multiple dials and Angel script still fascinated him.

After Mike tapped on the device, the dials glowed and moved.

"We're going somewhere, I guess," Jonah smirked.

It was odd to see Mike staring back with glowing eyes. "You trust me?" He held out a hand.

"Always," Jonah said as he gripped Mike's hand. When the destination locked in, the compass activated. One second, they were in the Hightowers' backyard; the next, they stood on a circular brick and stone platform that served as an overlook.

The muted late-afternoon sunlight, a stark difference from the darkening light back home, warmed Jonah's skin, and the wind carried the taste of salt. He walked carefully to the platform's edge since there wasn't a safety rail and peeked over.

He wished he hadn't because of the sheer drop to the ocean far below where waves pounded against the cliff side. He moved away from the edge but found the constant crashing of waves oddly soothing. Turning, he saw Mike halfway up the steps to a pavilion.

Jonah followed and sucked in a breath when a huge seaside monastery came into view. The structure was about a hundred yards away and connected to the pavilion by an ancient brick pathway. The bright blue dome of the monastery's main building had golden flecks that sparkled in the sporadic sunlight.

"Mike, where are we?"

"On the West Coast," Mike said. His eyes had returned to their normal light brown. "The Alliance has been mapping the designation stone network. Of course, we get as much information as we can about the locations. Then an Alliance Guard or Mage goes with me." Mike inhaled a long breath of sea air. "I loved this place the first time I saw it."

"Have you been inside?" Jonah took in every aspect of the quiet building.

"No, and the monks rarely come out. We'll be fine." Mike sat on the pavilion's rounded bench and waited for Jonah to join him before handing over the wrapped bundle. "I was at HQ most of the day working on this with Mage Trueblood."

Jonah paused. He had been unwrapping the item. "You were?" He peeled back the last fold of paper and three lacquered pieces of art clanked against each other in his hand. Jonah's jaw dropped as he balanced each on his leg. It was his mom's triptych. He gaped at his friend. "I don't get it."

Mike grinned. "Connect the pieces."

Pure curiosity caused Jonah's hands to shake as he snapped the pieces together. Immediately, the Underworld image appeared, along with the sets of coordinates for each. But something new happened. Five pulsing circles appeared over the image.

"Place your fingers on those," Mike explained.

Jonah did, experienced a jolt, and swore he heard an echo of Trueblood's voice muttering a spell. The pulsing circles disappeared, alarming him until the full page of writing replaced the image. His mouth fell open in amazement, and without thinking, he made a swiping motion with his finger. The page turned to another one.

"You know about Akashic records?" Mike asked.

"They're records in the nonphysical realm," Jonah answered, thinking. He sucked in a breath as something he learned from the Deliverer came back to him. "The Central Archives," he breathed. "All those are Akashic records."

"Yep. The total histories of every human being who lived and died. In the case of living people, it shows their possible futures." Mike touched the triptych. "This has an Akashic record overlay. I encoded the last segment of the Deliverer's Tales on it. The Prime Archivist showed me how to do it."

"You saw him too?" Now Jonah was getting jealous of his best friend. He hadn't been back to the Afterworld since their adventure last summer. When he noticed Mike was grimacing, Jonah suddenly remembered the loss Mike had endured on that trip. "Sorry. I forgot about…"

"Trevor?" Mike asked. "I'm fine. It was just odd going back there and being reminded of his sacrifice." Sighing to himself, Mike sat straighter.

Trevor, an Afterworld courier, had come to Mount Vernon to help them activate the Seeker's Compass and cross into the realm of the undead. Mike had grown close to Trevor but lost him in the battle to escape from the Central Archives.

Jonah watched his best friend for a moment before deciding to let the subject drop. He prodded the triptych. "Ah, Mike, why not just use a regular tablet?"

"Well, for one thing, you can't take electronics to camp."

Jonah nearly dropped the device. "You know about Mandara's visit?"

"Mage Trueblood told me. That's why we rushed to get this finished." Mike swallowed hard. "The Tales and the

Protector's Ring have been locked away by the Council Head of Security."

"Who's that?"

Mike looked apprehensive. "It's Mandara."

"Mandara!" Jonah shouted. "Not him again."

"I know," Mike hedged. "Trueblood suggested this so you could read the Tales. When Mandara found out, he wanted to lock this up. At least, that's what Trueblood told me. I had to wait outside the closed Council doors while they argued."

That shocked Jonah, "Mike!"

"I told you I wouldn't let the Alliance take your mom's triptych," Mike assured him.

Sensing his best friend's utter sincerity, Jonah relaxed. In fact, he was deeply moved that Mike, who liked working with the adults, would use his power to keep the device out of their hands. "Thanks again."

Mike smiled. "In the end, I didn't have to do anything because Trueblood came up with a plan. He promised the Council he'd add magical protections."

Jonah didn't envy his friend's trip to HQ after hearing that. "How did he protect it?" he asked, examining the triptych with deepening interest.

"He used a spell that only allows one person to read the Tales. Touching the glowing points activated that spell on you."

"And that satisfied Mandara?" Jonah snorted, not believing it.

Mike hesitated. "Trueblood worked in a backdoor. You can give someone else access if you both touch it and you say the counterspell."

Jonah nodded, but he caught Mike's hesitation before avoiding answering his question. "Okay. Is there more?"

"The Council wants you to find the Destiny Medallion. Actually"—Mike flipped to the last ethereal page—"they need you to solve the puzzle."

"Ah, it's blank," Jonah observed.

"I know. Mandara had experts from Alliance Archives read through the translation first," Mike said in a rush. "When they saw each section ended with a blank page and couldn't find any clues, their expert told the Council that you were the only one who could figure it out."

Wow, Jonah thought. Someone in the Alliance really believed in him. Even so, Jonah sensed the hesitation within his friend again. "What's the catch?"

"You can only keep this as long as you're at camp."

Slumping against the pavilion's side railing, Jonah pieced together the rest of the news. "Let me guess: Mandara is gonna be there."

"He's Campmaster."

That news made Jonah want to go to Florida immediately, but that wasn't really an option anymore. "Why not encode the Tales completely?"

"There wasn't time." Mike glanced away, looking embarrassed. "And I forgot to tell you that I translated the symbols on your dad's paperweight. They spelled out Destiny."

"Destiny?" Jonah sat up. "That's why the Alliance called the exhibit the Destiny Medallion. How could my dad make a replica of it?"

"The Prime Archivist worked with your dad and gave him access to real occult objects," Mike continued.

"True, including Lynn's real blades, Robert's archive box, and the Seeker's Compass." Jonah's gaze shifted to the device that hung around Mike's neck.

"And your mom and dad were able to find a real Protector's Ring," Mike added. "So, I thought that if your dad made a replica of a real medallion…"

Jonah snapped his fingers. "He must have seen it."

"More likely an image of it. Otherwise, the Prime Archivist would know where to find the medallion, and he doesn't." Reaching over, Mike tapped the triptych again. "Destiny's Sorrow is the story of the last medallion the Deliverer found."

The discussion about the medallion and the occult reminded Jonah of Fallen Reaper Mitchell. He told Mike all about his encounter with the twins and the Alliance adult.

"He's the expert who convinced the Council you have to solve the riddle. I met him once and he's cool." Mike sobered. "I heard about the twins. They're worse than Deyanira."

Jonah's excitement over Mike's upgrade to the triptych began to wane as his decision became more clear. That frustrated him more than anything else. He rose and crossed to the seaward side of the pavilion to face the ocean.

"Why can't I ever get a break?"

Mike came over. He hooked an arm over Jonah's shoulder, patting him lightly on the chest. "I get it. You have a group here that likes you. Now you have to go off and do it all over again."

"Exactly!" Jonah took a deep breath. "Why me?"

Mike rested his chin on Jonah's shoulder. "You're a hero, Jonah."

"I'm not a dang hero."

"Fine, you're heroic," Mike amended. "You like helping people. It comes from your parents and the Deliverer spirit inside you. If you stayed on the sidelines and something happened, you'd never forgive yourself. It's why the Alliance's secrecy angers you."

Jonah leaned his cheek against Mike's. "My wise Seeker gets a vacation in Florida while I go off to summer camp. Yay for me."

Mike let out a tired huff. "Kevin will be there so that you can spend time with him. Plus, he'll look out for you when it comes to the Council, right?"

"I guess so," Jonah hedged. He suspected his boyfriend had to walk a fine line when it came to Council decisions about him.

"Well," Mike said, sensing Jonah's doubt, "you'll meet new kids with powers."

"Powers?" Jonah stared at his friend. "I never even thought about that."

"Jonah, you won't be the only kid at camp learning to use his abilities. Don't worry. I worked with some of them over the summer and they're cool. I bet you have more fun at camp than we do in Florida. I wish I could go."

"You're serious," Jonah said, surprised.

"Yes!" Mike leaned to the side to look Jonah in the face. "Think about it this way. From what Mage Trueblood told me, the camp counselors will give you more information than you ever could ever want."

Jonah couldn't argue with his friend's logic. It was clear that if he was gonna find the Destiny Medallion, he had to attend camp. Besides, Lynn had told him the same thing. It seemed all roads pointed to Camp Alliance and not a fun summer with his friends.

"Fine," Jonah finally said, "but you're gonna help me disappoint everyone else."

CHAPTER EIGHT
THE ELDEST BROTHER

The Brentwood Baptist Church shuttle idled at the curb outside the Hightowers' home. Jonah sat beside Mike inside the bus as everyone else stowed their luggage and settled in. The Littletons, who agreed to be chaperones on the trip, were also there. The couple had the same sandy complexion as their son and were members of the Hightowers' church.

Jonah didn't envy Mike's need to hide his Seeker status from his parents, who hated anything remotely supernatural. They were friendly enough, but Mike warned Jonah that his mom couldn't understand why Aunt Imma would allow him to abandon the family.

When he caught Mrs. Littleton looking his way, Jonah turned and focused on his reason for sitting on the shuttle. He was glad he'd broken the news to the others last night. Everyone had reacted as he expected, but at least they had the night to adjust. Their spirits were high again this morning.

Glancing out the window, Jonah noticed that his relatives lingered on the front porch. Even Lynn and Wick joined them, leaving Rico and Tamara, on the bus. A white SUV sped up the street and pulled into the driveway. Everyone inside the shuttle pressed their faces to the windows, no doubt staring at the yellow-and-gold Monarch Summer Camp logo.

Kevin hopped out and crossed to the porch. He wore his camp clothes of tan khaki shorts and a tangerine-orange shirt. The word *Mentor* was stitched just below the golden Alliance Symbol.

Knowing it was time to say goodbye, Jonah stood. "Have a good time and send me pictures." His friends rushed forward to hug or bump fists with Jonah.

Mike gave him a one-armed hug and whispered, "Don't have too much fun without us."

"You know me," Jonah said, releasing Mike. Taking one last look around, he stepped off the bus, and strolled to the porch.

"Where're your bags?" Kevin asked.

"Inside."

As the Fallen Reaper went inside the house, Wick stepped forward and pulled Jonah's shield bracelet from a small sack. It had been a birthday present from Wick on Jonah's first summer in Mount Vernon. The young mage had polished the device so that it shined in the afternoon sunlight.

"Here you go." Wick pressed it into Jonah's hand.

The bracelet hummed with power at Jonah's touch. He glanced into Wick's expectant face, wondering when his friend had snagged it. "You recharged it?"

"Yep, Padawan. It should give you one good use, maybe two if you don't overdo it." Wick grinned. "When I first met you, you were just a Padawan."

Lynn held a fist under his chin. "If you finish that sci-fi quote, I'm swinging."

Jonah laughed, including Wick, who added, "Kick butt, Jonah." He glanced at Aunt Imma. "Sorry, Mrs. H."

Robert peered at Jonah, opened his mouth, and then stopped. "I was gonna say take care, little cousin, but you're as tall as me now." After a moment, Robert tapped Jonah's forehead. "Tell me everything you see when you get back."

Jonah knew his cousin wanted to draw detailed images from his thoughts. He and Wick still had plans to release a video game one day.

Lynn moved her brother aside. "Take care, geek boy," she said after hugging Jonah. "And remember, I can still take you down."

"Yeah, yeah." Jonah smiled as he watched his cousins and Wick march to the shuttle.

Aunt Imma gathered Jonah into a warm embrace. "Do your best." She stepped back and handed Jonah a bag of her chocolate, butterscotch, and raisin cookies. "Share them with Kevin." With a last hug, she followed the others onto the idling bus, leaving Jonah alone with his uncle.

Uncle James shook Jonah's hand. "I know my sister would be proud of you. She loved going off on new adventures."

There was something in Uncle James's tone that revealed his loss was still fresh. For the first time, Jonah considered asking his uncle if they could visit his parents' crypt next year, together.

"Do you want to go to DC—"

"Jonah," Uncle James cut him off. "We can talk when you get back. Go and enjoy yourself."

Jonah swallowed hard. He sometimes forgot his uncle had the same intuitive gift as his mom. Maybe not as strong, but he had it. "Yes, sir."

With a final, encouraging nod, Uncle James hurried to the shuttle.

Danita and the rest of the Mount Vernon Social Club waved from inside while the vehicle pulled off and drove down Morningside Drive. They had a five-hour trip ahead of them, Jonah reflected, a long, fun ride.

Kevin closed the rear hatch of the SUV, drawing his attention. "We'd better get going."

Jonah grabbed up his trusted book bag, another survivor of the Virginia fire, and climbed into the vehicle. He placed the cookies on the seat between them.

Kevin got in, started the SUV, and paused, watching Jonah. "You okay?"

"Yeah."

Kevin squeezed his hand before backing out of the driveway and pulling away from the Hightowers' home.

Jonah leaned back in his seat and stared out the window, letting his mind shift to what lay ahead.

~

The landscape of central Georgia swept by Jonah's window outside as they took the highway out of Mount Vernon. Only when he considered the length of their journey did something simple occurred to him.

"Why aren't we phasing to Camp Alliance?" he asked.

Kevin snorted. "I have to get this ride back. Plus, we'll need it while there. You'll see."

After giving it a little more thought, Jonah decided to trust him. He opened the cookies and sighed when the fresh-baked aroma filled the car. Offering one to Kevin, he took two cookies and settled in for the trip.

The first leg of the ride to Atlanta went well, with Kevin answering questions about camp. Despite his boyfriend's talkative mood, Jonah suspected Kevin deliberately kept the topic on business and away from anything personal.

That was irritating, considering this trip was their longest period alone in months, and the chance to learn more about Kevin excited Jonah. Reaching over, he intertwined their fingers. "So," he began, "what else do you want to talk about?"

Perhaps Kevin sensed his mood because he kept his eyes on the road. "Symon told me about the updates to your triptych."

"The triptych?" Jonah couldn't resist the stab of disappointment. "Can't we talk about something else? Like you?"

Kevin released his hand. "Just tell me about the triptych. Okay?"

"But why?"

"Jonah." Kevin eyed him.

Jonah opened his book bag with a jerk and pulled out the triptych. After taking a moment to calm his racing emotions, he explained how the device worked.

"Make sure you read it," Kevin warned. "Camp can get distracting,"

"Oh, I will." Jonah swiped through the pages, wondering if he could turn the conversation back to Kevin's life.

His finger stopped midswipe when specific phrases in the Tales caught his attention. Sitting forward, Jonah read a passage and realized the Tales weren't from the Deliverer's perspective. The story read as if someone else reported what happened. Despite his previous irritation with Kevin, this piqued his curiosity. Who could have written the Tales?

Immediately, he thought of the Prime Archivist who had been alive two thousand years ago. After all, Destiny's Sorrow, which contained six segments, was a record of the Deliverer's journeys. And the Prime Archivist's job had been to maintain the records.

The entire situation fascinated Jonah's nerd side. To him, the Deliverer's Tales was like having a fantasy novel, except the adventure was real. Flipping through the ethereal pages, he discovered the first five sections were about how each brother, or Ring Bearer, met the Deliverer. The last segment focused on Destiny herself and the epic war between Good and Evil over two thousand years ago.

Jonah began to appreciate the amount of work Mike put into the translation project and updating the triptych. Destiny's story alone required many pages. And considering there were six other medallions, each with five Protectors, the total number of pages was daunting.

Kevin's voice intruded on his thoughts. "Go ahead." When Jonah looked at him, Kevin added, "We'll have time to talk at camp."

Taking a moment to search their mutual connection, Jonah sensed Kevin's honest desire to spend time with him. So why the reluctance to talk about himself? Jonah wondered. Could it be that as a member of Marcus's inner circle, Kevin was following orders to make sure he read the Tales?

Of course, a lot depended on Jonah finishing the translation and finding the medallion. Like a punch to the gut, he realized he followed in his parents' footsteps. Just knowing that sobered him because they had paid the ultimate sacrifice while he had faced the Grim Reaper and survived. Had he been luckier than his parents?

Running a finger over the triptych's surface, he had no doubt the answers were in these ethereal pages. After squeezing Kevin's hand, Jonah slid lower into the seat, finding a comfortable position, and began to read.

Destiny's Sorrow: The Eldest Brother

The Deliverer journeyed from the realm of Sister Wisdom with a heavy heart. All the sisters valued Wisdom's strength and counsel, but that was gone, leaving Destiny alone in the world. Word had already reached the Deliverer about trouble among Destiny's sons. Thinking to gather his strength and prepare, the Deliverer camped in the hills outside the final Virtue's Realm.

News of his presence spread, and by dawn, a multitude of people had gathered to seek his counsel and justice. The Deliverer awoke and found the people below his encampment. As he gazed on them, he felt compassion for the suffering they endured. But he couldn't counsel everyone at once.

He called out to the crowd. "Choose from among yourselves representatives to speak. I will hear their words and render a decision for those aggrieved."

Excited at his pronouncement, the most vocal people argued among themselves. Eventually, a select group went uphill to speak with the Deliverer. When they came before him, all bowed low to the ground to honor his presence.

"Do not kneel before me," the Deliverer begged them. "I am just a person like you and will not make the same mistakes as the Grim Reaper and Grand Oracle. For they sought worship of others and hardened their hearts against all mortal kind."

At his words, the bravest of the group stepped forward. "Forgive us, great Deliverer. We have heard of your wisdom and discernment and how you help the poor and injured. We come before you with our grievances."

The Deliverer nodded and bid the speaker continue.

"Troubled times have overtaken the land. The glorious and brave Protectors have grown arrogant, cruel, and disdainful of the people they once served and protected."

Another person pressed forward. "I'm from the Eldest Protector's province. My family and I were driven from our homes because he accused us of serving the Grim Reaper!"

A third person spoke next. "He has become haughty and uses his power as a judge and jury to execute my brothers. I, too, was driven out lest I suffer the same fate and can never return to my land."

"And he takes advice from a stranger, someone who reeks of evil and the Grim Reaper's influence," another petitioner stated. "But to speak against his councilor results in banishment from the province."

The people's words troubled the Deliverer because the son's betrayal was a warning that the great Virtue's time of sleep was at hand. Once more, his heart moved with compassion for the suffering of the people and the coming darkness. After he considered their words, the Deliverer made known his decision.

"I will go to the province of Destiny's eldest son and see for myself and judge his actions."

Satisfied, the people thanked the Deliverer. After disguising himself as a lowly traveler so that he might observe the Eldest Brother's actions in secret, the Deliverer left on the next morrow.

⊂⊃

"How is it?" Kevin asked sometime later.

Jonah looked up from the Tales and discovered they had reached the Atlanta metro area with the downtown spires not far ahead. "It's cool. I wish it was like a novel instead of like reading the Bible."

Kevin raised a questioning eyebrow. "For real?" He snorted.

"Yeah," Jonah said, glancing at the rest of the story. "The first section is about this guy using his power to jack up the people he was supposed to serve."

"And he was a Protector? He sounds like a piece of work. What happened?"

"Oh, the Deliverer tricked him into a duel and embarrassed him. The brother ran for it." Jonah deactivated the triptych and frowned as he gazed out the window. "He was getting advice from a Wraith-possessed Advisor who played on his emotions. Sounds familiar, huh?"

Kevin tapped his fist on Jonah's leg. "You did the right thing with your Aunt Ruby."

Jonah accepted Kevin's comment, but mentioning his aunt reinforced the desire to be with his friends and family in Florida.

Nodding for Kevin's benefit, Jonah turned up the stereo, and they listened to music. Soon, the Atlanta cityscape gave way to the northern suburbs. Eventually, Jonah reconnected the pieces of the triptych and opened the Tales again.

He reread the ending of the Eldest Brother's story, and then he flipped through the rest. Could he skip to Destiny's section about the great battle? Skimming through to the end, he found the blank page Mike had shown him. His first reaction was Mike, and the Alliance, made a mistake by assuming there was a riddle or puzzle to solve. Then he sensed it, the slight beating of a pulse.

Moving his hand over the ethereal page, Jonah didn't expect anything to happen, but it did. A single star appeared in the center of the page as if drawn by an invisible hand. The star's rays began to rotate around the center while shortening and lengthening. The movement reminded Jonah of a cool 2D animation.

As he gawked, a circle of five more darkened stars appeared around the first. Unlike the animated center star, these remained static. Holding his hand close to the surface, he confirmed the heartbeat belonged to the pulsating center star. But why were the other stars darkened and still? Then he got it. The center represented Destiny, and the five dark stars were the five brothers!

"Wow," Jonah blurted out before he could stop himself.

"You read something good?"

Jonah held up the triptych to show Kevin the page, but the Fallen Reaper looked puzzled. "Oh. There's a pulsating star on the page. The outlines of five black stars surround it. Those must be the brothers." Jonah's excitement increased as he thought about it. "It's like reaching the end of the level on a video game where you have to find all the keys."

"That makes sense. The question is, can you find the keys?"

Jonah sank lower in the seat, staring at the triptych. "They have to be buried in the text. That means I have to read them all, and probably in order."

Kevin laughed. "What's the problem? You like to read."

"I do," Jonah said, shoving Kevin. "This feels like a deep game, but I don't know, I had hoped to read it and find the answer fast."

"If it was easy…"

"Anyone could find it. Yeah, I know," Jonah said. Turning back to the first segment, he began reading through it again. He continued for the next hour until Kevin slowed, pulled off the two-lane Georgia highway, and rumbled down a gravel road.

Within a few minutes, they broke from the cover of Georgia pines and passed a beautiful blue-green lake. Jonah deactivated the triptych and all but forgot about the Tales as they entered the Monarch Summer Camp. He alternated gazing out the left and right windows while trying to take it all in.

Sloping fields covered much of the area, with a solid ring of pine trees around the edge of the campsite. Numerous cabins and buildings dotted the landscape between pools, ranges, climbing walls, and ball courts. Jonah even spotted a horse grazing in a field.

"This is the camp for regular kids," Kevin explained.

He drove by groups of kids standing around a line of Monarch vans and continued until reaching two maintenance buildings. The structures bordered the high fence that encircled the entire camp. An adult stood there, with the gate opened for them to pass through.

The paved road led to an old wooden bridge that only extended for several feet over a deep ravine. Something had destroyed most of the bridge, leaving an abrupt twist of planks.

A similar surviving section jutted out from the opposite side of the ravine. There, the road disappeared into a dense blanket of pine trees. Jonah was perplexed and then shocked when Kevin didn't stop but continued out onto the broken bridge.

"Kevin?"

"Don't panic," Kevin said. "Everything's fine."

Jonah clutched at the door handle, nonetheless. What was wrong with Kevin? Was this a stupid joke?

"This isn't funny!" Jonah shouted when his boyfriend kept rolling forward, the ravine below looming closer and closer.

"I'm not laughing," Kevin said.

The next moment, the vehicle drove off the edge of the broken bridge. At the sight of the sheer drop to the river far below, Jonah nudged himself into a phase and discovered he couldn't do it. He was trapped!

CHAPTER NINE
CAMP ALLIANCE

Panic seized Jonah as he tried to phase a second time without results! Before he could try a third time, a dense forest appeared outside the windows. They hadn't plummeted to the depths below. Instead, the SUV continued along the smooth roadway.

"See?" Kevin said, sounding a little disappointed.

That angered Jonah. "What was that?"

"A mirage."

Jonah turned in his seat to glance behind them. The gate was visible with no ravine. "A mirage?"

"Yeah. It's a magical projection. Mages create them to camouflage things like entrances."

Embarrassment warmed Jonah's face, and he also got why Kevin sounded disappointed. "That was a test, wasn't it?" When the older boy nodded, Jonah punched Kevin's shoulder. "Why are you testing me?"

"To see how you'd deal with the unexpected." Kevin glared at him. "You failed. I know you tried to phase."

Jonah's anger finally receded until he could think about the situation in a more rational manner. "The SUV has sigils on it." Kevin nodded. "But how could I know you didn't go crazy?"

Kevin snorted in disbelief. "Even if I meant you harm, your Death Sense would have gone off. Did it?"

"No."

"Gee whiz, Jonah." Kevin watched him and softened his voice. "Just be prepared at camp. You never know when something's a test."

But Jonah's anger resurfaced for a different, more basic reason. He punched Kevin again. "You're my boyfriend. I need you on my side."

"It was a test—"

"Stop thinking like the Alliance Council. I need to be able to trust and relax with you and not worry that you're gonna spring something on me every second."

Kevin stared at him, dumbfounded. "I'm sorry. Actually, I thought you'd figure it out, but—" He broke off at Jonah's glare. "Okay. Okay. I'm sorry. I won't do anything like that again." He gripped Jonah's hand. "I promise."

Like before, when they promised each other something, Jonah heard a snap and goose bumps raised up along his arm. The certainty and sincerity of Kevin's pledge pushed aside the anger. Although he still didn't look forward to camp any more than before, he welcomed Kevin's promise. "Thanks."

Glancing back the way they came, Jonah added, "Wick's gonna flip out when I tell him about the mirage." He faced forward, allowing a guarded curiosity about camp to enter his mind. If the projection was any indication, he was about to see and find out some cool stuff.

By now, Kevin had finished a shallow turn, and two great posts made from stacked timber came into view on either side of the road. An arched sign connected both posts overhead, creating an archway. The letters on the sign spelled out *Camp Alliance*.

Beyond the sign, at the end of the road, was the small camp. The front gate was wide open, revealing a guardhouse just inside and to the left, a squarish log cabin to the right, and a large, two-story wooden building straight ahead.

Once they entered the gate, Jonah noted the adults bustling around the small camp. He spotted Fallen Reaper Mitchell and at least two people in blue mage tunics. And there were other vehicles parked outside.

Jonah's impression that the place looked more like a fort than a camp intensified. His confusion grew because this camp wasn't the same one Kevin had shown him two years earlier. Jonah certainly couldn't imagine spending four weeks here.

Kevin drove to the main building and parked out front. Without being told, Jonah climbed out. The fresh air was a welcome change from the recirculated air inside the vehicle.

Taking another moment to breathe in the scent of the nearby trees and flowers, Jonah grabbed his bags and followed Kevin into the building. The main floor had a decent common area, with plenty of chairs near a fireplace and numerous tables like a restaurant. Adults sat around sipping coffee, talking, or reading reports. The only thing missing were young campers like him.

"Come on, hero," Kevin said, leading Jonah out a set of rear double doors to reveal an incredible view of a deep blue lake and forested hillsides beyond. He could see the outer portion of a lower deck, but he couldn't see the entire deck from where he stood. Beyond that was a small pier with a boat moored at the end, rocking gently in the slight breeze.

Symon waved to him from where he stood near a gap in the railing, clearly the steps leading down to the lower deck.

"Jonah! Put your stuff with Eddy's."

Confused, Jonah crossed to the mage. His steps faltered when the full lower deck came into view. A group of kids about his age stared up at him in frank curiosity. They all wore the same sky-blue polo shirt and tan khaki pants. And, Jonah noted, each shirt had the Alliance logo with the words *Monarch Associates* beneath that.

Trueblood gestured at a beanpole Hispanic boy wearing a lopsided Atlanta Braves ball cap. "That's Eddy. Go ahead. We'll get going in a minute."

A blond girl broke away from the group and hurried over to Jonah as he descended the steps to the lower deck. "Hi! I'm Lisa." She gripped his hand with both of hers. Her uniform was the neatest, as if she took special pride in wearing it.

"Everyone," Lisa announced with a tour guide's bubbly enthusiasm, "this is Jonah Blackstone."

The lackluster response was in stark contrast to Lisa's energetic introduction. The most reaction he received was a wave from Eddy, who also smiled, showing off braces. "Hey, I'm Eddy," he said with a Latino accent. Then he hooked a thumb toward a lanky biracial boy beside him. "He's AJ."

AJ, taller and with a light brown Afro and matching goatee, responded with a quick upward flick of the chin. He was the only one with an extra bag. Jonah wondered if the thin case might be a bow, like the one his cousin Robert had. AJ also held a Georgia Guidebook in his hands.

Jonah couldn't understand why the boy didn't just look up info on his phone until he recalled Mike's comment that they couldn't use electronics at camp.

"That's Darren," Lisa said, pointing to the third boy.

Darren was clean-cut and tall and had massive shoulders and biceps, making his slimmer lower body seem almost out of proportion. He simply glared at Jonah, with his muscular arms crossed.

Given the boy's size and his familiar face, Jonah blurted, "Hey, is your dad a Captain in the Alliance Guard?"

Instead of answering, Darren huffed and looked off toward the lake.

Oh no, Jonah thought.

The final kid, an athletic-looking girl whose confident stance reminded Jonah of his cousin Lynn, placed her hands on her hips. She'd been toying with her single long braid but flicked it over her shoulder while giving him the once-over. "You fought the Grim Reaper and Grand Oracle?"

Lisa patted Jonah's forearm. "Yes, he did, Monisha."

Kevin came up behind them. "Jonah also beat a Hunter and a goddess," he said, nudging Jonah in the back.

Getting the message, Jonah shuffled forward with his bag.

Eddy moved his bag aside. "You can put your stuff here."

"Thanks." Jonah sat his bag down and only then became aware the other kids still watched him. He gulped, uncomfortable with the attention. Finally, Monisha and Darren turned to face the lake while talking to each other. AJ opened the Guidebook and disappeared behind the cover.

When Lisa asked Kevin something about their work at Headquarters, Jonah learned she had a paid internship.

"You were right," Eddy said.

"What?"

Eddy glanced at Darren and Monisha. "Darren's dad is an Alliance Guard. He doesn't want people thinking he's gonna do the same thing."

"Oh," Jonah said. "Sorry, I mentioned it."

"No problem," Eddy said. "You might want to stay out of punching range." He held Jonah's worried gaze for a few seconds before laughing. "I'm kidding." Eddy moved off to hover near Lisa and Kevin.

Despite Eddy's reassurances, Jonah swallowed hard. He guessed Darren didn't want to be judged by his size; and Jonah got that. Once he realized everyone pointedly did not look his way, he released his breath.

Fearing that someone would come over if he continued to stand there looking lost, Jonah moved to the circle of tightly packed bricks at the center of the lower deck.

Studying the space inside the circle done in a lighter wood than the rest, he discovered a sigil drawn on it. The familiar symbol and the gap between the wood center and the surrounding brick alerted Jonah to the deck's real purpose.

Excited by his discovery, he crossed to the wooden, three-foot pole and found a circular, fist-sized hole near the top, large enough to fit a codex! This deck was much broader than the platform at the guesthouse. They had used Mike's compass to move that platform. The Alliance had expanded that concept.

"What's up?" Eddy asked, right over his shoulder.

Jonah's irritation flashed for a moment because the question drew the attention of the other kids. Did they expect him to explode or something?

"I know what we're standing on," Jonah answered in a low voice, hoping the others wouldn't hear.

Eddy looked down at the deck and shrugged. His response was anything but quiet. "It's wood, right?"

Jonah grimaced, but before he could explain, Mitchell came down to the lower deck. He skirted around the others and walked up to Jonah and Eddy.

"Excuse me, gentlemen." The Fallen Reaper gestured to the pole behind them. The boys stepped aside.

Trueblood and his sister Eleanor had joined the group.

Eleanor handed her brother a dozen heavy-duty zip-top bags, and the sibling mages moved among the group of kids, passing out the bags.

"Put your phone in the bag and zip it closed, please," Symon explained, handing bags to Jonah and Eddy last. "That includes any fitness watches and digital watches.

However, traditional watches are acceptable. Once you've done that, please seal the bags and hand them to Mage Trueblood." When someone snickered, Trueblood grinned. "I mean, my sister, of course."

The other kids relinquished their devices without a fuss. Facing the prospect of not having a phone for weeks, Jonah wished he'd called Mike one last time. Too late now, he decided, placing his phone in a bag. Within a few minutes, Eleanor Trueblood had collected the bags and stowed them in a larger secured pouch.

That done, Symon Trueblood checked his watch and motioned to Mitchell. "It's your show."

Mitchell reached inside his long coat and pulled out a codex in one smooth motion that spoke of a lot of practice. With a curt nod to Jonah that caused everyone to look him, Mitchell placed the device in the opening near the top of the pole.

Immediately, Jonah experienced the gentle tug on his power when Mitchell activated the codex.

—

The reserved kids let out a collective "Wow" when they reappeared at their destination. Though Jonah had been here once before, he still found the blue lake beautiful as it sparkled in the July sunlight. At the center of the lake was a small island with a profusion of green grasses, trees, and bright flowers, just as he remembered.

Symon clapped his hands and said, "Welcome to the real Camp Alliance."

While the others surveyed their surroundings, Jonah stared at the young woman who stood at a tall podium at the edge of the deck. A light shot up from the podium's top and into the air. High above, it intersected with a magical barrier.

"You have a ward over the whole camp?" Jonah asked, impressed and awed.

"The entire camp is protected from intrusion," Trueblood explained to them. "We use talismans to get through the protection at specified times for groups and supplies."

AJ moved to stand beside the mage. "Did you help design it?"

Trueblood half bowed. "Yes, I did. We also have the standard sigils to protect from phasing and creating vortices. The only way to enter or leave the camp is through the travel building or the back gate." He motioned the boys closer to the podium.

The young woman smiled and stepped back as Trueblood pointed to a round metal device about the size of a small plate. The beam of light flowed from it. Jonah saw sigils within the beam, some of which glowed or pulsed in a repeating sequence.

"That's a dialer," AJ exclaimed from over Jonah's shoulder. "Nice."

Trueblood nodded. "We use it to open a brief corridor through the wards."

"That wasn't here the last time I came with Kevin," Jonah observed.

"We've updated the camp's protections since then, Jonah."

"What about the talisman?" Jonah gestured at the beaded necklace Mitchell held.

"Ah, yes. Think of it like this. You know how a home can have a security system?" Trueblood began. "When you enter, you have to disable the alarm, but you also had to use a key to get in the door."

"The talisman is a key," AJ said. "And the dialer is the alarm code."

That made sense to Jonah, considering the pulsing symbols on the device.

"Excuse us," someone called out. Two men rolled dollies loaded down with boxes onto the deck.

Mitchell consulted with a guy holding a clipboard then returned to the round travel deck. As everyone watched, the Fallen Reaper fiddled with the codex, double-checking everything, then briefly met Jonah's gaze before activating the device. He, the travel deck, and all the containers vanished. A few seconds later, the light from the podium winked off.

"That's so cool," Monisha gushed.

Trueblood stepped to the front of the group. "Let's go. I want you checked in and squared away before this evening's assembly."

With the other crates and boxes gone, Jonah finally noticed a motorized flatbed cart. People grabbed their bags and loaded the cart. Jonah stuffed his on top of Eddy's.

Trueblood handed Darren a remote control. "Do you mind steering the cart?"

Darren nodded, eagerly took the remote, and fidgeted with the controls.

The mage started across a white stone bridge that connected this deck to a bamboo-covered pathway. He let everyone else follow before starting the cart.

Meanwhile, Trueblood began pointing out things. "That path on the right leads to the White Tower and the Practice Ranges. We designed these ranges with kids like you in mind."

Jonah didn't know what to make of that. How could a range be designed to deal with his phasing ability? Glancing around, he recalled Mike's comment that the other kids also had powers.

That idea intrigued Jonah as he and the group walked around the west side of the lake. They passed a Lavatory Building and a square courtyard with two smaller buildings and a boathouse. Jonah could hear the gentle lapping of water and muted bumps from the boats secured inside.

The other campers pointed and talked in expectant voices, but Jonah edged forward to walk beside Trueblood. "Can I ask you a question?"

The mage smiled. "I expect you'll have a lot of questions over the next four weeks." He chuckled, and Jonah took that as an opening.

"It's about the codex and the travel deck."

Trueblood blinked at him and said, "What's your question?"

"How did you get the designation stones?"

"We've always known about a limited number of stones. But with Mike's help, we uncovered a vast network around the world and discovered we could move them." He gestured back toward the building. "So this place got a designation stone."

Jonah fell silent as he thought about the designation stone at his parents' hideaway. Had they relocated the stone? He glanced at the mage as more questions burned in his mind. "Mitchell used a schedule?"

"Oh, yeah. We can't have people appearing on top of each other. The Alliance has a few Fallen Reapers who work our little network. It's a big help being able to move large groups of people and equipment around."

Jonah nodded as his mind shifted to the next questions. "So, about the wards and sigils you mentioned. Will they keep us from phasing around inside camp?"

Trueblood smirked. "Yes, they will. You won't be able to take any late-night trips." He laughed but quickly grew quiet, watching the surrounding area for a minute before speaking again. "I know you wanted to go to Florida, but give the camp a chance, okay?"

Jonah just nodded, wondering if the mage had guessed his plan to leave as soon as possible.

"We're here," Trueblood announced, gesturing to a gateway in a medium-high dark wooden fence.

Beyond the entrance, Jonah glimpsed a sprawling compound, the heart of Camp Alliance. Despite his earlier hesitation, he couldn't wait to explore the rest of the camp.

CHAPTER TEN
GROUP OF MAGES

This is what a camp should be, Jonah thought to himself.

Camp Alliance's central compound contained four buildings, including a large, covered pavilion and a mesmerizing flower garden, all spaced around a central courtyard. Light stone tiles that cushioned his footsteps covered the areas between the buildings: no sidewalks or outlined paths in sight.

Just inside the compound's entrance, they passed a formation of giant granite boulders with flattened tops that resembled ancient drums rather than rocks. As Jonah walked by, he touched one to make sure it was real. Just beyond the rock formation, the pavilion came fully into view. This building, like all the others, had the Asian-inspired tiled roof.

Trueblood continued toward a two-story building that could pass for a sky lodge. The profusion of colorful plants and bushes and the two ponds out front reminded Jonah of a theme park pavilion. He bit back the pang of regret for missing the Florida trip.

Mage Trueblood turned to face their group. "This is the Embracing Valley building. It's where you'll sleep and eat your meals and hang out when not in sessions. Dorm rooms are on the second floor. The kitchen, meeting rooms, and common areas are on the ground floor. Bathrooms and showers are in a building behind and to the right of this one."

Monisha frowned. "You mean we don't have any inside? This is just like a regular camp."

Trueblood smiled. "Not exactly, Monisha. The dorms are as large as nice hotel rooms. Two people per unit." He proceeded up the landscaped walkway, through the front double doors, and into the building.

A small reception area and office on the immediate left contained two desks, while the open room on the right had several round dinner tables inside. And, Jonah noted, a small sculpture sat on a pedestal beside a column. It changed colors like a wind sculpture.

Beyond the atrium and straight ahead was a welcoming area with a hearth, plenty of chairs, and a pool table in the far-right corner. The ceiling above this section opened to a second-floor railed balcony.

Monisha and Darren started toward that area when Trueblood called out to them. "Take your bags to your dorm rooms first and unpack. Lunch begins in thirty minutes. Then you have the rest of the afternoon to yourself." He grinned. "I suggest you try out the smaller lake just outside the building."

Excited with that news, people rushed outside to the cart, grabbed their bags, and hurried up the curved stairs just past the reception's area and office. Their excited muttering faltered when they reached the second-floor landing. A young woman, with vibrant golden skin and long dark hair, blocked their way. Despite her serious expression—arms crossed and eyebrows drawn together—Jonah smiled because he recognized her. She'd been the Memory Charmer who helped with Aunt Ruby.

The woman nodded to Jonah in greeting before extending a hand to Monisha and Lisa. "My name is Serena. I'm your mentor for the session." She stepped back and motioned the girls to the hallway across the open second-floor balcony area. "You'll stay in that wing." She shifted her gaze to Darren and added, "Guys to the left."

Jonah wanted to grin at Darren's shocked expression as Serena ushered the girls to the opposite hallway. Meanwhile, Kevin took her place at the head of the stairs and motioned them to the left. AJ and Eddy moved at once, but Jonah held back.

Darren also stood his ground and went up on tiptoes to see past Kevin. "Who's she?"

"She's a Memory Charmer," Kevin answered.

"You mean a Mind Bender?"

Kevin grimaced and glanced over his shoulder, as if making sure Serena was out of earshot. "They don't like that name, Darren."

"That's what they do."

Kevin pointed down the left hall. "Go unpack. Your girlfriend will be alright."

Darren whirled and marched off without another word. Kevin shook his head like he had been through this with Darren before.

Jonah realized that could be the case. Just as he knew all the kids back home, Kevin knew these kids too. Jonah's feeling of being the outsider increased.

"You okay?" Kevin asked.

"Yeah. Fine," Jonah lied and trudged to his dorm room with his bags.

He had the second dorm on the left, and he found Eddy inside, waiting. "Who assigned the rooms?"

"Mage Trueblood. Why?" Eddy asked, looking a little concerned. "You want to change?"

"No." Jonah didn't, but he had a hunch Trueblood had deliberately paired him with Eddy to change his mind about leaving camp. After entering, he dropped his bags at his feet.

Just as Trueblood described, the room resembled a hotel room. Instead of a bathroom, there was a short, narrow hall with two closets as soon as you entered. The open doors revealed three installed pull drawers at the bottom and a bar up above to hang clothes.

Two full-sized beds with exotic bird-patterned covers took up most of the space beyond the double closets. Against the wall opposite each bed were identical desks with reading lamps and plain chairs. The beds had large bamboo headboards that reminded Jonah of the pathway outside. Given their side of the hallway, he knew the room's single window faced the courtyard below.

He glanced at Eddy. "Which bed do you want?"

The boy hesitated and glanced between the two beds and Jonah, as if trying to gauge Jonah's feelings on the matter. "I'll take this one?" He dropped his bag on the bed closer to the door.

"That's cool with me," Jonah said and began unpacking his things and putting them all away. Finished, he sprawled on the bed, testing it out.

A bell sounded through speakers in the hallway. It was like the ding of an upscale elevator but loud enough to hear through a closed door.

Eddy wiggled his eyebrows. "Lunch is ready."

—

Jonah expected sandwiches and potato salad or something simple like that for lunch. However, the kitchen staff had put out a real lunchtime meal of pasta, salads, baked chicken, and jasmine rice. Plus, they had real plates and silverware. People spoke with excitement as they attacked the spread.

The dining area had more than enough tables for everyone to spread out, yet the group chose to sit together. The lunchtime conversations centered around speculations about what they would learn. Jonah spent most of the time listening to the others and getting a feel for them.

Darren came off as a little cocky and always sure of his ideas. Monisha didn't care what they studied if it wasn't dull, while Eddy hoped he impressed the instructors.

AJ tended to listen, but when he spoke, his answers were always well-reasoned and based on something he either read, overheard, or asked the adults. At seventeen, Lisa was the oldest of the group and seemed happy to facilitate the discussion like she did this every day.

About halfway through lunch, she rose from her chair and cleared her throat. "Now's a good time to get to know a little about Jonah."

With his face already warming from embarrassment, Jonah opened his mouth to stop Lisa when Darren spoke up.

"We already know all about him," the boy said, pointing at Jonah.

"Yeah," Monisha chimed in. She looked as irritated as Darren sounded. "Give it a rest, Lisa. Everyone's heard the stories." She glared at Jonah. "Don't expect us to bow."

Jonah's anger flared as he sat forward. "I didn't ask anyone to bow to me."

"Good, because I don't plan to. Right, Darren?"

"Dang straight." Darren gave Monisha a high five.

Jonah couldn't believe their comments and, out of reflex, glanced at Kevin, who sat at another table with Serena. But the Fallen Reaper seemed too engrossed in a conversation with his fellow mentor to look Jonah's way. That's when reality set in. Jonah needed to fight for his place among these kids.

"Well," Lisa said, clearly flustered, "um, we could at least tell Jonah where we're all from and what we can do."

Her comment surprised Jonah because he assumed everyone was from Atlanta since they all wore the Monarch uniforms. As far as he knew, he was the only kid from a small country town.

Turning to Eddy, he asked, "Where are you from?"

"I'm from Chattanooga, Tennessee," Eddy said and gestured at the others. "Monisha's from Birmingham, Alabama, and Lisa's from Lakeland, Florida. Darren's from Atlanta."

Jonah nodded to AJ. "What about you?"

AJ calmly laid his fork down. "I'm from Raleigh, South Carolina. Actually, I'm from all over, but South Carolina will do."

Jonah thought AJ had a cool, even voice without a Southern accent.

"Well," Lisa said, turning to Darren. "Show him."

Darren crossed his arms, refusing to budge until Monisha patted his shoulder.

"Oh, go ahead."

Everyone set down their cups or silverware and leaned back from the table. Jonah hurried to do the same, not understanding why, until Darren gripped the table with both hands and lifted the entire thing. The boy's face didn't show any strain as he waited a moment and lowered the table. Nothing had spilled or moved around.

Jonah clapped with the others until he noticed Monisha's devious grin. Without warning, she held out her hand so fast Jonah thought she would shoot lightning or fire at him. He jumped back in his chair, causing her to laugh. A second later, his silverware lifted from his plate and flew into her outstretched hand.

With a slight flicking motion, the silverware zoomed back across the table, stopped in front of him, and dropped onto his plate, knocking chunks of cold pasta salad into his lap.

"I'm sorry," she said. "I guess my control needs work."

Monisha's shocked expression didn't convince Jonah, nor Lisa, who frowned at her friend.

AJ stood, drawing everyone's attention to his closed fist. He blew on it and shook the fist like he had lucky dice, causing the others to laugh. When he made a throwing motion, three tiny green fireballs flew out and danced around in midair before puffing out. Everyone roared their approval.

Next, Lisa crossed her legs underneath her body. Once settled, she closed her eyes and wrinkled her forehead in concentration. Within seconds, she rose from her chair and stopped, level with the tabletop. Jonah stared at the levitating girl in amazement as everyone else clapped.

Monisha's piercing whistle seemed to distract Lisa, who wobbled and lowered herself to the chair somewhat hard. Jonah held the girl's arms to keep her from toppling onto the floor.

Although Lisa smiled, her hands shook a little when she took a gulp of her water. Jonah guessed the levitation had weakened her. Or maybe it was nerves.

Eddy pushed back his chair and stood. "I guess it's my turn." He raised his hands, palms upward.

That's when the hair on Jonah's arm began to rise, startling him. Lisa laughed and pointed at Monisha, whose long braid rose in the air behind her head like a tail. Lisa didn't seem to mind that her shorter blond hair stood out as if someone had spooked her.

Jonah's heart stopped when he saw the ball of lightning in Eddy's hands. Memories of Deyanira shooting lightning at his cousin Lynn roared into his mind. He jerked away from the boy before he could stop himself.

Eddy noticed. "What's wrong?" Noting the way Jonah stared at the energy ball, Eddy brought his hands together, and the ball of lightning disappeared with a popping sound. "Sorry, dude."

"It's…" Jonah glanced at the others. "Forget it."

Horrified now, Lisa shot to her feet. "Well, that's enough."

"Hold up!" Monisha pointed at Jonah. "What can he do?"

The idea that he'd have to do something had occurred to Jonah while watching the others.

Every eye turned to him as he stood. Before he could do anything, Kevin clamped a hand on his shoulder.

"Jonah can phase like other Fallen Reapers."

"But," Monisha stammered, "can't he show us?"

"No, he can't because the camp has protection against phasing."

The others deflated on hearing that. Discovering they didn't know about the camp's protections either, Jonah finally felt he was on even ground.

After Kevin's intervention, the discussion turned to the small lake. Everyone finished lunch and rushed outside to check it out. However, Mage Trueblood had neglected to tell them about negotiating a maze featuring a profusion of Asian-inspired plants like tall bamboo, camellias, and apricot blossoms.

The group's initial confusion soon turned into playful wandering along the scented pathways. Lisa managed to find the exit before anyone else and shouted, "This way," to the others. The inlet had a small artificial beach and a tiny pier. Everyone ran back to the main building, changed, and returned to the beach, eager to have fun.

Jonah only hesitated a moment before pulling off his shirt. With muscle-bound Darren there, no one would notice him. Soon, he splashed around with the others until the late afternoon turned into early evening. Everyone, including Jonah, was disappointed when Kevin called them back inside to change for that evening's opening ceremony.

Eddy reached the dorm first to discover seven forest green T-shirts and seven pairs of dull gray basketball-type trunks stacked on each bed. The shirts had Camp Alliance in yellow letters on the upper left chest, and the trunks had green bands down each leg.

"Wow," Eddy said. He lifted a shirt. "I wonder if we get to keep these?"

Shrugging, Jonah lifted a shirt and discovered it was made of a quality mesh material. He had just pulled a shirt over his head when a raised voice came from outside. Peeking through the curtain panels, he spotted six kids standing at attention in the courtyard below.

Mage Albrecht paced in front of them, causing Jonah to smile at seeing another familiar face. And he recognized the tall, lean boy standing among the other kids. It was that Thomas guy again.

The young mage, and the others, wore navy blue mage tunics with azure blue T-shirts underneath. Their athletic trunks were also dull gray but had matching blue stripes down the leg. There was one girl among them, sporting a complicated African head wrap of white and lavender fabric. Not only were they already changed, but they didn't have luggage with them. Had they already been at the camp?

"What's up?" Eddy crowded in behind Jonah. "Oh, the mages." Jonah gave him a blank look, and Eddy blushed. "Sorry. They have to train just like we do."

"Really?" Jonah stared at the group of kids, his fascination growing. "They missed lunch."

"Oh. The mages had lunch in Albrecht's cabin," Eddie answered. "One of them told me. It's a tradition or something like that."

Albrecht had finished his instructions. Thomas waited until the short mage walked off before leading the group of younger mages into the building.

Jonah rushed to his door and peeked out.

Thomas had just reached the second-floor landing and motioned the guys down Jonah's hallway. The young mage had a bossy attitude about him, something Jonah never noticed the first time they met.

The mages-in-training marched past Jonah's open door without looking at him and moved to the dorm rooms at the end of the hall.

AJ leaned in his doorway across from Jonah's dorm, frowning.

Raised voices drew their attention toward the stairs. Thomas stood with the lone girl of the group. "You have to stay with the other girls, Jennifer."

The tall girl crossed her arms. "I don't want to stay with them," she said in an African accent.

Jonah sucked in a breath.

Eddy peeked over his shoulder. "Dude, what's wrong now?"

"I think I know her."

"What, like you dated her?" Eddy leaned farther out.

By that time, Serena came up the steps behind Jennifer. "We've already been through this. All the women are staying in the east hall, including you."

Jennifer flexed her hands, and Jonah detected the crackle of magic. If Serena sensed the danger, she didn't let on. Instead, the mentor crossed her arms, staring down the girl.

Thomas gripped Jennifer's wrist. "Mage Rubio would throw you out in a second. Calm down."

"You're the mentor for the mages, and I'm a mage! Not a…" Jennifer flicked her hand at Serena like the woman was beneath her. "I'm not a Memory Charmer."

"It's just the way it is."

"Well, it's sexist," Jennifer shouted.

Thomas slapped a hand over his forehead. "Fine. I'll see if the Alliance Council will vote to change things just for you in their next meeting." He gathered power around himself. "Until then, you sleep with the other women." When Jennifer opened her mouth to continue protesting, Thomas raised his voice, drawing everyone out of their rooms. "Being a member of the Alliance is more than about power. It's about following orders."

The girl huffed and stormed off to the east hallway. Serena traded a sympathetic look with Thomas before following. Both Jonah and AJ stood straighter as Thomas turned and strode in their direction. Unlike the others, his eyes flicked to the left and right, checking out his surroundings.

As he passed, Jonah experienced a buffeting wave of power, like the onrushing air before a subway train entered an underground station. Jonah blinked, having never sensed so much magic from anyone. That made him wonder about Albrecht and Trueblood. Why didn't magic leak off the adult mages like this?

"Did you feel that?" AJ whispered to Eddy.

"Yeah."

AJ waited until Thomas slipped into the last room on the right before saying, "He needs to learn better control."

Jonah ducked back into his room with a more pressing concern on his mind. He'd finally placed Jennifer's voice. She was the niqab girl, Antwan's cousin. The one who had worked with the Alliance Mole and his wild Aunt Ruby!

CHAPTER ELEVEN
THE ALLIANCE COUNCIL

Jonah had to tell someone about Antwan's cousin. He intended to do it—that is, until he reached the main room and all thoughts about Antwan's cousin vanished. The entire Alliance Council stood around two reserved tables, one on either side of a podium. Each member wore their work clothes with a shiny Council pendant clipped to a lapel, tunic, or long coat.

Other adults, probably from Alliance Headquarters, Jonah decided, stood around. Most shocking, Marcus had a new beard. Jonah grinned, thinking it didn't look bad.

When his godfather noticed him, Jonah waved as he followed the others to their table. Eddy sat next to Jonah, AJ, on his other side, with Lisa, Monisha, and Darren taking the remaining seats. Kevin and Serena sat at the mentors' table while Thomas remained with the young mages. The various conversations quickly died away as Mandara stepped behind the podium.

"Welcome to Camp Alliance. My name is Cedric Mandara, and I am the Campmaster and Session Supervisor. Before I go further, I want to thank the Alliance Council for being here." He turned to regard the people on either side of him.

Jonah already knew that the Alliance Council had three Fallen Reapers, three mages, and three mortals. He recognized half of those present, but not the rest.

After the polite applause, the Campmaster cleared his throat to continue. "For those who've already begun formal training as future mages, today, you begin the final process before you join our ranks."

Eddy whispered through clenched teeth. "Is this the military?"

The Campmaster's head snapped around and he looked directly at Eddy. "Some of you may think this sounds like the military." He frowned at them. "We are in a fight that began over two thousand years ago when the Rulers of the Afterworld perverted the natural order of things. Destiny has called us to reset the balance."

Jonah froze with his glass halfway to his mouth. Had the Campmaster said *destiny* on purpose?

The man's eyes traveled over the two tables of young people. "The stakes are real, and you must hone your abilities. However"—he glanced at Trueblood—"we know that some of the things you'll learn at the camp may be frightening and unusual for you. Please remember that all of us are here to help. Go to your mentors if you have issues or concerns. If needed, they will refer you to Mage Trueblood or me. Also, do not hesitate to stop any of the teachers for additional help with their classes."

Jonah liked that idea since he assumed Trueblood had a session at camp. Likewise, he could always ask Kevin something, but he couldn't see himself going to the Campmaster with a problem. Then again, would the man teach a session?

As the Campmaster continued, Jonah scanned the Council members for their reactions. Marcus remained still, but Jonah knew his godfather well enough to tell he wasn't happy with the speech. He already knew the Campmaster was a Hardliner. Jonah knew Mage Trueblood and Albrecht weren't Hardliners because he had worked with them.

He didn't know the dignified older woman with wild reddish-gray hair, nor the heavyset older Black man sitting next to her. The woman's mouth drew down in a frown. And the guy didn't look happy either, although he leaned heavily on his cane as he listened to the Campmaster.

The only likely candidates, in Jonah's opinion, were a severe woman with short hair styled in a box braid bob, a shade lighter than her ebony skin, and Rubio. Jonah had worked with him on the Afterworld mission. Both nodded so much that Jonah thought they would jump to their feet and start clapping each time the Campmaster paused.

"Perhaps someday the world will know what you've done," Mandara said as he stepped from behind the podium. "But it all starts here, at this camp. So follow the rules, work hard, and make us all proud."

Mandara spread his long arms and smiled. "Enjoy the rest of the evening." A smattering of talking and clapping erupted as people moved about and mingled.

Eddy let out a breath. "Dude, I thought he heard me."

AJ nudged his friend on the shoulder. "Maybe he did."

"He's a Fallen Reaper," Jonah interjected. "They have enhanced hearing."

He would have laughed at Eddy's stunned expression, except AJ pointed at Marcus. "You waved to that Council member earlier."

"He's my godfather."

AJ's eyebrows rose high. "Introduce us."

Eddy nodded eagerly at the suggestion. Having no good reason not to do it, Jonah rose from his chair and made his way toward Marcus. He always thought the long coat was impressive, and tonight his godfather carried an extra bit of power about him. Maybe it was because the Alliance Council was here. As they approached, Marcus surprised Jonah with a big smile, accented by the beard.

"Jonah. I see you made it here in one piece."

When he shook Jonah's hand, Marcus's gaze lingered on the birthday watch Jonah had decided to wear tonight.

Either AJ or Eddy poked Jonah in the back. He couldn't tell which, but he got the message. "These are my friends, AJ and Eddy."

Eddy paled a little as he shook Marcus's hand. "Nice to meet you, sir."

AJ was more reserved when he shook hands.

Jonah had a lot of questions, but the first came out on its own. "Will you teach us something at camp?"

"I'm afraid not." Marcus nodded toward the Campmaster. "But I suspect the Campmaster may conduct a blade session."

"Really?" Jonah couldn't hide his frown.

"He's scary," Eddy said and clamped a hand over his mouth.

Jonah's godfather smiled. "You'll learn a lot from him," he said. "Just do your best, take it seriously, and you'll be fine."

Eddy and AJ nodded.

"He…" Jonah began. "He reminds me of my dad."

Marcus's jaw clenched. "He worked closely with your father and could have picked up some of his ways."

"But Mandara's a Hardliner," Jonah countered.

"Yes, he is. That's Council business. Don't concern yourself with it."

Jonah lowered his head, thinking that statement was interesting, considering Marcus was the one to say he'd have to enter Alliance politics soon. He met his godfather's gaze and, at that moment, decided not to mention his suspicions about Jennifer. He'd tell Kevin first.

"You're here to train," Marcus continued, as if sensing the source of his hesitation. "Concentrate on that, and you'll honor your parents' wishes. And don't be afraid to ask your mentors or adults for help." He gestured toward the food tables. "Why don't you gentlemen get something to eat?"

Jonah trailed Eddy and AJ to the food line, his stomach grumbling all the way. While the two boys talked about the food arrayed on the serving table, Jonah watched Mage Rubio with the short, severe councilwoman. Thomas stood beside her, listening to every word. Seeing the facial resemblance, Jonah realized she was his mother.

Eddy elbowed AJ. "Thomas looks so serious. Maybe he's getting instructions."

"Probably telling him how to jinx all of us," AJ quipped.

Jonah wouldn't go that far, but he realized his brief introduction to Thomas hadn't prepared him for the real boy. The line moved forward, and he started piling food on his plate.

AJ stood on the opposite side of the table, observing Jonah with a shrewd expression. "Your godfather tells you a lot about Council stuff?"

"No way." Jonah snorted. "He wants me to concentrate on my training."

"Then how did you know about Hardliners?" AJ asked, following Jonah to the dessert table.

Jonah hesitated to mention Kevin had been the one to explain everything. But this wasn't the Mount Vernon Social Club. These guys knew all about the Alliance. He'd have to pick his way around some details. "I'll tell you later. Promise."

Goose bumps raced up Jonah's arm, and he froze.

AJ glanced at his arms. "Interesting."

Lost in the meaning of the strong reaction, Jonah didn't notice Alastor until they were halfway to their table. The deceitful Fallen Reaper waved like they were buddies. The man's appearance surprised Jonah. Though Alastor sported the disheveled brown hair, and his unblinking eyes were as sunken as ever, the man's dark coat and slacks were clean and presentable. No shabby clothes tonight, Jonah assumed, since the entire Alliance Council was present.

No matter the man's neater appearance, Jonah changed direction to find a table on the opposite side of the room. AJ and Eddy were right behind him, but Jonah feared Alastor might come over until Kevin joined them, leaving two empty chairs because Lisa, Monisha, and Darren sat at another table.

Lisa and Monisha carried on a conversation with a Fallen Reaper. Darren focused on the Trueblood siblings as soon as the mages joined their group.

The young mages reclaimed their table and talked among themselves, except Jennifer. She watched Jonah with an intense expression, causing his Death Sense to stir.

Thomas appeared beside the mages' table and spoke to Jennifer, shocking her out of the gaze. Her head wrap wobbled as she shook her head, shot to her feet, and marched out of the dining room. Thomas flashed an irritated look and followed her.

Wondering what Thomas's mom thought of Jennifer's attitude, Jonah searched the gathering, but the woman had disappeared with Rubio and the Campmaster. Trying not to find anything ominous in that, Jonah ate his meal with the others while dodging AJ's incessant questions about his godfather.

"Do you mind if I sit here?" Thomas had reentered the room about thirty minutes later and crossed to their table.

Jonah, surprised at the young mage's presence, also thought it odd that Eddy and AJ looked at him instead of Kevin. Thomas noticed, and he too waited for Jonah to answer.

"Sure."

Pulling out an empty chair, Thomas plopped into it, then folded his hands on the table. Up close, Jonah noted the young mage's perfect, smooth brown skin, clear of any pimples or bumps. His short Afro was neat without a hair out of place.

With chiseled cheekbones and a strong chin, the guy could be a model, Jonah thought, if not for the constant brooding.

Eddy gestured at his second plate of food. "Dude, you gonna eat?"

Thomas waved him off. "I'm not hungry."

"Is something wrong?" Eddy persisted. When Thomas glared at him, Eddy moved his chair away. "Hey, dude. You're supposed to help us adjust."

The young mage let out a low chuckle and a long breath as his shoulders slumped.

"You look like a man with a lot on his mind," AJ observed.

Thomas chuckled again to himself. "You have no idea." On the last word, he shifted his intense gaze to Jonah. "Trueblood told me what you did back during Halloween."

His brown eyes took in Jonah's face, hair, and hands. It was a curiously open thing to do, but Jonah thought he understood. Thomas probably heard all kinds of stuff about him and now had a chance to see him face-to-face.

"Okay," Jonah said.

Without warning, Thomas sat bolt upright and slipped his hands off the table and out of sight.

Detecting the sudden crackle of familiar magic, Jonah spun around to find Jennifer at the hallway entrance. The fingers of her right hand moved in small circles, conjuring a hex.

Kevin leaned forward, his gaze on the door. "Do we have a problem, Thomas?"

Jonah opened his mouth, but Kevin waved him silent.

Thomas stared between Kevin and Jennifer, who finally moved off. Slowly, he raised his hands above the table. Jonah's Death Sense calmed as the tension disappeared. Looking around, he realized that all the Council members and instructors had moved outside. Only the campers, mentors, and kitchen staff remained.

"You need to relax, man," AJ said to Thomas. "You're leaking power like a broken water pipe."

Jonah wondered how Thomas would react, but the boy lowered his gaze to his hands. AJ's observation reminded Jonah of Wick's speculations that a person's emotions affected their powers. Thomas must have had some powerful emotions surging through him, judging from the buzz of magic around him.

It didn't bode well for the rest of the young group of mages, who, Jonah thought, all seemed moody. He imagined a mage should be more stoic. Well, he'd felt that way until he met Symon Trueblood.

Thomas pushed his chair back from the table and shot to his feet. Kevin stood, matching the young mage's move. He also held his deactivated blades in his hands. Jonah's mind tried to decipher all the roiling emotions and magic around him. While he had sensed magic from Thomas and Jennifer, only Jennifer had tweaked his Death Sense.

Thomas raised his hands now, proving he meant no harm. With a final glance at Jonah, he stalked out of the room.

"No offense," Eddy began in a low voice, "but we're supposed to ask him for help?"

"You come to me," Kevin said, still watching the doorway.

AJ laughed. "I feel sorry for the mages."

Jonah silently agreed.

The incident at dinner haunted Jonah. Did Thomas want to protect him or keep Jennifer from embarrassing the mages with the Council at camp?

Kevin didn't leave Jonah's side for the rest of the evening. He stood inside Jonah's dorm room with arms crossed and head cocked to the side.

Jonah had come up to read since Eddy had remained downstairs with the other kids. When he couldn't discover any clues in the Tales' first section, Jonah gave up the effort and tried to talk about Antwan's cousin with Kevin.

"It's her!" Jonah repeated yet again, only to have Kevin not respond. "What are you doing?"

Kevin gave him an impatient look. "I'm listening. But I can't hear anything from the mages' end of the hall."

Jonah scrambled to the end of his bed. "You mean the mages found a way to block you?" Jonah's eyes widened as he considered the idea. "Thomas spent a lot of time listening to Mage Rubio. I bet he told Thomas all kinds of ways to block you."

Kevin snorted. "Rubio may be a Hardliner, but he's also on the Council. Besides, Thomas is smart and doesn't need help creating a way to block us. No, that Jennifer worries me. I already warned Serena."

"So you believe me?" Jonah relaxed after Kevin nodded. "It's Antwan's cousin. And she worked with the mole."

"I didn't say that. Besides, you never saw the girl's face back in Mount Vernon."

Jonah blinked hard at that. "I recognized her voice and eyes."

That caused Kevin to smirk. "What happens when she says you're wrong?"

"Can't the Alliance make her tell the truth?"

Kevin's face turned serious and he worked his jaw. "You don't know what you're saying, Jonah. The Alliance doesn't work that way."

Something about his question worried Kevin, but Jonah also sensed the half-truth in the comeback. "We have to do something. By the way, Brandon's sure she did something to her cousin Antwan."

"How do you know that?"

Jonah squirmed. "Brandon told me just before a couple of KIN showed up."

Kevin's eyes widened. "Oh, yeah. I heard about that. But see? That proves my point. Why would she hurt her cousin?"

"Hello!" Jonah threw his hands up in frustration. "She's evil!"

"Whatever, Jonah. I'll tell Symon, but don't expect them to kick Jennifer out of camp without proof."

Jonah didn't like the answer, but at least Trueblood or someone else would watch the girl. That reminded him of another troubling issue. "Thomas waited until his mom and Rubio left the room before he came over. I thought he was cool the first time we met."

Kevin considered it a moment, then came over and kneeled beside Jonah's bed. "Let it go, little man," he whispered.

"I told you, don't call me that anymore."

"You'll always be my little man." Kevin stood up, smiling and keeping his hand in Jonah's.

Jonah tried to pull Kevin closer, but the boy stood firm. "I'm not breaking any rules around you."

"Whatever." Jonah had just released Kevin's hand when Eddy walked through the door. The timing was too close for coincidence, Jonah thought. Kevin's embarrassed grin confirmed he must have heard Eddy coming.

"See you in the morning." Kevin slipped out of the room.

Disconnecting his triptych, Jonah slid it under his pillow.

"What's that?" Eddy asked. He'd already changed out of his camp uniform.

"Nothing," Jonah lied. He rose and stripped out of his camp clothes while avoiding Eddy's curious expression. After placing his new watch on the bedside table, Jonah got into bed.

With a shrug, Eddy also hopped into bed and turned out the lights.

Jonah settled down, thinking; in all his bitterness about attending camp, he never anticipated danger to himself. Of course, things always happened to him, but Camp Alliance should have been safe. With Alastor, Mandara, and now Antwan's cousin here, Jonah wanted to be in Florida even more.

Thinking of his family and friends having a good time at this very moment strengthened his decision. If he found the clues in the Tales and discovered the medallion's location, maybe he could leave camp early and join everyone for the remainder of the vacation.

Yeah, Jonah thought. *It's a plan*. He rolled over and closed his eyes, imagining a fun time in Florida.

CHAPTER TWELVE
MAGICAL BARRIERS

The morning bell awakened everyone, leaving them plenty of time to prepare for breakfast. When Eddy crossed to AJ's room to chat, Jonah escaped to the showers. He felt a little guilty for not hanging out with the guys, but he had a plan. Solve the riddle and go to Florida.

Arriving on the first floor after taking a shower and dressing, Jonah found few kids there. One of the young mages, a tall one with a round Afro, sat in a corner chair, flipping through a textbook. Darren reclined in a similar seat on the opposite side of the room, reading a magazine.

Crossing to the serving tables, Jonah discovered the undisturbed mounds of steaming eggs and hot bacon, letting him know he was the first to eat. Cool, he thought. Maybe he would get a chance to read before the rest of the kids arrived.

Jonah spotted the Crunch Berries cereal at the cereal table and thought of his cousin. Smiling, he scooped some in a bowl, sat a small milk carton on top of his selections, and crossed to a corner table.

After attaching the pieces of the triptych and taking his first spoonful of cereal, Jonah paused, unsure of reading the device in the open. Why not? Everyone here was part of the supernatural world, and no one could see what was on it anyway.

He swiped to the section on the Eldest Brother and started reading as he ate. Searching for any clue he had missed, he considered single words, a spell, and even a phrase. The Deliverer conjured wind in his battle with the Eldest Brother.

Making sure no one watched, Jonah swiped to the Tales' last page, leaned close, and whispered, "Sakoto," the wind incantation.

Nothing happened. The five stars remained dark.

"Um, Deliverer's Speed," he tried. That was the traditional parting blessing among the Afterworld Rebels. When nothing changed on the ethereal page, he tried several words, including *destiny, protector, medallion*. After several more minutes, he gave up.

Eddy and AJ had returned from their showers while he had attempted to find a clue. After stowing their things upstairs, the boys came down and went through the breakfast lines. Jonah pretended to read, hoping they would snag the table they used last night and leave him alone.

No go. The boys came straight to his table and, Jonah noted, they got almost the same things he did.

As expected, Eddy noticed the triptych first. "That's what you hid under your pillow last night!" Dropping into a chair beside Jonah's, he asked, "What is it?"

AJ's eyes widened. "It's a triptych. Cool!" Eddy flashed a confused look, and AJ explained. "It's three pieces of art that create a single picture when combined."

Eddy leaned close to look and Jonah resisted pulling the device away. AJ was more restrained as he scanned the surface. "That's an interesting picture."

Jonah's irritation rose. *Why won't they let me read in peace?* Giving in to the inevitable, he pulled the segments apart and slipped them into his pocket. Catching AJ's disappointed look, he said, "It's a design from my cousin's video game."

"Wow," Eddy gushed around a mouth full of food.

AJ seemed to sense the lie but let it go. Besides, the rest of the mages came downstairs and drew their attention. Instead of crossing to the breakfast line, the mages huddled around their buddy and talked in whispered tones. Jennifer joined them when she arrived a few minutes later.

Lisa and Monisha weren't far behind and crossed to Darren. Jonah wondered if he, Eddy, and AJ would be the only ones to eat this morning. He was about to comment on it when Serena entered the room and paused to frown at the campers.

"Everyone needs to finish breakfast in time for your first sessions." She crossed her arms and waited for everyone to line up at the breakfast tables. Only once all the campers were seated together and eating, did Serena finally fetch a bowl of oatmeal and coffee.

Jonah watched the Memory Charmer sit alone at a table before it occurred to him: she shouldn't have breakfast duty by herself.

"This looks interesting." AJ motioned toward the entrance to the dining area.

Kevin and Thomas had just entered the room. Kevin crossed to the food table, filled a couple of bowls with cereal, and sat with Serena. She leaned close and talked to him. Kevin shrugged and shook his head several times before handing Serena a blue folder that he'd carried in.

Jonah shifted his attention to Thomas. The mage mentor also had a blue folder but didn't look through it. Instead, Thomas handed the folder to Vanay when the younger mage came over. Then he ate his bowl of oatmeal alone.

The boy's behavior still mystified Jonah, but he didn't have time to give it much thought because Serena approached their table, blue folder in hand.

"These are your session schedules for the next two weeks." She took out the printed pages and passed them out. The page had a chart with weekdays across the top, time of day down the left, and a grid showing his activities.

He had History, Introduction to Nature, Team Building, and Range Sessions on Mondays, Wednesdays, and Fridays. The even days of the weeks were for Meditation, Blades, Personal Development, and Independent Study.

Eddy moaned. "Why do we have History three times a week? It's my worst subject."

AJ laughed at him.

Jonah nodded, but his focus was on the Tuesday and Thursday sessions. "What's Meditation?"

"It's supposed to help us control our powers," AJ answered while scanning his schedule.

Monisha let out a squeal of glee. "We study blades!" She noticed Lisa's sad expression. "What's wrong, Lisa? It'll be fun."

"I'm no good with weapons." Lisa frowned at her schedule.

Jonah wasn't worried about blades. He'd do fine with that if he stayed. The Team Building seemed obvious enough, and the last thing he wanted to do. And having been here with Kevin, he already guessed what the Range Session meant three days a week.

AJ was the only one excited about the Personal Development and Independent Activity on Tuesday and Thursday. "It's a chance to practice on your talents and hobbies," he explained when Jonah questioned him. "I'll get to use the time to work on my music."

"That's fine if you have talent," Darren pointed out. Eddy nodded in agreement.

"That's why it's called Personal Development." When everyone stared at him, AJ shrugged. "I asked. The counselor who teaches it will help you find your thing."

Watching Darren, and before he thought better of it, Jonah blurted out, "But you have talent." Although Darren sat up in his chair, Jonah pressed on. "You do cosplay. I saw the costume you did for your dad. It was cool!"

Darren's shocked face didn't show any gratitude for the compliment, only a growing mixture of angry embarrassment.

"Cosplay?" Monisha asked, eyeing the boy like she didn't know about this.

Only then did Jonah realize Darren kept his interest in sci-fi and cosplay a secret. "Sorry, I didn't mean…"

Darren rose from the table and walked to the corner where he'd sat that morning. Monisha hurried after him.

Jonah never meant to out anyone for being a nerd, of course, and he suspected Darren would never consider himself a nerd.

"What's cosplay?" Eddy asked.

"It's when fans of a movie or show wear an accurate costume of their favorite character," AJ told his friend. "Darren makes the costumes for people." Eddy shrugged, and AJ let out a breath. "It's a nerd thing, okay?"

AJ met Jonah's gaze and flashed a knowing grin.

At that moment, AJ reminded Jonah of Mike. Not only did he understand nerd culture, but he was also smart. Could he help with the Tales? Jonah shook his head, remembering his plan to leave as soon as he figured out the clues.

Telling AJ about the Tales would mean discussing it with Eddy, and that would slow Jonah down. No, he'd solve the clues on his own and hopefully before Darren punched him.

⸺

The temperature was already in the low eighties, and the cloudless blue sky promised a scorching day, despite the slight breeze. Jonah grimaced, expecting that he'd have to run to make his first session and work up a sweat. At least, he thought that until Lisa pointed out the building locations on the camp map. All they had to do was cross the courtyard.

Eddy paused, staring at the names of the buildings. "Agreeable Mist? Embracing Valley? Quiet Fragrant Hall?" He waved his schedule at the group. "Who named these buildings?"

"I bet Mage Trueblood did it," Lisa answered. "I think the names are nice."

"You would," Monisha said and laughed at her friend as they approached the large pavilion.

"Mr. Blackstone," someone called out.

Jonah spotted Trueblood and Mitchell exiting the Admin Building.

The Fallen Reaper seemed eager as he approached. "I know the first session is Supernatural History. As someone who loves to do research, you'll love it."

A sigh came from behind Jonah. He glanced back to find Eddy and AJ standing there.

"You're a geek too?" Eddy asked Jonah with another exaggerated sigh. "You should have AJ as a roommate. He loves to study all the time."

"Not all the time," AJ objected.

Trueblood stepped forward to pat Eddy on the shoulder. "You'll be a perfect roommate for Jonah. And, since you and AJ benefited from attending the summer program before, I expect you two to make Jonah feel part of the group. Understand?"

The boys nodded.

"Good. Well, don't be late for your first session." Trueblood escorted Mitchell toward the compound's entrance.

Jonah whirled on Eddy. "You don't have to show me around. I'm cool on my own."

"Oh no," Eddy said. "That was an order." He faked saluting then playfully pushed Jonah forward.

Only one of the pavilion's courtyard-facing doors remained open. Jonah imagined it to be stifling hot inside, but as he followed the others through the opening, a gentle, steady breeze caressed his face. The door on the east-facing side of the space was open, creating the cross current.

The room's front wall displayed a large, colorful mural that surprised Jonah because it featured scenes throughout human history. Scanning the images, Jonah realized they represented magical or gifted humans through the ages. The final image to the far-right included the Atlanta skyline.

"Whoa," Jonah said.

Eddy had crossed to a wall-mounted panel covered with protective plexiglass. The panel featured a black-and-white etching of an old rustic church with a description below. The sign on the building read Alliance Freedom Church.

"Camp Alliance started as a church?" Eddy asked. "Weird."

Jonah agreed, but AJ shook his head as he read the panel.

"Not really. A lot of congregations build their churches on Ley lines."

Eddy gave him a puzzled look.

"Magic power lines," Jonah offered.

AJ nodded. "It would make sense to locate the camp in the same place."

Jonah sucked in a breath. Of course, locating Camp Alliance on Ley lines would make it easier to keep up the camp's magical protections.

By now, AJ and Eddy had moved off to look over the mural. Jonah took a moment to take in the rest of the room. There was a leather desk chair up front, and a small table on which sat a projector. Beyond that was a blank screen.

Hearing the machine's low whine and seeing the rows of hard metal chairs reminded Jonah of a classroom. Darren, Monisha, and Lisa took the front row nearest the east door. Jonah sat behind them and AJ and Eddy joined him.

A center aisle divided their rows from the next. Jonah glanced at the extra chairs just as he heard footsteps outside. The young mages entered and took the remaining spaces, sitting two mages on the front row and three on the second.

Jonah never expected to have sessions with the mages. He assumed they'd go off with Albrecht and practice spells or something. Unlike Jonah and his friends, who lounged in their seats, the mages sat straight and didn't talk.

Eddy whispered to Jonah, "They love to show off, don't they?"

A door behind the desk opened, and the heavyset Council member from the previous night clumped into the room. He favored his right leg and leaned hard on his cane. Jonah thought he'd sit down immediately, but the older man walked around his little table to stare at them in his solemn way.

"I'm Alliance Council Co-chair Ambrose Sterne. This class is in session." Without warning, Sterne whacked the cane on the tabletop. Everyone jumped and sat straighter, including Darren, who slipped his arm from around Monisha's shoulder.

Sterne placed the end of the cane on the ground, leaned heavily on it, and said, "Power concedes nothing without a struggle. And the current Rulers of the Afterworld will fight to hold on to what they have built. In this class, you will learn how and why we got to where we are and how to set things right."

Jonah's insides froze because he never considered the issues from that angle. He, Marcus, Kevin, and his dead parents were trying to destroy the current situation. It was a fight, just like the Campmaster had said. Jonah shook himself and found Sterne staring at him.

"I know what you're thinking." Sterne leaned forward, hands resting on the cane's head again. Jonah wondered if the man was talking directly to him. Then Sterne's large, sad eyes turned to look at the other kids. "I was like you. No, I didn't have powers, but I was clueless about the reality around me until the day someone opened my eyes to the supernatural world."

Sitting back on the table's edge, Sterne sighed as he took the pressure off his leg. "I'm sorry to say that you can never go back, no matter how you choose to deal with the eye-opening knowledge. You are forever changed and different from everyone else."

Jonah winced at Sterne's comment. Even now, he wished to be normal, like any other nerd. Watch movies, play games, talk geeky things, date. You know, normal stuff.

"There's a saying that knowledge is power," Sterne continued. "I say, knowledge is knowledge. It's what you decide to do with the information that can make a difference. I will train you to use what you learn in these sessions. And"—he raised a pudgy finger in the air—"as a former judge and attorney, I'm also tasked with teaching you the ethical use of your powers."

Campers stirred in their seats. Jonah was surprised and a little embarrassed, considering his vigilante stuff back in the fall. He glanced around at the others, coming to terms for the first time with the idea that maybe he hadn't been the only one.

Sterne watched, and a smile tweaked the corners of his mouth. "For example, repeatedly snuffing out all candles in a town church until the minister believed it was a message from God wasn't ethical."

AJ's pale face darkened with embarrassment.

"Zapping a bully from concealment or creating a mirage of a Hindu god to frighten the local religious leaders wasn't ethical either."

The Indian mage covered his face, but Eddy sat up straighter. "He deserved it!"

"Never admit guilt without consulting counsel first, Mr. Corvera," Sterne said, enjoying himself. "Using your gift to make a quick buck is not illegal as long as the person agrees to the act, yet some may consider it unethical."

When Jonah squirmed in his chair, Eddy gave him an envious look, like he wished he'd done the same thing with his gift.

"Or, how about casting a hex to injure an innocent?" Sterne continued. "There are many more examples that the

Alliance is aware of and I won't mention. To address the issue, you'll have quizzes in this class and essays that offer situations describing power used and whether it fell under ethical conduct. Understood?" Everyone nodded.

"Good!" The Councilor fetched the remote, pointed it at the projector, and clicked. The course title appeared on the screen.

"You won't have a text in this class because there aren't any out there. In the back are about twenty bound composition books. Please get up and get one. You'll take copious notes. My hope is these notes will become your manual that you pass on to others." Sterne paused, then said, "Go on. We have things to cover."

People jumped from their seats before they knew where to look. Then one of the mages pointed to a table against the back wall. Everyone hurried over, but Darren reached the table first and handed out the notebooks in an orderly fashion. Jonah found it interesting that not even the mages wanted to mess with the large boy, taking their notebooks without any fuss.

By the time they settled down, Sterne had a new slide on the screen displaying two words: *The Afterworld*. He pointed his cane at the screen.

"Write this down. The Afterworld. The Domain of the Undead. Who are the Undead? People who've died, but instead of their souls moving on to their final destination, they received afterlife duties. This process has existed since mortals have been on Earth."

Jonah settled in, listened, and wrote everything down, even if he knew some of it. After two years of being frustrated with Marcus's trickle of information, everything was opening to him. Not only would he train to use his power, but he would have all the information he ever wanted.

For the first time since arriving at Camp Alliance, Jonah decided that wasn't such a bad thing after all.

CHAPTER THIRTEEN
TOKENS & TALISMANS

"Long Corridor Bridge," Lisa announced to the group on their walk from History class. They approached the covered bridge, which extended for a couple hundred feet over a lush meadow.

A pleasant breeze from the lake wafted through the openings on the bridge's sides. Jonah took a deep breath, beginning to like the air here. When the clump of their shoes on the bamboo surface echoed in the narrow space, everyone shouted. Their voices bounced off the walls.

Smiling, Jonah kept quiet while gazing out at the camp's scenery.

Soon, the group exited the covered bridge and followed a curved path down a shallow hill. The sparse shrubbery on the north side of the pathway tapered away, exposing the camp's high wrought iron perimeter fence.

At the bottom of the hill, the path curved back toward the lake and a grouping of buildings. Jonah noted the top of a greenhouse and a larger squat metal building that reminded him of a workshop or mechanic's garage.

He longed to investigate these buildings but couldn't. After all, Mage Trueblood stood near the fence with arms crossed and five backpacks on the ground beside him.

When they halted in front of him, Trueblood spread his arms wide. "Welcome to the Introduction to Nature class. During our time together, I'll teach you what I know about the forest and how to survive in it."

AJ sighed. "I've been in Boy Scouts."

Trueblood laughed. "Then I expect you to take the lead in helping your classmates." He gestured at the backpacks. "You'll use these during our class hikes into the surrounding hills and overnight stays in the forest. They're all the same, with basic camping gear. So come up and take one."

After everyone had selected and slipped on a backpack, Trueblood unhooked a small tan leather pouch from his belt. Jonah had missed it because the mage wore a tan, sleeveless leather shirt, matching pants, and tan hiking boots that closely matched the color of the pouch. As far as Jonah could tell, the Counselors didn't wear the Camp Alliance shirts. Only the campers and the mentors did.

Opening the leather pouch, Trueblood lifted out a small wooden token with a square hole at the center. "This is a talisman. You need this to pass through the protective ward over this entrance. And, since I'm responsible for this and other doorways around the campsite, that means what?" He raised a questioning eyebrow at Jonah.

"You're the only one who can make the talismans," Jonah answered. "But that token is different from the necklace."

"Correct. The gate is like the dialing device and creates a corridor through the main ward. As such, you need a different talisman. By the way, the fence and gate are also enchanted against attack and the gate will only open to someone with a special key."

Trueblood surveyed the rest of the group. "If you ever lose the talisman, come to me."

The mage handed the pouch to Darren, who took a talisman and passed the bag along. When Jonah pulled a token, he discovered it was made of wood with small symbols around the surface's curve.

Lisa pulled hers last. "This is beautiful."

"Thank you, Lisa." Trueblood retrieved the pouch from her and reattached it to his belt. "I want everyone to raise your tokens."

Jonah glanced at the others as he did so, holding it at chest level.

Trueblood raised his hand and muttered a spell under his breath. "Now, speak your name to the token."

"Jonah Blackstone," Jonah said, ignoring the others. When he spoke his name, the token flared in his hand and grew warmer for a second. Gasps came from the others as the same thing happened to them.

"You've just marked the token with your name. Each time you go through this gate, your name is recorded." The mage eyed each person. "In other words, I'll know who goes in and out of camp."

Raising his hand, Jonah asked, "Do the mages get tokens?"

"Yes. They have to leave the camp for their sessions." Trueblood motioned to the tokens. "Keep those in a safe place. Is everyone ready?"

Jonah was confused because he didn't see a gate. Were they standing at the wrong spot? All they saw was an unbroken section of wrought iron fence.

Trueblood didn't seem bothered as he withdrew a small key from his pocket. When the mage placed it flat against a particular iron bar, the bottom of the bar retracted from the ground with a loud clink. Three more bars to either side did the same thing.

Everyone gasped as a real gate appeared, complete with hinges and a heavy lock.

"That was cool," Eddy gushed.

Trueblood used the key in the heavy lock. With a clunk, the gate groaned as it opened. The mage walked through the nearly invisible barrier.

The occasional distortions in the air let Jonah know it was there. Darren and Monisha didn't hesitate to follow, though Lisa hunched her shoulders like she expected the passage to be painful.

"You next?" Eddy asked Jonah.

He laughed, stepping close to the ward. The hairs on the back of his neck and arms rose, and when he crossed through, it felt like parting a heavy curtain that disappeared within seconds.

On the other side, Jonah paused to watch Eddy and AJ walk through the barrier. AJ turned to close the gate but it swung closed and locked on its own. The hinges and lock disappeared, leaving a normal section of fence again.

"Nice!" AJ observed. "I wish I could do something like that for my bedroom door at home."

The guys laughed until Eddy looked over their shoulders. "Oh no."

Trueblood and the others were already halfway across the open grassy field, heading for the tree line. The boys hustled to catch up.

Hiking the surrounding Georgia hillsides filled the first half of the session. All the while, Trueblood conducted a walking lesson, pointing out and naming every plant, tree, animal, and bird that came within sight. Jonah's awe of the man grew as he indicated transplanted species that the Forestry Commission allowed them to place.

At one point, Trueblood reached a small clearing and told them to take off their packs.

"Inside, you'll find a weatherproof notebook. Take that out. I want you to record everything I tell you about the edible plants, how to identify them, and where you'll most likely find them."

When the kids grumbled, Trueblood crossed his arms and said, "Take this seriously. During the second week, I'll began picking two of you at random to spend the night in the forest. You'll leave before dinner and return after breakfast the next morning. So, if you don't want to go hungry, you'd better listen up."

After he dropped that little bomb, nobody dared to say anything as they slipped off their packs and took out the notebooks. Jonah heard five people furiously scribbling while Trueblood started into the next part of his lesson.

The mage finally sent everyone out to find something edible and bring it back for inspection. They had twenty minutes. Jonah didn't know if he was lucky or not because five minutes into his search, he found berries. He collected a handful and hiked back to Trueblood. Part of the test was to see if people could also retrace their path to the clearing where the mage waited.

Jonah arrived to find AJ was already sitting down with his back against a tree. The boy's eyes were closed, and his right hand tapped out a rhythm on his leg.

"What do you have for me?" the mage asked.

Jonah held out the berries. Trueblood took them and popped one in his mouth.

"Good. You can relax and wait for the others."

Grabbing his pack, Jonah sat it at his feet and remained near the mage.

Trueblood scanned the surrounding trees as he spoke in a quieter tone. "How's the reading going?"

"Ah, okay." The question surprised Jonah. "I'm stuck," he admitted.

"How so?"

"You know I have to find the hidden clues to complete a puzzle at the end, right?" Jonah sucked in a breath as his frustration bubbled to the surface. "Well, I don't know what the keys are. And it's hard to find space to read with people always around."

Trueblood remained quiet for a moment. Finally, he said, "You're too close to the problem, and the frustration is making it worse."

At that moment, Lisa returned with some leaves. Trueblood inspected them. "Good job, Lisa. You can relax."

When the girl sat near AJ, Trueblood turned back to Jonah. "You understand what I'm saying? Sometimes when we set our minds on something other than the immediate problem, the answer to a pesky question often presents itself."

"What else is there?" Jonah glanced at the others, who didn't appear to be listening. "Finding the medallion is so important."

"Yes, it is. But you need to step back, Jonah, and not push yourself into exhaustion."

Jonah didn't know what to do to relax, except solving the clues, getting out of there, and going to Florida. Somehow, he didn't think that's what Trueblood meant.

"Focus on your sessions here at camp." Trueblood gestured at the other campers. "And get to know your classmates. Have fun and relax. I guarantee the answers will come to you."

Darren returned next with berries like the ones Jonah had found. Monisha followed a few minutes later. Only Eddy hadn't returned, but Trueblood didn't seem worried.

"When you commit to something, Jonah, you need to see it through," Trueblood said.

Jonah heard the serious undertones in the mage's voice, and his shoulders slumped slightly.

He had given his word he would come to camp and read the Tales. Just as Mike suggested, he had met a new group of kids, all with powers. And he'd had a history session on the Alliance and learned more information in one setting than he could ever want.

Was it so bad here, even given the danger? He guessed it wasn't, but a part of him, the stubborn side, wasn't ready to give up.

Eddy returned and broke Jonah's train of thought. After inspecting Eddy's leaves, Trueblood clapped his hands.

"Our two hours are almost up. Everyone back to camp for lunch."

Cheerful talking broke out as the campers slipped on their backpacks and hiked out of the hills. Jonah trailed behind Eddy and AJ. The boys noticed and made space for him to walk with them while they talked about internship experiences. Jonah enjoyed listening to the stories, and he had to admit the first two sessions at camp had been fun.

Camp Alliance's kitchen staff put out another tasty lunch spread. Jonah eagerly wolfed down two Sierra turkey sandwiches and had started on a third when the mages trooped into the dining room. He wondered where they had gone for their second class. From the expressions on their faces and the clothes stained with what looked like bits of strange-smelling plants, it had been an exciting session.

After lunch, and with a free hour before afternoon sessions, Jonah decided to pour over the Tales again. When he reached the second floor, he found Eddy standing near their dorm, staring toward the mages' end of the hallway.

Despite his desire to get the triptych and find a quiet place to read, Jonah's curiosity stopped him. "What are you doing?"

Eddy glanced over his shoulder at Jonah, looking perplexed. "You ever notice how quiet they are?" He gestured at the mages' dorms. "I know some of them are up here, but no noise."

The observation surprised Jonah because Eddy had a point. "Yeah, now that you mention it. They make plenty of noise downstairs." He reached out with his senses and detected the subtle magic.

Being more practical, Eddy had started forward. "I'm gonna listen by a door."

"Eddy," Jonah warned. "Don't. Come back."

"They won't catch me." Eddy bumped into an invisible wall and let out a grunt of surprise as he sprawled back on his butt. He and Jonah stared, slack-jawed, at the waving lines of light blue energy and faint sigils that appeared. Tendrils continued radiating out in a pattern from where Eddy had smacked into the invisible barrier.

"Who put up the ward?" AJ asked, coming up behind them.

"The mages," Jonah answered.

One of the mages, a burly Hispanic boy, left his room and walked through the ward without breaking his stride. He glanced down at Eddy with a smirk and kept moving. Jonah knew the boy must have had a talisman to get through the ward.

The young mage was about to step past Jonah and AJ when he stopped in his tracks.

Kevin stood in the center of the hallway with his arms crossed. "You can't build wards in the hall."

"You'll have to take it up with our mentor. He's the one who made it." The boy nodded toward the stairway. "Can I go?"

Kevin nodded but didn't bother to move aside, forcing the boy to squeeze by him. Once the mage was out of sight, Kevin hauled Eddy to his feet.

Jonah tensed when Kevin turned back to the ward and reached out to touch it. His prodding produced more of the blue tendrils of energy and sigils, but that was all.

He stepped away and crossed his arms again. "I'll give Thomas credit. He didn't design it to hurt, just to keep people out."

The fuller implication of the barrier finally occurred to Jonah. "That's why you couldn't hear them last night, isn't it?"

"You might be right about Rubio," Kevin grumbled while stroking his chin.

"Can't you make them take it down?"

"No. Thomas is a mentor like me."

Jonah glanced at Eddy and AJ and lowered his voice. "They could be doing anything on the other side. Can't you phase over—"

Kevin turned on him. "Didn't you pay attention yesterday? Trueblood told you we couldn't phase around the camp."

"I remember that but—"

"You're gonna have to start thinking things through whenever a Counselor tells you something. It's not about memorizing and putting it down on a test. It matters."

Kevin stalked off, forcing Eddy and AJ to jump aside. Jonah's anger prickled at his boyfriend's tone. Was Kevin just angry that Thomas had outwitted him?

Eddy stared after their mentor. "Is he gonna make Thomas take it down?"

AJ poked Eddy in the back. "He can't."

"Why not?

"Rubio, Thomas's mother, and Mandara are all Hardliners on the Council," AJ said in a sure tone, but he glanced at Jonah for confirmation.

Jonah nodded. "Plus, chances are the Campmaster would congratulate Thomas for doing it."

"So Kevin knows that, huh?" Eddy asked.

"Yeah."

"Where did he go?"

"Probably to tell Mage Trueblood about it."

Eddy relaxed when Jonah told him that bit, but Jonah didn't find any comfort in it. Mandara was Campmaster and could no doubt run the camp any way he wanted.

Gazing down the mages' end of the hallway, Jonah suspected Thomas and crew had other surprises for them. And this only increased his desire to finish the Tales and get away from camp.

CHAPTER FOURTEEN
PRACTICAL APPLICATIONS

News of the mages' ward had spread among the kids by the time everyone headed off to the Team Building session. The campers discussed the ward as they followed the bamboo pathway to the smaller courtyard they saw the first day.

This pavilion wasn't as big as the central pavilion. Yet it had an added benefit: it bordered the large lake, offering a beautiful view.

"I would love to take a rowboat out on the water," Lisa gushed, checking out the boathouse.

"Ask Trueblood," Monisha suggested, not sounding too enthusiastic.

The group paused in front of the pavilion because there were two doors with signs above them. The one on the left read Meditation, and the sign above the right door read

Team Building. Darren opened the right door and stood back to let everyone else in first.

Inside, Jonah discovered a divider wall bisecting the pavilion's interior. The walls on the Team Building side were sage green with several motivational posters attached. Like Sterne's class, the side facing the lake had sliding panel doors. Fresh air flowed in from two open panels.

AJ pointed at a dozen scattered folding chairs. "That's a lot of seats."

"Yeah," Eddy agreed.

A few moments later, the mages entered the pavilion and stopped. Jonah noted that most of them spent the free hour after lunch cleaning up and changing shirts. He wondered if they had extras.

Both groups of campers stared at each other before Darren and Jennifer moved simultaneously and each snatched a chair from the grouping. After a hesitant second, the rest of the kids copied them, pulling the remaining chairs into two separate collections.

The distrust was palpable in the air, and the groups left a fair amount of floor space between each other.

Mage Trueblood entered, walked into the very center of the space, and clapped his hands. "Welcome to Team Building. I'm sure all of you can decipher the meaning and intent of the class." People shuffled and looked at the ground or their fingernails or even out at the lake.

I don't care, Jonah thought. He still planned to leave camp.

"The chairs were a test," Trueblood said, his earlier, cheerful voice earnest now. "I do it every session, and each time the result is the same." He peered at each person. "I assure you that by the end of camp, you may not be friends, and that's okay because you may not click with everyone. That's life. However, you will learn that working together has nothing to do with agreeing or liking everything about another person."

He waited again, letting his words sink in. "Even saying that, once we go through the exercises in class, you'll see we're all the same, no matter the power, color, culture, sex, gender, or any other identity." He clapped his hands. "Now. I want you to form two lines, with the first person in each facing me. The rest of you line up behind."

Jonah's group lined up as they always did. Darren was first, with Monisha behind him, followed by Lisa, Jonah, Eddy, and AJ in the back.

"Good. Now I want you to turn and face the other group."

Oh boy, Jonah thought to himself, not liking where this was going.

He faced the Hispanic boy; the one Kevin questioned this morning about the hallway ward. The boy didn't look pleased to see him. Darren stood across from Jennifer. Monisha seemed to have more problems with that than Darren did.

Monisha's partner was a short, thin kid with thick glasses and droopy, light brown dreads. He tried to maintain his snobby air, but when Monisha crossed her arms, clearly unimpressed, the boy hunched his shoulders and looked at the ground. Lisa stood across from the Indian kid, who held his chin up, looking as superior as Jennifer.

Eddy stood in front of a shorter, pale, slender kid with dirty blond hair. The boy gave Eddy a shy wave before pushing his thick glasses up on his nose. And AJ faced a confident-looking boy with an Afro shaped like a bowl on his head. He was AJ's height and was the only mage not to frown as much.

Trueblood watched everyone, letting the silence weigh on them. The tension built until Jonah thought kids would bolt for the door.

That's when the mage spoke. "You are here to learn to defend the Alliance and fight for humanity. The word Alliance implies teamwork. That is the common goal that supersedes all else. That is what bonds us together."

Trueblood's voice didn't carry a trace of humor, and power and conviction crackled around the man. Everyone stood straight and paid attention.

"Shake hands with the person across from you." He waited as everyone moved.

"My name's Alex," the young mage said. His hand seemed to swallow Jonah's hand whole.

"Jonah—"

"Blackstone. I know." Alex didn't say it with any trace of hatred, just curiosity as he gave Jonah the once-over.

"You've just met your team partner for the rest of the summer camp," Trueblood called out and received muted grumbling in reply. "You'll do everything together, every task, every test, every assignment in the class. You will become working teammates. We'll work on being friends later."

Their teacher was true to his word. Alex and Jonah had to grab two chairs and set them up as part of a larger circle of chairs. Each camper had to present the seat to the other instead of sitting in the one they chose. Trueblood walked around and made each pair leave space on either side to separate them from the others. He also had the kids alternate, so no mage sat next to another mage, and the same went for Jonah's group.

Looking over the results, Trueblood took a chair, placed it in the middle of the circle, and sat down.

"Now, I want each pair to turn to the other and tell your partner about yourself. Who are you? Try not to focus on your name, ability, or where you live. Tell your partner something unique about yourself." Everyone groaned. The mage raised his voice. "You have ten minutes, and then each pair will tell the rest of us about your partner. Got it? Go."

Turning to Alex, Jonah shrugged and motioned for him to start.

The young mage frowned. "Let's see. I'm half Puerto Rican and half African. My mom was from Nigeria. Oh, wait. We weren't supposed to say where we're born or live. Dang. Okay. I used to play football. And, huh, Mage Trueblood discovered me."

Jonah noted that he'd been right about the football thing. He also found it interesting that Trueblood had discovered Alex. With the little he knew of Council politics, Jonah wondered if Alex was part of Rubio's fan club but didn't think that would be a good thing to ask. He decided to focus on safe ground.

"Do you speak Spanish?"

Alex smiled. "Only when I visit my dad's folks back in Puerto Rico. It's more Spanglish." He pointed to Jonah. "Your turn."

Jonah gulped. "What don't you know about me?"

Alex's eyes widened. "Ah, I don't know anything." He lowered his voice. "I hear things, but it's all general."

"Oh." Jonah let the comment go as he decided to copy Alex. "I know I'm part Indigenous American, on my dad's side."

"Indigenous?" Alex frowned.

"Native American. My mom was an archaeologist, and she always used *indigenous*." Realizing he sounded like a know-it-all, Jonah hurried on. "I also like basketball, and my dad used to be on the Council, so here I am."

"What happened to your dad?"

Jonah hesitated, though not from shame about his parents. They were heroes, despite what some people might believe. "They were killed while fighting the Grim Reaper."

Alex sat back so quick he nearly toppled out of his chair. "He didn't tell me—I mean, hey, I'm sorry."

"It's okay. I have a lot to live up to." Jonah narrowed his eyes at Alex. "Who didn't tell you about my parents?"

"It's nothing." Alex paled. "Look, I understand about living up to expectations. That can be a lot of pressure."

Jonah sensed fear and evasion in Alex, but he let it go. It was clear someone had talked to him. Jonah's bet was on Jennifer and Thomas, who, in his opinion, were too close to Rubio.

And did Rubio know about Jennifer's feelings toward him? Would Trueblood pass along Kevin's information? Having dealt with people's reluctance to believe his suspicions about Alastor, Jonah guessed Rubio would do the same with Jennifer. Kevin admitted as much with Jennifer's identity. He'd have to keep his guard up, Jonah decided, while he completed the assignment.

~

"That was pathetic," Monisha complained as she walked from the Team Building class with her arms crossed. "Did you see who I got stuck with?"

Darren nodded and tried to put an arm on her shoulder, but Monisha ducked from under it. Jonah didn't think the class went too badly, and his opinion of the young mages had shifted, as Trueblood had predicted. They weren't as standoffish and snobby as he'd first thought, and guys like Alex seemed more relaxed alone.

He followed the rest of his group north along the bamboo pathway and onto the ranges. Jonah grew excited because this was where Kevin had trained him almost two years ago. The section of the camp contained four large grass-covered fields. Each had a sturdy lean-to at the far end, and waist-high shrubbery served as separation walls.

Kevin, Serena, and Mage Albrecht waited for the campers in the nearest range. The little mage had on his ever-present shades, and the looping mustache looked as curly as ever to Jonah. His group fanned out in a close line, facing their mentors. When footfalls came from behind, Jonah glanced back and groaned.

Mage Trueblood led the young mages down to the fourth range.

Albrecht made a deliberate cough as he bounced on his feet.

"Pay attention. We have a lot to do today. For the next hour and a half, you will engage in practical applications of your various talents."

A whoosh came from the far range where Trueblood had just produced an enormous ball of green fire.

"Your powers are like muscles," Albrecht continued. "The more you use them, the more they grow. We will push each of you to extend your control, so this won't be easy." The mage clapped his hands. "Now, each range is set up to test different skills. Mr. James and Corvera, you will come with me to the third range." Albrecht gestured to Lisa and Monisha. "Ms. Randolph and Ms. Owens, you will take the next range and work with Serena."

Jonah glanced over the shrubs into the next field. There were rocks and other objects of all sizes piled near the front of the range. He wondered if Lisa would have to levitate them while Monisha tossed them around. That stumped him because he didn't know if Lisa could levitate anything but herself.

Albrecht pointed at Darren. "Mr. Watkins, Reaper Mitchell will meet you at the back gate. Do you know the way?"

Darren nodded, backed out of the range, and strode down the bamboo path all alone. The boy didn't look happy, just determined, causing Jonah to wonder what kind of training he would get out in the woods.

"Well, please move to your posts," Albrecht announced.

Jonah raised a hand. "Sir, you didn't assign me a range."

Kevin snorted. "You're with me."

Albrecht turned without any comment and set out for the third range. Eddy waved and hurried to follow while AJ walked off in a more sedate manner.

"Eyes forward," Kevin ordered while circling Jonah.

Clamping down on a retort, Jonah snapped into a perfect ready stance. "What am I gonna practice? I can't phase."

"Why not?"

Jonah caught himself before he turned his head and waited until Kevin came back into view. "You already yelled at me about not being able to phase in the camp."

"Oh, well, sorry about that," Kevin said, pausing. "Mage Albrecht made a zone of exception just for us."

Jonah's eyes widened, and he looked around as much as he could without moving his head.

Kevin sensed the next question and answered, "The exception covers this range. So don't phase out of here by mistake, or you'll regret it."

"What'll happen?"

"Pain. That's what happens. We'll let you get a taste of that later."

Kevin smirked, and Jonah broke his stance. "I don't want to do that. I'll take your word."

"Oh, no. Marcus wants you to get a feel for it."

"Why?" Jonah thought Kevin joked, but the boy didn't smile.

"He thinks you should experience it in a controlled environment."

That had to be the truth, Jonah thought, because that sounded just like his godfather. When he started to protest, Kevin spoke over him.

"Think about it. You want to know what's happening if you ever get jerked out of a phase."

"I guess so."

Kevin smirked again. "Don't worry. We'll save that lesson for last. Are you ready?"

Jonah had a split second to prepare before Kevin came at him using hand-to-hand techniques. Struggling to remember the forms he'd learned in Practice Club, Jonah thought he did okay until Kevin mixed in microphases. The Fallen Reaper succeeded in dumping Jonah on his butt.

"Had enough, hero?"

"Lynn's the only one who can call me that." Jonah stood, rubbing his sore behind. "And, you're supposed to be teaching me."

"I am. You countered some of my moves. But if you want to pout, come here."

Jonah wasn't sure if Kevin was about to play a trick on him. But his boyfriend showed him the techniques and moves using the microphases. Jonah concentrated on the rhythm of the combination as Kevin demonstrated again. Start the movement, phase, complete the action. It looked so simple, but when Jonah tried, his movements came out jerky.

"Watch me again." Kevin began the move, slipped into the phase, and came out, completing the action. Jonah got the problem. While he started the movement, he paused just before he phased. Plus, he reappeared too far out of position instead of a few feet away. He wasn't doing a true microphase.

Imitating Kevin, Jonah started his move while thinking about the spot where he wanted to phase. The result? He finished the motion as soon as he reappeared.

"Good!" Kevin said. "See if you can shorten the time between starting the move and phasing."

Jonah repeated the steps until he lost count, but kept going, thrilled at learning a new fighting technique. Ignoring the passage of time, he was shocked when Kevin halted the training.

"I got it right." Jonah wiped at his sweaty forehead and flapped the bottom of his sweat-soaked camp shirt to fan himself.

Kevin grinned and nodded at the others, who were already leaving their ranges. "Time to head back."

As they joined the group, Kevin patted Jonah's shoulder. "You're doing fine." He walked close, occasionally bumping against Jonah. "How's the reading coming along?"

"Trueblood already asked me that."

"And?"

Even though Jonah loved the physical contact with his boyfriend, his frustration with the Tales intruded. "I can't solve the riddle of the blank pages. When I told Trueblood, he said I'm too close to the problem."

Kevin grinned. "You have to relax and focus on other things, right?"

"Yeah." Jonah lowered his voice, aware of the others trailing behind them. "I thought if I found the Destiny Medallion—"

"You want to run off to Florida and skip the rest of camp," Kevin finished. "You can't do that, Jonah."

"I only promised to come to camp and solve the riddle. Once I do that, I can leave."

"First," Kevin began, "don't tell me you didn't enjoy camp today." When Jonah didn't answer, Kevin poked him in the side, making him squirm. "Plus, if you find the medallion, who do you think they'll send to get it?"

Of course, Kevin was right about an enjoyable day, but when it came to the medallion, Jonah assumed the adults would do the usual. "They'll tell me to keep my head down." Even as he said it, Jonah knew it sounded half-hearted, and the persistent frustration returned. "This sucks!"

Without warning, Kevin hooked him in a headlock. "Stop complaining."

"Okay!" Jonah stammered while squirming free. He was about to shove Kevin when he remembered they weren't alone and glanced back. AJ watched them, but Jonah couldn't decipher the boy's expression.

"If you leave, we'll never get a chance to have that serious talk," Kevin said.

"You're trying to distract me," Jonah accused. "I'm gonna find the clues, and then we'll see if I can leave."

Kevin moved to the front of the line, leading the group back to the main compound.

With the distraction of conversation gone, Jonah noticed a slight dizziness from the constant use of microphases. He'd pushed himself today and felt better for it. Glancing back toward the ranges, he wondered if his parents had also walked this trail while tired after a long training session.

The sense of tradition made it difficult for him to reconcile their wishes with his desire to run away from camp. One thing was sure, he had a renewed determination to solve the riddle.

Staring at Kevin's back, Jonah wondered if that had been his boyfriend's, and Trueblood's, plan all along.

CHAPTER FIFTEEN
OUT OF BOUNDS

"One, two, three!" everyone shouted in unison.

Darren heaved Jonah into the air like he weighed nothing, which was probably true for the large boy.

Jonah yelled at the top of his lungs as he made a graceful arc through the air and plunged into the water like a cannonball. The cool water on his body was exhilarating and welcome after the hard Range Session. Jonah swam back to the fake beach amid clapping and laughing from the others.

Plopping down beside Lisa and AJ, he hooted at Eddy, who was up next. Darren continued to heave volunteers into the water for the rest of the early evening.

After changing into dry clothes and eating dinner, Eddy and AJ grabbed a table by the unlit hearth and pulled out the playing cards.

Eddy caught Jonah watching and patted an empty chair. "Come on."

Jonah's first thought was to say he couldn't play cards until he recalled Trueblood's suggestion. Feeling a little guilty, he dropped into the offered chair.

In no time, he and the guys lost themselves in the game. Almost two hours later, Jonah glanced at his watch, shocked. He'd done as he had promised and spent time with his campmates. But he still needed to read the Tales. "I have something to do."

"Really?" Eddy looked disappointed.

"For the Council," AJ suggested, pausing in shuffling the deck.

Jonah blinked at that and imagined others in the room listening. "Nah," he lied. "Just something for Trueblood." Before AJ could point out that could still mean the Council, Jonah rose and crossed to the stairs, trying to ignore the renewed buzz of conversation.

When he closed the door to his room, he leaned his head against it, thinking of a snatch of advice from Mike, who'd warned him to be careful how he appeared to others.

Listening to the excited noise from downstairs, Jonah experienced a moment of uncertainty in his mission. Should he go back and continue playing cards with Eddy and AJ? No, reading the Tales mattered to the Alliance, he thought to himself while retrieving the triptych from his drawer.

Trying to tune out the occasional bursts of distant laughter, he connected the pieces and plopped on his bed.

"Let's see," Jonah mumbled to himself. "We're on the

Second Brother." He found the spot and started reading.

Just like the Eldest Brother, the Deliverer encountered citizens of the Second Protector's province and learned about the issues they faced. It seemed the Second Brother had developed a hatred of solving citizens' problems as a Protector unless there was something new to learn, discover, or teach people.

Things worsened when strangers entered the territory, claiming to possess information the Second Brother did not have. They had been welcomed into his Grand Repository and were now his advisers. The word repository worried Jonah because it reminded him of his time in the Afterworld. His enemy, the Grand Oracle, had a private repository of precious artifacts he stole from mortals and the supernatural alike.

Sensing where this part of the story would go, Jonah settled into the narrative just as the Deliverer prepared to visit the fallen Protector.

⊂⊃

The Second Brother

After sojourning among the people of the Second Brother's territory and hearing all they had to say, the Deliverer finally consented to address their needs. On the morrow after his last meeting, the Deliverer ventured into the borderlands, where he found a wealthy governor who had run afoul of the Protector.

His region had suffered much from the enemy's encroachment, and the people suffered so that nothing worked anymore. The governor's situation suited the Deliverer because he had a plan and required the governor's help. Having no need for a false identity, the Deliverer presented himself to the rich man, who immediately agreed.

"If you can restore my favor to the Protector, I will gladly offer all that I have."

"Do not fear. I will repair the breach that has occurred and return prosperity to this land," the Deliverer promised. "Please, take a short vacation from this place, and when you return, all will be set right. Only, may I borrow some of your best attire for a short time?"

The governor agreed and gave the Deliverer all that he asked. Then he departed his manor house, leaving it to the Deliverer's care. Once the Deliverer had changed into the beautiful garments, he called on his Seeker to bring a unique item from their hidden chamber. That done, he set out to the Second Brother's Repository.

Upon reaching the towering edifice, the Deliverer's heart filled with sadness. Already the structure resembled that of the Grand Oracle. He suspected the new advisers were agents of the Afterworld Rulers and had seduced the Protector. The Deliverer approached the guards, making sure to display his fine clothing.

"What business do you have with the Protector?" the guard asked.

"I am an emissary of my master, the governor of the outlying provinces. He has heard of the Protector's great storehouse of knowledge and his desire to obtain new items for his collection."

"What do you offer?"

The Deliverer shook his head. "I will make my offer only to the Protector and no one else. Send word to your master."

The guard obeyed, and after a time, word came back to allow the Emissary into the building. Shelves, stuffed with ancient books and manuscripts of knowledge, lined the wide passage to the main room. The Second Brother didn't sit on a throne but busied himself between tables stacked with more books and writings.

He regarded the Emissary. "Well, what news have you brought me?"

The Emissary spread his hands. "I have not brought you anything, but my master has obtained a rare scroll that once resided in the Grand Oracle's repository."

The Second Brother was well pleased with the news. "Bring it to me, and I will grant your master whatever he wants."

"Alas, but I cannot bring it here. You must journey to the governor's manor and take possession of it thyself."

At hearing this, the Protector's advisers were troubled and counseled against accepting the Emissary's terms. One even suggested he go and fetch the valuable document for the Protector.

"That will not do," the Emissary said. "My master will only release the scroll to the Protector."

"But what of his security?" another adviser asked.

"He is a Protector, a powerful and wise ruler. He is more than able to overthrow anyone who would oppose him."

Flattered by the Emissary's words, the Protector agreed. "I will go." He raised his ring hand. "The power of my ring will transport me there."

"Please, that will not satisfy my master, either. You must journey on foot or horse. It is his request."

Again, the advisers objected, but the Protector's eyes showed keen interest in the scroll. "I accept," he announced.

And so, the Protector boarded his paladin, and he, the three advisers, and the Emissary set out for the governor's manor. In all, twoscore people traveled through the land.

Very soon, they came upon an engineer whose foundation was flawed so that the building's structure leaned to one side. The Emissary noted the Protector's impatience and desire to ignore the man, so he intervened.

"Oh, wise Protector, surely you can assess the engineer's problem and properly guide him to remedy his issue."

The Protector frowned, and his advisers grumbled, but the engineer bent low in respect. "I humbly ask your words of wisdom, noble Protector."

"So be it," the Protector said and ordered his paladin lowered. He crossed to the engineer and consulted the plans and damaged structure. "There is the problem. Your measurements didn't account for the weight of the substandard material." With confident orders, he told the engineer just what to do to fix the issue.

Afterward, the engineer bowed low in deep respect. "Thank you, brave Protector. Your knowledge is a blessing to us all."

Somewhat pleased, the Protector stepped into his paladin and motioned his group to continue. Two more times, the Emissary intervened to convince the Protector to help his people. And each time, the people praised the Protector's great wisdom and power. As the day drew to early evening, the group reached the governor's manor. The Emissary led the Protector and his advisers into the great hall.

As planned, the Seeker had placed the scroll on a pedestal at the center of the room. The Protector saw it at once and hurried forward to take the document.

"Your master will be rewarded for this, Emissary." His countenance fell as he unrolled the parchment and read.

The Deliverer knew that the scroll was from the Grand Oracle, but it was only a list of records and nothing of great value.

"What is this? It is not new knowledge," the Protector yelled. "It is useless." Power gathered around the Protector, and his ring glowed brightly in the chamber. He turned on the Emissary, who had remained by the door. "You have tried to deceive me, Emissary. I will punish you and your master. I will bring this manor house low so that no stone remains atop another."

Reaching the end of the deception, the Deliverer discarded the borrowed clothes and confronted the stunned Protector with two fiery blades. "It is good to see you can yet call on the power of the ring, noble Protector."

"You!" The Protector's eyes widened. "My Eldest Brother warned me of you. Because of your evil, the people turned against my dear sibling."

"Your brother lost his way and stopped listening to the promptings of his ring or his mother, Destiny," the Deliverer said. He brandished the blades and pointed one at the Protector.

"You, oh Second Brother, are a most knowledgeable Protector," the Deliverer intoned and bowed in recognition. "But in your selfish pride and desire for recognition, you have become a braggart who dismisses, insults, and scorns the people you swore to protect." The

Deliverer's voice grew loud and sure. "Heed the call of your ring and let it renew your soul and mind!"

The Deliverer's words pierced the Second Brother's heart. Though his advisers protested, he raised the ring to his mouth and whispered to it, "Protect my soul. Open my eyes."

Immediately, a protective shield of understanding covered the Second Brother. The deception parted, and he understood the evil influence of the advisers. "What have I done?"

"You are human," the Deliverer said. "But it is not too late."

With his mind free and his understanding restored, the Second Brother turned on his evil advisers. "You are the children of the shadows and of the Grand Oracle. I banish you from the mortal realm!"

The Protector's ring glowed brighter than the midday sun. When it faded, the advisers were gone. From that day forward, the Second Brother used his considerable knowledge to help his people. And his repository became a new school to train and uplift the mortals under his protection.

⊖

Jonah paused at the end of the section. While he liked the story and the obvious lesson, he still had no idea about the clues. What about the midday sun reference? The final page had the outline of stars. Swiping to the end, he held the triptych close and whispered, "Midday sun." Jonah held his breath, but nothing happened.

Fighting back the frustration, he reread the segment again and again, but still, nothing else occurred to him. On a whim, he waved his fingers over the term *midday sun*, but he sensed nothing. Not able to avoid the disappointment, yet again, he deactivated the triptych and put it in his drawer as Eddy thundered into the room.

The boys met each other's gaze for a moment and continued their preparations for bed. Jonah had changed and was under the covers before Eddy.

Waiting for his roommate to get into bed, Jonah said, "Sorry about cutting out early."

"AJ insisted it was something for the Council." Eddy yawned and said in a tired voice, "All fun and no play makes Jonah a snob."

Shocked, Jonah sat up, but Eddy flashed a lopsided grin and rolled over.

Jonah yawned himself and curled up under the covers. Something had to give because ignoring the others while getting nowhere with the Tales couldn't continue. He tried to figure out a solution until he slipped into a light doze.

Unfortunately, he dream-walked, but this one was unlike any of the others. He couldn't move, which became more alarming by the second. And his view was partially blocked, as if something pressed against his face. The object itself was too close to bring into detail, yet it obscured enough of what was beyond to make it impossible to complete a mental picture.

Even the sounds were strangely muted and wavered. All of it overwhelmed Jonah, and he struggled to move again. His heart raced and panic rose. It was one thing to be stuck in a dream-walk until he saw what he needed to see or hear. This dream was taking the experience to another level.

"You should learn to use your powers without panicking."

Marcus's admonition from two years ago had referred to his phasing ability, but the words penetrated Jonah's current panic. Relax and listen, he told himself.

He concentrated on the heavy thuds of metal against metal punctuated by a loud ticking noise, like a clock. Something bubbled on an open fire, the way thick soup did on a stove. He heard the lick of an open flame, and he decided the room must be hot.

Letting his eyes move back and forth, he pieced together the bits he could see. He stood near a wall. Golden light reflected off glittering clocks on an adjacent shelf. Thin metal cylinders and spare parts littered a workbench. And, resting on a dark cloth, lay a long dark blue blade with swirls in the metal surface.

A shadow moved across the visible part of the workbench, and a man stepped into view. The deep tawny, well-muscled arm, lifted the blade to examine it.

"That blade is coming along, Campmaster," Alastor said from somewhere close but out of sight.

"I've had the mages cast spells on each layer of the metal during the forging process."

Jonah gasped because even through the distortion, the Campmaster's way of talking reminded him of his dead dad.

"That's impressive. Perhaps I could witness the forging?" Alastor suggested.

"You know that's out of the question." The Campmaster returned the blade to the cloth. "What do you want, Alastor?"

"I wondered if the Memory Charmers have made a breakthrough."

"No, they haven't." The Campmaster picked up a tool. "Give it time, and we'll know what our enemies are planning."

Alastor snickered. "What do you think of Isaiah's son?"

"It's too soon to know. He seems bright enough."

"Everyone thought his father was smart, including Isaiah himself. Look what it got him. Killed!"

Mandara's voice grew cold. "I warned you, Alastor. I had my problems with Isaiah, but he was still…"

Jonah's anger boiled up inside him, and he heaved himself, trying to break free. For a few precious seconds, the workshop came into sharp detail. At the same time, a device on the workbench illuminated like a warning.

The Campmaster whirled, looking around the space. "You told me those sigils would block Jonah's dreamwalking."

"It works on Wraiths."

"The boy isn't a Wraith. You should augment the sigil. Ask Rubio."

"Why, so he can have Thomas put sigils on the boy's dorm?" Alastor snorted. "In a way, this proves what you wanted to know about Blackstone."

"Get him out of here now!"

Jonah's view of the workshop grew obscured again, but he saw Alastor reaching for him and tried to move or do something.

The next moment, Jonah awoke in his bed with a muffled cry of pain. He clapped a hand over his forehead and sucked in ragged breaths until the slicing feeling dulled to a throbbing ache.

What the heck did Alastor do to me?

Jonah tried to recall the conversation but found it difficult to think straight. He remembered the question about the Memory Charmers and sigils to block his power. Throwing off his cover, Jonah swayed as he lurched to his feet. He gripped the window seal to steady himself and leaned his head against the glass.

He didn't move for several minutes, allowing the pain to recede and his head to clear. A creak came from the hallway as someone moved outside the door. Jonah's heart raced, and he froze. If not for his aching head, he would have reached out with his Reaper sense. Eventually, he heard the person move away.

After a long, anxious moment, the only sounds were the metallic clinking of the AC unit punctuated by Eddy's low snores. Jonah took deep breaths, pushing aside a slight nauseous sensation while trying to relax. Finally convinced he wouldn't collapse or hurl, Jonah lifted his head and opened his eyes.

That's when he caught movement in the courtyard below. He wasn't sure at first, and then a person moved beneath the nearest lamp, and he recognized Thomas's tall frame and small Afro.

Had the Campmaster told Thomas to put the sigils in the dorm room? But how? They'd just had the conversation. Even so, Jonah turned and scanned the walls, but he couldn't detect anything in the dark.

Anxious and unwilling to go back to sleep, he gave in to the intense feeling of unfairness. How could he develop his talents if people were scheming to block him? Well, he wasn't going to sit around and let Thomas or Alastor mark his dorm room.

Turning back to the window, he spotted Thomas moving toward the compound's exit and not the admin building. Confused at first, Jonah reminded himself that the Campmaster and Alastor were in a workshop! So Thomas could still be on his way there.

Making up his mind, he grabbed a shirt and his shoes, determined to catch Thomas and use that as leverage to go home.

CHAPTER SIXTEEN
CAMPMASTER'S LAIR

One benefit of the soft courtyard stones was that Jonah's shoes only made soft thumping sounds. Even so, he tried to keep to the shadows until he reached the exit to the central compound. Given Thomas's head start, Jonah feared he might not find the young mage. Then he spotted a distant flare of blue light on the meadow bridge.

Jonah ran full out but slowed as he neared the bridge. He didn't want his footsteps to echo inside the pitch-black passage and alert Thomas. Forcing himself to take shallow breaths, he entered the bridge. Where was the Campmaster's workshop? Was it in one of the outlying buildings he saw when they gathered for the Nature session?

Jonah considered the options during the nervous minutes before he reached the long corridor's end. Following the sloping path, he stopped seconds later because Thomas paced back and forth in front of the unlocked gate.

He dropped into a crouch behind a row of shrubbery to watch, wondering if Trueblood's ward was still in place. He received the answer when Thomas reached out to help someone through the opening. *Of course!* Touching Thomas, who wore a talisman, allowed the person through the barrier.

The mysterious stranger wore a dark cloak. In the weak moonlight, and with the hood pulled forward, the person's face was impossible to see. When Thomas and his visitor turned to look through the gate, Jonah darted forward to crouch behind the last bit of bordering shrubbery. At least now he could hear their conversation.

"I don't want to do it," Thomas whined.

"Your mom wants you part of the action," the stranger answered, sounding as young as Thomas.

"If the other Memory Charmers haven't succeeded, what can I do?"

The stranger shrugged. "I don't know."

Thomas whirled around, throwing his arms up in frustration. "I didn't sign up for this. We're not Mind Benders!"

Jonah sucked in a breath at the same time his Death Sense spiked. Not giving it a second thought, he dived to his right as a blinding flash of light engulfed the bush behind him. Jumping to his feet, Jonah spun around to find his attacker emerging from the bridge with a raised hand and glowing energy gathering around the fingertips.

Pain spiked in Jonah's head as he leaped aside, avoiding the green fire that shot over his head next. The spell ignited a bush on the opposite side of the bamboo path and bathed the immediate area with an eerie, pale green light. Fear pumped Jonah's legs as he regained his feet and sprinted past a stunned Thomas.

Rounding the sharp curve in the path, Jonah angled for some nearby trees and more buildings that offered cover from his attackers. Thomas yelled out, but Jonah ignored the camp mentor as he raced toward a service building. Just when he thought he'd make it, his sense prickled again. Before he could dodge, something caught his legs, and they clamped together as if tackled by a linebacker.

Unable to maintain his balance, Jonah pitched forward, his arms flailing around. He just managed to avoid smacking his chin on the ground. Even so, the impact rattled his skull, dazing him.

Terrified, Jonah struggled, but his legs refused to respond. Footfalls shook the ground moments before a pair of hands roughly rolled him onto his back. Thomas leaned over him. The visitor stood back. The third person who had attacked remained out of Jonah's line of sight.

Thomas made a gesture in that direction. "Stop!"

"Why?" Jennifer shouted back.

Jonah's breath hitched when he sensed the buildup of magic from the girl. Before she could cast the spell, lightning zipped overhead, followed by a painful yelp.

Heaving himself onto his side, Jonah saw what had happened and his jaw dropped. Eddy and AJ had followed him from the main compound. While Eddy attacked Jennifer again, AJ hurled green fire at Thomas.

But the camp mentor was quicker than Jennifer and blocked the ball of green flame with an almost casual flick of his hands.

The hooded stranger pointed at Jonah's friends without calling on any defensive magic. "This is Alliance Council business," the guy said, putting bass in his voice, though Jonah heard a little shakiness. "Lower your hands and stop attacking!"

Eddy wavered, but AJ kept his hands raised. "You tell her to stand down."

Thomas whirled, caught Jennifer about to cast a spell, and sent a counterspell, causing her building hex to burst with a loud bang. She glared at Thomas, but he stood his ground. "I told you to stop!" Pure anger radiated off the young mage now, so much so that Jennifer backed off.

"Lower your hands," the stranger ordered Eddy and AJ again. This time, the boys complied. The visitor gestured at Jonah. "He heard us. Maybe you should take the memory, Thomas."

"Me? Why can't you do it?"

"It's time you proved yourself."

Thomas shook his head. "I'll do that when it's needed."

"Look, dude—" the man began.

"I said no." Thomas tossed his token and key to the guy. "Get out of here. I'll handle this." The young man hesitated before turning and hurrying back to the gate. Thomas snarled at Jennifer, "And you get back to the dorm before someone catches you out of bounds."

When Jennifer opened her mouth, Thomas shouted, "Go!" Once she had moved off, he gazed down at Jonah and muttered a spell under his breath. Light shot from his hand, enveloping Jonah's legs. All at once, he could move.

Then Thomas produced a glowing Alliance sigil in the air that faded after a few seconds.

Anger surged through Jonah as Eddy helped him stand. "You stunned me!"

"You ran when I caught you out past curfew."

"That's a lie!"

Thomas raised one of his manicured eyebrows. "Then why are all of you out here when you should be in bed?"

Jonah's frustration overcame his ability to argue. Eddy and AJ looked just as angry.

By now, a vortex appeared, and a young mage stepped through. "What's up, Thomas? I can't leave my post…" The guy trailed off as he took in the situation with a glance. He was slender, with brown, spiky hair, a pencil beard and goatee, and a gleaming diamond stud in one earlobe. He also wore a somewhat wrinkled blue tunic. "Dang. What did the kiddies do?"

"Take them, Damian," Thomas said, pointing to Eddy and AJ.

"Sure thing." The newcomer flipped Thomas a mock salute and gripped each boy by a shoulder.

"What about Jennifer?" Jonah objected.

A devilish glee entered Thomas's expression. "I only see you three."

Damian let out a snort as he steered Jonah's friends along the path.

Jonah followed before Thomas could shove him. Only now did it occur to him how much trouble they faced.

The Campmaster's office wasn't the workshop Jonah had seen in the dream-walk. Neither was it like anything else Jonah expected. Instead of a harsh interior with blank walls and hard chairs, Mandara had a dark and cozy office. Between the earth-green walls, the dark wood desk, and the deep brown leather chair, the similarity to his parents' former home office bothered him.

Shelves covered two walls, and they contained Reaper blades, medallions, watches, and clocks of all types and sizes. Fascinated, Jonah moved closer to inspect the glittering objects. Glancing down at his bare wrist, he realized his new watch was like these timepieces, particularly the off-gold and silver highlights.

One of the metal sculptures shifted in the light, drawing Jonah's attention. He guessed it was a kinetic piece, like the ones he'd seen in an outdoor nursery. And he realized this sculpture reminded him of his Aunt Imma's starburst art piece. Instead of rings at the end of thin spikes, this sculpture had little stars.

At first, Jonah thought they floated free, as if a mage had cast a spell on them. But moving closer, he saw tiny filaments attached to each one. It had to be a wind sculpture, but indoors?

"Why have this inside when—" Jonah stopped because his voice produced ripples across the filaments, subtly changing in color as they rotated. "Whoa!"

Damian, who hovered nearby, cleared his throat, pulling Jonah's attention back to the current situation.

Turning, Jonah was stunned to see Kevin staring at him from the opposite corner. He couldn't feel his boyfriend's irritation, indicating Kevin had clamped down on his emotions. Gulping, he shifted his glance to Thomas and back, hoping Kevin would sense that something was up.

Mandara strode into the office and crossed to his desk.

Damian nudged Jonah, Eddy, and AJ to stand right in front of the Campmaster. The man's eyes bore into their faces, subjecting them to a full, undisguised Reaper stare as he sat.

While Jonah didn't know what his new friends felt, he was sorry for getting caught and embarrassed someone had called Kevin. Beneath those emotions was his fury at Thomas's lies. Jonah let all his twisting emotions flow free.

The Campmaster's eyes widened slightly, and he let out a low grunt of dissatisfaction.

"Gentlemen, your emotions are all over the place tonight, particularly yours, Mr. Blackstone." Mandara paused, but Jonah remained quiet. "I understand Thomas caught you three out of the dorm room after curfew. Why?" The man steepled his fingers, waiting.

Jonah swallowed again, casting a venomous glance at Thomas. "He let someone in the back gate." Jonah's voice gave out. He caught the frown on Thomas's face and plunged on. "Why was he meeting someone late at night?"

The Campmaster rubbed the visible stubble on his chin as he peered at Jonah. "The question is, why were you out of your bed? A camp mentor has leeway to move around the camp, Mr. Blackstone. You don't."

"But he stunned me."

"And Jennifer was out there," AJ protested. "Why isn't she in trouble?"

"Yeah," Eddy added.

Damian stirred when Mandara glanced his way. "I only saw these three, sir," he said, nearly repeating Thomas's words.

Jonah wanted to scream that was a lie but kept his mouth shut.

"Mage Pledge is a full member of the Alliance," the Campmaster continued to Jonah. "As such, he has other duties that are none of your concern." Mandara's voice rose as he leaned forward. "You're here to train so that one day you'll serve the Alliance. Until then, you follow the rules." Mandara paused, going back to stroking his chin. "Two days of detention in the kitchens. I think Chef Patelli could use your help with breakfast."

He stood, glancing over their heads at Kevin. "I expected you to watch the people under your charge, Mr. Brown. Escort these gentlemen back to their dorms."

"Yes, sir." Kevin motioned the three boys out the door.

Jonah's legs shook with embarrassment as Kevin herded them out of the building and across the courtyard. Kevin's free hand balled into a tight fist. The veins bulged in his neck as he stared straight ahead.

Jonah swallowed past a lump in his throat. "I'm sorry—"

"Shut up," Kevin snapped.

Too miserable to speak again, Jonah remained quiet. Eddy and AJ exchanged nervous glances and didn't say a word as they entered the main building. Kevin hustled Jonah to one of the armchairs then turned to the other boys.

"Eddy, AJ, up to bed. Now." The Fallen Reaper's mouth worked as if trying not to shout as the others hurried upstairs. Jonah suspected Kevin didn't want to yell in front of them but wouldn't hold back once they were alone. Kevin paced back and forth, reminding Jonah of the time Marcus had lost his cool and shouted at him.

"Kevin…"

The young Fallen Reaper spun around, leaned right over Jonah, and said in a furious whisper, "How could you be so stupid?"

"What…"

"You heard what the Campmaster told you? Thomas is a full mage. He could've hurt you."

"Well, he didn't, and he told the others not to."

"Yeah, because he's also smarter than you." Kevin poked Jonah in the forehead, rocking his head back. "If they had injured you, Mandara would have to deal with that. But since Thomas used a simple stun spell, you look like a rule breaker who he caught."

"You believe me, right? Thomas was talking to someone."

"I'm sure he was. But that's none of your business." Kevin smacked a fist into the chair's armrest. "You could have been hurt."

The raw concern from Kevin and the worry in his eyes stunned Jonah. Kevin allowed his true feelings to come through, and the simple, undeniable fact made all this even worst for Jonah.

The shame became too much, and his voice quivered. "I'm sorry."

"You have to be smarter than that," Kevin bit out.

While some of the anger disappeared from his boyfriend's voice, Jonah still sensed the worry and concern. He wanted to say sorry again but couldn't.

"Remember what I said," Kevin continued. "All camp mentors are members of the Alliance. Serena is a certified Memory Charmer. I'm a Fallen Reaper, and Thomas is a full mage."

"And he's a Memory Charmer," Jonah thought to add, hoping to salvage something out of this evening. "I heard the other guy say it."

Kevin blinked in surprise. "I didn't know that. But it proves my point. Someone else would have blocked your memories of tonight. All of us have real duties with the Alliance. I'm sure Thomas had a legit reason for the visit."

"But why at midnight?"

Kevin slapped one of his large hands over his face, letting out a deep breath as if dealing with a kid. "Jonah, members of the Alliance work all around the world, in different time zones. Maybe tonight was the only time they could meet."

"Why are you taking his side?"

"I'm not taking his side. That's just the way it is."

"Then why was the Campmaster surprised when I told him about the person? He kept Thomas back."

"I'm sure he's asking Thomas about it." Kevin shook his head. "But again, that's none of your business." He jabbed a finger in Jonah's chest. "The next time you suspect something, you tell me. I'll decide if it's worth investigating. Do you hear me?"

Jonah nodded, wondering if he suspected Thomas because the boy's mom was a Hardliner. And then there was his dream-walk. "Hey, I dream-walked tonight."

Kevin knelt beside the chair. "Did you see Thomas? Is that why you followed him?"

"No. It was about the Campmaster and Alastor. They talked about Memory Charmers getting information. What does that mean? Memory Charmers mess with people's thoughts. Is that it?" Jonah asked in a rush. Kevin winced and tried to cover by rubbing his hand over his face, but this close, Jonah saw the look. "Then Thomas let a Memory Charmer through the gate."

"How do you know the other guy was a Memory Charmer?"

Now that Kevin asked, Jonah realized he'd connected the bits of conversations he'd heard. "He told Thomas to block my memories instead of doing it himself," Jonah recalled. "And what about Jennifer? She was out there and tried to kill me!"

Kevin waved that bit of information off. "Probably just a nasty hex. Even she's not that stupid. Besides, she'll be in bed and asleep by now."

"It all means something." Jonah watched Kevin, sensing his boyfriend's hesitation. "What's happening?"

"Nothing that involves you."

"That's not true."

Kevin stood and hauled Jonah to his feet. "It's time for bed."

Jonah didn't struggle, letting Kevin nudge him up the stairs. When they reached the top landing, he thought of another snatch of the dream-walk conversation and stopped, causing Kevin to bump into him. "When Alastor talked about my dad, in the dream-walk, Mandara got angry."

Jonah turned and was sure of it when a spike of dread washed over Kevin, and the boy averted his eyes. "It's nothing, Jonah."

He didn't believe that, but he'd already done so much to get Kevin into trouble, he wouldn't argue. He would, however, remember and get to the bottom of it before leaving camp. "Fine."

He marched to his door with Kevin right behind.

"One day, and you're already in trouble." Kevin leaned close and whispered, "If you slip up again, I'll kick your butt back to Mount Vernon." He crossed to his room, went inside, and closed the door with a snap.

Jonah entered his room to find AJ standing beside Eddy. "Why did you two follow me?" He quickly closed the door, so Kevin wouldn't hear.

Eddy looked embarrassed, but AJ stood tall. "I knew something was up, so I told him to keep watch."

"Thanks, guys." Jonah crossed to his bed. "That was brave, but I don't want you in any more trouble."

AJ gestured at the door. "I have to wait for Kevin to fall asleep, or he'll hear me, right?" When Jonah nodded, he added, "So, there's time to tell us what's going on?"

Jonah considered keeping his mouth shut until he met their gazes. These guys had helped even though they barely knew him. Plus, the idea of withholding information sounded like Marcus and the Alliance adults, and he didn't want to be like them.

AJ, who had been watching his face, suddenly sat and pulled Eddy down beside him.

With a sigh, Jonah hopped on his bed and told them about the Tales and the Destiny Medallion.

CHAPTER SEVENTEEN
CALMING WINDS

Jonah Blackstone! the voice whispered his name in the darkness of the dream.

Jonah opened his eyes to find himself soaring over the darkened countryside. Somehow, he knew this was still Georgia.

"Jonah!"

His name echoed around him as he descended closer and closer to the trees! Jonah raised his hands, expecting to crash into the branches, but they parted and allowed him to hurtle along a moonlit pathway through the woods.

"Jonah," the voice taunted him now. It was a woman's voice, and she laughed.

Up ahead, a dark opening appeared on a hillside. Jonah's speed increased as the cavern yawned wider, like a mouth about to swallow him. He struggled and tried to backpedal, but he couldn't stop from plunging into the darkness.

"Jonah Blackstone!"

Thera Rasmussen's face appeared. She laughed and pointed at him. *"We are coming for you, Jonah Blackstone!"*

As her finger touched his forehead, pain exploded in Jonah's mind. He screamed.

"Ow!" Jonah groaned then struggled when someone shook him. "Huh?" he asked, opening his eyes.

"Wake up," Eddy said.

Jonah rubbed his aching head as he sat up in bed. "What time is it?"

"Six thirty. Kevin said we had to be in the kitchen by seven fifteen."

Jonah rose and grabbed his clothes while shaking off the ominous sensation the dream had created. He knew the KIN wanted to kill him. That was nothing new.

Eddy stood by the door, clutching a small bag with his toiletries inside. "Do you think he'll make us run laps if we're late?"

Jonah didn't offer an answer as he left the room in time to join a sleepy AJ in the hallway. Kevin waited downstairs and shadowed them to the showers. But when they finished up and came out of the Lavatory Building, Kevin was nowhere in sight. Shrugging to each other, the boys hurried to their rooms, put away their things, and headed for the kitchens.

The clicking of pots and pans and the muted conversation reached them before they pushed open the kitchen's swinging doors. The cooking staff bustled around amid aromas of oatmeal bubbling away in a large pot, fresh rolls, eggs, and savory bacon. Jonah's stomach grumbled in response.

Chef Patelli stalked around, shouting directions. When he noticed the boys, he paused to run his thick fingers over the wavy silver-gray mustache.

His eyes narrowed, appraising them. "I think we had a kid who beat you guys by four hours."

Jonah exchanged a confused look with the others.

The Chef nodded while tapping a finger to his temple. "Yes. Technically that boy got in trouble on the first day. You three at least waited until after midnight," he joked, waving them toward the large pots.

With that, they were off. Eddy served as the gofer, running here and there, following the Chef's orders, while Jonah and AJ cleaned the pots and pans used to make the breakfast. And when people came down to eat, evident by the increased noise on the other side of the swinging doors, they started washing the incoming dirty breakfast dishes.

At least he and AJ could have a whispered discussion about Thomas, Memory Charmers, and the information the Alliance hoped to find. Or Jonah tried. AJ's answers were short, as though the boy was bothered. Jonah let it go for now and kept his thoughts to himself. Deep inside, he sensed something more significant going on with Hunters and Memory Charmers. And whatever it was involved people here at camp.

When the Chef placed a tray containing an antique tea set and three carafes beside him, he came back to reality. "Clean these, please." The man pointed to a side space where the coffee brewers sat. "Put them there when you finish."

Jonah groaned, but he started on the items. The various latent aromas from the opened carafes let him know the adults liked their unique coffees. He recalled seeing a kitchen worker carrying the tea set to one of the meeting rooms down the first floor's west hallway.

"Here goes," Eddy announced in a sad voice, leaning against the swing door. A blast of noise rolled into the kitchen when he pushed the door open and went out front to retrieve empty trays.

Jonah didn't think he could stand the astonished looks from the others, nor the smug grins of the young mages. He didn't have to worry because Chef Patelli didn't release them until after everyone had finished breakfast and headed off to morning sessions.

The boys grabbed sticky buns off a plate and raced upstairs to get their things.

⁓

When AJ, Eddy, and Jonah entered the Meditation class, everyone was sitting on floor mats in a semicircle, facing the teacher. And the young mages were with them again. The Councilwoman with wild reddish-gray hair stood in the center of the group clad in a loose-fitting dress and see-through scarf, despite the summer weather.

Making pushing motions with her hands, the Councilwoman said, "Move back a little. Give yourself more space."

Like the Team Building room, this space had light sage green walls and a floor done in a dark wood. A large print of a rain forest covered the divider wall, and someone had placed a low stone bench in front of that. The setup struck Jonah almost like an altar, with two bunches of flowers in earthen vases.

Once satisfied with everyone's spacing, the woman pulled her salmon-colored scarf around her thin neck and tied it in a loose knot. She tilted her chin up, ready to speak, when a couple of mages snickered, and she finally noticed Jonah, Eddy, and AJ standing in the doorway.

"Gentlemen," she announced in a slight Creole accent like a judge about to sentence a prisoner, "are you part of the class or not?"

"Yes, ma'am," the boys said in unison, grabbing floor mats from the stack by the door.

They claimed the bit of floor space behind Lisa, Darren, and Monisha, and sat.

Lisa glanced over her shoulder. "Where were you guys this morning?"

"Long story," Eddy whispered back.

The Councilwoman peered down at them with a frown. "As I was about to say, I'm Mrs. Bertonneau, the Alliance Council Co-Chair, and this is Meditation class. During these sessions, you will learn to tap into your center of power. To accomplish that, you must meditate. And why must you learn to meditate?"

"It clears your mind," AJ answered.

"It gets rid of any distractions blocking your connection to your power," Jennifer said, though her voice sounded like she was countering AJ's answer.

"Correct! I see some of you have meditated before." Bertonneau continued walking among them. "Pay attention to your classmates. When you meditate and clear your mind of distractions, you can connect to your power. But you can't do that if you are worried about your family, resentful of a fellow camper, or concerned about your girlfriend or boyfriend."

Jonah nodded, but he also remembered Wick's comment about emotions and raised his hand. Bertonneau paused and gestured to him. "Don't your emotions help you gain more power?" he asked.

"You can indeed activate your power when you experience sudden strong emotions, Mr. Blackstone, but any uncontrolled emotion, positive or negative, will eventually interfere. You will strain yourself and do potential damage to your body." She watched his expression, no doubt trying to see if he understood. He did, but this was new.

As if sensing his thoughts, Bertonneau said, "This may be a new way of thinking for some of you, but give it time. We're here to help. Your advantage over most people is that your powers are a literal manifestation of your ability to tap into your inner source."

She turned, meeting every eye, and received nods from the class.

"Good. Now, I'm going to teach you techniques to increase your ability to access your power."

Eddy looked doubtful, and AJ once again showed keen interest in the new information. The idea intrigued Jonah. He knew a little about concentrating and reaching out to touch his power.

"Close your eyes," Bertonneau said. "Relax and focus inward. Imagine you're on a calm lake." Someone laughed. "I know we have a lake right outside. That's good. Picture yourself sitting on the lake in a boat. Concentrate on the sound of real water, and if your mind strays, refocus yourself. Don't worry if you don't get it right at first."

Jonah did as instructed, and immediately, thoughts about the Tales intruded. He remained calm and refocused his mind several more times upon the sound of the gentle lapping waves until, finally, he relaxed. Maybe the slight breeze from the actual lake helped with the mental image. Or perhaps it was Bertonneau's voice, which was as soft as the breeze.

"Feel every part of your body. Now go within, deeper and deeper, until you can touch the energy."

Sudden doubt assailed Jonah because the last time he did something like this, he had on the Protector's Ring, or he had a chamber full of power to call on. He wasn't a mage; nor was he like the other campers. Sure, he could defeat a Wraith or open a rip to the Underworld, but what else could he call on?

Bertonneau spoke from nearby. "Believe you can do it, and when you reach inside, you'll touch your power."

Slowing his breathing, Jonah refocused on the mental image of the boat. He imagined a slight wind blowing across his face, legs, feet, head, hair until he could feel a breeze. Latching on to that, he went deeper, opening himself to the sensation until his entire body tingled in response.

At first, Jonah held his breath because he was afraid, but then he relaxed. It was like standing in a soft wind as it caressed you. Out of pure curiosity, he imagined throwing his arms out wide and calling the wind to him.

The force of the imaginary wind increased, feeling too real against his body until something solid bumped into him, breaking his concentration. He opened his eyes.

Eddy had bumped into his arm while holding up a hand against a strong gust of wind.

"What the…?"

Everyone in the pavilion held up their hands, shielding their faces. Bertonneau stood apart from them with her flowing dress flapping in the breeze. While everyone looked out at the lake, she watched Jonah with an unreadable expression.

Darren stood. "Should I close the sliding doors, ma'am?"

Bertonneau tore her gaze from Jonah and shook her gray-haired head. "No. I think it will calm down." She waved Darren back to his spot. "All of you continue. This situation is perfect to practice concentration."

Poor Jennifer had the hardest time because she had to keep a tight grip on her head wrap. Then the young mage muttered under her breath, and a greenish distortion encircled her. She turned to give Jonah a sneer before going back to meditating in her bubble of calmness.

The only other mage to achieve a personal shield was the thin blond mage named Crosby. Unlike Jennifer's, his shield was blue and not very good, judging by the visible distortion lines. Yet the boy seemed unruffled as he motioned to his friend, the mage with the droopy dreads, to try. His friend produced a shield; however, the shield snapped out of existence within seconds with an irritating pop.

Jonah would have laughed if a pair of bony hands hadn't clutched his shoulders.

"Concentrate, Mr. Blackstone. Calm the wind," Bertonneau whispered.

She released him, and Jonah didn't question how she knew he was the culprit. It didn't help that each gust of real wind broke his progress when he tried to call up his mental picture of sitting in the boat. Instead, Jonah imagined himself pushing against the wind with his arms.

Calm. Quiet.

He willed the wind to die down until nothing but a gentle breeze rocked the boat.

"Thank God," Monisha said.

Jonah slowly opened his eyes. The real wind was back to a whisper again.

Bertonneau tapped him on the shoulder. "We're aiming for control. Don't forget that." She moved away.

Glancing around, Jonah noticed the other campers' various talents. Eddy had a tiny tendril of current jerking around his palm as he commanded it to move.

AJ held a blue flame in his hand, making it grow then shrink to a ball at will. Jonah had seen Trueblood train Wick do the same thing. He was impressed because AJ's flame ball was already well defined.

Monisha let out a frustrated grunt. She had a pen in midair and her brow furrowed. Jonah realized she was making the point shift in graceful motions like she was writing. Her best friend Lisa hovered a few inches off the mat, her face also showing deep concentration as she kept herself aloft.

Across the room, Jennifer, Marvin, and Alex all produced complex sigils in the air. Beraki continued to try the shield while Crosby's barrier grew noticeably more stable.

Jonah blinked in surprise at the Vanay guy because he sat beside a cave. He hadn't noticed that, and it made no sense to have a cave inside the pavilion. As he watched, the details of the cave wavered before winking out of sight. A mirage!

Impressed with the others, Jonah doubled down and continued channeling a calm wind until the class ended. Outside afterward, in the muggy summer heat, he realized another benefit of his power. The steady breeze he had created kept the meditation room comfortably ventilated. After half a dozen steps, he wished he had that breeze now.

Up ahead, Crosby talked in excited gestures to his friend. "Did you see it, Beraki? I made a shield. Well, it wasn't as good as Jennifer's, but it was cool."

Beraki shrugged. "Mine didn't last."

Before Jonah could stop himself, he blurted out, "You have to believe you can do it." Crosby and Beraki whirled to face him. Jonah swallowed and plunged on.

"Don't think about it, just do it, and bypass the doubts."

Crosby pushed his glasses up on his nose, peering at Jonah with open curiosity. "What can you do?"

"I can phase."

"Whoa. Awesome." The boy's face broke into a grin, and he tapped Beraki's shoulder. "He's right." When Beraki pulled a doubtful look, Crosby added, "We can practice it in the dorm."

Vanay, who stood a short distance away, called out to them. "Crosby, Beraki. Get in line."

Crosby waved to Jonah as he and Beraki joined the other mages. The group marched away in single file.

Eddy gave Jonah a speculative look. "Was that extra credit work for the Team Building class?"

"No. They're cool. Just like us."

As they followed the rest of their group, Eddy asked, "So, how'd you do?"

"I don't know." Jonah glanced back at the pavilion roof visible above the sculpted shrubbery that bordered the smaller courtyard's wall. "It's not like I can shoot lightning or fire."

"Maybe." Eddy laughed. "I bet you'll do okay in the blade session."

Jonah shrugged, but he enjoyed Eddy speculating how blade training would go. At one point, Jonah caught AJ glancing back at them. The boy walked with Lisa, and his strange behavior began to bother Jonah.

He nudged Eddy. "What's up with AJ?"

The question caused Eddy to stare at his feet as they moved along. "It's about last night."

"I don't want you guys to get in trouble."

"Not that," Eddy started then swallowed. "You see, AJ's convinced you're not telling us everything."

That surprised Jonah. "I'm not. I mean, we didn't have time and you don't need to know everything." Jonah squeezed his eyes closed, aware again he sounded just like his godfather.

"I get it, but AJ likes learning things he didn't know."

Jonah glanced at AJ's back. As irritated as he felt, he also noted the relaxed sway of the guy's walk. Out of nowhere, Jonah wondered if AJ was a good dancer. Maybe an excellent slow dancer. The heat in his face added to his frustration with the boy. "So, he decides to be pissed with me?"

"Hey, you wanted to know," Eddy offered as they neared the junction in the path and headed toward the ranges.

Everyone had another hot topic of discussion when they arrived. Damian, the young Alliance Mage who had helped Thomas march Jonah and his friends to Mandara's office, stood at the crossroads with Kevin and Serena. Instead of his wrinkled mage's tunic, the guy wore the mentor uniform without tucking in the shirt or lacing up his hiking boots.

"What's he doing here?" Eddy asked.

Jonah heard the dislike in his friend's voice, and he shared it. Damian had been more than willing to back up Thomas's lie the night before.

AJ answered, "He's stepping in as mentor for the mages."

Jonah couldn't stop himself. "How do you know?"

AJ turned and raised an eyebrow, looking as if he debated speaking to him again.

"How do you think?" Eddy blurted out. "He asked someone."

"You weren't there for breakfast this morning when Trueblood made the announcements," Lisa added. "Mandara and Thomas left camp this morning."

"Oh." Jonah was too intrigued by the development to worry about AJ.

And where the heck did Thomas and the Campmaster go? Jonah was sure it had something to do with the Memory Charmers. For once, he felt a bit of sympathy for the brooding young mage. He wouldn't want to work with Mandara and could never imagine a situation where he'd trust the Campmaster.

CHAPTER EIGHTEEN
CHOOSING OF THE BLADES

When Jonah spotted Fallen Reaper Rex Montgomery on the ranges, his concerns about the Campmaster's whereabouts and the Memory Charmer mystery vanished.

"Rex!" He ran over to the big, blond Fallen Reaper.

"How ya doin', Jonah?" Rex asked, shoving a large gym bag under a table near the lean-to. He stood and shook Jonah's hand.

"I didn't know you'd be here."

Rex scratched the side of his large nose. "This week, you have me. Next week, the Campmaster will have someone else here, or he'll take over."

Jonah grimaced and caught himself before Rex noticed. He definitely didn't want Mandara as a blade teacher.

"You know everyone?" Jonah asked as Rex shook hands all around.

"Sure. I met all the interns during the summer."

Although Jonah knew about the summer internship by now, the reminder that all the others had that shared experience still bothered him. Why hadn't his godfather told him about the program?

At that moment, muted clinking drew everyone's attention. Jonah turned toward the range opening, fearing the mages would join them. Instead, Alastor rolled a large black box into the field. It resembled one of those pieces of luggage with the pull handle and had a rolled-up black cloth secured on top.

Alastor pushed the box to a long side table near the field's lean-to. As they watched, the Fallen Reaper unfurled the black cloth and draped it over the table with a flourish.

"Now, all of you know that this session is about blades," Rex began, his voice full of excitement. "Except for Jonah, none of you have ever used blades before, right?" He paused while the others either nodded or shrugged in agreement.

"I'm gonna teach you the basic techniques for holding the blades and defending yourself. If you come along better than I expect, maybe I'll get into some advanced things."

More clicking sounds came from the table as Alastor began arranging rows of gleaming silver cylinders on the velvet cloth.

Jonah's anticipation spiked at seeing the deactivated blades.

Rex clapped his hands together. "Reaper blades are special weapons from the supernatural world. Spells cast on the blade's metal imbues the weapon with power. It's a dang hard craft to make one, and I know only one person who can do it."

Surprised at that bit of information, Jonah whirled to face the Fallen Reaper. His thoughts went to the snatch of dream-walk about Mandara. The man talked about enchanting that long blade. *No way!* Jonah shook himself, trying to dispel the sudden, shocking thought.

"Blades are deadly to supernatural creatures of all kinds," Rex continued, "and they can cut and kill regular humans like any other blade." He held up his beefy hands. "I don't want you to get concerned about the killing part. We're focusing on defense today, but before we get into the lessons, you need to choose your blades." He stepped back and waved toward the table.

"Go on."

Everyone raced to the table and jostled against each other to look over the cylinders. There were three rows of over twenty blades. The setup reminded Jonah of a vendor's table at a sci-fi convention he once attended. The seller had replica fantasy blades and knives. Yet these Reaper blades were the real thing.

Jonah didn't expect the varying sizes and lengths of the devices. Some cylinders had rounded edges, while others were flat and square or tapered toward the bottom ends.

"Whoa. I never noticed how different each pair could be," Jonah observed, looking at Alastor.

"Yes, Mr. Blackstone," Alastor said, snickering. "Think of the blade cylinders like tennis racket handles. Each person should pick one that fits their grip."

Darren reached for a long cylinder that was also the thickest. Jonah hesitated, remembering using Lynn's blades and wondering how his mom knew what size to give his cousin. *She must have used her intuition.*

Alastor snapped his fingers, getting Jonah's attention. "Rex doesn't have all day."

Jonah ignored the sting of bitterness for being singled out. Everyone took their time pawing the blades. He picked up a couple of cylinders right in front of him and tested their weight. The weapons reminded Jonah of Lynn's blades, but after a moment longer, he put them down. As he tested each pair, he liked them less and less.

Darren went back, hefted the first ones he tried, and walked from the table. AJ also found a suitable pair of blades and moved off, while Eddy and Lisa looked as lost as Jonah felt. Monisha didn't seem to care if she took all day as she tried every pair.

Alastor let out a sigh. "The Campmaster personally selected these blades from the storehouse with your group in mind." He raised an eyebrow.

Jonah didn't catch on, in part because hearing that the Campmaster chose the blades strengthened his shocking conclusion about the supernatural weapons.

Rex walked over. "When creating blades, the time of year makes a difference."

With that clue, Jonah realized his mistake. Though laid out in three rows, he finally noticed the gap between groups of three or four blades. The significance of that registered on him. "They're grouped according to the Zodiac symbols?"

Alastor leaned over the table. "When's your birthday?"

"The twenty-third of June."

"Ahh, you're a Cancer. That would be the pearl birthstone." He waved his hand over a group of blades in the center row, near the right end.

As soon as Jonah picked up a pair of the supernatural weapons in that group, he knew these were a better fit because a tingle shot up his arm.

This is more like it! He fought the immediate urge to activate the weapons.

The first cylinders were too thick, but Jonah grew excited as he moved on to the next pair of blades. Like the first pair, these seemed to react to him but didn't satisfy the tug he felt on his soul. Something called out to him, but not these blades. Jonah gripped the next set of cylinders with slightly widened ends so that his hand fit snuggly in the center.

A sharp tingle raced up his arm, and the internal tug morphed into a deep sense of familiarity. He moved away from the others without hesitation, activated the blades, and whirled them in his hands. They were even better than Lynn's, and just for a second, he heard the echo of a song in his head.

Eddy, Lisa, and Monisha gaped at him. Alastor smirked. When the slippery guy turned to wink at Rex, Jonah suspected something was up. Rex hid his reaction as he helped Eddy and Lisa pick their blades. Alastor turned to Monisha, helping her quickly find the perfect pair.

Jonah didn't notice any of the other kids having the same reaction that he had. So why did he get a response? As soon as Rex finished with the others, Jonah stepped in front of him. "What happened?" He held up the blades he'd chosen. "Why did they respond to me like that?"

Rex scratched the side of his nose and traded a quick glance with Alastor. "Well, you'd find out eventually. Your mom and dad helped to make those blades."

Jonah's eyes widened as the cylinders began to hum in his hands with a haunting melody again. He sucked in a breath because the tune sounded like one his mother used to hum to him.

"There are two strands of their hair intertwined through the stone inlay." Rex patted Jonah's shoulder. "Alastor and the Campmaster wondered if you would choose the blades." He hesitated. "Your parents would have given them to you in person if they were still here."

To Jonah's surprise, the news didn't sadden him. Instead, the haunting song filled his soul with peace. He moved through the fighting positions, the blades swishing and humming even more. *My parents touched these blades. Now they're a part of me.*

Jonah deactivated the blades. "Thanks," he told Rex and walked out to where the others waited.

AJ pointed a slender finger at Jonah's cylinders. "You didn't know about the birthstones?"

"No." Jonah had noticed it on Lynn's Reaper blades the first time he ever held them, but he'd never asked about it.

"Wow. That's odd since you've used blades before." Perhaps AJ saw Jonah's flash of irritation because he turned over his cylinders and pointed to the thin, deep red lines down the grips.

Turning his cylinders over, Jonah found a pearl inlay with the thin, dark line down the center, the strand of his mom and dad's hair. "Is this…?"

"Yep. Each blade has a bit of the birthstone in it."

Jonah stared at the boy. "I guess you asked about that?"

"It's amazing how some people don't mind sharing information."

The boy's challenging tone made Jonah want to yell at him.

"I was born in January," AJ continued before Jonah could respond. "So, my stone is garnet." He nodded to Darren. "He's a Taurus."

The large boy showed Jonah the diamond inlay on his cylinders. The only thing that Jonah didn't understand was how plain the blades appeared. "Rex? Where's all the Angel script?"

Rex, who helped Alastor collect the remaining blades, smiled. "The Angel script imprint comes later when you've reached a certain level." He activated his blades and held them up to show off the etchings covering the blades and handles. The others gathered close to gawk. "The blades will grow on you and become part of you. Because of that, every inscription is unique to the individual. Okay," Rex said, motioning them back. "Space yourselves out about six feet apart."

Once they had spaced out, Rex held up his blade cylinders. "Now, the first thing you need to learn is how to activate the blades without cutting yourself."

He showed them the process. Jonah recalled his first time learning to press the cylinder near the top. The wrist twist took him some time to get right before the blade activated. He demonstrated for AJ and Eddy.

AJ activated his blades on the third try. "That felt weird," he said in an awed voice. "The metal shifted in my hands."

"Why don't my blades work?" Eddy blurted out. Jonah helped and by the time Eddy succeeded in activating the blade, Rex was ready to move on.

"Okay," the Fallen Reaper called out, "put the blades away now."

Everyone grumbled while they slipped their cylinders in pockets. Rex crossed to the now bare long table and pulled a large gym bag from underneath. Dropping it on a patch of grass, he unzipped the bag to reveal multiple pairs of dull-ended wooden sticks with handles.

"Practice batons," Jonah said, taking a pair out of the bag and slipping off the rubber band that bound them together. "We used batons like these in our Practice Club."

"Exactly. I don't want anyone getting hurt the first day," Rex explained, "so everyone gets a pair. The sizes vary a little, but they don't need to be a perfect fit like the real blades."

Jonah stood back as the others crowded the bag, grabbing pairs of batons. Once everyone had a set, they lined up, facing Rex Without being told. The Fallen Reaper went through the basic self-defense stances and moves. Soon into the lesson, Rex asked Jonah to work with Monisha and Lisa. Monisha took to the batons with an intensity that frightened Jonah, whereas Lisa seemed afraid to handle the weapons.

"Lisa, think of them as a part of you," Jonah tried to explain.

"I know," she whined, "and I'm trying. I just don't like a lot of violence."

"Me neither, but this stuff will save you."

"Can't I float above it all?"

Monisha snorted as she went through the basic moves. "That's smart. No one will think to attack you while you're hovering over their heads."

Noticing the way Lisa observed Monisha's moves, Jonah had an idea. When Monisha paused, he whispered to her, "You're doing well. Why don't you let Lisa follow you through the positions?"

With Monisha showing her friend the moves, Jonah used the opportunity to back away and observe. He was right. Lisa did better without him standing nearby.

"Perhaps you have a calling as a teacher," Alastor suggested. The Fallen Reaper had propped himself against the side of the rustic lean-to, observing the session.

With the newness of having personal blades wearing off, Jonah's distrust of Alastor returned. "Why are you still here?"

"I wanted to make sure the blades were okay."

"Liar."

"Hate me if you will, Mr. Blackstone," Alastor said, leaning on the table, "but we both know I helped you."

"You tricked me. I could have been stuck in the Underworld forever."

Alastor pulled a skeptical face. "That was never going to happen. And here you are, safe and sound. Plus, you discovered a lot about yourself." Alastor peered at Jonah. "Do you regret that?"

Jonah opened his mouth, only to shut it without responding. He wouldn't let Alastor nor the Campmaster off the hook. After the last dream-walk, Jonah was sure that Mandara had been the one to send Alastor to Mount Vernon back in the fall. The Council's Hardline faction had manipulated him like he was a weapon and not a person.

"I don't care how many sigils you use. They won't keep me from finding out what you're doing," Jonah challenged.

Alastor laughed. "Really? So full of ourselves, aren't we?"

"Just go away," Jonah snapped.

Alastor raised an eyebrow.

"Our session's over," Rex announced. "Everyone did mighty well."

Alastor grabbed the travel box and drop cloth and rolled it out of the Range ahead of the others. Jonah wondered if the man was on his way to report to Mandara until he remembered the Campmaster was gone.

Catching up to Rex as the big man waved the others through the gate, Jonah asked, "Hey, Rex?"

"Yeah, buddy?"

"Where's Alastor taking the blades?"

"To store them in the workshop for now. Someone will take the blades back to Atlanta." He turned to close the gate.

"So the Campmaster makes the blades?"

"Yeah, he's a Master Blade-maker." Rex scrutinized Jonah's face. "He's the only one left who can do it. You didn't know?"

Jonah shrugged as his conclusion about the dream-walk descended on him like a heavy weight. Not only had he been in the Campmaster's workshop, but all the glittering items in the man's office were other things he had created. Yet Jonah was still perplexed.

"Why would he put my parents' hair in a blade for me? He doesn't like me."

"Jonah, your father did that."

"My dad? But you said only one person could do it…" Jonah's voice trailed off. Mandara was the only one who knew blade-making because his dad, who had also learned the technique, was killed by the Grim Reaper.

Rex flashed him a worried look. "The blade-making talent runs in your family, so…"

The Fallen Reaper cut off the rest of what he was about to say, but Jonah got it. If his dad could do it, did that mean he could learn to make blades too? A strange sensation came over Jonah—that would give the Campmaster and him something in common, and Jonah didn't like that idea.

CHAPTER NINETEEN
PERSONAL DEVELOPMENT

Personal Development began with a person-to-person chat with Bertonneau. Jonah was first on her list right after lunch. After his session, Lisa, AJ, and two mages would go in turn. Eddy, Darren, and AJ were lucky and got Trueblood for their sessions.

"During this time with me," Bertonneau began, "I want to help you learn to use a different power that all campers possess."

That statement piqued Jonah's interest. What power did all the campers share? Before he could try to figure it out, the teacher continued.

"You have the power to feel any way you want at any time and in any circumstance." Bertonneau folded her hands in her lap and waited, no doubt wanting him to figure out her meaning.

Jonah screwed up his mouth as he tried to understand the woman. He knew about emotions and feelings in ways others didn't. As a Half-Reaper, he could sense and see the aura around people. The most remarkable aspect was how the field around the person constantly changed colors depending on the person's emotions. "I can decide my emotion any time I want? Even if someone gets me angry?"

"Yes."

"How?"

"You simply decide to embrace a different emotion." Bertonneau placed a hand over her heart. "As I said in the first Meditation class, controlling your emotions is fundamental to tapping into your power in a controlled way."

"I can sense people's emotions if I try, and the emotion is strong," Jonah decided to add.

The Councilor nodded. "Yes. I knew your mother well. Although sensing a person's aura is a Reaper power, I suspect you inherited the ability to decipher emotions from her. That's a powerful tool if you can develop it properly. That journey of personal development"—she pointed at Jonah's head and then his chest—"begins with learning to identify and control your own emotions."

The woman's words fascinated and excited him. He'd never considered learning to go that deep with his ability.

"Of course," she added, "going deeper doesn't mean you should use it to get money from your classmates."

Did all the Alliance adults know about the lie detector stunt? He sank lower in his chair until Bertonneau raised a critical eyebrow. Jonah sat straight again.

"Mage Trueblood and I will introduce all of you to an emotional scale. With it, you'll identify your current state and then move to the next emotion on the scale."

"Whoa," Jonah said.

"You do it by thinking of things that produce a specified emotional reaction inside you. This process may seem hard or impossible at first, but you will learn to do it with practice. Keep in mind that you can't go from boredom to joy. However, if you're bored, you could try to think about things that make you content. Understand?"

"Yes, ma'am." He was eager to try this new thing.

"Good. Now, how do you feel?"

With that question, Bertonneau spent the next twenty minutes working with Jonah to identify his current emotions and ways to change them. Most of the work would happen during his day and on his own. It was like an ongoing homework assignment and Bertonneau would check in on his progress.

⁓

After a good start on the emotion scale, Bertonneau switched to asking him about his hobbies and other things he liked to do. Once she discovered an area of interest, the camper spent the rest of the individual study time focusing on that. He was surprised to discover that included using the library in the main building to do any needed research.

Jonah didn't know what to tell the aloof woman. Of course, he liked to read, but he doubted the Councilor would let him spend all his time in the camp library. "Um, I like to listen to soundtracks, practice with the blades, and play video games."

"Well, you won't do that here." Bertonneau looked a little put out with him for a moment. "Remember, we're here to help you connect to your abilities and use them. Personal Development has helped many individuals discover additional talents that connect to their power. The time spent here expands your core identity."

Jonah thought about that and regretted his first answers. He liked to read and study all kinds of things. He also thought about his mom and dad. His mom had a beautiful voice, like Lynn. And his dad, well, he could make blades. Jonah never saw anything like that at home.

Only now did it occur to him that his dad probably had a workshop somewhere else.

Bertonneau watched his expressions without saying a word. "Mr. Corvera is doing woodworking. Why don't you try that for now?"

Did she know about his dad? He'd only found out he might have a talent for making things that morning, but he doubted the camp had a course for it. Maybe wood carving was the closest thing to metalworking. Not having a better idea, he nodded and made the long trek to the outlying buildings not far from the back gate.

The wood carving took place in the squat metal building he'd noted on the first day. Seeing all the carpentry tools, he wondered if the carpentry teacher, Mr. Tippens, a bland man wearing a plaid shirt and jeans, had a carpentry business.

As he peered around the interior, Jonah noticed a closed section in the back. The wooden door looked heavy and had a large silver lock securing it. "What's that?"

"That's the Campmaster's workshop," Mr. Tippens answered. "We won't be going in there."

The teacher motioned him toward Eddy, who waited beside a wooden table with tools spread out on top. Jonah glanced back at the secured workshop.

So, that's the place from the dream-walk, where the Campmaster makes the blades. Did my dad work in there?

Jonah found it challenging to pay attention while Tippens explained the various tools. The man's monotone voice defied all attempts to focus, so Jonah thought about the Campmaster's workshop.

"Are you listening, Mr. Blackstone?" Tippens had paused in demonstrating the tools.

"Yes, sir."

Tippens grunted and continued his instructions. Afterward, they were free to pick a piece of precut wood and start. At least hanging out with Eddy for the hour and a half turned out to be fun. They could talk among themselves if they kept busy.

Darren was also there, working on wooden sculptures for what Jonah guessed were segments of fantasy armor. He thought about the costume Darren had done for his dad and a sudden crazy thought occurred to him. What if Darren worked on something for the Alliance Guards? But that didn't make sense, not if the guy hated the idea of being a guard.

Knowing better this time, he didn't make a big deal about it, yet he couldn't resist. "I don't get it," he whispered to Eddy. "Yesterday, Darren got mad when I mentioned his talent, yet he's working on a costume."

"Yeah, alone," Eddy said. "With Monisha doing beading and taking Lisa with her, Darren can keep the armor a secret."

"Really? I'm sorry," Jonah said. At the mention of the others, he noticed someone else was missing. "Where's AJ?" Jonah feared the guy decided to work alone because of their ongoing disagreement.

"Bertonneau's letting him work on his music," Eddy answered. "Lucky."

"That's right. He mentioned that when we got our schedules."

"Yeah. AJ plays the keyboards and makes beats on the computer," Eddy explained. "The keyboard was in the long case."

"But," Jonah stammered, "I thought we couldn't bring electronics?"

"Oh, the Campmaster let him bring one keyboard and laptop because there's a talent night the last weekend of camp." Eddy nodded his head. "AJ can rock."

A talent night? Jonah decided he'd have to find out how good AJ was at music. And apologize. The thought he was making plans for camp and not concentrating on leaving surprised Jonah. Watching Darren and Eddy work, he knew he had decided to stay. At least, for now.

Before dinner, the campers headed to the fake beach again. Jonah tagged along, and, seeing his chance, he plopped down beside AJ, who seemed happy to watch the others splash around. He wondered if AJ would move, but the boy remained, even after glancing at him.

Without waiting for AJ to say anything or change his mind and get up, Jonah said, "Eddy told me you play the keyboards?" AJ nodded, and Jonah took it as a good sign. "My cousin Robert plays the trombone in the school band. And my cousin Lynn can sing."

AJ listened, and after relaxing, he asked Jonah several questions. The boy's thirst for information relieved Jonah as he answered. Soon, AJ leaned back on his elbows and talked about his love of music. In no time, the boys forgot their little disagreement.

Jonah returned to the main building in high spirits and entered a hive of activity. Thomas had returned, and the young mages surrounded him, talking in excited voices.

For once, the older boy didn't sport his usual frown. He looked exhausted. Jonah considered that as he, AJ, and Eddy rushed upstairs to change, then came back down to claim their usual spot near the hearth.

Half an hour later, Eddy tapped the table and asked, "I wonder what's up with them?"

Jonah sensed the tension as Thomas gazed at the entrance. He turned, but all he saw was Damian talking with Kevin and Serena.

Darren, who had changed and left the building earlier, reentered carrying a wrapped bundle and stopped inside the entrance. Jonah wondered if he brought some of the armor he'd been working on during Personal Development. He wasn't the only one interested.

AJ nudged Jonah in the back. "Go find out what's going on."

Jonah agreed with AJ, but before he could stand, Mandara and Mitchell entered the common room. The Campmaster wore his Reaper's coat and paused beside the mentors. "I'll need you three to watch everyone."

Serena nodded. "Yes, sir."

Mandara motioned to Thomas. The young mage said something to his mentees, then crossed to the Campmaster.

"They're going to HQ," AJ observed.

Jonah agreed. Watching Mitchell fetch a cup of coffee from the refreshment table, he had a sudden idea. The thought had occurred to him after his last session reading the Tales. Now, the notion had popped back into his mind.

"I'll be back." He strode over to Mitchell. The Fallen Reaper nodded in greeting while sipping his coffee. "Can I ask you a question, sir?"

Mitchell lowered the cup and smiled. "Of course, Mr. Blackstone. What is it? Is it about your work?" The familiar sparkle returned to the man's eyes.

Jonah should have known Mitchell would sense the nature of his question. But he knew better than to talk about the Tales in the open. "Can we go inside the office?" At Mitchell's nod, Jonah crossed to the small office and stepped inside. When he turned, he noticed Mandara giving them a speculative expression.

Once Mitchell entered and closed the door, Jonah considered how to ask his question, then decided just to do it. "Can I see the Deliverer's Tales?"

Mitchell took a pause from sipping the coffee and looked at him, perplexed. "You have a copy on the triptych."

"I mean the actual Tales."

"It's locked in the Archives, Mr. Blackstone. Can I ask why?"

"The triptych works," Jonah explained, "and I can sense things in the text with my Deliverer power."

"Ah, interesting," Mitchell mused. "If having that Akashic record worked, what's the problem?"

"Well, I've only been able to get so far, and I wondered if I needed to touch the real thing to find the answers."

"So you want to test your theory on the actual book."

"Yes, sir. Since you're all going to HQ, I wondered if I could go and take a look at that section and touch the real pages."

Mitchell nodded, only to have his curious expression dampen moments later as he turned to glance out the office window. "I'll have to okay it with the Campmaster." After a moment, he brightened. "I can't see him saying no." He reached for the door, only to pause. "Please, ask Mr. James to come along."

AJ?" Jonah asked, wondering at Mitchell's request.

"Yes. Mr. James worked in Archives this summer and helped me in the Artifacts department. He'll be excited about a quick return to the department."

Jonah's jaw dropped. "Okay."

Once they left the office, Mitchell pulled the Campmaster into a quiet conversation.

Jonah couldn't determine what Mandara thought of his idea and hurried to AJ. "You wanna go to HQ?"

"Yeah." AJ sat up. "Why?"

"Mitchell said you worked in Archives and can help me with something."

AJ shot to his feet. "Is it the—" He broke off, his eyes wide with excitement. Then he nudged Eddy. "You wanna come?"

"No way. They're not putting me to work." Eddy sat back, determined to enjoy the rest of the evening.

Jonah laughed and turned to find Kevin standing behind him.

"I know why Thomas is going back. Please tell me you aren't involved in that," Kevin hissed. "Marcus would go crazy."

Perplexed, Jonah shook his head. "No. I'm not. It's about my project. Okay?"

Kevin relaxed. "You'd better go."

Looking at the entrance, Jonah noted that Darren's dad had joined the Campmaster, and they spoke in hushed tones.

When Mitchell flashed the boys the thumbs-up, Jonah let out a relieved breath. He was eager to get to Alliance HQ, try his theory, and hopefully make some headway on the Tales.

CHAPTER TWENTY
ALLIANCE HEADQUARTERS

Jonah's group reappeared on a smooth metal platform in a dim, glass-walled room at Alliance Headquarters. Not knowing what to expect, the sudden change in environment disoriented Jonah for a few seconds. When he adjusted as best he could, he scanned his surroundings.

The blue-black platform was similar to the brick-and-stone platforms at the hideaway and the Afterworld locations. Four more glass-walled rooms ringed the area around a central space with a tall reception desk.

As they stepped off the platform, Mandara guided Jonah and AJ toward their room's opening. The telltale tug of a magic barrier washed over Jonah's skin as he crossed the threshold.

A vortex opened in a room to their right labeled V-1 and two older mages exited. The sign piqued Jonah's curiosity, and he noted that a second room on the right was labeled V-2. He turned back to the chamber they had used and saw it marked as P-1.

Mandara caught the direction of his gaze. "P-1 means phase room one. The other rooms are vortex rooms. Mages can use them to create a secured vortex in and out of this building. This system is the only way for Fallen Reapers and mages to enter Headquarters using their powers. Of course, we have magical protections and sigils throughout the rest of the building."

Shocked at Mandara's sudden information, Jonah nodded, taking it all in as they passed the reception desk. The young woman there, wearing a blue tunic with the Alliance Emblem embroidered into the left breast, stood straighter.

Her voice squeaked when she spoke. "Good evening, Council Member and Mr. Mitchell." She gave the adults a respectful nod, then flashed a quick smile at Thomas.

The attendant, a pretty girl with a deep tan complexion and long black hair, looked about Thomas's age. Jonah suspected they had completed their training together. When a beep sounded on the attendant's computer, she shifted her gaze to the screen and then to Jonah. "You have weapons on you."

"He's been cleared to carry his blades around HQ," Mandara interjected.

The attendant nodded and typed something on her keyboard. Once the group stepped into the well-lit hallway, Jonah glanced back to watch as the young mage replaced a barrier over the exit.

Only then did he notice the thickness of the entrance wall.

"That heavy steel door can drop into place to close off this section," Thomas explained, pointing up, "just in case someone makes it this far."

Jonah looked above his head and was shocked to see a thick door recessed in the ceiling. Imagining the door's heaviness, he quickly backed away from the entrance.

"The plan is to make that an automatic feature, so it doesn't depend on someone pressing a button," Mandara said.

Jonah gulped. "Why not keep it closed and let people open it when they arrive?" Even as he said it, another mage appeared in a vortex room.

"Because that would take too long," Mandara grumbled. "The Alliance Council doesn't want people to feel like they have entered prison. The compromise was an old-fashioned mechanical spring mechanism."

The man's sour tone revealed a lot about his arguments in the Council.

Thomas frowned until he noticed Jonah watching his reaction. "The door has sigils etched into it."

Jonah assumed it did, but thought he still missed something.

AJ tapped his arm. "That kind of heavy magic can interfere with electronics. It would probably cause the door to malfunction all the time."

Mandara grunted but didn't contradict anything AJ said. Jonah marveled at all the protections and the problem of mixing magic and modern electronics. It never occurred to him that Alliance Headquarters would have to plan and protect itself from the enemy this way.

"Is my godfather here?" Jonah asked.

"He's in Washington," Mandara said, pressing the call button for an elevator and stepping inside as the doors opened.

The floors went up to the fortieth level of the Monarch Law firm that served as cover for the Alliance. When the Campmaster swiped his key card, precisely like the royal blue card Jonah had received as a birthday gift, another row of buttons appeared in the space below the regular panel.

In contrast to the opaque floor buttons, these glowed a rich jade color, and the numbers weren't regular numerals but Angelic script. Mandara pressed the last button, and the elevator kicked into motion without a sound and only a minor vibration.

The doors opened a minute later, and Mandara gripped Jonah and AJ's shoulders to guide them forward. The tug of yet another ward tickled his skin within half a dozen steps. Belatedly, Jonah realized why Mandara gripped their shoulders at each doorway. The man had a security talisman that let him enter all the protected spaces.

Beyond the ward and just ahead, a guard sat at a desk, wearing a dark blue coat that stretched over his slightly out-of-proportion upper body.

The man nodded to them as they continued to a set of thick double doors, with the Alliance Symbol spanning both. The doors swung open at their approach.

Jonah let out a surprised, "Nice."

Considering they were far underground, he had expected the Alliance Headquarters to be something like the President's command bunker from the movies. Instead, he saw a sunlit atrium with a trio of glass-encased elevators to one side.

Small groups of people sat around the open area, talking or eating. Mandara led Jonah into the center of the space and slowed his pace so Jonah could gawk. He did, glancing all around and then upward. Several balconies curved around the open atrium.

A domed rock ceiling with large rectangular vents was far above the top floor. Sunlight streamed through the vents, bouncing off gigantic ceiling panels that directed the light into the atrium below.

The configuration was so cool to Jonah that he wanted to tour the place now and ask a thousand questions. He'd only gone to the rooftop patio the last time he had visited. Of course, his parents had brought him to the aboveground law offices a few times when he was younger, but he couldn't recall ever being inside the heart of the Alliance.

Well, he was here now and wanted to remember every detail, like the small figurines around the atrium and the art pieces just like the wind sculptures in the camp's main building and Mandara's office.

At least here, the art made more sense to Jonah because he felt the air current on his skin. Focused on the sculptures' subtle shifts in muted color, Jonah did a double take when Alastor appeared behind one in the far corner.

The Campmaster nodded to Alastor and moved on, so Jonah clamped down on any questions. Even so, he didn't like the way Alastor watched their progress. Noticing

Jonah's attention, the devious man didn't bother to hide a gloating smile. Jonah's insides squirmed in response.

Once they reached the elevators, the group separated. Mandara and Thomas continued across the atrium to where Trueblood waited by an entrance into a dark hallway.

Meanwhile, Mitchell ushered the boys into the elevator, and Jonah found himself beside Darren and gave in to his curiosity.

"What's in the package?"

"I have some new armor concepts for the Assistant Chief Armorer. I worked with the Alliance Guards as a summer intern. He was my sponsor."

"Wow," Jonah said, a little envious that the other campers had worked with chosen Alliance adults.

"Level six, Ancient Artifacts and Occult Translations," Mitchell announced.

Jonah knew the Fallen Reaper said that for his benefit and didn't mind. When they stepped off, Darren remained behind.

"I'm up on level eight, the same floor as the Alliance Council." He wiggled his eyebrows before the doors slid shut.

Mitchell led them into the Artifacts department.

Jonah didn't know what to expect when Mitchell led them into the Ancient Artifacts section of HQ. The low lighting and subdued, hushed feeling of the place unnerved him. The atmosphere was a cross between a bank, with all the endless drawers behind thick protected glass to his left, and an elegant jewelry store.

Mitchell talked with the receptionist, checking that Mandara's approval had come through.

Meanwhile, AJ, who seemed used to the procedure, had moved to the atrium's inner window to gaze into the distant artifact storage room. It was all rows of drawers in various sizes, like a library file room for maps and precious documents.

The level of technology and type of security puzzled Jonah. This area was so different from all the wards they had encountered. "Why aren't there any wards here?"

"Magic," AJ responded. "Remember where we entered HQ? Heavy spells don't mix well with modern technology." He turned. "You never noticed that Trueblood and the other mages don't pull out cell phones?"

The notion struck Jonah as odd, but as he thought back, he realized Trueblood and his sister rarely used mobile phones. Neither did Thomas. Glancing at the entrance and the keypad, he began to understand. "They hope the wards and spells on the building and that room we entered will stop supernatural enemies—"

"And key cards and modern security should stop mortal enemies," AJ finished.

Maybe, Jonah thought, realizing all the protections depended on the loyalty of everyone in the Alliance. People like Alastor, Jonah thought, were always suspect, at least to him. And the mole was still out there.

"Okay, gentlemen," Mitchell announced. "We're ready." He gestured toward the door to the department's inner sections. With a nod to the receptionist, who must have pressed a button because the door's lock clicked, Mitchell opened it and let them through first.

If the outer atrium was quiet, this hallway was even more silent. Only muted sounds reached them as they walked down a long hallway. Halfway down the passage, Mitchell turned to the right and stopped in front of an open doorway. Beyond was a bare room with a large table at the center and four chairs around it. The dark, expensive wood reminded Jonah of the library study rooms back home.

"Wait here," Mitchell said, "and we'll bring the item." He and AJ left Jonah alone.

Pulling out a chair on the side facing the door, Jonah sat at the large table. He didn't have to wait long before the door opened, and AJ pushed in a cart with a sealed Seeker's Box on top.

Jonah gaped at the device and nodded to himself. It made sense to protect the Tales inside a Seeker's Box. Even without the added security of a blood seal, it was safe against supernatural tampering.

Mitchell stood nearby, observing as AJ, who wore a pair of white gloves, opened the Seeker's Box, withdrew the actual Tales, and put the ancient book on the table. To Jonah's surprise, AJ also took out the translation documents and placed them beside the Tales. Jonah was thankful because he could use the translations to help him find his place in the Tales.

"I'll leave you here for a few minutes." Mitchell exited.

AJ handed Jonah a pair of gloves, then dropped into the chair beside him. The boy's eyes were wide with intense interest.

Jonah opened the Tales and flipped through the ornate pages full of unreadable Angel script. His appreciation of what Mike had accomplished increased. The sections had clear separations, so he could find the last one about Destiny.

Going to the final, blank page, Jonah held his gloved hand over the page, but nothing happened. Pulling off the right glove, he tried again while willing the center star to appear. It did.

"Wow!" AJ exclaimed. He pulled off his glove, waved his bare hand over the page, then drew it back.

"What?" Jonah asked.

"I-I felt something. That's all," AJ said, seemingly worried.

AJ's admission triggered something inside Jonah. It was something about the Tales and the Protectors. He narrowed his eyes at his friend. "Has anything like that happened before?"

AJ met his gaze, but before the boy could answer, the room's lighting turned red, and they heard a muffled alert sounding. Ground-shaking bangs followed that.

The door to the examination room banged open, and Jonah was on his feet in seconds with his blades drawn!

CHAPTER TWENTY-ONE
LOST TRANSLATIONS

Jonah's heart thudded in his chest, but he was ready to defend AJ and the Tales from anyone who came through the door. He didn't expect to see a serious-faced Thomas barrel into the room and slam the door.

The capable young mage placed more than one spell on the door and then backed away, his chest heaving. He glanced at them and pointed to AJ.

"Put the Tales back in the Seeker's Box, and code-lock it."

"Yes, sir," AJ stammered and moved to do it.

Thomas nodded at Jonah. "I'm glad you have your blades, but stay behind me."

"What's happened?"

"The KIN and Wraiths are inside Headquarters," Thomas spat out.

Jonah wanted to ask how, but he knew it in his gut. The mole!

More bangs shook the ground and rattled the walls. One seemed to come from right inside the department.

AJ had just reached for the translation when the room's door took a direct hit, causing the boy to jump and drop the translation document on the ground.

Jonah wanted to help him, but they didn't have time. The door buckled and splintered. Thomas used a ward to protect them. Then he went to work firing off spells at two guys with glowing white eyes. Wraiths!

A hex flew over the guards' heads, and Thomas had to duck to the side to avoid it. It hit the back wall leaving a huge scorch mark.

That allowed a Wraith to get through the door. Jonah didn't even think twice before darting forward to fight the possessed man. It was close, but he blocked the attacker's scythes and jabbed the man in the chest with a blade.

He winced as the guy screamed, and the Wraith inside died. Before falling to the ground, a hex hit the guy from behind, and he dissolved into dust. Jonah backpedaled and rammed up against the table as another Wraith entered. In the corridor beyond, Fabian Rasmussen continued to fire hexes at Thomas.

The strategy was clear. Keep Thomas on the defense and let the Wraiths take out the kids and get the Tales. Well, Jonah wasn't gonna let that happen.

Neither was AJ. He grabbed the Seeker's Box off the cart and activated the code-lock. Pushing the box behind him, AJ started conjuring green fire, which caught a third Wraith in the face. The guy screamed and fell back.

Jonah's next attacker body-blocked him into the wall, knocking the breath out of him. Immediately, the Wraith grabbed the translations off the floor! Jonah cut a gash in the guy's arm just as Fabian dashed forward to try to kill him with a hex.

But Thomas jumped between them and produced a complicated shield. It stopped the spell, but it also knocked the young mage back into AJ and Jonah.

As he raised his hands to cast a killing hex, the KIN's triumphant sneer vanished instantly at the scream from behind. The evil sorcerer barely had time to whirl aside before an Alliance Guard surged forward, glowing baton in hand. He took down the Wraith with the translations with one swipe and continued for Fabian.

The KIN was better than the Wraiths and blocked the baton with his glowing hands. Still, he grunted with effort as the baton neutralized spell after spell. In between, he hurled lightning around the room to keep Thomas back.

If not for the man's evil actions, Jonah would have been impressed. The KIN hurled a hex overhead in desperation, exposing piping above the false ceiling. Cackling to himself, he hit a particular pipe and produced an explosion that knocked the Alliance Guard into the opposite wall.

Unfortunately, the explosion also ignited Mike's translations. Fabian screamed in frustration, but it was too late. The pages seemed incredibly flammable and burned down to smoking ash in seconds. The furious KIN struck the downed guard with a nasty folly of lightning in retaliation.

Jonah's insides burned with anger at the brutality and the lost translation.

When more Wraiths crowded into the shattered hall, he jumped through the opening and cut down the first to reach their doorway. He rolled to the side to avoid a hex from Fabian while Thomas moved forward to cover him.

Once again, someone helped from behind by slamming a Wraith into another section of surviving wall. Darren ran forward, snatched up the dropped baton, and swung it hard enough to knock another Wraith into Fabian. The KIN sensed his trouble and hurled hexes at Darren so he could escape.

Darren roared in anger and raised the baton, ready to run after the KIN, until Thomas gripped his shoulder.

"It's too dangerous to chase him, Darren. Other guards will catch him before he can get away."

Darren turned and dropped the baton when he saw the injured guard. Hurrying over to the man, whose chest still heaved in spastic jerks, Darren clutched the man's hand and lifted his head. "Help's coming."

Tears streaked Darren's cheeks, leading Jonah to conclude this man must have been Assistant Chief Armorer. Jonah's insides turned cold as the man mumbled something to Darren, and then his body went limp.

"Oh my God," AJ whispered from the broken doorway. He clutched the Seeker's Box in his hands, one of which had a nasty cut and dripping blood.

Only now did Jonah notice he bled from cuts on his head and thigh and his back hurt from where he had rammed into the table. Every time he moved, his back would spasm, causing him to wince.

Thomas hovered near the junction with the main hallway, looking toward the atrium. Weariness hit Jonah, causing him to slump to the ground, leaning against an intact splinter of a wall.

Darren had a glazed expression and hadn't moved from holding the dead guard.

"I'm sorry," Jonah choked out. His throat hurt like he'd been yelling.

After a moment, Darren stirred and looked at him. "Why're you apologizing?"

Jonah winced as he raised a hand to gesture around them. He heard people nearby and knew help was coming, but it was too late.

"This was all my fault."

"No, it wasn't. The KIN killed our people." Darren's voice faltered, and he sucked in a breath. "I don't want to be a guard, but that doesn't mean I won't use my strength when needed. This fight is why we're training."

When his dad entered the battle scene, Darren laid the dead guard head's down and stood. His dad hurried over to hug his son.

Jonah gulped, reminded that he didn't have a dad to hug. He jerked when AJ squeezed his shoulder.

"Darren's right," AJ said. "This wasn't your fault."

Jonah understood why they said that, but if he hadn't asked to see the Tales, the mole wouldn't have attacked and killed people.

Frantic voices rang through the hallways now, but Jonah barely registered the noise as he stared in shock at the dead

Alliance Guard. Mitchell arrived with Trueblood, and they escorted Jonah and AJ from the room. With a start, Jonah realized AJ didn't have the Seeker's Box anymore.

"Where's the box?"

AJ pointed down a hallway where shattered glass littered the floor. "A lab tech and guard took it back to the vault."

The group boarded an elevator and descended to the first floor. The doors opened to reveal controlled chaos in the café area that had become a staging ground for Healers and other Alliance workers. As Trueblood led them to a quiet section, Jonah took in the scope of the horror.

A still presence alerted him. Looking up, Jonah spotted Alastor lurking in the entrance to a side hallway. The devious man didn't seem shocked at all. He looked smug and satisfied. Yet when he spotted Jonah, he hurried up the stairs and out of sight.

Without thinking about it, Jonah charged after Alastor. He didn't have any proof but wanted to know why the Campmaster's Assistant lurked around the hallways instead of trying to help like everyone else. By the time Jonah reached the exit, Alastor was gone.

A nearby wind sculpture moved as if caught in a sudden wind. Thinking that odd, Jonah crossed to it and stroked the delicate filaments. He had the feeling that someone had bumped into the thing because his touch also produced a riot of reactions. *Vibrations.*

Trueblood caught up, looking worried. "This shouldn't have happened. I'm sorry."

Jonah knew the mage assumed he ran because of what had happened in the Archives and not because he wanted to catch Alastor. Poking the sculpture at various spots, he continued producing micromovements and riots of colors that mirrored his surging emotions.

"I'm okay."

"No, you're not," Trueblood insisted. "Come." The mage led Jonah to a closed cafeteria. He took a chair beside AJ. Just then, two Healers rushed by them and toward the door the Mandara and Mitchell had used earlier.

Jonah stared at the atrium activity, resisting shuddering as images of Fabian killing the Alliance Guard returned. "What else happened?"

Trueblood took a deep breath. "The mole managed to smuggle Wraith agents and a KIN through HQ security. I'm afraid they killed the attendant on duty and smuggled a mind-booster to a captured Hunter in custody."

Jonah grimaced. "You mean the girl we saw when we arrived is dead? Does Thomas know?"

"He's there now," Trueblood answered. "That's not all. We had a captured Hunter. He used a mind-booster to send a charge directly into his mind."

AJ blanched and lowered his head to his hands.

"I'm sorry I asked to see the Tales." Jonah stared at his feet, trying to deal with everything.

"Jonah, this was a coordinated attack. We believe the initial goal was the Hunter. Stealing the Tales was an unexpected opportunity. Reaper Mitchell had warned us about the Rasmussens' interest in the Destiny Medallion."

"Fabian sent the Wraiths to damage Headquarters and divert our people from the captive's cell. But we've got them all." Mandara entered the cafeteria. Stains smudged his long coat. "You understand about the Cognitive Enhancers?"

"Yeah, the mind-boosters give you temporary brainpower." Jonah could never forget his buddy Mike's exposure to a mind-booster, but in his case, the boost was permanent once he became a Seeker.

Mandara stroked his chin as if choosing his next words. "We never knew the mind-booster could be used like that, not deliberately."

"You mean the Hunter's not dead? He's…"

"He turned himself into a vegetable," Mandara explained.

Jonah leaned back in his chair as images of a brain-dead Hunter flashed through his mind.

AJ looked as shocked as he felt.

"It had to be the mole." Trueblood said, sounding angry. "We had searched the prisoner for weapons."

Mandara frowned as he watched the activity around the atrium. "This is my failure to catch the mole. But perhaps now the Council will allow the changes to security I suggested."

The Campmaster's confession shocked Jonah. After all, Mandara was head of Security. For the first time, Jonah considered things from the man's point of view. He felt sorry for Mandara. But it didn't take away his feeling of guilt for the dead guard.

Thomas came over, his sleeve cut open and a bandage on his upper arm. Mandara walked off with him, talking.

Trueblood's quiet voice startled Jonah. "How do you gentlemen feel?"

"Pissed." Thinking more about it, Jonah added, "Guilty."

Did Trueblood really expect them to do emotion shifting right now after what happened? But then, maybe that was the point?

"I'm just scared," AJ added after a moment. "And worried. The translations are gone."

Choosing to reflect on how his best friend would respond instead of wallowing in his own anger, Jonah said, "Mike's not gonna like this. He worked hard on those."

"Yeah, I know, But we still have—" AJ cut his statement short.

Trueblood nodded. "It's not wise to talk about details until we've located the source of leaks."

Jonah sat up, keeping his comment to himself. He'd been about to explain why the digital copies of the Tales wouldn't help. In fact, Jonah doubted Thera could have used the written translations either, even if they stole them. The triptych worked to his touch because of the way it was encoded. While that was a relief to Jonah, it made tonight's violence and deaths seem more of a waste.

Darren shuffled over with his dad, interrupting Jonah's train of thought. The Guard Captain patted his son's shoulder before moving off to work.

"Let's get out of here," Darren said, glancing around.

The silent kids trudged along behind Trueblood through the damaged Alliance Headquarters in a daze. Thomas caught up to them as they used a different location to leave the building. The necessity of doing this was like a punch to the gut for Jonah. He knew the regular location was closed because the attendant had died there.

Any desire to explore the place had evaporated in an instant. All Jonah wanted to do was get far away from Alliance HQ.

CHAPTER TWENTY-TWO
MENTOR HEALTH

Kevin waited for them at the arrival building. Jonah could tell the news had already reached camp and dreaded facing the others, fearing they would blame him. Trueblood's comments echoed in his mind, but Jonah had difficulty accepting them.

The quiet group started down the path toward the main compound. No sooner had they reached the junction in the trail, than Darren swore under his breath and broke away. He strolled toward the darkened lake and stood along the shore looking out.

"Wait here," Kevin said and walked over. Thomas joined them, and both mentors talked to Darren nonstop.

Jonah feared the guy would leave camp. The boy's dad hadn't insisted, which he found surprising. Then again, Darren's dad was an Alliance Guard and probably dealt with this type of thing before. Plus, Jonah didn't want Darren to leave. It would make everything so much worse.

"It's real now," AJ muttered, watching the trio by the lake.

His words mirrored Jonah's thoughts. "Yeah. This whole evening sucks."

"At least Thomas and Kevin understand. I bet they can cheer up Darren," AJ insisted.

Jonah swallowed hard as the reality of the situation dawned on him. Of course, Thomas and Kevin would understand. Thomas had lost a friend, while Kevin, only a couple of years older than Darren, could relate. With a shock, Jonah realized he, too, understood Darren's pain. The enemy had killed his parents. So much death surrounded them.

He and AJ stood, nursing their thoughts, until the mentors led Darren back to the path. Darren didn't meet their eyes, and Jonah left the boy alone. No one said anything else on the way back to the compound. Inside the main building, Thomas patted Darren's shoulder before heading to his end of the hall.

Jonah's feelings toward the mage had changed. After all, Thomas had charged into the Artifacts wing to protect them from Fabian and the Wraiths. He'd risked death, just like the unlucky Alliance Guard.

He considered this as Darren and AJ went into their dorm after waving good night. Jonah still hadn't moved when Kevin touched his arms to get his attention.

Because of their unique connection, any physical touch from Kevin usually sent a jolt of excitement through Jonah. Instead, a cloud of weariness threatened to overwhelm him again. When Kevin pulled him into the mentor's dorm room, he wasn't even surprised at his own annoyance.

"I'm okay. Darren and Thomas had it worse," Jonah found himself saying as Kevin closed the door and faced him. His boyfriend ignored his protest and gathered him into a warm embrace.

"I'll keep an eye on Darren. And Thomas is an Alliance member with experience. You're the one we're worried about."

Jonah nestled against his boyfriend despite his initial protests, not wanting to let go. He loved the above-normal body heat of the Fallen Reaper. But the guilt wouldn't relent, and he sensed that something troubled Kevin. He grunted in dissatisfaction as he let go and stood back.

"What's wrong?" When Kevin didn't meet his gaze, Jonah jiggled his boyfriend's hand. "Tell me."

"Since Trueblood and Mandara already told you about the Hunter, I'm not under oath anymore." He let out a breath as if preparing himself. "You probably guessed they used Memory Charmers like Thomas to question the Hunter, right?"

Now that Kevin asked, Jonah realized he hadn't made the final connection until Trueblood talked to him at HQ. But he said, "Yeah."

"Well, some on the Council discussed another option." Kevin swallowed hard and added, "They talked about putting you in the room with the Hunter."

"Me? Why? I was never gonna suck out his soul," Jonah insisted. "I can't even do that, can I? Besides, why not use a Fallen Reaper?"

The grimace on Kevin's face finally stopped Jonah. "They didn't want you to suck out somebody's soul. Not quite.

And for your information, Fallen Reapers can't do that anymore. Only Reapers and you can do it."

When Jonah started to complain, Kevin held his hand over Jonah's mouth. "Let me finish, alright? Marcus nixed the idea, and Mandara supported him, believe it or not."

Jonah didn't believe it. Why would Mandara, a Hardliner, agree with not using him? "I don't know how to interview anyone. And I'm not a Memory Charmer. So, why put me in the room?"

"They wanted to bluff the information out of the Hunter." Kevin tapped Jonah on the chest. "What better way to bluff him than to put him in front of you?"

"Wait. The Hunter knew about my fight with Agent Ramsey?" Jonah asked. "That was supposed to scare him into talking?"

"Jonah, you took Agent Ramsey's power. You shocked the Grand Oracle by also taking Trevor's power in the Afterworld," Kevin explained. "And you put on and used the Protector's Ring and freed a goddess from the Wraith King. Marcus says what you did sent shock waves through the Afterworld and Underworld."

Kevin's words sank deep, and Jonah sat on the bed when the implications became clear. It was the idea of using him as a weapon again, even if it was just a bluff. Instead of anger, he found the whole situation disappointing. He wanted to crawl in a bed and stay there for a month.

"See? I didn't want to make things worse, but you're right. You need to know." Kevin pulled Jonah to his feet again and tugged on his ripped and dirty shirt. "Take that off." At Jonah's look, he added, "Don't get excited. It's not that kind of party. I have something to clear your negative feelings and help you rest."

Jonah shook his head. "I'll sleep fine."

Kevin gripped Jonah's chin. "Trueblood sent a message. He told me you started blaming yourself. We've helped Darren. Now I need to help you, so take this off." He began pulling the shirt over Jonah's head until Jonah gave in and took it off himself. That done, Kevin turned and nodded toward the far wall.

Glaring at the large hanging pattern on the wall, Jonah said, "Yeah. So?"

"You've never seen this setup before?" Kevin asked, resting his chin on Jonah's shoulder.

Thinking that if he answered, Kevin would give up on the special attention he didn't deserve, Jonah focused. Beneath the hanging was a wooden stand with a polished wooden box resting on top. Despite his raging emotions, Jonah finally recognized the setup. His dad had used something similar when he meditated and recharged. "I get it."

Kevin snorted, crossed to the box, and opened it to take out various-sized candles. "You sure about that?"

"I saw my dad use candles and the pattern to meditate." Now that Jonah knew Kevin's intention, he took the candles and placed them on the ground in a circle, with the thickest candle closest to the hanging pattern.

"I can hide in my Reaper side," Jonah objected as he stood.

"You can't do that, Jonah."

"Why not? It worked before."

"The more you do that, the more you lose touch with your emotions." Kevin lifted Jonah's chin, looking him in the eyes. "You have to deal with your emotions, not hide from them."

"You sound like Trueblood," Jonah accused.

"Well, he's right."

"You don't do it?" Jonah asked his boyfriend. "You never hide in our Reaper powers? I know you can do it."

"I did for a while after I fell," Kevin admitted, "but not anymore."

Jonah snorted and regretted it when he saw Kevin's hurt expression. "Sorry."

"It's not your fault. I never talk about falling or—" Kevin broke off.

He'd never told Jonah much about his First Life either.

"Coming back to my fifteen-year-old body wasn't easy. I'd seen more than most guys my age would ever see in a lifetime." Kevin added a few more candles to the circle until there were thirteen in all.

"Trueblood and Mabel helped me. She was like a mom to me," Kevin continued. "It was rough at first. The only thing that got through to me was Trueblood saying I was like a child soldier." He met Jonah's gaze. "The things I saw and experienced as a Reaper made me grow up fast." Kevin smirked and added, "Or should have if you listen to Mandara."

Jonah didn't know what to say. This conversation was the most honest Kevin had ever been about the process of falling. His boyfriend's honesty also revealed how much they still needed to learn about each other. Kevin sat on the bed. Jonah sat beside him and squeezed his hand.

"I didn't know."

"Because I never told you. It's embarrassing in a way. I had to get used to everything." Kevin emphasized the last word. "You know, Hackett was the one to help me once I arrived. Your dad had him waiting that night." Kevin stared at the wall hanging as if calling up the memories. "He warned me I was in a mortal body again and had to get used to eating food, even going to the bathroom."

Jonah winced. "Too much info." He nudged Kevin, who smiled.

"Hey. You wanted to know more about me," Kevin joked. Then he sobered. "My voice squeaked and changed my first year back, just like it's gonna happen to you. Marcus claimed I had a better transition because of my short time in the Afterworld. But other Reapers—"

Kevin shook his head as he continued, "It's why they don't have real relationships, Jonah. Your dad wasn't odd just because he had you. He was different because he fell in love with your mom and got married."

The torrent of information and feelings rolled over Jonah, forcing him to focus on what their closeness meant to Kevin for the first time. He could sense Kevin's emotions, but he had never truly considered their closeness from Kevin's angle. "Am I your first boyfriend?"

The question seemed to go further than Kevin could handle at the moment. It was like Jonah had touched on a sensitive subject.

Kevin stood and snapped the box shut. He paused to take a deep breath. "Yeah, you are."

All the complications of their relationship rocked Jonah. Kevin never had a boyfriend before, which hinted that he had less experience in this situation than Jonah. In addition, Kevin was a Fallen Reaper still getting used to being mortal, and he was an Alliance member.

Perhaps Kevin sensed Jonah's thoughts because he pointed to the floor. "Sit crossed-legged at the center of the circle."

Jonah sat in a daze of swirling thoughts and rested his palms on his knees. He knew clearing his mind now would take some effort. He'd been over a range of emotions tonight.

Kevin pulled two pillows off his bed and dropped them behind Jonah. He stretched out on the floor and grabbed Jonah's left hand, intertwining their fingers. At that moment, Jonah recognized Kevin wanted to share another part of his life he considered deeply personal.

Closing his eyes, Jonah took deep, steadying breaths. With Kevin's touch and the shared connection, he felt their heartbeats sync as he descended into the meditation. Soon, the horror of the evening faded until all that remained was their mutual touch.

CHAPTER TWENTY-THREE
RANGE WAR

The Alliance HQ attack was a dull, manageable memory for Jonah the next morning, thanks to Kevin. Yet Jonah was restless. Taking advantage of the early hour, he grabbed a shower and carried his notebooks to the kitchen.

Eddy and AJ had the same idea, and Chef Patelli allowed the boys to stow their things in a corner during their work time. After finishing their final day of detention, the guys made it to the History class on time.

Councilor Sterne shocked them again by banging his cane on the table. Jonah winced, coming to the unpleasant conclusion the man would do it every session. *Gee whiz*, he thought, taking out his notebook and jotting down Sterne's information on the Afterworld. Jonah itched to ask the man about Memory Charmers, but the teacher lectured straight through to the end of the class.

Jonah noticed Thomas appeared okay today as he worked with the mages. Darren was a little quieter than normal and stuck close to Monisha. Otherwise, the camp continued as if last night never happened. Jonah guessed they wanted to keep things consistent here. It sounded like something Mandara would do and Jonah didn't blame the Campmaster.

On the walk to the next session, Jonah flexed the fingers of his writing hand. AJ and Eddy carried on a conversation so he could just listen to and not participate. Everything went well enough until they passed the spot where Thomas had caught him. In the light of day, Jonah realized his stupidity in following Thomas.

The embarrassing memory of the encounter added to his restless, distracted mood throughout the Nature class and lunch period. Things didn't get any better when he arrived for Team Building that afternoon.

Despite Trueblood having them form the large circle again, the two groups of kids remained miles apart. In Jonah's opinion, the session was devoid of any real sense of teamwork and made him glad when the class ended.

Stepping onto the range for his last session of the day, Jonah realized a slow tension had built inside him. Aside from a quick wave, Kevin didn't speak as he waited for Jonah to get into a ready stance.

"Can we talk about what's going on?" Jonah asked since this was their first moment alone all day.

"Nope," Kevin said. "Follow me." With that, he phased. Caught off guard, Jonah took longer than he should have to make the mental nudge and phase. In an instant, he entered the in-between state, what Marcus called the aether, the substance of the Spirit World.

A simple phase only lasted seconds and would appear almost instantaneous to outside observers, but following someone else took a little longer. Jonah cast about, searching until he sensed the pinpoint of heat that represented Kevin's path through the aether. He focused on it, and the mortal world exploded into view, and, Jonah saw, he stood at the opposite end of the range.

Kevin made a show of impatiently tapping his foot and frowning. "You need to get it down to three or four seconds."

Jonah's jaw dropped, but his boyfriend didn't wait for him to reply before he phased again. Jonah's own words to Beraki came to him. He was trying too hard. Sure, he hadn't followed someone through a phase in months, but he had to stop struggling. Diving into the aether again, he detected the heat trail and followed it.

This time, Kevin moved quicker when Jonah reappeared, but Jonah was ready and followed.

Kevin continued the constant phasing around the range until Jonah couldn't take it anymore. He may have increased his sensing ability, but the fatigue had also worsened until Jonah stumbled and gripped the lean-to's side when he reappeared. Plus, his vision wavered. Was that a side effect of too much phasing?

"What're you doing?" Kevin had appeared beside him.

"I'm dizzy."

"Tough."

"I already know how to follow someone through a phase."

"Yeah, you do," Kevin agreed, "but not without puffing after a few phases. You heard Albrecht. The more you push yourself, the more you can handle. Shake it off."

When Jonah glared at him, Kevin raised an eyebrow. "You wanna cry about it?"

"No."

"Then move your butt. Come on." He phased again.

Jonah's irritation and dizziness increased as he followed Kevin through a series of phases. When the fatigue reached a new high, Jonah couldn't continue and stopped.

Kevin appeared nearly on top of him. "You're letting yourself give up."

Jonah whirled on him. "What's wrong with you?"

"Things are getting bad out there. You need to be ready."

The genuine concern in his boyfriend's voice worried Jonah. The attack on Alliance HQ and the Hunter's attempted suicide had affected Kevin after all. And, Jonah admitted, maybe he was giving up too soon and on more than just the phasing. What about the Tales? He'd been stumped and made no progress. With the situation growing worse outside, shouldn't the Alliance have the Destiny Medallion on their side?

"I get it, okay?" Jonah said.

"Sorry to push you like that." Kevin's shoulders relaxed a bit. "As I said, we're worried about you. And I know it hurts, but try for me. Okay?"

At Jonah's nod, Kevin phased, leading him around the range, sometimes going back and forth between the same two spots. Without warning, he'd suddenly change up, but Jonah kept on him and shaved a few seconds off his reaction time. Despite the building pain in his head and body, Jonah shook it off. No matter what, he wouldn't disappoint Kevin; nor would he give up.

Eventually, Jonah imagined himself a machine, locking on and phasing while not acknowledging where they reappeared. Knowing if he ever stopped, he'd topple over from fatigue, Jonah stayed focused, letting the dizziness become a constant element of his existence.

The entire outside world vanished. All that remained was the in-between and the changing position of Kevin's pinpoint of heat. Jonah pressed himself until he imagined he drew closer to the heat source. At some point in the never-ending process, he began to move in perfect sync with Kevin.

No sooner had he reveled in the accomplishment, than the mortal world exploded into existence around Jonah, along with the intense July heat, gravity, and dizziness. Collapsing onto his knees, he vomited up his lunch. When the ground vibrated, he opened his eyes to see Kevin kneeling beside him, breathing and sweating hard.

Jonah smiled, even though he dared not move. "Got you."

Kevin tapped Jonah on the arm, causing his world to tip sideways. He collapsed onto his back, feeling dizzy and bone-tired. Someone slid their hands under his arms and lifted him.

As Darren shook Jonah, his face swam in and out of focus. Jonah felt like his head floated off his shoulders.

"Here, give him a piece of candy," Albrecht ordered.

"Are you serious?" Darren asked, his voice skeptical. "Does he have diabetes?

"Goodness no, Mr. Hawkins," Albrecht replied in a testy but teacherly tone. "When they phase, it drains their soul's power. Something sweet like candy improves a mortal's emotional mood and aids in their soul's recovery. Now, if you'd please."

"I'll do it." Lisa came into view. "Open up, Jonah," she said, pressing something hard into his mouth.

As soon as the candy's flavor exploded on his tongue, Jonah's head began to clear.

Kevin still knelt on the ground with his head bowed. Albrecht leaned down to speak as he passed Kevin a piece of candy. Eventually, the Fallen Reaper stood and took a deep breath.

Albrecht motioned to the others. "Campers, get back to the dorms. We've gone past time here."

"Time?" Jonah stammered. "We've only been at it a few minutes."

The stares from the others caused Jonah to check his watch. That proved a mistake because the delicate dials refused to focus, making his dizziness worse.

Eddy came to the rescue. "Dude, you two were going around for over an hour."

Jonah couldn't understand how he'd lasted that long. It seemed like a few minutes, maybe ten. Then the reality of his body's condition made sense. Although the candy cleared his head, he remained tired beyond anything he'd experienced before.

When Darren offered a shoulder to lean on, Jonah accepted because he doubted he could make it back without the help. Kevin rose and walked on his own. The rest of the kids followed. No one spoke, but Jonah caught Eddy glancing at him in admiration.

—

A knocking at the door woke Jonah out of an exhausted nap. He tried to rub the sleep out of his eyes with sluggish movements. That's when the knock came again. "Yeah?"

"It's me, Lisa. Can I come in?"

"Oh, sure." He sat up in bed, feeling better than before.

Lisa peeked inside and smiled as she stepped into the room, leaving the door open.

Jonah noticed. "You're not gonna get in trouble with Serena, are you?"

She cocked her head to the side, and a little fire came into her eyes. "First of all, I'm an adult. Second"—she glanced out the door—"Serena knows I'm here."

"Sorry."

"It's fine. The others thought someone should check on you."

"I'm surprised Eddy didn't do it."

"He wanted to, but I won the coin toss." Lisa smiled as she came over and sat on Eddy's bed. Her expression changed as she glanced down and traced the exotic bird pattern in the bedspread with a finger.

"What's wrong?" Jonah asked. "You look spooked."

"I'm not. Honestly. I thought it was awesome what you two did."

"What did we do?"

"You and Kevin were like ghosts. You didn't stay visible long enough for us to see you. It was, it was…"

"Weird?"

"No, amazing," Lisa gushed, her gaze almost adoring.

Jonah squirmed. The last thing he needed was Lisa thinking him even more special. He didn't want a fan club either. "Maybe."

"What were you trying to do?"

"Oh, Kevin made me practice following him through a phase."

Meeting his gaze, Lisa spoke with wonder. "Jonah, you two were moving so fast that it looked like you were phasing together."

He slumped back while replaying the incident in his mind. They did move together or so close together that it didn't matter. And time had stopped for them. *A whole hour?* No wonder he and Kevin collapsed on the ground afterward.

"Kevin!" Jonah shouted and tried to get out of bed.

Lisa placed her hands against his shoulders and pressed him back down. Any other day and he would have moved Lisa aside, but not today.

Jonah struggled to contain his frustration with the aftereffects of the Range Session. "Where's Kevin?" he blurted out.

"Kevin's resting." She flashed him a reassuring smile. "Mage Trueblood says he has to recharge himself."

Jonah could imagine Kevin in his room, sitting in the circle of candles and meditating so his patterns could recharge. Still, his insides knotted in tension. "Is Trueblood angry with us?"

"No, he isn't mad, but he's had a lot of conversations with the other Councilors and the Campmaster."

Jonah groaned.

A commotion came from the hallway moments before the young mages filed by. Lisa jumped to her feet just as Alex glanced in the open door.

Jonah saw the smirk on the mage's face before he moved off.

Lisa wrung her hands. "It's dinnertime. I'll bring you something to eat."

"No. I can go down."

"You sure? It's no trouble."

"Yeah, I'm sure." Jonah swung his legs to the floor and tested his ability to stand. When he didn't topple over, he took a few steps and concluded he'd survive the trip down to the dining hall. Lisa helped him out the door.

"I want to stop by Kevin's room anyway," Jonah said, pausing outside Kevin's door.

"Oh, he's not in there."

"Where is he?"

"Mandara took Kevin to his office." At his stunned expression, she hurried to add, "I heard him tell Trueblood."

That made no sense to Jonah.

As they descended the stairs, Lisa whispered, "I always knew you were special, Jonah. Today proved it. And, well, Mandara smiled. Can you imagine that?"

Jonah *could* imagine that. He'd pushed himself beyond anything he'd done before, and that played right into the Campmaster's hands.

—

Except for Lisa, who kept the conversations going, the other campers put a little distance around Jonah. Even Eddy appeared unsure of what to say. This sudden isolation increased Jonah's desire to see Kevin, but the Fallen Reaper didn't show up for dinner.

When people flooded into the common room to play games, Jonah approached Serena, who sat in a corner near a window reading a book.

She gave him a curious look when he approached her chair. "Yes?"

"Can I go see Kevin?"

"No."

"Why not?"

She closed her book with a snap. "The Campmaster left strict orders that Kevin was not to be disturbed."

When Jonah opened his mouth to object, she stood. "He said those orders were meant especially for you." She motioned him to the common area. "Go spend time with your campmates."

Not deterred by the mentor, Jonah began making plans to sneak out and see Kevin anyway.

"Mage Trueblood put a seal over the Campmaster's office door," Serena said, as if sensing his intention. Sitting down again, she opened her novel and continued reading.

Jonah whirled to watch the others. Sure, he should stay inside with his friends instead of avoiding them, but he couldn't do that tonight. Besides, the others would relax without him around. Crossing to the front doors, Jonah stepped outside.

The fresh air and being away from the others relaxed him. After all this time, Jonah still found it easy to be alone when he needed to think. He recovered faster than Kevin and was the Son of Isaiah. *The One.* The only person to activate a ring in over two thousand years.

Being different widened his feeling of separation from everyone else and made him crave those alone times even more. Feeling alien, even at a camp for kids with powers, Jonah strolled through the courtyard.

The compound's western wall, near the entrance, was clear of obstructions, and he moved in that direction. He had a perfect view of the brilliant sunset and the riot of colors. Stopping, he breathed in, trying to calm his turbulent emotions.

Movement on top of the rock formation startled him, and he tensed, half expecting to see Jennifer. Instead, Mage Trueblood sat atop one of the large boulders, shirtless and with his arms spread wide. The mage's mouth moved as he spoke silent words to the setting sun. Jonah backed away and considered going inside when Trueblood called out to him.

"I'm done." The mage scrambled down the opposite side of the boulder and stepped into view with his prayer cloth and tunic clutched in his right hand. "You look like a person with the weight of the world on his shoulders."

Not knowing how to respond, Jonah shrugged and watched the darkening sky.

Trueblood pulled on a tunic and folded the prayer cloth. "You had a question for me?"

Jonah hesitated, trying to see if the mage was annoyed.

He couldn't tell in the fading light. "I wanted to see Kevin, but Serena told me you put a seal on Mandara's door."

Trueblood crossed his arms. "Kevin's still recharging. According to Mandara, he severely depleted himself."

"Why did he check on Kevin?"

"Mandara is head of the camp," Trueblood answered in a serious tone. "He's a very capable Fallen Reaper. Don't let the unsettling events at Alliance Headquarters cloud your judgment."

Jonah sensed the gathering power around Trueblood and regretted his question. "Yes, sir."

"Mandara has saved many of us in the past. One day you too may come to depend on the Campmaster." He continued to scrutinize Jonah for a few moments. "You'll find that people aren't purely good or evil. Everyone has a story." Finally, the mage turned to regard the dark purple sky until it shifted to black.

As the stars became visible in the night sky, Trueblood added, "You've had a busy day. Why don't you turn in early and get some rest?"

Jonah took that as an order and returned to the common room. Some kids glanced his way but quickly went back to their conversations. He expected, and secretly wanted, AJ and Eddy to call him over, but the boys remained focused on their card game. So, he shifted directions and headed upstairs.

After fetching the triptych, he chose a chair in the second-floor atrium corner and curled up to read. Finding the section on the Third Brother, he paused, reflecting that he was fine being alone right now. Yet as he began reading, he briefly wondered what tomorrow would bring.

CHAPTER TEWNTY-FOUR
TROUBLED MEMORY CHARMER

Jonah awoke feeling refreshed, physically. However, his mind refused to focus on anything or anyone else besides Kevin. He wanted to understand what they had experienced and couldn't shake the concern for his boyfriend.

Kevin was also his source for what was going on with the Alliance. On top of those concerns, Jonah still had to solve the riddle of the Tales. Last night, he'd read about the Third and Fourth Brothers. One was arrogant, and the other the opposite and full of self-doubt. Still, he hadn't found any clues. All of this reminded him how much things had gone wrong the past couple of days.

First things first, he told himself. Find Kevin. He rolled out of bed with a determined mood and gathered his things for the showers. When he opened the door, he almost collided with Eddy.

"Morning," Eddy said in a cheery voice.

Jonah's worry for Kevin made him irritable. "You're talking to me now?"

Eddy paused, the grin frozen on his face. "What do you mean?"

"Last night, you wouldn't say anything to me."

"Wow, dude. Sorry." Eddy held up his hands. "We thought you were out of it. That's all."

"So that's why you all stared at me? I bet you had a lot to say behind my back."

Eddy opened and closed his mouth, trying to decide what to say.

"We weren't talking about you like that," AJ said, walking up behind Eddy and leaning against the wall. "We didn't see what happened, but Monisha did, and she was impressed."

"Yeah, and…" Jonah didn't finish his statement because Eddy pulled him out of the dorm and shoved him toward the stairs.

AJ added a push, so Jonah didn't have any choice but to let them have their way.

"Off to the showers with you," AJ joked. "You can use one."

⸺

Halfway through breakfast, Kevin entered the dining room. Jonah paused in eating as he watched the Fallen Reaper go through the food line. When Kevin turned for the mentor's table, he flashed Jonah an embarrassed grin and then avoided making eye contact for the rest of the meal.

Why would Kevin be embarrassed? Jonah asked himself. *Because he was an Alliance member and shouldn't have gone too far?*

The frustration over the lack of answers worsened for Jonah. He needed to talk to Kevin. Well, he wanted to hug him, but how could he if his boyfriend continued to avoid looking at him? Jonah made up his mind to catch Kevin alone and find out what was going on.

—

Jonah's concentration in Meditation class suffered, and he called up a blast of wind again. This time, however, he calmed it right away.

Still, Bertonneau came over and whispered to him, "Try having the wind touch one finger." She walked off.

Jonah spent the rest of the class trying to focus his attention down to one finger. All he could achieve, though, was a faint breeze across his hand. Nevertheless, he gave the Councilor a quick grin when the session ended, and he headed off for the blade session.

—

Jonah welcomed the chance to work alone with Lisa and Monisha during blades. They knew the routines, and he could stand back and watch while thinking about Kevin. That didn't quite happen because Lisa's improved attitude required his attention as she worked her way through the moves.

Judging his friends ready, Jonah began to spar with them. Unlike Lynn, who had whacked him with a practice baton the very first time he hadpicked up the blades, he lightly tapped the girls' arms if their batons weren't in proper position.

"I think you're ready to spar on your own," he told the girls, stepping back. He lingered, making sure everything went well before he crossed to the range's fence to gaze at the lake.

The distinctive swish of activating blades cut through his attempt to focus on Kevin. Jonah whirled around to discover that Monisha had activated her real blades.

"Monisha, don't do that!" Jonah warned.

"She's doing fine," Monisha objected and hacked Lisa's baton. Like a slow-moving tragedy, Lisa didn't shift her left baton into place, and Monisha's blade cut a thin line across the girl's forearm.

Lisa yelled and dropped her baton as droplets of blood blossomed on her pale skin. "Ow!" She fell to her knees, cradling the injured arm.

"Oh, my God!" Monisha dropped her blades to rush forward and press the bottom of her shirt around Lisa's injury.

Jonah was at her side in an instant, pulled his camp shirt over his head, and used it to wrap Lisa's arm. Monisha stood back, the bottom of her shirt red from Lisa's blood

Rex hurried over with a huge kit in hand. Jonah had no idea where the Fallen Reaper got it, but he watched as Rex unwrapped Lisa's arm, cleaned, and bandaged the cut. "There you go, young lady. It wasn't a deep cut at all. We'll have to get you back to the Healer's station." He handed over Jonah's ruined shirt and then helped Lisa stand.

"I hate blades," Lisa said while gingerly touching her arm and looking miserable.

"I'm sorry," Monisha managed, twisting the bottom of her shirt around her hand. "I didn't mean for that to happen."

"Oh, you're not the first to draw blood." Rex smiled at her. "Learning the blades ain't easy." He clapped his hands. "That should do it for today."

Jonah found Monisha's discarded blades on the ground, deactivated them, and handed the weapons over. "Never forget to deactivate these." He leaned closer. "And listen to what I tell you next time."

Monisha took the cylinders, hurried to catch up with Lisa and put an arm around her friend's shoulder. Darren joined them but turned to stare at Jonah before walking out of the range with the girls.

—

"The Healer said Lisa's gonna be fine," Monisha reported to everyone in a shaky voice. She huddled on the common room sofa with Darren.

Jonah could sympathize with Monisha because he felt a little responsible for what had happened. Focusing on the good news, he felt less guilty for shifting his attention to a pressing question. Did the Alliance Council plan to involve him with other captured people?

Sitting in one of the low-slung chairs near AJ and Eddy, who played pool, he mulled over the problem until a possible solution occurred to him. Well, the idea wasn't new because he had considered it when he chose his blades.

He sat up in the chair when he saw Bertonneau leave the west hall and stroll toward the exit.

Jonah leaped from the chair, slipped around his curious friends, and followed the Councilor outside. "Councilor Bertonneau? Ma'am?" he called out.

The stately woman turned to regard him. "Yes, Mr. Blackstone?"

"Sorry to interrupt your walk. I just wanted to know if I could talk to you at the start of the next session."

The woman raised one of her eyebrows, considering his request. "Be on time," she muttered and walked off.

Eager to reach Personal Development, Jonah set off ahead of the others at the end of the free hour. The idea was simple: ask to learn blade-making from Mandara. Convincing the Campmaster to train him was the unknown factor. Jonah figured he could claim this was part of honing his skills or something like that.

Sprinting up the bamboo path, he wasn't prepared as he passed the boathouse and felt a quick twinge in his Death Sense.

He stopped in his tracks and turned to peer into the darkened interior. Everything was quiet except the boats creaking as they bumped around in their separate berths.

The inside of the structure was as dark as he'd originally thought because bright sunlight reflected off the water, allowing him to see into the corners. No one was there. Just when he considered leaving, he heard the quiet whoosh of an igniting flame. Spotting the new glow, he walked along the row of four boats to the far corner and discovered the ball of blue fire.

He reached out with his senses, knowing a mage had to be around. He thought AJ could be playing a joke, but that didn't fit because he left AJ in the main building. Then who was this? Thomas? Jonah didn't think the mentor would sneak around playing games.

Like a warning flare, his Death Sense spiked at the same time he sensed the movement from behind. Acting on instinct, Jonah tried to phase first. Only when he realized his mistake did he dive over the bow of the nearer boat. Something slammed into his shoulder and knocked him against the next boat and down on the deck.

By gripping the boat at the last second, he avoided falling into the shallow water. Ignoring the throbbing in his left shoulder, he pulled out his blades and rolled to his feet with both weapons activated.

Jennifer stood in the opposite corner, grinning at him as she moved around the end boat. Her hands crackled with magical energy. "Got you!"

"Are you crazy?" Jonah brandished his blades.

She eyed the weapons and didn't come close. Her face twisted in a disappointed frown. "You're faster than I expected, given you can't phase to safety."

"Why're you attacking me? I helped you at Center Point!"

"Me? I wasn't there." Jennifer's mocking tone turned bitter. "Besides, you did that to help your stupid cousins."

Jonah couldn't believe she would lie to his face. He also couldn't argue with her comment. While in the Underworld, he'd had a vision of the mole severely injuring Robert and helping Aunt Ruby kill him. Freeing Jennifer from his aunt's trap was the only way to change that vision, and it had worked.

Waving his blade at her, Jonah thought he could still trap her into confessing. "If that wasn't you, then why attack me?"

"Simple. You lied to the Alliance by claiming I worked for the mole."

"You do!" Jonah shouted. "Who is he? Do you know?"

"Because little Jonah said it," Jennifer continued, ignoring his question, "Mage Trueblood started asking questions. I can't have that." On the last word, she flung a hex at him.

Jonah deflected it and called on the wind to blast the girl. The boats rocked back and forth, and water welled up to splash her.

Jumping aside, she moved to block the exit. "Of course, I told them it was all lies."

"No one will believe that."

"Doesn't matter," she shot back. "The Alliance is too principled to subject me to a Memory Charmer interrogation, especially after their little accident."

Her joke about the Hunter's attempted suicide angered Jonah. The man had been the enemy, but no one deserved to have their brain fried. Tired of Jennifer's lies, he charged the young mage as she wove her hands around, conjuring another hex.

Caught by surprise, Jennifer didn't have time to avoid Jonah as he rammed into her at an angle. With a grunt, she stumbled sideways and banged against the boathouse wall, leaving the exit clear. But she was quick and rolled to her feet, her face full of rage. Still, she hesitated when she heard the other kids arriving.

"You got lucky," she spat, producing a vortex and diving through. Jonah stared at the closing vortex, thinking it was unfair she could do that while spells prevented him from phasing inside the camp.

—

What else is gonna happen? Jonah wondered as he rushed into Bertonneau's room and flopped down in a chair. His entire body vibrated with pent-up anger at Jennifer, yet Jonah forced himself to let it go. He had a plan and a reason for the meeting.

Taking a deep breath, he used one of the meditation techniques to settle and focus himself. He also thought of something that produced an emotion other than anger at Jennifer.

"It's good to see you using the techniques," Bertonneau said, watching him. "At least some of what I say matters to the campers." She placed her hands on her lap. "Well, Mr. Blackstone, how did the wood carvin' go?"

"It was fine, ma'am."

Bertonneau raised her eyebrow. "Well, you requested this meeting."

"I, ah, wanted to ask you if I could change my project." The teacher waited, and Jonah rushed on. "I wanted to know if I could learn to make blades."

Bertonneau rocked back in her seat, her eyebrows raising so high on her forehead they disappeared into her full head of hair. "Blade-making? Why would you ask…" Her eyes widened.

Reaching into his pocket, Jonah pulled out the blades. He activated one and held it up, letting the inlay show.

"Rex said my dad knew how to make blades and that the talent could run in families."

"Yes, your father was a blade-maker." Bertonneau stared at the blade as if she thought it would burn her. "It's why I suggested wood carving."

Jonah lowered the weapon. "Can I learn to make blades?"

Now the Council member shook her head. "It's a possibility, but something like this would have been better if arranged ahead of time. I'm sure Rex also told you that the Campmaster is the only one left who understands the art and process of making a Reaper's blade."

Jonah nodded. "Yeah, he did, but—"

"Well then, even you can see that the Campmaster's extremely busy."

No, Jonah thought to himself. The best way to find out anything about the Alliance plans was to go to the source, and that was Mandara.

"Please?" Jonah asked.

"As I said, he's a busy person."

With his hope to get close to the Campmaster failing, Jonah deactivated the blade and slumped in the chair. "This isn't fair. I didn't even know about camp, let alone independent projects. And even if I did, no one told me anything about blade-making or that my dad made them."

He didn't mean it, but his voice had risen in volume until just below a shout. He slumped in his chair again. "I'm sorry. I didn't mean to yell." Before the woman chided him, Jonah tried to focus on another emotion, but her next words stalled his attempt.

"You have a right to be angry. So much was hidden from you." Bertonneau's hand shook as she toyed with the pale green scarf around her thin neck.

Jonah sensed her anger, but he didn't think it was about his situation. "What are you going to do next? Does the Council know what the KIN and Hunters have planned?"

"That's confidential."

The answer reminded Jonah so much of his godfather, someone he'd grown used to sparring with, that he let himself flip into a partial Reaper stare. At once, he could see Bertonneau's aura bathed in the vibrant red of anger.

"Young man!"

Jonah blinked hard and dropped the Reaper stare. He didn't need it to see the emotion on the woman's face. "What?"

"I've been around enough Fallen Reapers to know that stare from a mile away."

"I'm sorry. I didn't mean to do it." At that moment, though, he sensed she wasn't furious but more disappointed in him. Or was she disappointed in the current situation with the Alliance?

Instead of sending him from the room, Bertonneau adjusted her scarf while avoiding his direct gaze.

"You didn't like using the Memory Charmers to question the Hunter?" he asked.

"No, I did not."

Taking that as progress, Jonah risked going deeper. "You don't want them becoming Mind Benders."

Bertonneau frowned. "An out-of-control Memory Charmer could create havoc. The same ability that allows them to suppress or take a memory can stoke or even suggest a horrible memory." She shuddered again as if she was cold.

Jonah wondered if she recalled past instances of what she described.

"In the old days," Bertonneau continued, as if sensing his thoughts, "they burned alive a person they caught using their abilities in that way. That's why we have strict rules that require a Memory Charmer to have the utmost character. That's what I demand of all who aspire to be among our ranks."

"You train Memory Charmers?"

Bertonneau tilted her chin up. "I not only train, but I also developed the rules and obligations for all Memory Charmers." She made a derisive sound. "To willfully take the memories from another being is ghastly."

The woman's Creole accent grew more pronounced, and the air became charged with tension as she continued. "It all leads to a Charmer becoming a Mind Bender. I'm afraid we're headin' down a dark path, young man, a very dark path. We become like our enemies, causing good people to suffer."

Bertonneau stood, breaking Jonah's train of thought. "We've talked too long. You should get to your wood carving."

"Yes, ma'am." Jonah stood and crossed to the door.

"Mr. Blackstone," the Councilwoman called. He turned to find her gazing out a window. "Your father was an inspiring man, and I was proud to serve with him on the Council." She lowered her head. Jonah started to respond when she met his gaze. "I'll ask the Campmaster about teaching you blade-making, but don't get your hopes up. I doubt he'll be able to rearrange his schedule to accommodate you."

"Okay. Thank you." Jonah slipped out the door, leaving the Meditation teacher alone with her troubled thoughts. At least Bertonneau would ask the Campmaster about the lesson, so his plan wasn't dead yet.

CHAPTER TWENTY-FIVE
DESTINY'S SORROW

As evening came on, Jonah looked forward to finding Kevin before dinner and talking. However, that didn't happen because Kevin disappeared from camp with another Alliance adult. Not in the mood to play cards, Jonah apologized to AJ and Eddy and headed upstairs. As he reached the second-floor landing, he heard someone enter the building.

Peeking over the railing, he saw Kevin below, looking around. As if sensing Jonah, the Fallen Reaper glanced up and saw him. Kevin mounted the steps and crossed to him, a little uncertain.

"Sorry about avoiding you."

Those were the best words Jonah had ever heard. He pulled Kevin to a corner, and they sat, facing each other. "Are you okay?"

"Yeah. I was just…"

"Embarrassed? Why?" Jonah didn't get it.

"With all that's happening, I let my binding patterns run too low on power. Then I went too far with you." Kevin rested his elbows on his knees, leaning forward. "Mandara lectured me on proper Fallen Reaper protocols. That's why I had to recharge in his office."

"So I wouldn't disturb you," Jonah grumbled. He stroked Kevin's chin. "You don't have to be embarrassed with me."

"I know." After a moment, Kevin held Jonah's hands and told him the nonclassified bits about the aftermath of the HQ attack and the whole story of the Hunter's capture and the loss of the paperweight medallion.

Though Jonah welcomed the information, he just wanted to listen to Kevin talk and confide in him.

—

Friday morning was overcast and slightly cooler, providing a welcome respite from the typical summer heat during the Nature class. But by midmorning, a thundershower rolled through Camp Alliance, pelting everyone with rain as they darted between the buildings. Jonah grumbled when he saw the wet and muddy ground at the practice ranges.

The condition of the field didn't stop Kevin from resuming his hand-to-hand combat training; nor did it send Jonah face-first into the muck. The one consolation was he had finally countered Kevin by the time the Range Session ended.

Returning to the main building, exhausted and filthy, Jonah went straight upstairs to gather his clothes for a shower. That's where he found Eddy, standing outside their dorm, reading a note taped to the door.

"What's up?" Jonah asked.

"Saturday's a free day, so we can stay up until eleven tonight," Eddy explained and opened the door.

That's cool, Jonah thought, deciding how he'd spend Saturday as he grabbed his clothes.

He'd seen the all-day trip announcements posted on the main room's message board. He nudged Eddy. "What are you gonna do?"

"I'm going on the half-day trip to Camp Monarch." They reached the stairs and started down. "Lisa wants to go horseback riding. I like the zip line over the lake!"

A zip line sounded like fun to Jonah. Best of all, when they returned, he could grab one of the study desks in the west hall after lunch. He doubted anyone else would use them on a Saturday, so he'd have the entire room to himself. Jonah imagined finding a nice spot and spending quality time on the Tales, even taking notes.

That plan died, however, when they reached the common room and discovered Mage Trueblood standing with AJ.

"Gentlemen," the mage said, "I need a word with Jonah."

AJ and Eddy flashed Jonah a look that said he'd better share later, and they moved to stand by the front doors.

Trueblood glanced around and said, "You should come on the canoe trip tomorrow."

"That'll take all day," Jonah objected. "I want to catch up on my *reading*."

The mage smiled. "I understand. However, remember what I suggested? Sometimes a break helps, and the Flint River is nice this time of year." He paused when the young mages, including Jennifer, rose from their chairs and left the room, still engrossed in a conversation. "I want to keep you close."

"What good is that if Jennifer can go around using vortices to attack me?"

"As part of Jennifer's advanced study, Thomas requested permission for her to create a vortex inside the camp," Trueblood explained.

"Why?"

"Jennifer's a mage, and it made sense, but we've asked Thomas to keep a closer eye on his advanced mages."

"She's also Antwan's cousin and worked with the mole in Mount Vernon. I know it."

Trueblood worked his jaw. At last, he said, "Proving allegations requires time to gather the evidence." He paused, clearly choosing his words. "I've found that people eventually show their hand. Until then, be vigilant, and I'll see you tomorrow morning."

Jonah's shoulders slumped as Trueblood left the building.

"You know what this means?" AJ asked as soon as Jonah joined them, and they set off for the showers.

"Yeah, I need to catch Jennifer and prove she's bad."

"Obviously," AJ said dryly. "I meant you should never be alone." He took a deep breath. "That's why I'm going on the canoe trip with you."

That caught Jonah off guard because he would never have thought AJ a rafting type of person. While he appreciated his friend's help, it bothered him to lose the chance to dig into the Tales and find those clues.

After dinner, the boys claimed three comfortable chairs and a coffee table by the fireplace and played cards until ten thirty.

Jonah yawned for his fourth time and said, "I'm done."

"Already?" Eddy asked. "You're leaving because I'm winning."

"No, I'm not," Jonah answered, amused. He could see why Eddy thought that. It was his friend's first time winning. "I wanted to read tonight since I won't have a chance tomorrow."

AJ exchanged a knowing look with Eddy. "Deal two hands."

Waving good night to his buddies, Jonah trudged up the stairs, thinking it cool he didn't have to lie to his friends anymore. At the top of the stairs, he crossed paths with Beraki and Crosby, who nodded as they hurried down to the common room.

Jonah watched the undulating barrier blocking the mages' end of the hallway, wondering what they used for a talisman. Maybe he could ask Alex during one of their Team Building classes. He shook his head at the likelihood the young mage would answer and entered his room.

Pulling out the pieces of the triptych, he turned for his bed, then changed his mind. The buzz of conversations from below grew louder as he crossed into the balcony area and chose his favorite set of chairs in the back corner.

With the voices below serving as familiar background noise, Jonah curled up in a chair and flipped through the sections he had already read, including the final brother, the youngest, who was the loyal one, almost to a fault.

All the sections and trials the Deliverer put them through fascinated Jonah, yet nothing helped with the riddle of the last page. Maybe, Jonah hoped, something in the section about Destiny would help him.

⊖

Destiny's Sorrow

In the final days of Destiny's journey in the land, violence and evil sprang up everywhere. The first six Virtues had fallen asleep, one by one, until Destiny was the only one remaining. Despite the Deliverer's effort to strengthen the five brothers, evil forces expanded their influence until the brothers were called home to guard Destiny's sanctuary.

The province was near a mountain the locals called Catawba for the grapes that grew there. The Deliverer journeyed to the region, and on his third day of travel, he came across the five brothers. Knowing that Destiny was the strongest Virtue and fearful because of what had happened to her sisters, the Deliverer determined not to approach the brothers in the open.

He camped and watched them for several days and learned that the brothers fished and hunted in the same spots. On the eighth day, the Deliverer stepped from concealment and presented himself as a poor traveler who'd lost his way.

The three younger brothers were inclined to help the stranger and send him away. But the second oldest of the brothers was weary of the Traveler. Being cleverer and more intelligent than the others, he leaped to his feet and confronted the stranger.

"You are no Traveler," the Second Brother said. *"You deceived me once with a disguise, but I see through it now."*

When his brothers heard the claims, they too saw the Traveler's true self. Grabbing up their weapons, the brothers moved to lay hold on him. The Deliverer threw off his coat and made ready to fight. Not understanding their fall toward doubt again, he implored the brothers.

"Why do you seek to slay me, noble Protectors? I am the one, the Deliverer, who helped each of you free yourselves from the influence of the evil ones. And I gave the Virtues aid in their time of need."

"Why are they silent?" the Eldest Brother demanded, stepping into the clearing. *"We hear our mother cry every night for want of contact with her sisters. She tells us they are gone."*

The Deliverer accepted their words with a heavy heart and witnessed the doubt produced by the Eldest Brother's words. "I know your mother grieves for her sisters. They answer not because they are asleep. The Virtues could not remain in this world."

"Lies," the Eldest Brother yelled and drew out his sword.

The Second Brother, wiser than the others, held him back. "This Deliverer is known to be a mighty man. All who went up against him failed, including you. I cannot deny he freed me from the Grand Oracle's minions."

"Tell your mother that I have come to talk to her. Let Destiny weigh my words and decide. If she refuses to hear me, then I shall leave this place."

The brothers argued among themselves. The eldest tried to hold sway, but the others wouldn't lift their swords against the Deliverer until they received word from their mother. Finally, the Second Brother revealed their conclusion.

"We will ask our mother whether she will consent to see you or not. Return here in three days at this hour to know the decision. Do not

come before the appointed time, nor return late, or we will take that as a sign of bad faith."

The Deliverer accepted their conditions and withdrew from the area. He was true to his word and did not return, watch them, or come near their territory for three days and three nights.

⇥

Jonah jerked, and the triptych slipped from his hands. The device's dull thud on the ground woke him. Sitting up, he blinked his tired eyes while he scanned the area. Had anyone seen him dozing? After retrieving the triptych, he went to his dorm and quickly stripped for bed. After sliding under the thin cover, Jonah scanned a little further through stories about the Deliverer wandering the land and meeting various people.

He couldn't imagine why these people's names would be necessary, but the writer clearly thought they were. Settling into the task, he continued through as much as he could, until he reached the place where the Deliverer went back to meet the Protectors.

⇥

When the Deliverer arrived at the appointed place and time, he sensed a state of discord between the Protectors.

"What is the issue among you five brothers?" the Deliverer asked.

The Eldest Brother stood apart from the others and glared at the Deliverer but held his tongue. The Youngest Brother, and bravest of the five, spoke for the rest.

"Our Mother has consented to listen to the words you will speak."

"Then why the division among you?"

"Because our Eldest Brother didn't like our mother's decision. He argued long with her over the past three days. But our mother would not relent and bade us come and give you her decision."

"Then you are bound to follow your mother's wishes in this matter."

The Youngest Brother nodded.

"Take me to Destiny. I will have my say, and then she will choose her future."

Disappointed with their eldest brother, the remaining four heeded the Deliverer's words and led him up into the mountain. Soon they reached the encampment high near the peak of the mountain, where the siblings lived. Yet their mother took shelter in the safety of a large cave. When the group approached the opening, five whirlwinds of fire appeared and barred their way.

In unison, the brothers held their rings aloft, and the whirlwinds obeyed their commands and parted. Once the group moved into the cave, the fire guardians closed ranks so no one could enter the mountain, except by passing through them. This display of power reassured the Deliverer.

The Eldest Brother noticed his countenance. "Why are you pleased with the sign of the whirlwinds? If not for our presence, the guardians would have burned you to a cinder."

The Deliverer inclined his head. "That may be so, but it pleases me to see that your mother is yet strong and able to defend herself."

The Youngest Brother, who trotted beside the Deliverer, jumped in excitement. "We protect our mother. We are strong, and no one can overcome our combined strength."

"I hope that remains so. But I fear that even now, your Mother's enemies sow distrust among you."

Everyone grew silent because they knew the Deliverer spoke of the Eldest Brother. He had been against their mother fleeing to this location.

The Deliverer sensed their distress and said to them, "Need I remind you the enemy overtook and slaughtered the other Protectors because they allowed distrust to manifest itself within their midst? Clear your hearts and remain true to the purpose, lest you too are overthrown in this wilderness."

The Eldest Brother fled from their sight, leaving the four to present the Deliverer to their Mother. When he was brought to the inner chamber and before the last Virtue, he and the Protectors bowed to the ground.

"Oh, Great Mother of Virtue and Destiny. I have come to give you warning and aid," the Deliverer said.

Destiny leaned forward in her chair of polished gold and rebuked him. "Six times you have approached one of my sisters, and six times they have fallen silent so that even I cannot touch them." Destiny rose. "Have you come to take my light from the world as you did my sisters?"

Her words saddened the Deliverer, but he stood tall and addressed her. "As I told your sons, I did not take their light from the world. Your sisters gave up their burden or passed it to those not fit to accept the responsibility. As a result, the Rulers of the Afterworld subverted and led their Protectors astray. Many fell because of their vices and turned away from the path. I urged your sisters to sleep to save themselves. You alone, of all the Virtues, have remained true and have survived to this day. But the time draws near when you will not be able to stand against your enemies."

All those gathered were deeply troubled at the Deliverer's words. The Eldest Brother stepped from the shadows where he'd listened with disdain.

"See, Mother? He is the reason your sisters no longer hear your call. I know you weep for them every night. Bid us slay him now before he can work his evil against you."

The Deliverer drew near the Eldest Brother without fear of him. "This is how it begins, dear Destiny. Mistrust spreads among the Protectors. The Grim Reaper preys on distrust, and the Grand Oracle loves misinformation. These are the tools of the Rulers of the Afterworld and their evil servants. Did your sons not give testament to the evil influence from which I freed them?" The Deliverer pleaded with the Eldest Brother, "Resist the Grim Reaper, and the power of your ring will put a shield around your heart and mind. And he will not have dominion over your soul. Heed me, Protector, before it is too late."

Moved by the Deliverer's words and convictions, Destiny saw the truth of his path and understood what had become of her eldest son.

"Come back to us, my son. Listen to your ring. Let it renew your spirit."

The Eldest Brother shook with fury. When his siblings sought to comfort him, he fled once again from their presence. The Youngest Brother wanted to pursue, but the Third Brother held him back. "It is not wise to follow, lest you also be trapped. He must come to his senses. Only then can the ring renew him."

"Is there nothing I can do to save my son and the world?" Destiny asked the Deliverer.

"Alas, there is not. The only way to protect you from the evil that spreads over the world is to sleep until another in the order of the Deliverers comes and releases you all from slumber."

The remaining brothers surrounded the Deliverer.

"Do not fear, Protectors. It has been decreed that the Grim Reaper and Grand Oracle can overcome you only for a season, lest they prevent mortals from seeing the light of truth forever."

⊖

When Jonah's vision wavered, he decided he'd have to finish later. More than ever, he wanted to stay back at camp tomorrow and finish reading instead of going on the canoe trip. But that wasn't an option. Sliding the triptych under his pillow, he rolled over just as someone knocked on his door. "Yeah?"

AJ peeked inside. "Where's Eddy?"

"Probably making a pit stop."

"Well, here." AJ tossed something small to Jonah.

He sat up to catch it. It was a back gate token.

"Eddy dropped his token again. He's lucky I found it instead of Trueblood." AJ yawned. "Night."

Smiling to himself, Jonah sat Eddy's token on the boy's night table, got back in bed, and closed his eyes. Before he knew it, he was asleep.

CHAPTER TWENTY-SIX
BLOOD MOUNTAIN

The Flint River canoe park was over sixteen acres, featuring breathtaking views of the river. At least that's what AJ quoted from the brochure in his hand. Trueblood smiled at Jonah and the other campers' muted responses as he went off to the outpost pavilion to secure their reserved canoes.

Meanwhile, Kevin turned to the waiting group. "We'll travel with two people in each canoe." He pulled Jonah over to him. "You're with me. I need to keep you out of trouble."

"Ha ha." Jonah stared at the row of colorful canoes along the riverbank. Beyond those were the kayaks. Not being a big water park person, he was glad they'd use the canoes instead. They were bigger and seemed a little less likely to roll over.

Trueblood returned, carrying a bundle of flotation vests for the group, and pointed to four canoes halfway down the riverbank. "Those are ours," he said, handing out vests.

The young mages acted like a string connected them as they donned the vests in unison, then took hold of a canoe. Darren, torn between wanting to talk to Trueblood and sticking close to Monisha, didn't move. She folded her arms and gave him a stern look that settled the matter. That left AJ to ride with Trueblood.

Once everyone chose a canoe, Kevin helped AJ and Monisha wrap the lunch cooler in waterproof tape and stow it in Trueblood's canoe. With that done, everyone got in their boat, and after a final check, they pushed off from the bank.

As they started down the river, Jonah squirmed in the vest.

"You'll get used to it," Kevin said, nudging him in the back.

"Maybe," Jonah grumbled. Despite the irritating vest, he had to admit the forest on either side of the slow-moving river was beautiful and the air fresh.

Their journey began slowly because several other canoe parties set off at the same time, creating a bottleneck. Thankfully, the various groups separated as people took different branches of the river.

"Why aren't we going that way?" Monisha shouted, pointing at a passing sign indicating rapids along one course.

Trueblood called back to his group, "We're not doing the white water section today."

"Nothing at all?" Monisha complained.

"Maybe next time."

Monisha scowled, but Jonah glanced at their quiet course and was okay with never seeing rapids. Besides, the profusion of plants and birds was incredible. And, staring deep into the green water, Jonah caught glimpses of fish below. Soon, the sound of their oars slicing into the water relaxed him. Maybe this was better than sitting in the Embracing Valley building and reading, he thought.

As the morning wore on, the clouds thickened overhead, blocking out the sun and providing a break from the rising temperature. Just as suddenly, a rain shower started. The sound of the heavy raindrops hitting the water was deafening and exciting. Monisha let out a whoop ahead of them. Marvin returned the yell, but Beraki looked miserable. His already droopy dreads lay plastered to his forehead, leaking water down the boy's face.

Jonah's Afro soaked up as much rain as possible before rivulets of water ran down his face. Swiping at the water didn't help, and neither did the snort from behind. Turning, he found Kevin had pulled on a ball cap to keep water out of his eyes.

"You could have brought me a cap."

"No way, hero. Eyes forward."

Jonah turned around and endured the shower that thankfully ended a short time later. The July sun peeked through the storm clouds again and baked their backs dry. Half an hour later, they entered a quiet branch of the river with large, flat rocks and leveled ground, where they stopped for lunch.

When Trueblood had them sit in a loose circle to eat, Jonah knew the Team Building teacher had planned for the mages to come along, almost like an arranged date. Thankfully, they didn't have any team exercises, just comfortable talking about camp and what they liked.

Forty minutes later, the group packed everything, taking care not to leave any litter, and continued on the second leg of the trip.

They reached a shallow bend in the river where the hills on either side began to close in. At some spots, sheer drop-offs spilled directly into the water. The expansive feel of the waterway vanished as the clouds blocked out the sun again. The sudden change created a sense of dread in Jonah.

Trueblood allowed his canoe to float, only using the oar to keep it in the center of the river. The others copied his motions. Judging from the furtive glances, Jonah knew they experienced the same heavy feeling of loss in the air. He slid an oar into the still water and paddled.

"What are you doing?" Kevin plunged his oar into the water to create drag. "We're floating along. Relax."

Jonah doubted anyone could relax in this creepy section of the river. He looked over his shoulder. "I want to ask Trueblood something."

"Oh." Kevin helped Jonah maneuver past Beraki and Marvin. As they came even with Trueblood's canoe, Kevin slowed them to match speeds.

"You sense it?" Trueblood spoke without turning.

"Yeah," Jonah whispered, aware everyone listened to the conversation. The eerie stillness and coldness of this stretch of the river caused his Death Sense to tingle and goose bumps to rise along his arms. "What is it?"

"You're sensing the presence of untold numbers who lost their lives here." Trueblood peered into the trees along the river.

Scanning the banks himself, Jonah slowly nodded. "You think there're Wraiths around?"

"No, probably not."

Though he tried to speak low, Jonah's voice carried to the others. "I've been to cemeteries, but I've felt nothing like this."

"Cemeteries are where the dead go to rest." Trueblood focused on the river ahead. "However, this place carries neither a peaceful rest nor a transition into the beyond."

"Guys. Please," Monisha complained, hugging herself. "This is creepy enough."

"Monisha, you're going to face the Rulers of the Afterworld," Trueblood said. "You should get used to the notion of death and what comes after."

A light fog rolled across the water and the canoes, casting a hazy edge over everything, like a misty picture.

"Are there a lot of places like this?" Jonah asked, trying not to shiver.

"Battlefields are like this, to people who are sensitive to it." Trueblood raised his chin as they slid deeper into the fog. "Perhaps the most oppressive place in Georgia is called Blood Mountain. Tribes of Indigenous people battled each other there."

"I've never heard of Blood Mountain."

Trueblood took a deep breath, and when he spoke, he did so with a more traditional Native American cadence. "Blood Mountain is the sixth highest peak in Georgia and is part of the Blue Mountain Range. Its Indigenous name was Entaon." He drew in another breath and continued in the strange voice. "The Cherokee and Creek peoples fought many battles over it. Eventually, after a fierce battle at Slaughter Gap, the Cherokee claimed the mountain. Legend says the land is called Blood Mountain because of all the warriors who lost their lives."

A shiver went down Jonah's spine when he sensed the broader meaning behind Trueblood's story.

The mage lowered his head and didn't speak for several moments. Everyone watched him, stunned. Then Trueblood flipped his head up, causing his long dreads to snap around.

"What did you think of the voice?" Trueblood asked.

Jonah stared back, unsure of how to answer. Anyone else doing the voice would be called insensitive. Yet Trueblood was full Choctaw and wasn't making fun of his culture.

AJ spared Jonah from answering when he observed, "That's how your dad or grandad spoke, isn't it?"

Trueblood turned, smiling. "Yes, it was. Remember the native oral histories exhibit I took everyone to see? I had considered volunteering as a narrator for that project, you know."

"Oh, cool," AJ replied.

The mage's comment reminded Jonah of that snippet of news clipping he had read in Mike's AJC newspaper. But he had a more pressing question for Trueblood. "Was that a true story?"

"It's an old part of the oral history passed down among the Indigenous people." Trueblood shrugged. "Today's society relegates those stories to movies and fairy tales." He snorted. "We love things carved on a cave wall but discount oral tradition, even though it can be as accurate."

Jonah leaned back because of Trueblood's stinging words. His parents had been researchers. And he put a lot of faith in the books he read. "I don't understand. How can the oral history be as accurate as written history? Doesn't it get changed?"

"Yes and no. Normally there's a ritual that goes with passing along the histories." Trueblood paused. "Do you know the term, Griot?"

"A Griot's a storyteller," Jonah answered.

"Good. Well, consider this. What happens if you write something down that is inaccurate? Because it's in a permanent form, is it accepted?"

Jonah's eyes widened. "Yeah, I guess so."

The mage held up a hand. "But what if the original information was wrong? The error is accepted and passed along."

"Then how can you know what's true?" The conversation was making Jonah uneasy.

"Facts are true," Trueblood stated. "The interpretation and presentation is always tainted." He saw the confusion on Jonah's face. "Be open, Jonah. A true researcher never overlooks or disregards something because it doesn't fit a preconceived notion."

"So you listen to the oral histories and read the ones in the books?"

Trueblood nodded. "Think of it as a puzzle. What happened in the past happened. The more pieces you have, the more the true picture takes shape."

The mage's words set Jonah's mind ablaze. He'd never thought of the things he read as an incomplete part of a larger puzzle. As the broader meaning nibbled at his mind, Jonah sucked in a breath.

He had the Tales, a history that no mortal had seen in two thousand years. And they were also a part of the puzzle. Suddenly, Jonah wanted to get back to his triptych. Maybe with this new awareness, he could finally solve the mystery and find the Destiny Medallion.

Kevin poked him in the back. "Hey, you awake? We're falling behind."

Jonah blinked and looked around. The others used their oars again and had pulled ahead. As he slipped his paddle into the water and they began moving, something odd happened. A sudden, cold sensation washed over Jonah's arms, making him shiver. Then he heard Thera's voice.

"Jonah Blackstone."

He glanced around, only to realize the voice had echoed in his head.

"Give me the translations," Thera hissed again. Jonah saw a faint image of her face floating in his mind's eye.

"No." Jonah barely moved his mouth, hoping no one would hear.

"Why Not? You hate the Council. Why do their bidding?"

How could she know that? Jonah wondered. *Unless the mole told her.*

"I could help you. With the medallion's power, I could avenge your parents by killing the Grim Reaper and Deyanira."

Jonah sucked in a breath. "Yeah. And become the new head bad guy in charge."

"Are you talking to someone?" Kevin asked.

"Shhh." Jonah motioned for Kevin to wait.

"But, your parents' killers would be dead. You're the Deliverer. You'd deal with me in time." Thera let the last word drag out. *"Or watch your friends suffer."*

Though Jonah wasn't tempted to give the sorceress the translation, threatening his friends made the answer easier. Why didn't they ever learn this didn't work with him?

"Not a chance," Jonah answered.

The oppressive feeling of gloom didn't lift. Instead, it increased until Jonah's Death Sense buzzed!

"Sir! It's Thera!" Jonah called out to Trueblood, but the mage sat alert, his hands raised and glowing with power.

The sudden, high-pitched screech shocked Jonah. He turned and spotted a Phantom zooming out of the fog and right at Beraki and Marvin!

"Look out!" Jonah shouted.

Beraki created a weak barrier right before the Phantom rammed into him. The force of the collision knocked the young mage over the side of the canoe. Marvin spun and shot a ball of fire at the spirit, but the Phantom used its shield to bate the fire aside as it spiraled away, punching a swirling hole through the fog.

Jonah activated his blades and heard Kevin do the same.

Marvin yelled, "Beraki!"

The young mage surfaced and splashed around, still in trouble.

With his anger at the attack building inside, Jonah prepared to defend himself just as two Phantoms dive-bombed the group from the cover of the fog-shrouded trees.

Trueblood fired a hex, hitting one of the dangerous spirits on its shield. The other angled at Monisha, but she ducked out of the way in time. Using her telekinesis, she reached out for a log visible through the mist along the shore and flung it at the Wraith.

Meanwhile, Marvin nearly overturned their canoe, but he got his friend inside and erected a solid ward. Beraki huddled close, shaking and rubbing his arms.

Hidden in the trees, the Phantoms screamed in their ethereal voices. The sound echoed, making it hard to pinpoint the source. But Jonah knew the next target. As expected, a Phantom swept out of the fog and dived right at him. It brought its sword down in a chopping motion as it approached, and Jonah met the swing with his blades. After blocking, he managed a microphase inside the canoe and cut the Phantom on the back before it disengaged.

Kevin let out a frustrated yell and phased away, forcing Jonah to adjust his balance with the sudden loss of the boy's weight. Kevin appeared on the misty riverbank and charged into the trees. Moments later, they heard a shout of pain. The second Phantom, which had just emerged from the trees, gave out a shriek of torment and vanished. Jonah realized Kevin went for the human host. He started to cheer when the second Phantom came around and dived into the water near his canoe.

Jonah didn't have time to react before the Phantom hit the canoe from underneath and turned it over. He pinwheeled, plunged into the water, and his blades slipped free. Before he could reach for them, the Phantom gripped his ankle and pulled him into the watery depths.

Panic seized Jonah as he struggled to get free while holding his breath. The surface grew dimmer as he sank into the deepest part of the river. The Phantom's head glowed, allowing him to see the black holes that served as eyes.

The Phantom's skeletal mouth moved. *"Diiiiiieeeeeeee!"*

Jonah tried to remember the meditation lesson, but he couldn't focus when his lungs were about to explode. Bubbles escaped his mouth as his breath fought to burst free. In a desperate attempt to survive, a part of him awakened. Power surged through his hands and into the Phantom. The evil spirit screamed in agony and vanished.

Free of the spirit now, Jonah looked up to see the ice-cold river closing around him. He made frantic motions, trying to swim. As river water flowed into his mouth, choking him, he felt the surge of energy again. This time, a distortion wave sped toward Jonah and engulfed him.

In seconds, a vortex of air formed around his head and stabilized into a bubble. Jonah coughed up water and sucked in the precious air as he rose toward the surface. Moments later, he burst out of the water.

Kevin grabbed hold and lifted him onto the overturned canoe. Jonah hung on, coughing up the last of the river water. Patting him on the back, Kevin watched for more Phantoms.

At a motion from Trueblood, the Fallen Reaper used his strong legs to propel them toward a bunch of tree roots sticking out of the water. "Grab on," Kevin said.

Jonah did and watched as Kevin also gripped a root with one hand and used his other hand to heave the canoe over.

Pulling it close, he held on while Jonah rolled into the boat. Kevin came last and pushed off.

Darren and Monisha had retrieved their floating oars and passed them over.

When Trueblood and AJ drifted over to them, Jonah said, "Thanks for saving me."

Trueblood frowned. "I didn't do that."

"You mean, I saved myself?" Jonah stammered. He glanced at the spot where he had toppled into the river.

"I got these for you," AJ said.

Jonah looked down to see his wet blades in his friend's hand. He'd recalled that Eleanor Trueblood had used a summoning spell to save the Seeker's compass once. He didn't know AJ could do the same spell.

Cradling the metal cylinders in his hands, Jonah gazed at AJ, impressed. "Thanks."

"No problem," AJ said, blushing a little.

Trueblood motioned to the others. "Let's move out."

The sunlight broke through the clouds, and the riverbank angled back and away. Jonah let out a relieved breath and realized the canoes moved on their own. He turned and saw Trueblood using a spell to propel them into a safer part of the river. The mage had also drawn the canoes closer together.

Checking on the others, Jonah saw Beraki looked better but had a spooked expression. Monisha seemed ready to kick butt, and so did Darren. AJ snuck quick glances at him.

Jonah fought down the embarrassment that his presence had led to another attack. He glanced back the way they came to avoid looking at anyone. "They used that section of river to keep us from sensing them, didn't they?" he asked the mage.

"Yes, they did." Trueblood surveyed the others, and added, "This wasn't a coincidence. Phantoms are Underworld creatures."

Kevin's soft voice intruded. "Who'd send Phantoms after us?"

Jonah knew the answer. "The mole. Or someone working with him." He glared at Kevin because, in his mind, Jennifer was the logical person. Yet, once again, he didn't have direct proof.

No one spoke until Trueblood said, "Everyone did well."

"I didn't," Beraki grumbled.

"We were all surprised. Let that be a lesson. Expect the unexpected and be ready to recover."

Jonah accepted the mage's words because he had let his guard down and almost lost his new blades. Why didn't he think of phasing to the riverbank and going after the mortal host? Well, no one told him a Phantom needed a human host. After taking a second to reflect, Jonah admitted he should have known that. Despite their powerful presence, Phantoms were Wraiths.

"Kevin and I have more experience," Trueblood continued as if sensing his thought. "That's why you're here at camp."

Everyone nodded. Jonah imagined the other kids nursed their private thoughts as they completed the journey down the river. When the group reached the canoe park at the end of the course, they found a few Alliance members waiting.

CHAPTER TWENTY-SEVEN
TUNICS & LONG COATS

By the time the Flint River group arrived at the Alliance fort, their collective shock had receded. Jonah couldn't wait to get back to Camp Alliance, strip out of the damp clothes, and take a nice hot shower. He clambered out of the van and followed the others inside the main building, where Eleanor Trueblood handed out juice bottles.

As Jonah sipped a mango-grapefruit, his thoughts went back to Trueblood's story. Did the mage have another reason for making him come on the trip other than watching over him? Trueblood was the one who stopped paddling, so the canoes could drift slowly through that weird section of the river. Of course, Jonah figured the Councilor regretted that now.

Also, he couldn't shake the notion that even the adults who looked out for him had hidden agendas inside of agendas for everything they did. He wasn't angry with

Trueblood because the mage had been his mom's best friend and wouldn't trick him into doing anything crazy. No, the Hardliners were the only Alliance members willing to do that.

Trueblood wanted to open his mind, Jonah concluded. An unexpected pang hit him because it was something his dad would have done. He was so focused on that observation that he didn't notice Mitchell wasn't at the travel deck when they gathered out back.

Eidelman, a thin Black Fallen Reaper who met them at the river, assumed the controls.

Monisha watched the Fallen Reaper, marched over to Kevin, and blurted out, "Do you have one of those long coats?"

"Yeah, I have one."

"I think the coats are cool, but"—Monisha tapped her bottom lip, scrutinizing Eidelman"—don't they get hot?"

Kevin's jaw worked for a moment. "No, they don't get hot."

It was Eidelman who explained in a deep voice, "The coats are made of enchanted cloth."

"And Jonah has one too," Kevin offered, to get the attention off him.

Sure enough, everyone turned to stare at Jonah now. He gulped and said, "My godfather sent me a long coat for my birthday."

"Interesting," Eidelman observed. "Normally, the long coats are given after you've completed your training and become a member of the Alliance."

"Mages do the same with the tunics," Marvin agreed.

Jonah hadn't known that about the mage tunics, but it made sense. And it also raised an interesting question. "My best friend put on my coat before I did. He wore it for Halloween." Jonah's face warmed as the other kids laughed. "I think it adjusted to him and then to me when I finally tried it on."

"Was he magical or gifted?" Eidelman asked.

"Yeah." Jonah smiled. "He's my Seeker, the one who made that codex."

Eidelman's eyes widened.

"Wow," Monisha said. "You never told us about him."

AJ nudged Jonah's shoulder. "Why didn't you wear the coat for Halloween? That would have been cool."

Jonah's ears warmed even more. "I went as a Grim Guard."

Eidelman hissed while Trueblood gave Jonah a keen look. *That's right,* Jonah recalled, *Trueblood and Marcus were on a mission and never saw my Halloween costume.* Like the mage, AJ seemed to get the reference.

Monisha huffed, looking impressed as much as pissed. "So why does Jonah get a long coat?"

"He's Half-Reaper," Kevin explained, gesturing at himself and the other Fallen Reaper.

The glum looks on her and Darren's faces forced Jonah to wonder if the whole setup was unfair. "But why can't other people wear them?"

Eidelman stared at Jonah. "We wear the Reaper long coats and mages wear the tunics that are also enchanted. That's the way it's been for decades."

"What about us?" AJ asked. "I'm not a mage or a Fallen Reaper, but I'm magical, and Darren and Monisha are gifted."

"Yeah," Monisha joined in. "And why don't the Memory Charmers get a coat or tunic?"

"I don't know." The Fallen Reaper looked baffled, as if no one had ever asked this.

Trueblood raised his hands to get their attention. "First, Councilor Bertonneau made the decision not to have Memory Charmers brand themselves in any way. They can affect the minds and memories of others. That's not something to parade around, and the Council agreed." The mage took a deep breath. "As for individuals with a single power or ability, most have chosen to keep their lives as normal as possible."

The very sight of the flustered adults awoke something inside Jonah. "Are you sure? Maybe they didn't have a choice since they weren't mages or Fallen Reapers. They're like second-class Alliance members."

"That's an astute observation." Trueblood let out a small sigh. "I'm afraid the structure of our Alliance may have coerced some into acting normal while others can strut around like we're the elite."

Eidelman stirred, but Trueblood motioned him to stay silent.

"No one ever tried to change it?" Jonah asked.

"We've just settled into our little groups. In a way, you and your friends represent a change that we'll have to face."

Although the mage didn't say it outright, Jonah could sense the unspoken sentiment. Things were different this time because he was here. Once again, the pressure of expectation weighed on him. Everyone thought he'd do something big to change everything.

Trueblood clapped his hands, dispelling the tension. "I think we should get back, don't you?"

Jonah didn't know if the mage had used a spell or not, but he did feel less irritable and was ready to head back to camp.

Kevin leaned close to him. "Didn't I tell you to stop causing trouble?"

Eidelman activated the codex before Jonah could respond, returning them to Camp Alliance two hours before dinner.

The Flint River group didn't feel like swimming, considering they spent the day on the river and sometimes in it. They all changed out of their damp clothes and lounged in the common area. And, of course, he and AJ had to tell Eddy all about the river attack.

When Jonah headed to the snack table to get some juices, Mitchell came over. The mage had been standing in the atrium talking with the Healer. Jonah noted the man looked exhausted. That was something, considering Fallen Reapers had extraordinary stamina.

Suspecting Mitchell wanted to ask him a question, Jonah lingered over the snacks.

Mitchell glanced at AJ and Eddy while filling a cup with coffee from the carafes at the next table. He took a sip before saying, "I guess you told your friend about the river adventure?"

The tired voice caused Jonah to wonder if the Fallen Reaper got any sleep. "Yeah. Everyone knows," Jonah added, a little defensive.

"Of course," Mitchell smiled and sipped more coffee. "You know, the phantoms attacked to keep you from finishing the Tales. That's how important that document is to our enemies."

"I'm almost there." Jonah put as much sincerity in his voice as he could but feared Mitchell sensed the lie.

The young mages came downstairs at that moment. Mitchell watched them as if hesitant to say any more. With an abrupt nod to Jonah, he headed for the exit. That was odd, Jonah thought, going back to his friends. AJ wanted to know about the brief conversation, but thankfully, Marvin came over.

"Let's play cards," the outgoing mage announced, pulling out a chair. He waved over Beraki and Crosby, who hovered in the background.

"Someone can have my seat," Jonah offered.

"No way. Sit," Eddy ordered him.

Jonah did, and he had to admit after a while, it was fun. The mages were pretty cool and after all, just like them. Crosby turned out to be a true sci-fi nerd and discussed his favorite movies with the group.

During a lull in the conversation, Eddy caught the boy sneaking glances at Monisha and poked him in the side. "You want our buddy Darren to break you in two?"

Crosby blushed, causing everyone to roar with laughter.

Though Beraki laughed, he didn't rag his friend. Watching this, Jonah realized the quiet guy probably didn't like attention on himself. But Marvin thrived in the spotlight.

"Where you all from?" he asked.

AJ and Eddy recounted what they had told Jonah on their first day at camp.

Marvin listened, then barked out a laugh as he slapped his cards, faceup, on the table. "Ha! I'm out." He grinned at everyone. "Count up the points, gentlemen."

Jonah's hand was awful and set him back enough that he'd never win this round. He leaned back against his chair as Marvin shuffled the deck.

"What about you?" Jonah asked the obviously extroverted mage, who had more of a Southern accent once he relaxed.

"I'm from the ATL. Big family," Marvin announced and dealt the cards. "My folks don't know anything about my powers." He glanced up at Jonah. "Church folk. You know the kind? They'd think I had the devil in me or something."

Marvin laughed it off, but Jonah could see the tension in the boy's movements.

"I have a sister," AJ said, holding up one slender finger. "She's older than I am and thinks she's smarter." He paused a moment to arrange the cards in his hand. "My parents are scientists for the government and moved us all over the place. They'd never understand magic."

"Yeah. But traveling had to be nice." Marvin eyed him.

AJ shrugged. "It was alright, I guess."

The boy's comment didn't fool Jonah at all. He knew AJ soaked up all the information he could in each location the family had traveled.

"My parents don't know about me either," Eddy chimed in, studying his cards. "It's hard to hide your power with a cousin and four brothers and sisters at home. Someone's always around."

"Whoa, dude." Marvin nudged him.

"I like it in the summer program and camp," Eddy said, looking a little guilty. "I got space here and all I can eat!" He wiggled his eyebrows.

Marvin grinned and glanced at Jonah and then quickly away without asking about his family.

Jonah suspected the mage already knew about his dead parents. Not wanting to bring down the mood, he said, "Well, I got lucky with my aunt's church. They thought my thing was a gift from God."

Marvin paused as he set down the deck. "For real?"

"Yep." As they played the next round of cards, Jonah told the boys about his trip to the state park his first summer in Mount Vernon. As he talked about his aunt, uncle, and cousins, he relaxed.

Everyone had a ball until Thomas and Jennifer entered the common room, with Alex and Vanay trailing behind them. Jonah noted Jennifer's snide expression at once and glared back at her.

Thomas paused by the table, took in the cards with a frown, and motioned Marvin, Crosby, and Beraki to follow. The boys jumped to their feet. Crosby gave them a what-can-I-do look. Marvin, being bolder, at least waved before he stepped into line and trooped upstairs with the others.

Eddy stared open-mouthed at the departing mages. "Dang."

Darren strolled over with Monisha, a smirk on his face. "You shouldn't try to get too close to those guys."

Jonah shook his head. "*Those* guys were cool. And Alex seems okay in Team Building."

"Yeah," Darren said, rubbing his chin. "They're cool until Thomas snaps his fingers, and they go running like little puppies."

"That's not fair, Darren. Thomas saved us at HQ, remember?"

"Yeah, I know. Which is why I don't get him sometimes. But remember what Trueblood said? Who else besides us knew we were on the canoe trip?" The big guy nodded toward the stairs, then glanced at AJ. "I'm glad you aren't part of that crew."

Monisha patted Darren's arm and nodded in agreement. "And everyone can see that Jennifer girl has it in for you, Jonah."

Hearing someone else voice his concern about Jennifer without knowing all the details reassured Jonah.

Unable to find anything else negative to say about the young mages, Darren and Monisha crossed the room to sit near the large back window, alone.

Eddy threw down his useless hand. "Who knocked Darren's ice cream on the ground?"

Jonah wanted to defend the mages, yet he couldn't deny Darren's point. He noted the thoughtful expression on AJ's face and asked, "Do you think he's right?"

AJ shrugged and tore the sheet of paper with their scores out of his notebook. "I'm sure Thomas knew where we were going, but he's a mentor and I don't think he works with the mole. The Phantoms tried to hurt Beraki and Marvin. And before you say it, I'm sure they're keeping an eye on Jennifer."

"Yeah, maybe," Jonah agreed, watching the stairs. "Still, I wonder what they're doing?"

AJ gave them a lopsided grin. "Probably plotting something else awful for you."

When he came down for breakfast on Sunday morning, Jonah was in for a surprise. Someone had posted a stylish, printed sign at the end of the breakfast table announcing a nondenominational service. He thought that was an odd event for Camp Alliance and shook his head as he chose cereal and crossed to his usual table. Eddy was already into his second helping of eggs and bacon.

Jonah tapped Eddy's glass. "Did you see that sign at the buffet table?"

"Yep," Eddy said. He swallowed the rest of his food before adding, "I'm gonna go."

"A church service?" Jonah poured his cereal and milk in the bowl while considering going himself. Aunt Imma would like it if he did. Plus, with Eddy going, the service would be fun. "Do you think AJ will go?"

Eddy paused with a strip of bacon hanging out of his mouth. It slipped free when he tried to talk. "Oh, AJ will be there. You'll see."

"Cool. I'm in." Eddy's comment mystified Jonah, but he decided to wait to discover what his friend meant.

After the boys had changed into nice, casual clothes, they crossed the courtyard to the main Pavilion. The number of people already inside amazed Jonah. The only changes from the usual classroom setup were the large stardust sculpture in front of the history mural and a slender black podium.

Most shocking was the source of soft piano music. AJ sat on stage right, behind his keyboard, playing hymns. The way he nodded to people while his slender hands never ceased producing harmonies impressed Jonah.

He glanced sideways at Eddy. "You knew."

Eddy didn't answer as he continued down the center aisle and toward the second row.

Camp staff sat in the front row. Thomas and a couple of his mages sat across from the adults. Jonah smiled at not seeing Jennifer, only to have the girl ruin the moment by striding into the pavilion with the rest of her group.

The boys wore slacks and polo shirts. Jennifer had donned a more elaborate headdress today with vivid oranges, yellows, greens, and mango colors. Her traditional tribal dress was a deep tangerine. A lot of people watched as she took a seat.

Jonah's group grabbed the two rows behind Sterne and Albrecht. AJ's music continued while late arrivals filled the remaining seats. Soon, everyone waited in anticipation. Finally, a door beside the front mural opened, and Trueblood entered, carrying a sizable black Bible. He also wore a black robe with a multicolored clergy stole around his neck.

"No way." Eddy sounded as shocked as Jonah felt.

Trueblood stood behind the podium, placed the Bible on it, and clasped his hands. "For those of you too shocked to ask," he paused as people chuckled, "I'm an ordained minister."

Jonah whispered to Eddy. "Yes, way."

Trueblood conducted a nondenominational service in which he talked about God but used names like Divine Source and things like that. The gathered crowd sang a variety of hymns from different denominations.

As they worked through the final song, Jonah heard Monisha and Lisa harmonizing. Their voices drew appreciative glances from those closest to the girls. Meanwhile, Jennifer didn't look too enthused by the services, nor did Marvin. With all they knew about the Afterworld, Jonah thought the other kids should have more open minds.

An open mind. The very idea brought back Trueblood's comments on the Flint River, causing Jonah to lose his place in the song. He was more convinced than ever that the mage intentionally did that to open his eyes.

The question was, had the mage done that to help Jonah with the Tales, or to open his awareness to the larger things going on around him?

CHAPTER TWENTY-EIGHT
NET DARKNESS

Eddy's back gate token lay on the floor in front of the closet. Jonah gazed at it a moment before shaking his head. The thing must have slipped out of Eddy's trunks when he changed for bed. Right now, he was in AJ's room.

Jonah plucked up the token and thought of barging across the hall to embarrass his friend when another idea occurred to him. Crossing to his bed, he picked up his token, which he kept on the bedside table. He got in bed and held up both, searching for their names.

Finally, after staring at the tokens from every angle, he spotted the tiny names on the innermost edge. "Wow."

Jonah put Eddie's talisman on the bedside table but lay back with his token on his chest. He spent some time thinking about the level of magic required to imprint their names on objects. Could Wick do something like this for the club? Long before Eddy slipped into the room, Jonah's eyes closed, and he slept.

The next conscious moment, he dream-walked. This time, he stood on the bamboo path near the back gate. The last person he wanted to see also stood there. Alastor pressed his staff key against the proper bar, making the actual gate appear. When he looked around, Jonah froze.

After several tense moments, the devious man stepped through the open gate. Jonah found himself in a dilemma. He wanted to follow Alastor and find out what the guy had planned. However, even with the gate open, the camp wards would stop him without a talisman, even in a spirit body.

That's when Jonah realized he held something clutched in his left fist. Opening his hand, he saw his glowing token.

Of course! He'd fallen asleep with it resting on his chest. He hurried forward and through the gate, not sure this would work. But it did! Jonah's excitement at the discovery only lasted until the gate clanked shut. Even with the astral token, he didn't have a key for the gate. Before the panic set in, Alastor phased. Jonah put aside his concern over the gate and followed.

Moments later, he reappeared in the darkened forest-covered hillside. Alastor had stopped near a large tree, watching the way ahead. Following the man's gaze, Jonah saw a circle of blue fire scattered around a section of woods.

A dark shape moved past one of the flames, and Jonah recognized Mage Rubio's stocky features. The mage strode through the trees, inspecting bright spots on several trunks. Jonah moved closer to get a better view and to put distance between himself and Alastor. He discovered the bright spots were glowing sigils burned into trees.

Rubio finished his inspection and turned in Jonah's direction. "Are the rest of the sigils done?"

Jonah whirled around just as Thomas jogged right by him and into the supernatural light.

The boy wiped the beaded sweat from his brow. "Yes, sir."

"Excellent." Rubio gave him an energetic nod. "I'm taking part in the overnight test tomorrow." He clapped his hands together in anticipation. "We have a big surprise planned for the hikers. I trust any mages chosen will perform well."

"They will," Thomas said and looked off into the darkness.

Nearby, leaves crunched a few seconds before Jennifer entered the flickering light wearing a simple head wrap. No doubt she worried the more elaborate ones could snag on a branch in the dark.

Jonah's insides squirmed when Alastor also stepped into view. With Mage Rubio too focused on whatever he had up his sleeve to detect him, Jonah repositioned himself behind a different tree.

"What are you doing here?" Thomas asked. At first, Jonah thought he spoke to Jennifer, but Alastor smiled at the young Alliance Mage.

"I'm here to represent the Campmaster. He wants to make sure the net is in place."

Thomas shook his head, disgust evident on his shadowy face. "Don't you think this net kind of unfair?"

"Oh please, Thomas," Jennifer scoffed. "Like you care about the Blackstone brat, aside from a chance to play the hero."

Jonah bristled at the comment. The only other person to call him a brat was the Alliance Mole.

"You aren't supposed to be here," Thomas said to her. "Get back to your dorm room."

"The net isn't aimed only at Blackstone. It also dampens a mage's ability to do much more than simple spells, Thomas. Now, stand back!" Rubio commanded, ending the little argument.

Thomas and the others stepped farther into the darkness, strangely mimicking Jonah's move.

Rubio held up his hand and shouted, "*Nishati*," in his military voice.

A beam of energy shot from his raised hand and struck the nearest tree, causing the sigil to flare with magical power. A line of energy shot from that tree in two directions, connecting with other trees around the hillside.

Staring at the nearest glowing symbols, Jonah finally recognized the sigil to prevent a Fallen Reaper from phasing in or out of the area covered by the net. At that moment, high overhead, the lines of energy crisscrossed each other, making a bright red net. Pain exploded in Jonah's head, not only from his Death Sense but from an intense spike behind his eyes. It was the same pain he had experienced in the failed dream-walk about Alastor and the Campmaster.

More ominous to Jonah, the lower the energy net descended, the greater his pain, until he cried out. Alastor's head snapped around to look right at him, but the next second, the hilltop disappeared, and Jonah smacked into a glowing, solid wall.

His astral body recoiled and landed on the ground. His entire front ached with pain, and his head throbbed. He bent over as nausea hit, but when he heaved, nothing came out. Distantly, he realized his physical body threw up. All at once, he began choking.

He gasped for breath while clutching his throat. He had to get the gate open! What would happen to his astral body if his mortal body died? He took another painful heave.

Someone ran up to the gate. *Jennifer.* She used a key to open it. Before he could wonder where she got a staff key, he felt the jerk on his spirit body, and the next second, he awoke back in his dorm room. He leaned on his side, coughing and gagging. Someone patted his back.

He smelled the vomit, but he didn't care as he sucked in a precious breath.

"Hey? You alright, dude?" Eddy said. "I heard you gagging and turned you on your side."

Jonah nodded as he squeaked out, "Get Kevin."

Eddy's footfalls retreated to the door. Before Jonah knew it, Kevin burst into the room.

"Go get him some water and a towel from the kitchen," Kevin ordered, moving around to the clean side of the bed to press a hand to Jonah's forehead. "What happened?"

"Dream-walk," Jonah managed in a weak voice.

Kevin's eyes widened. "Who was it about?"

"Rubio, Thomas, Alastor, and Jennifer. They're in the woods putting up an energy net to keep us out."

"Us?"

"Fallen Reapers," Jonah said.

"Are you sure?"

"Kevin! My dream-walks are never wrong."

Kevin stood as Eddy entered with the water and towel. After handing Jonah the cup of water, Kevin came around the bed, dropped the towel over the vomit, and used his foot to wipe it up.

"What's wrong?" Eddy asked. He screwed up his face and squeezed by Kevin to open the window.

"Bad dream." Kevin rolled the soiled towel into a ball and glanced out the door.

Jonah knew his boyfriend was thinking about the ward protecting the end of the hallway. He slowly sat up because his head still pounded. Wincing, he took time speaking. "Forget Thomas. You can prove Jennifer's outside."

Kevin shook his head. "She's with a Council member and her mentor. Plus, you said the Campmaster knows."

"I'll check," Eddy volunteered and sprinted from the room, only to yell in the hallway a minute later, followed by a heavy thud. By the time Kevin helped Jonah to the doorway, Darren and AJ had left their dorm and crossed to the opposite side of the second-floor balcony, where Eddy lay sprawled on the ground.

Everyone gazed at the green, translucent wall of energy blocking the entrance to the girl's side of the hallway.

"I don't get it," Eddy complained, rubbing his head and looking dazed. "The other one didn't push back that hard."

"Thomas put up the first one," AJ pointed out. "I bet this one was all Jennifer. I've heard her talking about being the best at this type of magic."

Jonah peered at the green wall of energy as he came over. "Yeah," he agreed, keeping his voice low. "She made a green shield that first day in Meditation class."

"We can yell and wake up Serena," Eddy suggested.

AJ shook his head. "She won't hear you, will she, Jonah?"

"No, and she won't be able to take it down." Jonah moved right up to the barrier, causing the faint sigils to grow more distinct. "Jennifer's the only one with a talisman to get through."

Darren cracked his knuckles, looking prepared to hit something. "If she's hurt Monisha or Lisa, I'll break her neck. Magic or no magic."

Jonah believed the boy could do that at this moment.

"They're fine," Kevin offered.

Eddy snorted, then backed away when Darren glared at him. "What I don't get," he said in a hurry, "is why use a ward if she has permission to be outside?"

"Because she's evil," Jonah said, though he agreed with Eddy. He turned on Kevin. "This isn't fair. You know it'll have something to do with me."

Kevin raised a cautioning eyebrow, but Jonah had already told the guys everything.

"We should tell Mage Trueblood," Eddy suggested.

"First of all," Kevin said, "he isn't here."

The boys stared at him in disbelief.

"Where is he?" Jonah asked.

"Busy."

"What about Albrecht?" AJ pressed.

"He's in a staff cabin on the other side of the camp. Besides, it won't matter. Rubio will say he gave Jennifer special permission to go outside the camp. He's her sponsor."

Reacting to their disappointed faces, Kevin added, "I'll tell Trueblood when he comes back in the morning, and he'll decide what to do. Okay?"

Darren and AJ still looked mutinous. "But—"

"If you two try anything stupid," Kevin warned, "the Campmaster will send you home. Do you want that?"

"No," Darren muttered. AJ nodded, never taking his eyes off the ward.

"Then go to bed." Kevin motioned them back.

Eddy, Darren, and AJ crossed to their rooms, went inside, and closed the doors, leaving Jonah alone in the hallway with Kevin.

Feeling he was too paranoid, he turned to say something, when Kevin covered his mouth. "For the last time, you stop causing mutinies."

Jonah smacked the boy's hand away. "I didn't do anything."

In response, Kevin pulled him close to kiss him but pulled back. "Ah, you need to wash out your mouth."

"Oh, thanks," Jonah mumbled, trying not to open his mouth too far. Kevin grinned and kissed him on the neck instead.

Stunned and excited now, Jonah nodded and turned to his room when he heard the quiet click of AJ's door closing. Jonah froze. Had the observant boy peeked out the door? Or was it Darren? Did they see the kiss with Kevin? Jonah didn't know what to do.

Before he could change his mind, he crossed to their door, his heart thudding in his chest.

AJ opened it before Jonah could knock. "What's up?"

"Ah, did you…" Jonah gulped. "I thought I heard your door close."

"Yeah, when I came in here a few minutes ago. Why?" AJ peeked out the door and offered Jonah a stick of gum. "Did something else happen?"

There it was, Jonah thought. The opening. "Nothing. Just saying good night." He took the gum and backed toward his door, hating himself for chickening out.

"You sure?" AJ's voice shook with a hint of disappointment.

They peered at each other, unblinking. Without thinking about it, Jonah opened his Reaper gaze and knew at once. The emotion he saw wasn't the same intense attraction Kevin shared with him. AJ was more uncertain, but the longing was there. Just as quick, Jonah released the Reaper stare, feeling guilty. He never did this to a friend or family.

"Wow," AJ said, stepping into the hall and pointing at Jonah's face. "Your gaze went out of focus. What was that?"

"Nothing." Jonah gripped his doorknob.

"Please," AJ said. "Tell me."

"Shhh. Kevin will hear you," Jonah whispered. "And Eddy's inside."

AJ's shoulders slumped a little, and he twisted his hands together.

Jonah swallowed hard. "I'll see you in the morning." He slipped inside his room. Closing the door, he leaned against it, listening and trying to ignore his rapid heartbeat. He sensed AJ just outside, not moving. Would the boy knock? What would he do then?

The click of AJ's door closing was a relief, and Jonah crossed to the bed while crushing the gum in his hand without realizing it. He replayed every conversation he'd had with AJ at camp. So his friend had seen Kevin and him kiss. Part of Jonah wished he had suggested they go to one of the second-floor sitting areas or even downstairs to talk.

At the same time, he suspected that a bad idea. He had sensed AJ's real emotions underneath, and well, Jonah was afraid something would happen. And how could he do that when he already had a boyfriend? The situation was so complicated and unexpected that he wished he could talk to Mike, but he couldn't, not until next week.

Wait! Mike was his Seeker. He could reach out to his best friend from anywhere. Lying in bed, he closed his eyes, pictured Mike, and reached out with his mind.

"Mike, can you hear me?" he whispered. "Mike?" Jonah sensed the abrupt awareness, but it was distant and weak. He strained, but the interference seemed to increase. Dumb, dumb, dumb! The wards over the camp prevented them from connecting.

Out there, in Florida, Mike had sensed his call, but couldn't come to him. Frustration welled up inside Jonah at the feeling of being cut off. He rolled over and stared at the window while his mind raced with too many thoughts.

Despite Kevin's warning, he retreated into the calm of his Reaper side so he could at least rest.

Arriving for breakfast before most of the other campers, Jonah looked forward to reading more of the Tales. That task wasn't easy with his late-night dream-walk intruding on his mind. Choosing his breakfast of scrambled eggs and bacon, he sat at his regular table.

A sharp bark of laughter drew his attention. The camp teachers were already at the staff table. Rubio and the Campmaster talked like old buddies trading stories.

Wishing he had some earbuds, Jonah tried to tune them out and read before the others arrived for breakfast. He didn't get far before Trueblood entered the room and crossed to the table.

"Kevin told me everything, including that Jennifer erected a barrier."

Jonah put the triptych aside. "Are you gonna make her take it down?"

"Thomas says it's for training," Trueblood explained, "so she'll be able to keep it, only at her end of the hall near her door, just as the guys did on your side."

Irritated, Jonah lowered his fork. Glancing at the head table, he asked, "What can I do about the other thing?"

"You keep to your lessons. Nothing changes as far as that is concerned."

"But the dreams always mean something's up."

"I also know that you have to wait and see how things work out," Trueblood said. "At least now you're prepared for what comes."

That was true, Jonah thought, slumping in his chair.

The mage searched his face. "A lot of people would love to have your gift."

How could Trueblood expect him to look on the bright side, Jonah wondered, when his dream-walks often led to something terrible happening?

"You're here to learn to use them," Trueblood added. "Never forget that. By the way, make sure you put aside your talisman before bed."

Jonah should have known Trueblood would figure out how he had dream-walked outside the camp. Recalling how the camp's ward prevented his soul from returning to his body, Jonah wasn't going to argue. "Yes, sir."

Trueblood moved to the staff table, where he greeted Rubio, showing no hesitation in his movements.

Was the mage demonstrating how he should act around the others? Picking up his fork, Jonah dug into his breakfast again, giving that some thought. Maybe it was better to know what the enemy was up to while not revealing your hand. But he couldn't accept the idea of Jennifer walking around as if nothing had happened.

He pushed his cold eggs away just as the other guys entered the dining room, with Kevin walking behind them. As soon as they piled their plates with food, AJ and Eddy came over to the table.

AJ mumbled good morning and quickly focused on his food, leaving it for Eddy to ask, "What did he say?"

Jonah held up a hand and checked the staff table. Mandara had his head turned away from them while talking to Trueblood. Tapping his ear, Jonah nodded toward the adults.

Eddy's eyes widened. "That's right he can—"

AJ poked him hard in the side. "Don't say it. Gee-whiz."

"Sorry." Eddy turned back to Jonah. "Well?"

"Trueblood says work on our classes."

"That's it?"

"What did you expect?" AJ threatened to poke Eddy again.

"Okay! I get it. What's wrong with you this morning?"

"Nothing," AJ lied, his face blushing a little. "We just have to see what happens, right?" He met Jonah's gaze for a moment before focusing on his breakfast.

"Yeah," Jonah agreed, not liking either situation.

CHAPTER TWENTY-NINE
SPIRIT OF LOVE

Being alone was something every introvert understood and craved at times. Jonah certainly wanted ed that as he crossed the courtyard, on his way to the History of the Afterworld. He didn't feel like waiting for Eddy this morning, who had misplaced his back gate token. Avoiding AJ was easier, considering the boy talked to Lisa while refusing to look Jonah's way.

The profusion of birdcalls floating out of the morning shadows in the maze soothed his guilt over ditching his friends. While Jonah enjoyed the natural sounds, he also focused, keeping his senses alert.

The only warning that someone crept upon him was the double, long shadows on the soft stone. Not sensing danger, he relaxed, knowing Jennifer wasn't about to try something again.

Just as he reached the History Pavilion, Eddy clapped him on the right shoulder. "What's up, dude?"

"Nothing. Why?"

Eddy leaned forward over Jonah's left shoulder, looking him in the face. "You didn't wait for us."

Glancing back, Jonah confirmed AJ had followed his friend. "Oh. Sorry," Jonah hedged. "I got a lot on my mind."

"Blood Mountain?" AJ studied Jonah's expression but refused to say anything else.

Eddy blew out an exaggerated breath. "AJ figured you might wanna ask Sterne about it."

"He's a supernatural historian," Jonah pointed out. "Not a regular historian."

"The story involved the supernatural," AJ countered, then went silent again, like he remembered he wasn't talking to Jonah.

"Maybe Sterne's heard about the mountain's history," Eddy offered, watching both boys.

Jonah considered the point as they entered the pavilion and took their usual seats. Darren, Monisha, and Lisa arrived a short time later. As expected, the mages marched into the room and sat across from Jonah and his crew. The group kept their eyes on the front and sat straight in their seats.

Eddy tapped Jonah. "Do you think Thomas warned them to stay away from us?"

"Maybe Jennifer did it," Jonah whispered. He didn't have time to give it any more thought because Sterne clumped into the room. When the Councilor reached the small desk, he rapped the head of his cane against the tabletop.

"Class is in session." Sterne activated the projector. "Today, we will talk about oaths and agreements among supernatural beings." The heavy man sat on the edge of the table, taking the pressure off his bum leg. "All of you are of age, meaning you're older than thirteen."

A few people chuckled. Jennifer actually glanced back at Jonah with a smirk.

Except for Beraki, Jonah was the youngest person there.

"Why is that important, you may ask?" Sterne continued. "The age of thirteen has been the traditional age when powers manifest themselves. No one knows how far back this goes, but there it is. When a person with supernatural abilities reaches that age, any formal oath or promise takes on a new meaning."

Jonah sat straighter in his chair because this was the type of information he craved. While he knew about oaths, he had deeper questions about how they worked. In particular, he wanted to understand his connection to Kevin and the immediate reaction to any promises they made with each other.

Sterne waved his hands in the air as he talked. "The very forces of the universe, or whatever makes your abilities possible; that source is engaged when you speak an oath or promise. It creates a binding oath on you and your powers. As a result, all of you must understand the dangers of making careless promises to other beings with powers."

Eddy's hand shot up into the air. "Sir?"

"Yes, Mr. Corvera."

"Does that apply to family members? I mean, if they don't have powers?"

Sterne searched Eddy's face. "A promise made between a supernatural and nonsupernatural sibling would not be binding, in my opinion. However, a promise made to a parent or by a parent to you may carry additional importance above a simple promise between regular mortals.”

Monisha’s hand went up. Sterne pointed to her. “Yes, Ms. Owens?”

“How can that be if they don’t have powers?”

“Love is the most potent force in the universe, Ms. Owens. None of us truly understands it, but only a fool would deny its power. A parent’s love for a child can be the most powerful of all.” Sterne turned his gaze back to Eddy. “I’m afraid, Mr. Corvera, that whatever you so obviously promised your parents, you’ll have to keep.”

Hearing the teacher’s response, Eddy lowered his head, apparently deep in thought.

Jonah raised his hand next.

“Yes, Mr. Blackstone?”

“What about other types of love?” Jonah didn’t intend to ask the question; it just came out on its own.

Everyone turned in their seats to watch him. Jonah saw a few smirks, and his face grew warm, but he couldn’t take back the question now.

Sterne scratched one of his ears, and Jonah wondered if the man preferred not to get into this subject. “What type of love, Mr. Blackstone?”

“You know,” Jonah glanced around. “Love, love.”

“Be specific, Mr. Blackstone. Do you mean romantic love?” Jonah nodded and slid low in his chair under the pressure of everyone’s gaze.

"Yes, romantic love. You can make that type of bond, but please understand that love between two individuals can only strengthen an oath. Does that answer your question?" Jonah nodded, and Sterne continued, "Oaths and promises in the supernatural world function the same as contracts in the mortal world."

At that point, the Councilor mentioned things Marcus had told Jonah, only with more detail. Jonah took lots of notes while ignoring the occasional looks from the others, including covert glances from AJ. Certain that he'd be the talk around the camp for the rest of the day, he wanted to kick himself for asking his question.

When class ended, Jonah held back. AJ and Eddy noticed and paused at the door. "I need to ask Sterne a question," Jonah told them.

Eddy frowned. "For what?"

"Just go on. Hey, get my hiking pack for me, okay?"

Eddy subjected Jonah to a curious look. "Sure."

After the boys left the building, Jonah waited quietly for Sterne to collect his things. He could feel the time slipping by, but he had to risk being late.

The Councilor eventually finished with turning off the projector. That's when he noticed Jonah. "You have another session, Mr. Blackstone. Is there a problem?"

"Yes, sir. It's about my question in class."

Sterne leaned against his desk, waiting.

"Can two people have a strong reaction to a simple promise, even if they just met?"

Sterne rubbed his chin, causing his jowls to move up and down. "You mean love at first sight?"

"No," Jonah lied, embarrassed. "Just a strong reaction."

"It's possible." Sterne tapped his cane against the floor, thinking. "I understand. You're at that age when these things can overshadow all else. Since I don't have any special power, this rule doesn't affect me. You should ask Mage Trueblood. He seems to get on well with you. And he knows more about this than I."

Jonah nodded, thinking that was a good idea.

Running full out, Jonah reached the back gate just as the others prepared to leave. Trueblood paused to let him slip into line; then the mage stepped through the gate and led the class around the camp to the south along a fast-moving stream.

As the group followed the stream's course into a new set of hills, Jonah's mind returned to the information about oaths. His godfather mentioned nothing about love. And considering the quiet comments and smirks from his friends, Jonah lost his nerve to ask Trueblood about it.

He was so lost in his own thoughts that, without realizing it, he found himself walking beside the teacher. Confused, Jonah looked around and realized the others hung back as a group, leaving him to catch up with Trueblood. Even more telling, no one met his gaze except Monisha, who grinned.

Jonah didn't get it until he turned around to discover the mage holding an open leather pouch toward him.

"Eddy misplaced his token," Trueblood explained. "We found it, but I decided to offer everyone a way to secure their talismans."

Jonah peeked into the pouch. It contained various lengths of leather strings, a few lanyards made of knotted leather with clasps, and two thin wrist straps, also of leather. Those had Native American symbols burned into the deep tan surfaces.

"Wow," Jonah said, picking through the offerings.

"I was worried you might not have much of a choice, given that the mages also took pieces."

After Jonah quickly chose a wrist strap, Trueblood pulled the drawstring on the pouch and reattached it to his belt. "May I borrow your token?"

Jonah handed over his token and the wrist strap. He watched, fascinated, as Trueblood secured the token to a holder that made the leather piece resemble a thin watch and band. The mage handed it back.

Slipping on the band, Jonah used the drawstrings that connected the two ends of the straps to tighten it around his wrist. The leather wasn't stiff, and the band felt cool against his skin. "I like this."

"My sister, Eleanor, made the straps. I'll pass along your compliment." Proving he had a sixth sense when it came to determining people's moods, Trueblood asked. "What troubles you today, Jonah?"

"He's in love," Darren said from right behind them, causing Monisha to giggle.

Giving the duo a rare severe look, Trueblood pointed out ahead. "Darren, why don't you and Monisha lead the group today? Take us out for about forty-five minutes, then find our way back. That'll be your test."

Darren's smile disappeared in an instant. "Yes, sir."

He and Monisha moved to the front of the group. As Trueblood held Jonah back, Lisa went by next, followed by Eddy, who flashed a smile. AJ paused to say something but thought better of it and hurried to catch up with the others.

Once the rest of the class pulled ahead and out of earshot, Trueblood started walking. "I can see from your expression that Darren wasn't exaggerating."

"I'm not in love. I just…"

"Yes?" Trueblood spread his arms when Jonah didn't explain. "I'm a certified youth counselor as well as an ordained minister. So, anything you say to me is covered in more ways than I can count."

Relaxing on hearing that, Jonah dived in. "Mr. Sterne told us about oaths and promises. He said love was the most powerful force in the universe, but he talked about families." Jonah lowered his voice. "I wanted to know about other types of love."

"I see."

Jonah didn't know if he liked the way the mage said that. The tone carried a lot of meaning. "Can two people who don't know each other have a strong reaction to an oath?"

"I'm assuming this is someone to whom you are attracted?" Trueblood glanced ahead.

Jonah's stomach clinched up because AJ's hesitation hadn't gone unnoticed by the mage. Unwilling to reveal too much of his feelings about Kevin or AJ, he was tempted to clam up. But he also wanted an answer, and Trueblood seemed willing to explain. His voice shook a little when he spoke. "I wasn't at first. Not when we made the promise, yet the feeling was so strong."

Trueblood folded his hands behind his back in a strangely contemplative pose.

"Jonah, there's a verse in the Christian Bible that talks about prayer and the Spirit. The author of the verse speaks of the Spirit, making utterances on behalf of the person praying, asking for the deep things that the person truly needs." Trueblood lapsed into silence again for a moment before continuing.

"I believe it happens all the time with oaths. It's why they are binding on supernatural and magical beings. The power of the universe understands the deepest meaning of the oath and binds us to it. If we break the agreement, then we court disaster, even the loss of power or life."

Jonah's eyes widened because he never knew a person could die from breaking an oath. That brought up a larger question for him. "How does that apply to love?"

"If two people who don't even know each other make an oath and have a strong reaction to it, I believe it's the power of the universe stepping in and revealing the deeper truth."

"You mean God?"

Trueblood smiled. "I'm sure your relatives call it God. As you heard at the service, there are other names for this energy."

"So, you're saying that this power, this energy, knew what we really wanted and that made the promise so strong?"

"Yes."

"Then it has nothing to do with being attracted to each other?"

Trueblood grinned at him. "You've found a soulmate."

Jonah stopped in his tracks. "For real? A soulmate? How can I meet a soulmate?" If Kevin were a soulmate, then he could trust his boyfriend, even when the Alliance interfered.

"This is about you and Kevin phasing in perfect sync last week, isn't it?"

A sudden knot of fear twisted Jonah's stomach, leaving him feeling exposed. He knew Trueblood suspected the truth that night at Alliance Headquarters.

The mage placed a hand on Jonah's shoulder, giving him an understanding look. "Marcus and Omar are two of my closest friends. I will never judge you if you have feelings for Kevin. How could I if the universe is bringing you two together?"

Jonah winced. "Is it obvious?"

"Ah, the eternal fear of all young people. I know what to look for, so…"

"Oh, that's great."

"Your new friends like you, Jonah. I'm sure you'd find acceptance among them if you'd be your whole self. This camp is about you learning to be your best self. We're here to help." Trueblood cocked his head to the side. "I'm curious. Why haven't you talked to Marcus about this issue? He would seem the perfect one to understand what you're going through."

"No way." Jonah couldn't see himself having this kind of talk with his godfather.

"You could always talk to Omar," the mage suggested.

Jonah wondered why he hadn't considered that before. Omar had told him to call if he had any questions.

"I bet," Trueblood said, eyeing him. "Omar will tell you the same thing I did. Talk to Marcus."

"We don't have any cell phones."

"You'll get a chance to call him on your third weekend. That is, if you stay out of trouble." Trueblood grinned.

"Cool. Then I'll try Omar."

The mage laughed and walked on.

Jonah followed, concerned that the others were out of sight. "They left us behind."

Trueblood shrugged. "Not a problem. They need to learn a thing or two about being quieter in the forest."

As Jonah watched, the mage barely made a sound moving through the trees. Even if he had made a sound, Jonah's friends made so much noise themselves they would never have heard anything. Trueblood used that to his advantage until he and Jonah appeared right behind the others. At that point, he whirled his right hand and produced a magically amplified clap.

Lisa yelled and levitated off the ground. AJ and Eddy whirled around, hands ready to cast fire or lightning. Darren and Monisha stood together, also prepared to fight. Trueblood stood tall and waited for the lesson to sink in. After their initial surprise and looks of shame for allowing the mage to sneak up on them, the group moved on.

Jonah noticed the glances they gave him, but no one was brave enough to ask what he and Trueblood had discussed. Yet Jonah expected AJ and Eddy would corner him later in the dorm room, so he started preparing a cover story.

A soulmate? Wow.

CHAPTER THIRTY
DESTINY'S FINAL BATTLE

"Who do you love?" Monisha crossed her arms like an interrogator and waited for an answer.

Jonah sensed Kevin nearby but refused to look, not with Monisha eyeing him. AJ hid behind a magazine. Then, to Jonah's horror, Eddy hooked an arm around his shoulders.

"We discovered our true feelings about each other," Eddy said sweetly, pressing his cheek against Jonah's.

Monisha's jaw dropped for a hot second before her eyes narrowed. Just as fast, she burst out laughing and pulled Lisa along with her to where Darren sat.

Jonah pushed Eddy away. "Why'd you do that? Now, everyone will start gossiping."

Eddy's eyes widened as he watched the girls. "You don't think Monisha likes you?"

Now Jonah laughed until Darren glanced his way and he stopped. Why did jealous boyfriends always come after him? He was about to complain about that when he caught AJ scrutinizing him.

Jonah gulped and gestured to Eddy. "Deal the cards."

But Eddy's attention was on the front door where the mentors had gathered to speak with an Alliance adult. They broke off their conversation when Trueblood came into the common area carrying a shiny clay bowl.

With all the talk about love, Jonah had forgotten Trueblood's promise to send campers out for a night in the forest. He sat up, studying the bowl. Painted symbols in greens and blues covered it, reminding him of a sunny day without actually picturing that. Given the bowl's handmade look, Jonah suspected a former camper made it.

"As a tradition, the beginning of the second week of camp means the start of overnight stays in the forest," Trueblood announced, holding the piece of pottery high. "This contains the names of everyone taking my Intro to Nature class. Tonight, I'll draw the first two people to go."

The mages sat up, clearly interested in the activity, even though they didn't take the Nature class. Trueblood shook the bowl, making sure all eyes were on him as he drew out a piece of paper.

"Eddy!" he announced.

Everyone clapped while AJ tapped a fist with Eddy.

Trueblood held the bowl high again and shook it. When he pulled the second piece of paper out, the mage hesitated before reading the name. "Darren."

Jonah's group clapped for Darren. Alex, Marvin, and Beraki were the only mages to applaud. Yet Jonah watched Trueblood because he noticed the flash of indecision.

When the mage gave him a guilty glance before turning to the others, Jonah knew. *He pulled my name.*

Plastering a smile on his face, Jonah turned to congratulate his campmate when a stilted clapping attracted everyone's attention. Quiet spread through the common room as the Campmaster entered with Alastor lurking behind him.

The serious man surveyed everyone and nodded to Trueblood. "Excellent choices for tonight."

Trueblood frowned at the Campmaster's tone. "It was random."

"Of course." Mandara's eyes passed over Jonah for a moment before he continued. "I want to make a change. Mr. Corvera will stay here tonight. I want a mage to go out with Mr. Watkins."

"The young mages haven't taken my nature class," Trueblood countered as he surveyed the campers.

Mandara smiled. "They received training last summer in basic wilderness survival techniques. They will do just fine."

"Cedric, I choose the campers going out."

"Yes, we can see that. I'm changing up the routine a little. Given your Team Building sessions, you should want to help the young people bond even more."

Raising his chin in a way that said he wouldn't take any more argument, Mandara said, "Good. Now I believe that trainee-mage Crenshaw will join Mr. Watkins." The man motioned to a stunned Marvin.

Jennifer was Darren's buddy in Team Building class, but Jonah thought the boy looked relieved to have Marvin going out instead.

"You have ten minutes to gather your hiking packs. Mage Trueblood will escort you to the back gate. Good luck."

Jonah didn't know if the Campmaster meant his last comment as genuine encouragement. Neither Darren nor Marvin smiled. Instead, they headed upstairs to get ready. Everyone fidgeted and whispered to each other, even after the Campmaster and Alastor left the building.

When the boys returned, the crowd followed them into the courtyard. A few more adults stood outside talking in informal groups, but they quieted to watch the campers' procession.

Exchanging quick goodbyes, Trueblood led Darren and Marvin away. No one else could go along, not even the mentors.

Eddy watched the glum faces around him in confusion. "It's just an overnight hike. Why's everyone so quiet?"

"It's the Campmaster," Jonah told Eddy in a tired voice. "The whole idea of staying in the forest overnight sounded fun until he jumped in the middle. Even Trueblood didn't like it."

He peeked at AJ, who had followed them back inside and to their favorite seats but hadn't said anything.

When Beraki and Crosby sauntered over, Eddy brightened. "Hey, you guys wanna play cards?"

Beraki pulled over a chair and sat down. Crosby shook his head but leaned against the back of his fellow mage's chair to watch. At Eddy's urging, AJ sat forward to shuffle the cards on autopilot, Jonah thought.

After several disappointing hands of cards, Jonah decided to let Crosby take his place, and turned in early. With the exciting evening ending, his mind returned to solving the riddle of the Tales. He stripped down to his boxers and paused before removing the leather wrist strap. Deciding to keep it on, for now, he grabbed the triptych and slipped into bed.

His spirits brightened when he saw the segment was about the big battle.

⊖

The Final Battle

With Destiny's consent, work began on the final resting place for her and the Protectors. The Second Oldest Brother oversaw everything and led the artisans in completing the tunnels, and the Hall of Remembrance. In the hall, etchings detailed all the stories of the other fallen Protectors as a testament to what had happened. They also completed the inner chambers that would serve as a shrine to the last of the Virtues.

The Eldest Brother never returned to the company of his younger siblings. The remaining four drew closer and worked with the Deliverer to protect their domain from the occasional raiders and minions of the Afterworld. In time, the Youngest Brother ventured far and wide outside their territory, hoping to persuade his lost brother to come home.

The day arrived when the Youngest Brother returned to the original encampment. When he appeared in Destiny's chamber, the Deliverer, and all present, approached the young man. "What have you found?"

The Youngest Brother regarded the Deliverer. "All people in the surrounding countryside who did not join the Evil One or flee were killed. Their lost souls were imprisoned in the Underworld lest they give aid to our mother Destiny."

"As I expected," the Deliverer replied. "Evil has descended on the mountain, and the Grim Reaper's power to sow fear has rolled over the land." He gripped the young man's shoulder. "But you, the Protectors, can resist that paralyzing fear."

"That is not the worst of it, brothers," the youngest continued. "I saw the KIN and agents of the Grand Oracle as well as the Wraiths. Many of the living and those that have passed beyond are rallying to overwhelm us."

More distress greeted these words, forcing the Deliverer to calm the people. "Your Eldest Brother has lost his way, but you four are strong in the rings' powers. You will prevail so that Destiny can sleep in peace."

Destiny regarded the Deliverer. "But how can we defeat such a large army?"

"It has been decreed that the balance be maintained. Your enemies will fall in great numbers on this mountain, so that those who come long after will remember and tremble."

The Deliverer's power shook the very walls of the cave. And the brothers, with rings glowing brightly, were fortified in their mission. Bearing witness to their renewed conviction, Destiny prepared herself for the battle and the long sleep to follow.

And it came to pass that the army of the Grim Reaper and Grand Oracle encompassed the entire base of the mountain. A hush fell over the countryside. Even the army of the Rulers of the Afterworld was quiet.

As the Deliverer maintained his vigil, a lone figure ascended the pathway to the encampment. The stranger wore all black with a white skull on the left breast and rode upon the back of a Grim Hound, a beast of the Underworld.

Stopping the stranger outside the encampment, the Deliverer forbade him to come any closer. The beast snapped and growled, but the Deliverer stood his ground.

The stranger dismounted and faced the Deliverer with an arrogant stance. "I was sent to offer you a way out. Give us Destiny and her Protectors, and you can leave here."

The man's words stoked anger in the Deliverer's chest. "Get you back to your Masters. I have been called for this very purpose. With the universe as a witness, I tell you that all gathered below will have no place for their souls in the Afterworld. Relent from the evil you would do, member of the KIN. It is not too late for even one, such as you."

The man scoffed at him, and his laugh caused the air to waver as a red mist appeared. It swirled faster and faster, descending on the KIN and fashioning itself into flowing red robes.

The Deliverer became alert, for he recognized the living robe. This stranger was the Grim Reaper!

The Evil One spoke in his true form. "All of you gathered here will die."

"Careful, Serapis," the Deliverer said, shaking his head and frowning.

"You dare use my mortal name?"

"You're just a Reaper with grand delusions."

The Grim Reaper raised his hands in fury. "I'll burn you and this entire mountain to the ground." He conjured red flames and hurled them at the Deliverer.

Yet the Protectors came to his aid, calling on the living flames from the cave's mouth. They sprang up as a wall between them and the Grim Reaper, who didn't stop the barrage.

The Deliverer stood his ground. "By your mouth, Serapis, you condemn yourself."

The Grim Reaper's fire was eaten by the living flames, which sprang forward and swirled around the Evil One. He fell to his knees but produced a shield so the flames did not consume him. As the air inside the shield wavered from intense heat, the Grim Reaper cried out, and his once smooth skin blistered.

The Deliverer held out a hand. "Relent from your evil, Serapis."

Filled with hatred, the Grim Reaper didn't relent, thus prolonging his agony until his screams echoed along the mountainside. Not until his burned skin had turned a reddish-bronze color did the man let the shield go and phase away.

The brothers inched forward, horror on their faces. The Deliverer turned to them. "The Evil One was sorely injured, but he will return. Therefore, we have to redouble our efforts in the extra time allotted us."

One hundred and fifty days from the encounter with the Grim Reaper, word came that the Afterworld army moved again toward the mountain to engage the Protectors and the Deliverer.

The battle was fierce, but the Protectors were unassailable. The Deliverer went between the realms, fighting and killing the KIN and Hunters seeking to use the aether as a passage into the very heart of the mountain.

In his betrayal, the Eldest Brother led the enemy through a gap and right to the encampment entrance. Mother Destiny was so distraught by her son's betrayal of his office that she strode into the battle.

Standing at the edge of the gap, she summoned lightning and fire from heaven and windstorms and hail to punish the invaders.

"You will not survive, oh, Mother," the Eldest Son declared.

The Deliverer discerned the Eldest Brother's strategy. His attack covered the approach of a powerful sorcerer who emerged to challenge Destiny. The man was an elemental and could control the lightning.

He drew a storm that struck the medallion. When Destiny stumbled under the assault, the Deliverer came to her aid.

"Stand aside, Deliverer," Destiny commanded. She rose to confront the elemental. Calling on her connection to the elements, she took control of the lightning and commanded it to strike her enemy. She defeated the sorcerer, but a crack marred her medallion from that day forward.

The Deliverer unleashed his fury and slew the KIN and Hunters with his fiery blades. When he captured the last KIN and slew him, the others retreated. The Wraiths were caught and killed by the Protectors so that they would never know anything beyond.

In all, over fifty thousand souls died on the gap in the mountain. The bodies were so high that the survivors' feet never touched the ground.

Weakened from the display of power, Mother Destiny allowed the Deliverer to hold her up. At that moment, the Youngest Brother appeared on the outcropping with the broken body of his slain Eldest Brother cradled in his arms.

He laid the body at his mother's feet, and she shed tears for her lost son. After a time, Destiny gathered herself and said to the others, "We won this battle, but not the war. It is time for us to sleep, as the Deliverer has said. We cannot continue to resist the Grim Reaper and Grande Oracle without my sisters."

The four brothers made ready to escort mother Destiny into the special chamber prepared for them. When they moved to take the body of their Eldest Brother, the Deliverer bid them stop.

"He must remain here, in the world, as a sentinel for what he has done."

The brothers wanted to argue, but Destiny agreed. "It will be so."

Once the others had gone beyond to the inner chamber to rest, the Deliverer raised his hands, sealing that room and the Hall of

Remembrance from the unworthy. To all but the Elect, the entrance into the mountain would seem a harmless, deep cave.

With the fallen brother's body and all the blood and bodies of the slain, the Deliverer called up a powerful spell. "I decree that no Shaman, Priest, Wraith, or any supernatural being may work their spells or power on this mountain until the time comes for another in the line of Deliverers to call forth the sleeping sisters."

The power flowed to his open palm, flared, then receded. In its place was a small, gnarled seed. He used his bare hand to dig a shallow hole to drop the seed inside. When he covered it over and stood back, a mature tree sprouted and grew up at the entrance to the cave, which was at the top of the gap.

"This tree will be the first," he intoned. "As it grows and others come, the prohibition will become a lasting barrier to all except mortals."

According to the Deliverer's decree, over time, the one tree multiplied, and the spell extended to the mountain's very base. No one of magical means, spirit, or member of the Afterworld could ever breach the barrier until the new Deliverer's time. Even the slain souls were imprisoned in the mountain so that all mortals who dared to claim this land became haunted and obsessed with war.

He who wrote of these things says, "May the Deliverer quicken your steps."

⊖

With a final swipe of his finger, Jonah came to the single animated star that still pulsed at the center of Deliverer's

Tales' last page. Holding his hand close to the surface, Jonah confirmed the heartbeat was still there. But the circle of five darkened stars remained dormant, like they were *asleep*.

That's it! Destiny and her sons, or the rings, went to sleep! Well, all except the one brother whose body remained in the mortal world. Jonah sat bolt upright in bed, reminding himself the Tales were about the supernatural objects. If a Protector remained in the mortal world, was that the Protector's Ring his parents had found? Somehow, Jonah knew it was true.

He was the Deliverer now, so he must be the one mentioned in the Tales. And the most exciting thing of all? There were four more Protector's Rings hidden with the Destiny Medallion!

CHAPTER THIRTY-ONE
DARREN'S RETURN

*F**our more Protector's Rings.*

Jonah leaned back from his breakfast, amazed by the thought. Of course, he knew there were over thirty rings out there. Mike's uncle, Mr. Hackett, the owner of the secondhand bookstore in Mount Vernon, had told them all about the rings nearly two years ago. Yet this was the first moment he had put it all together.

Reality settled in as Jonah focused on the Tales, still held loosely in his hand. His oatmeal and raisins sat half-eaten and growing colder by the minute, just like his search for clues.

When AJ and Eddy came downstairs for breakfast, Jonah gave up and put the triptych away. Staring at the unappealing oatmeal, he suddenly felt in the mood for something else. He returned to the food table loaded a plate with eggs and bacon.

As Jonah snatched a couple of slices of bread, he almost bumped into AJ, who also went to place his bread in the toaster. The boys awkwardly avoided meeting each other's gaze.

"I'll toast that for you," AJ offered.

Jonah's eyes widened in surprise. "Thanks." Waiting for Eddy to walk to their table, leaving them alone, he added, "We're cool, right?"

AJ paused before starting the toaster. "Yeah."

"I mean it," Jonah insisted in a whisper. "You gonna talk to me today?"

"I've been talking to you."

"Yeah, right. Not like before. Half the time you're just staring at me, and when you do say something, you act like I did something to you."

"I thought you didn't like attention," AJ shot back. Then a smile twitched the corners of his mouth. "Or, maybe you don't mind attention from me." And for a moment, AJ met Jonah's gaze before focusing on the toaster again.

"No, I don't mind it," Jonah answered. "I like it when you talk to me."

This time, AJ held his gaze, and the smile was unmistakable and genuine.

Jonah's heart skipped a beat as he crossed to the table, not bothering to hide his own smile.

Eddy noticed, glanced at AJ still at the bread table, and grinned. "Good, you two kissed and made up."

Jonah's face warmed because Eddy had no clue that an overseen kiss had led to the current awkwardness between friends.

"You think he'll teach us blades next?" Eddy gestured at Mitchell standing at the head table.

"I doubt it," Jonah answered. "I don't think he likes to use his blades."

"How do you know that?" Eddy said.

"I asked him." Jonah realized the Fallen Reaper had arrived while he talked with AJ at the food table. "He said he doesn't like dueling the KIN."

AJ dropped into his chair and slid Jonah's toast across the table on a small paper plate. Not only had he toasted the bread, but he also spread strawberry jam on it.

"Thanks," Jonah said, wondering how AJ knew he liked strawberry jam until he realized his friend had been observant again. Jonah dug into his breakfast and had a mouth full of food when Mitchell approached their table.

"Hello, gentlemen. How's the camp going?"

"It's cool," Jonah choked out as he tried to swallow his food. "I like it here."

"You fought the KIN?" Eddy blurted out.

"Once or twice, yes." Mitchell nodded, then turned his attention to Jonah. "I was just telling the Campmaster it's a shame that your cousin Lynn and her friend Wick could not come with you."

Staring at his food, Jonah carefully picked his next words. "They had other plans for the summer."

"As I said, it is a shame. I hear your cousin Lynn's a gifted blade user. And the young mage has already made shield bracelets. Maybe next summer?"

"Yeah, that would be cool." Jonah had been so focused on leaving camp that he never thought about coming back next year.

"Well, I am off to Headquarters," Mitchell announced. "Enjoy your second week at camp, gentlemen."

AJ stared after the Fallen Reaper before turning to Jonah. "You and your cousins get around, don't you?"

"What does that mean?" Jonah asked, catching the edge in his campmate's voice and suspecting the source. "You got a chance to work with the Alliance people in the Translations department. I never did that."

AJ didn't answer, and he also didn't talk much as they finished breakfast. Afterward, he cleared his plate and headed off to the Meditation session without waiting for them.

"What did I do wrong now?" Jonah whined to Eddy as they dumped their plates in the trash. "We were good like twenty minutes ago."

Eddy lowered his gaze as he headed to the front door. "Well, like he said. You get around."

"You mean he's jealous because I know these people? He knows Mitchell too." He walked beside his friend in a daze. He'd hoped they were past the awkwardness.

"Yeah, but you and Mitchell faced real KIN," Eddy pointed out.

The idea that some people envied his life had never occurred to Jonah. Surprisingly, he had received his deepest wish because his life was standard teen stuff most of the time. Then there were the terrifying short bursts of extreme danger when someone plotted to kill him.

"If AJ wants people threatening his family and friends, I'll swap places with him."

Eddy stopped. "Is that what happens?"

Jonah groaned. He'd avoided telling the others any truly personal details about the incidents in his life.

But his new friend deserved an answer. Jonah swallowed and said, "Well, it's like a bad movie where the villain tries to hurt the hero's friends to get to him."

Eddy's eyes widened, clearly reevaluating their current friendship.

To Jonah's relief, he laughed and said, "Well, I guess we don't have a choice, huh?"

"No, we don't," Jonah said.

"AJ will come around. He knows a lot of things," Eddy continued, "but you've been out there with some cool people. With everything you've done, AJ can't impress you and, well, I think he's a little jealous."

Jonah didn't think AJ jealous. He did think the boy wanted to impress him because of what he sensed the night AJ caught Kevin and him kissing. Of course, keeping that to himself, Jonah continued to ponder the rest of Eddy's comments as they left the compound.

Back home in Mount Vernon, Jonah's cousins and friends had decided to go along with him and investigate the things that happened. And the rest of the Mount Vernon Social Club wanted to be part of the action, too, even though they didn't have powers.

Despite his initial intentions, Jonah sensed a new group of kids developing around him at camp, all of whom had come here because they chose to fight.

He elbowed Eddy. "We have each other's back, right?"

"Yeah."

"Cool."

As for AJ, Jonah decided he would set things right.

—

Jonah's newfound determination to smooth out his friendship with AJ hit a snag in Meditation class. He tried to joke with AJ, but the boy remained quiet and wouldn't open up. Jonah thought he'd prefer an actual argument rather than nothing.

Eddy talked with Lisa near the door, purposely giving them a few minutes alone. Knowing he had little time before Bertonneau arrived, Jonah drummed his fingers on the open book AJ held. "You promised to talk to me today." The most reaction he got was a quick flick of AJ's eyes in his direction.

Taking that as progress, Jonah said, "So what. I know people. Most know me because of my parents. It's not fun and doesn't mean much to me." He waited. "My friends are what counts. It's not a competition, because all of you impress me."

AJ snorted. "Yeah, right."

Glad for the response and a clue that Eddy had been right, Jonah leaned close. "I'm impressed that you play the piano. You were so confident and smooth at the service. Remember, I told you I wish I had a talent like that."

AJ finally looked at him. "You're just saying that to be nice."

"No, I mean it," Jonah insisted. "Your music is a real part of you, just like the flames. Your talent isn't fake or part of some stupid destiny." He hadn't expected the sudden bitterness, but he didn't hide it either.

In response, AJ produced a blue flame in his palm and extended the hand toward Jonah. Without stopping to consider it, Jonah brushed his palm over the flame. Though it tickled at first, the sensation was rather pleasant.

The boys met each other's gaze, ignoring everyone else in the room, until Monisha let out a piercing squeal of surprise.

Everyone turned as she sprang from her floor mat and rushed to Darren, who had just entered the pavilion. Monisha wrapped him in a tight embrace, staggering the large boy.

Muttering broke out, and Jonah's jaw dropped because Darren had visible scratches and a bandage on his left forearm.

Monisha released him and grabbed that arm. "Oh my God! What happened?"

Everyone crowded around to hear his answer. But Darren gave them a sad look and shook his head. "I can't tell you."

Monisha's shock morphed into fury in an instant, and she smacked Darren on his massive right shoulder. "What do you mean, you can't tell us? I want to know what happened. You look like cats attacked you!"

Chattering erupted as everyone insisted he tell them something.

Darren dropped his backpack and held up his hands. "I can't."

"Darren—"

"Monisha! I'm serious." Darren paused to take several painful-looking gulps. If Jonah didn't know any better, he would've thought the boy was having trouble talking.

"Ah." AJ's voice came out in an awed whisper. "They made you take an oath?"

Darren nodded.

"Why?" Monisha looked from AJ to Darren.

"They don't want us to know what happened," AJ explained. When everyone gave him disbelieving stares, he smiled. "It's not ominous. My guess is the overnight hike is a test?" He looked at Darren for confirmation, but the boy remained still, afraid to acknowledge that much. "Yeah, they don't want the rest of us to know what we'll face. Get it?"

Lisa frowned. "I don't like it."

And Monisha made frantic gestures at Darren's cuts and injuries. "Look at him. He's hurt."

A movement came behind Darren and he stepped aside to let the mages troop into the room. They didn't crack a smile or smirk when they noticed Darren's condition, and Jonah found out why.

Marvin had a small bandage on his forehead and numerous scratches as well. Even injured, Marvin gave Darren a discreet thumbs-up before sitting with his fellow mages.

Monisha pulled Darren to their usual spot and continued to whisper to him, but he repeatedly shook his head. Jonah didn't envy the guy, not with Monisha determined to get answers.

"She's wasting her time," AJ observed. "Darren can't break an oath."

Bertonneau swept into the room, and all talk about Darren ended.

The rest of Meditation didn't go so well for Jonah. With his mind dodging between fascination with AJ, concern about the dream-walk, and now the mysterious oath Darren had taken, he wasn't able to concentrate a bit.

Councilor Bertonneau's patience with him wore thin when he produced a blast of wind that knocked over the stacked chairs along the back wall. As if mirroring his chaotic thoughts, intermittent rain pelted the building with fat drops of water that punctured his concentration even more.

When the session finally ended, Jonah craved to do something more physical, and a session of blades sounded like the perfect remedy.

CHAPTER THIRTY-TWO
THE BLADEMASTER

The summer rain left the camp's ground muddy once again and the bamboo paths slick. Blotches of gray clouds still covered most of the sky, offering a welcome respite from the July sun for Jonah and the rest of the campers.

His eagerness for blades waned a little when the range came into view, and he saw Mandara standing at attention with his hands behind his rigid back. The Campmaster looked as prepared as ever for battle in his long reaper's coat, making Jonah wish Rex's smiling face was still around.

Instead of waving or saying hello, Mandara waited for the group to fetch pairs of practice batons, gather around, and quiet down. When he continued to gaze at them, Darren caught on and motioned for the others to line up.

Mandara nodded. "I expect you to fall into line immediately at the next session and every time I call you together. Understood?"

Jonah answered, "Yes, sir."

Giving them his coolest Reaper stare, Mandara waited until everyone said, "Yes, sir."

Eddy, who stood beside Jonah in the line, gulped. It didn't help that Mandara remained in one spot while turning his upper body to gaze into each pair of eyes as he spoke.

"Blade combat requires hours of training to condition your body and your mind. When you're in a battle, you have to make split-second decisions."

He continued to scan each face as he continued. "I know that Fallen Reaper Montgomery taught you the basic defensive moves for blade work. When you fall out, I want three teams of two people each."

The Campmaster pointed to Darren, Lisa, and Eddy. "You three will be the attackers. The person to your right will defend. I'll assess what you have learned. Fallout."

Everyone jumped to fetch the practice batons from the bag. In short order, Jonah faced Lisa, ready to defend himself. Lisa seemed extra nervous this morning. While Rex had been a bit more understanding of her hatred of real violence, Mandara didn't offer her a reassuring smile.

Without the usual support, Lisa's confidence wilted.

Noticing she still favored her right arm, despite the Healer having mended the wound, Jonah flashed an understanding smile. "You can do it, Lisa. Just remember the moves."

"Do not engage your opponent with talk," Mandara shouted out to everyone. "Unless"—he turned to stare at Jonah and Lisa—"you're doing it to distract."

Lisa's eyes widened. "Is he serious?"

"Ms. Reynolds?" Mandara called. "Are you posing for a picture?"

Lisa swallowed hard and attacked Jonah. Her technique had improved since the previous week, but her moves were slow and uncertain. Jonah didn't have to try hard because she telegraphed her intentions in the way she leaned and looked. When Mandara stalked near, and his black boots made soft squishing noises in the wet grass, the girl's concentration worsened. Checking the other pairs, who weren't doing any better, made Jonah want to groan. How much more did Mandara needed to see?

Sudden clapping punctuated the air, causing everyone to lower their batons, confused. Jonah's stomach clenched, even before he whirled around to confirm his hunch.

Mandara surveyed the young people. "Uninspiring." His tone prickled Jonah's sense of unfairness.

Had the man meant the comment for him? Jonah wondered until Mandara's eyes scanned everyone before settling on Lisa.

"Ms. Reynolds, you act like you're swatting flies. Mr. Corvera," Mandara called to Eddy, "I've seen children show more finesse. And Mr. Watkins, if I see you pull your blows on behalf of your girlfriend again, it's fifty laps around the entire camp."

The Campmaster strode over to Jonah. "Mr. Blackstone. How will Ms. Reynolds ever learn the error of her ways if you hold back? You do her a disservice." He whirled on the group. "You'd fall to the first KIN or Hunter that crossed your paths."

The others stirred uncomfortably, yet no one dared to object as they watched the Campmaster prowl around the range.

Jonah's Death Sense gave off a mild warning when the Campmaster turned toward him. *Why does everything have to happen to me?*

"You disappoint the most, Mr. Blackstone. With the stories about you and all that's happened, I expected you to help the other campers. Instead, you hold back, never pushing yourself nor letting them know what it's truly like."

Mandara activated his blades in a second. "Stand ready."

Everyone gasped and scrambled out of the way.

Jonah dropped his practice batons and pulled his blades from his pockets. As soon as he activated the weapons, Mandara circled to the right. Jonah wearily moved in the opposite direction.

While he held the blades against his forearms, Mandara's blades were pointed right at him. That's when Jonah realized the weapons weren't in the man's hands. The blades extended from inside the cuff of the black coat and out over the back of his palms, leaving the hands free. And the blades were a bit longer than any Jonah had seen before.

Without warning, Mandara attacked, hammering at Jonah with blow after powerful blow. The ferocity of the assault staggered him, causing him to stumble back and forth as he tried to regain his balance on the slippery ground.

Kevin's warning blared in Jonah's mind, and he planted his feet, desperate but also determined. Mandara disengaged with a sweeping motion of his arms. Almost before Jonah could catch a breath, the Fallen Reaper attacked again, delivering staggering strikes that Jonah barely managed to block.

Just when Jonah thought the pain would overwhelm him, the Campmaster pulled back, not even breathing hard.

"Yes! That's much better, Mr. Blackstone. See class? He's conditioned his responses, so the blades are always ready to defend." Mandara pointed a steady blade at Jonah. "You still disappoint me. Just because I attacked doesn't mean you can't." On that last word, Mandara lunged.

Prepared now, Jonah defended himself a little better. He even added a few moves that Lynn and Kevin had taught him. The change in tactics produced an opening that Jonah seized. Coming in under Mandara's attack, he channeled all his frustrations into a kick to the man's midsection.

The force of impact surprised Jonah and Mandara. A moment of shock crossed the Campmaster face. Then he turned his sudden backward momentum into an impressive somersault and landed on his feet. A collective gasp escaped the other kids.

"Now, you're learning," Mandara said, grinning at Jonah. "The KIN and Hunters will use everything they have. Some were sorcerers in their first lives and would burn you with fire or hex you in the middle of a blade duel."

Jonah's heart thudded in his chest, and his breaths came hard. This duel was unfair and increased his animosity toward the Campmaster. Once again, heeding Kevin's warnings, Jonah clamped down on the anger, focusing on Mandara's words instead. The man talked about doing the unexpected.

I can do that. Jonah lunged at Mandara, hoping to catch him off guard. For one fleeting second, Jonah thought he'd succeeded until the Fallen Reaper blurred into motion and repelled the attacks.

Jonah pushed his fear aside and didn't let up, even though he thought his heart would explode out of his chest. Moving in, he landed well-placed hits on Mandara's forearms, impacting something extremely hard beneath the coat's fabric.

Of course, Jonah thought. The Fallen Reaper had a blade holder underneath, which provided him added protection.

Mandara nodded at the look of awareness on Jonah's face, and moving incredibly fast, knocked Jonah's arms aside and stabbed him in the upper left shoulder.

Jonah screamed as the pain numbed his left arm. His hand loosened on the blade for a split second before he regained control and rolled away from a possible follow-up attack. But Mandara didn't attack. Instead, he stood several feet away, watching.

"Keep away from him," Mandara yelled at Lisa when she moved toward Jonah. "That goes for you too, Mr. Brown. Mr. Blackstone is Half-Reaper. He will heal."

Jonah finally noticed Kevin standing at the practice field's entrance.

Mandara waited for Jonah to regain his feet before he continued, "You assumed that because I was Campmaster, I wouldn't draw blood. Never believe that you know the opponent."

Tears streamed down Jonah's face from the shoulder pain, but his wavering blades remained activated and up.

Mandara finally nodded and deactivated his blades. "I think I made my point, Mr. Blackstone. You will challenge and push yourself at my camp. That goes for everyone. Rex took valuable time out of his schedule to train you. Respect that. Playtime is over."

When the Campmaster crossed to him, it was all Jonah could do not to drop into a ready stance. Mandara loomed close, scrutinizing his face for several uncomfortable moments. Jonah blinked because he sensed curiosity flowing off the man. No. It was something else. Opening his Reaper's ability to read emotions, Jonah gasped when he recognized the feeling underlying the Campmaster's curiosity. Hope.

Like other Alliance adults, once Mandara realized what Jonah was doing, an impenetrable mental wall snapped into place. Not even the disappointment the Campmaster had displayed earlier seeped through now.

The familiar frown returned to the man's brown face. "I can't adjust my schedule to teach you blade-making. Perhaps later, if you prove yourself worthy with your new blades."

Mandara started to turn away but paused as if something invisible tugged on him. He peered at Jonah's shoulder, and his expression lost some of its sourness. "I didn't mean to cut that deep. You're excused from of rest of the lesson to visit the Healer." Again, he paused as if wanting to say something else. Eventually, he nodded and turned to give Kevin a curt bow. "Finish the session, Mr. Brown." He stalked out of the range but didn't head back to the main compound. Instead, Mandara strode down the bamboo path toward the travel building.

Jonah stood in a slight daze because a feeling of hopefulness and the last comment of concern didn't square with what he'd just experienced at the beginning of the duel. Nor did it square with what he sensed from Mandara at other times. The painful throbbing in his shoulder underscored that fact.

It must be something negative, he concluded. Yet a small part of him resisted that idea. And didn't he want to train with the Campmaster so he could ask him questions?

Eddy patted Jonah's uninjured shoulder, shocking him out of his private thoughts. Jonah offered his friend a weak smile.

AJ came over, peering at Jonah's injured arm and then into his face. "I guess you're right. It does suck to be you sometimes."

"You think?"

AJ laughed. Jonah started to join in but grimaced when his arm spasmed and throbbed.

It was a sign of their respect or fear that no one said anything about Mandara when they lined up again without being told. It seemed the Campmaster's impromptu visit had sucked the play out of everyone.

"Fall out into pairs," Kevin ordered. He paused next to Jonah and lowered his voice to a whisper. "You can go see the Healer."

"I'm okay."

Kevin searched his expression a moment before he nodded and moved on. Lisa raised her batons, intent on being the attacker again. Jonah didn't mind because his shoulder still hurt, and the blood had soaked through his shirt. As soon as he readied himself, Lisa attacked. Her moves were more intense, if a bit frantic, as he absently knocked her batons away.

"Don't do that," Lisa yelled. "I'll never learn if you keep being nice to me."

Jonah glanced at Kevin, who watched their exchange but didn't come over.

"I'm sorry," he told Lisa. "I just thought…"

"Don't think. Just fight the way you did with the Campmaster." She lost a little of the fierceness in her voice. "Please."

Jonah nodded. This time when she attacked, he blocked with a lot more force. Lisa recoiled, then caught herself. It bothered Jonah to do it, but he continued to block harder, forcing Lisa to get into the rhythm. Kevin called for them to switch, and Jonah scored early hits on Lisa's unguarded forearms. The girl winced but shook her head when Jonah hesitated.

Honoring her request, Jonah didn't hold back. Each time he scored another painful hit on Lisa's forearms, his conflicting impressions of the Campmaster intensified.

⁓

With his failed attempt to learn blade-making and losing the duel, he experienced a new emotion related to the Campmaster: disappointment. He truly wanted to know the craft because everyone in his family had a talent.

His mom had a beautiful voice, as did his cousin Lynn, though she downplayed it. Robert was a musician and could paint and draw, and Aunt Imma was a sculptor. Even Uncle James was a writer. Jonah needed to know what mortal gift he had.

That's why, after exchanging his bloodied shirt for a fresh one and a quick stop by the Healer's office, which Kevin had insisted on after blades, Jonah hurried to wood carving to test a new theory. The sharp scent of fresh-cut pine tickled Jonah's nose as he pawed through the pieces of wood in the carpentry bin. Jonah wondered if he could carve a blade. Buoyed by that notion, he searched in earnest and found a longish piece of pine that seemed perfect.

When he asked Mr. Tippens to make a few modifications, the teacher raised one of his bushy eyebrows. Jonah didn't know why he was so sure. It just made sense. Already he could see the carved blade in the block of wood. Once Tippens cut the piece, he hurried to his space, his excitement growing.

Eddy peered over his shoulder. "Dude, that's really thin. What are you gonna make?"

"You'll see." Jonah flashed him a grin.

Darren let out a curse as his carving tool slipped from his hand. That's when Jonah noticed the boy's curled fingers. "Darren?"

The big guy tried to hide his hand. Of course, Eddy blasted through Darren's attempt at a little privacy and gripped the boy's wrist. Jonah thought it significant that the super-strong Darren didn't fling Eddy clear across the room. Instead, he allowed Eddy to lift his hand free of his pocket.

"Dude, what happened?"

Finally, jerking his hand free, Darren couldn't hide the embarrassed look on his face. "It was Monisha."

"Dang! Maybe you should break up."

Darren glared at Eddy, forcing the smaller boy to back away.

Jonah pointed at the gnarled hand. "What happened?"

"She kept asking about the overnight hike, and I figured that if I couldn't say it, maybe I could write it down." Darren paused, his face darkening with embarrassment. "Trueblood said it'll wear off by dinner." He looked miserable.

"Does it hurt?" Jonah asked.

"No, but Trueblood laughed! And Monisha got in trouble for bothering me."

Now that Darren confessed, Jonah did think it a bit funny, despite the sight of the cursed hand.

Eddy looked spooked. "Whoa."

"Well, don't you ask me anything about it."

"I won't." Eddy crossed to his project and started working.

After adjusting to the gnarled hand, Darren returned to his carved pieces of wood on a table. Jonah froze, reminded of the Alliance Guard armor Darren had taken to HQ.

Darren noticed Jonah looking and smiled. "Don't worry. It's fantasy armor this time."

"You okay?" Jonah asked, unsure if he should.

"Yeah. Using my hands helps. You know?" Darren hesitated then added, "Thanks for asking."

As Jonah watched Darren sand the fantastic sculptures, he experienced a bit of envy at the boy's talent. The sensation only increased when Jonah gazed at his piece of wood and realized he wasn't sure what to do next.

Almost out of habit, he cleared his mind and relaxed. Without any conscious thought, he took a wood-carving tool and held it poised over the wood. His eyes scanned the surfaces, and then, an image of a blade solidified in his mind. *Chip there*, the thought came. Jonah lowered his hand and did so, pleased by the result.

He relaxed and let his hand chip another imperfection and then another. Soon, the pauses in between disappeared as the motion of his hands became surer. With his concentration sharpened, he lost track of time. Tippens surprised Jonah when he announced the end of the session.

Jonah stepped back, taking a deep breath. He had zoned out, and, in his mind, had carved a perfect top half of a Reaper's blade. Instead, what Jonah saw on the table was a block of wood with numerous gouges and chips. From a certain angle, it could resemble a blade if he also squinted.

"Ah, that's interesting," Darren observed.

"Is it a submarine?" Eddy asked and nudged Jonah.

"Sure," Jonah lied. He set the carving tool aside, not sure if he'd ever pick it up again.

"Hey, it's cool." Darren leaned close to peer at the wood. "I can tell it's a blade."

The doubt in the boy's voice deflated Jonah even more. He covered the ruined blade with a cloth.

Eddy stared at him. "Hey, you just need a little practice, the same way all of us need to practice with the blades."

"It's why we're here, I know. I get it," Jonah said. Of course, he wasn't good at everything, but given his dad's talent, he thought he would have the same skill. Maybe this was the real reason the Campmaster rejected teaching him blade-making.

"Tell you what," Darren said while watching his sad expression. "You show me some advanced blade moves, and I'll teach you to sculpt wood. Deal?"

Jonah blinked in surprise, not sure if Darren's offer was just a friendly gesture or genuine. He decided he didn't care. "Okay. Deal."

CHAPTER THIRTY-THREE
MOTION BLUR

Now that everyone had seen the results of breaking an oath, they listened in rapt attention in Sterne's next lecture. Darren's hand was back to normal, but as expected, the Councilor took the opportunity to use the muscular boy as an example.

Sterne paused in front of Darren, who slumped low in the chair while avoiding the teacher's amused stare.

"Don't hate me, Mr. Watkins, but I made sure to include that curse and other bits of fine print in the oath to which you agreed." Darren couldn't hide his shocked expression. The teacher turned to the class. "Mr. Watkins and Mr. Crenshaw consented to abide by an agreement that they didn't bother to read. That being the case, the oath they took bound them to all the terms of the deal."

Marvin raised his hand. "You mean it's really like a mortal contract?"

"Yes, Mr. Crenshaw. Let that be a lesson. Always read the fine print, especially with a supernatural oath." Sterne turned back to Darren. "Don't beat yourself up, Mr. Watkins. Every summer, young people always try to get around the oath without fail. Your reaction was mild when compared to others."

Sterne continued with his usual practice of firing off details about the subject. He also gave them an interesting ethics case about a mage who got off because he used a vortex to place himself hundreds of miles from a crime scene just seconds after committing it.

AJ kept whispering, "Albrecht," under his breath.

Jonah agreed and wondered if that was the reason the mage always wore the shades. A pleasant buzz of conversation filled the room at the end of the session. The topics were popular with everyone, Jonah thought. Even the mages talked more than usual as the groups parted ways.

—

"Are you sending out more people tonight?" Monisha asked at the start of Trueblood's Nature class.

Trueblood smiled in his relaxed way. "Of course, Monisha."

The girl held her chin high. "Well, I'm not coming back scratched up."

Darren covered his face with his hand, and Eddy laughed.

"Each experience is different," Trueblood said as if accepting her challenge. "Getting scratched up may not be a problem. Besides, Mr. Owens and Mr. Crenshaw chose the harder option for their test, hence the injuries." That caused an excited stir because Darren hadn't been able to provide any details.

Meanwhile, Trueblood strode past Monisha and headed out into the forest. Though they remained in the lower elevations today, Jonah sensed Rubio's net and suspected Trueblood kept the class far from the net's source on purpose. Instead of relaxing, Jonah grew more anxious because the net had the Campmaster's approval, which could only mean trouble.

～

While Jonah still nursed misgivings about the net, everyone else returned from morning sessions in high spirits. Sure, playtime was over, as Mandara had put it, but Jonah didn't want his group to start acting like Jennifer and Vanay.

When Darren cracked the first joke about Mandara, everyone peered around even though the Campmaster rarely lurked in the main building outside of mealtimes. Eventually, they relaxed and, to Jonah's horror, made fun of his attempt to best Mandara.

Replaying the duel in his mind, Jonah's face warmed with embarrassment. He sank lower in his chair.

Eddy nudged his foot. "Hey, I couldn't have done that."

"Me neither," Lisa seconded.

Monisha and Darren held out their fists, and Jonah, surprised, touched his fist to theirs.

Last, he met AJ's gaze, and the boy smiled. "Hey, you literally got a chance to kick the Campmaster." Everyone laughed at that.

"What did he say to you?" Lisa asked.

Jonah gulped. "He apologized for stabbing me."

That received almost identical shocked expressions from everyone. They broke into hushed speculations about the Campmaster.

Leaning back and observing the others talking and laughing before lunch, Jonah realized everyone had gathered around him. The thought that Mandara had brought them together as a group bothered him. He didn't want to believe that had been the Campmaster's plan all along.

A movement down the west hallway caught his attention since his chair faced that way. Fallen Reaper Mitchell and a group of Alliance people stepped from a conference room. Jonah expected the adults to leave the building, but the group descended on the coffee table for refills and sugar cookies.

Mitchell spotted Jonah, smiled, and came over. "Mr. Blackstone, it's good seeing you again." He shook Jonah's hand like they'd never met before, then nodded to Lisa. "Ms. Reynolds." He motioned to Jonah. "Can I have a word with you?"

Confused, Jonah rose and followed Mitchell. The Fallen Reaper didn't head outside. Instead, he paused near the wind-sculpture and turned, so he faced the main room.

"I'm sorry about my abrupt exit the last time we talked," Mitchell began as soon as Jonah reached him. "I wanted to ask about the Tales." The man's voice carried the same guarded eagerness Jonah heard the first time they talked in Mount Vernon.

"Ah. What about it?" Jonah asked, watching the constantly changing colors on the sculpture.

"Did you discover something new in the texts?" he asked.

"No," Jonah admitted yet again. "I still haven't solved the riddle."

"Well, it has to be something that only you can figure out, as the Deliverer," Mitchell added. "Something about stars?"

Jonah found it odd to hear people refer to him as the Deliverer. "Yeah. Stars. I think they represent Destiny and her five sons. Her star shines, but the others are dark."

Mitchell leaned closer, his eyes alight with keen interest. "How did you get Destiny's star to shine?"

"Well," Jonah said, stuffing his hands in his pockets. "I didn't tell everyone this, but when I used the Protector's Ring, I could sense it had a pulse, almost like a heartbeat."

Mitchell's eyes widened. "That's astonishing."

"The same thing happened in the Deliverer's cave and with the seal," Jonah continued, explaining how waving his hand over the last page made the stars appear. "So, I figured I should sense a pulse from the other stars on the page."

"And nothing happened?" Mitchell's expression turned thoughtful. "Perhaps you share more in common with the last Deliverer than you think."

"How so?" Jonah asked. He was younger than the last Deliverer, so he never imagined they could have much in common.

"We know the last Deliverer inspired people." Mitchell nodded at the main room's buzz of activity. "Whether or not you realize it, I think you inspire your new friends."

Jonah didn't expect the compliment, but he considered it.

"Your godfather mentioned you don't like the attention," Mitchell said in a cheery voice. "But it's admirable that you've already established a place among the other campers. In a way, they're like your own Protectors."

Mitchell's group began leaving the dining area, carrying steaming cups of coffee and napkins full of cookies. "I'd better go. More meetings," Mitchell said with a dramatic sigh and shook Jonah's hand. "Let me know what happens."

The Fallen Reaper's observation intrigued Jonah, and he turned to gaze at the others laughing and talking together. Maybe Mitchell had a point, but how would that help him? Try as he might, the answer still wouldn't come to him. Giving up on the elusive key to the riddle, for now, he joined the others for their last two sessions of the day.

—

"What happened now?" Kevin asked, watching Jonah shuffle onto the field and come over to him. "Is it the cut?" Kevin pushed up Jonah's left shirt sleeve to inspect the fast-healing cut.

"The Healer said it's mending slower because it's a cut from a Reaper's blade," Jonah complained, even though he liked Kevin fussing over him. "But I'm fine."

Kevin grunted and lowered Jonah's sleeve. "Then what's wrong?"

"Let's see," Jonah began, ticking off the points with his finger. "There's a magical net in the forest designed to stop me. I found out this morning I suck at carving wood, even though I bet my dad had the talent, the Campmaster tried to maim me, and oh yeah, I still haven't solved the riddle of the Tales." For a moment, a brief idea tickled his mind, but then it was gone, leaving the mounting frustration behind.

"Wow." Kevin crossed his arms, striking a thoughtful pose. "Don't forget you're at a cool camp, learning more about the supernatural world than you can process, met a group of new friends, *and* have chances to do fun things. You're right. Life's tough."

Jonah slugged Kevin in the arm. "You're my boyfriend. You're supposed to cheer me up."

"I never signed up for that thankless job." He grinned at Jonah's moan of frustration. "I have an idea. Go stand at the end of the range."

"Why?" When Kevin raised an eyebrow, Jonah turned and trudged to the end of the range, knowing he'd soon find out. Reaching the lean-to, he looked back to discover Kevin had moved to the opposite end.

Would Kevin show him a new combination of moves and phases? No sooner had he thought that than the Fallen Reaper blurred into motion. A mere half second later, Kevin stopped in front of Jonah with a fist an inch away from his chest. Jonah stumbled back and into the lean-to before he could stop himself.

Kevin smirked and offered a helping hand. "You try it."

Jonah brushed off the help as he stood on his own. "Try what?"

"Blur your movements."

"I can't do that."

Kevin pointed at Jonah's forehead. "You've been taking the Meditation class for a reason. And this is Mandara's recommended next step for you."

"He stabbed me."

"And apologized. Plus, I thought you were fine?" Kevin crossed his arms. "Of course, I could tell Mandara you didn't follow the rules."

Jonah groaned. "No."

"Then man up."

Jonah flipped the middle finger at Kevin, but the Fallen Reaper blurred and held the offending finger in a tight grip.

"Jonah. You're starting to feel sorry for yourself."

The comment shocked Jonah and cut through his surly attitude.

Kevin let the finger go and blurred to the other side of the range. His body became a moving, indistinct, dark shape for the second it took.

"Show me what you can do, Mr. Blackstone," Kevin said in a wickedly good imitation of Mandara's deep voice.

Taking a breath, Jonah ran forward while trying the same mental nudge that sent him into a phase. All he succeeded in doing was sprinting halfway across the range before stopping. He tried again and again, but each time he moved at regular speed. Besides getting exercise and working up a sweat, he wasn't making any progress.

"It's not working." Jonah's frustration with the whole failed process mounted.

"That's obvious." When Jonah let out an agonized scream, Kevin walked over. "You're not thinking."

"That's *all* I'm doing!"

"I mean, you forgot you've done it before."

"When?" Jonah threw his arms up in exasperation.

Kevin waited as Jonah assumed a ready stance and calmed his rapid, angry breaths.

"That time you saved Antwan from cracking his head on the concrete."

Jonah's jaw dropped. Saving Antwan seemed so long ago that he'd forgotten. Yeah, he'd been desperate to save the boy because, well, he'd pushed Antwan. "All I thought about was getting to him in time."

"And saving your butt," Kevin smirked. "You were focused, and it jump-started your blurring power. Remember how it felt and try again." He blurred to the other side of the range and waited.

Picturing Antwan as a source of motivation created a problem for Jonah. The boy was Brandon's best friend and a bully. Not even focusing on Brandon's concern for the boy helped.

"Sometime today would be nice," Kevin taunted.

Scowling, Jonah willed himself to think back to that day. Instead of Antwan, he imagined Mike was in trouble. Jonah searched inside himself for that same feeling of desperation. Closing everything else out, he let the fear return, and he ran. In his mind's eye, he saw Mike tumbling backward over the bike rack, his head coming closer and closer to hitting the pavement.

Suddenly, time slowed, and Mike's fall stopped midmotion. Just as Jonah reached out his hand to stop his best friend's fall, he rammed into something hard and cushioning at the same time. His sense of the outside world returned as he and Kevin tumbled to the ground.

The Fallen Reaper let out a surprised grunt when Jonah landed on top of him. "Good." He smirked. "Now, get off me."

Jonah's face warmed with embarrassment because he straddled Kevin. But he also saw an opportunity. "I'll get up if you tell me what's happened with the Alliance."

Kevin sighed as he lifted Jonah off him with no problem. "You know I can't tell you anything." Instead of standing, Kevin leaned back on the grass, as if enjoying the sun.

Jonah sat beside him while looking across the Practice Range. The sounds of rocks hitting rocks came from the next field. Beyond that, he heard the whoosh of conjured fire from either AJ or the young mages. The noises reminded him of the prohibitions against his powers, and he frowned.

"Trueblood's still worried about Rubio's net. Our nature hikes are far from the source, but I can still feel it." Jonah watched Kevin, but his boyfriend remained mute on that point. "They expect me to get picked soon for the overnight hikes, don't they?" When Kevin didn't budge, Jonah fought down the disappointment. "Well, do you think I'll have to use the blur?"

"Maybe," Kevin hedged. "It's better to be prepared."

"Having some info would help me prepare."

Kevin shook his head, refusing to take the bait. After checking that no one was looking, he slid his fingers between

Jonah's. "You can't do anything about the net, so let that go. Give the wood carving a chance. It's about learning to do something, not being able to do it the first time you try."

Jonah winced because Kevin almost repeated Darren's words. His friends wanted to help, but something else nagged Jonah. "It's just… I'm supposed to be the One. I was the first to use a ring, blah, blah, blah. I come here, and I get more things wrong than right."

Kevin jiggled their clasped hands. "Let all that other stuff go. Be yourself."

"What about my mission?"

"I don't know what to tell you about the Tales." Kevin let out a long breath. "Did you find any clues?"

"Nope," Jonah said, a little irritated. "Hey, I think there are four more rings hidden with the medallion."

Kevin whistled. "That would be so cool if we had more rings."

"But who'd wear them?" Jonah held up his hand and wiggled his fingers. "Me? That's like overload."

When Kevin's eyes narrowed, Jonah suspected his boyfriend had more news about the search for ring bearers but couldn't reveal it. Since no one had mentioned the Protector's Ring in a while, Jonah didn't know how the search progressed. "I don't want to be the only one, Kevin. Know what I mean?"

"What's the matter? Lonely at the top?" Kevin quipped. He leaned close, so their shoulders touched.

Jonah searched Kevin's eyes. "When are we gonna talk?"

"Third weekend is free time. Maybe then."

"The third weekend?" Jonah frowned. "Nice of you to make time for me."

Kevin ruffled Jonah's bushy hair. "I was gonna suggest we could go somewhere, but not now." He stood and pulled Jonah to his feet. "Let's try adding a blur to the fight moves."

Like with the wood carving, Jonah messed up the combination move at first. But with Kevin's help, he began to get the hang of the routine. *I'm learning, and that's the important thing.*

CHAPTER THIRTY-FOUR
ANSWER REVEALED

The Range Session with Kevin had worked a subtle magic on Jonah's mood. He wasn't as irritable and bummed about his efforts at camp anymore. With the sour emotions gone, his mind returned to the issue of the Tales. That nugget of excitement he experienced when talking with Fallen Reaper Mitchell returned.

Standing at the second-floor balcony at the start of the free hour before dinner, Jonah watched his friends below. Darren, AJ, Eddy, Lisa, and Monisha talked, sharing stories and making plans for the next weekend trip to Camp Monarch. He experienced a sudden dual vision, one with his new friends at camp and the second vision with his hometown friends gathered in the Summit clubhouse. Two groups with a common purpose: protect mortals.

Protect. Mitchell said his camp friends were like a group of protectors. The root word echoed in Jonah's mind as a ripple of goose bumps raced up his arms. Though both groups of kids had different skills, they acted as a team, just like Protectors. *Of course!*

Jonah hurried into his dorm room to fetch the triptych. He debated putting the pieces of art together there and testing his theory. But, knowing AJ and Eddy, one of them would come up to investigate his absence, and he didn't want that.

Slipping the triptych pieces into his pocket with the deactivated blades, Jonah raced downstairs. His guess had been right on the mark because he met Eddy at the bottom of the stairs.

"Where're you going?" he asked suspiciously.

Jonah didn't have the time to explain. "I gotta take care of something before dinner," he answered. "I'll be back." He spotted Kevin and gestured to him while moving for the exit.

"Whoa, what's up?" Kevin asked, meeting him at the door.

Jonah searched the common room, spotted Jennifer with the other mages, and whispered to Kevin, "I have an idea about the Tales. I want to sit on the big rocks outside and work on it."

Kevin crossed his arms. "Okay. That's a weird request."

"No, it isn't. I saw Trueblood sitting up there meditating the evening you had to do the emergency recharge."

"Oh, well…" Kevin eyed the other campers.

"Jennifer's in the corner," Jonah said, "near the pool table."

After confirming her location, Kevin said. "Well, come back in time for dinner. Hear me?"

"Yeah, yeah." Jonah slipped out of the building and fast-walked to the formation of large boulders near the compound's entrance. The idea to sit out here had only just occurred him like a sudden inspiration. The only problem was he didn't know how to get to the top. As he reached the boulders, he assumed Trueblood used a ladder, or maybe footholds. He didn't know if the mage could levitate himself like Lisa.

Walking around the huge rocks in the dimming light, he stumbled on the answer. The east-facing boulder was flattened on that side and had a row of handholds carved into the surface. Testing the lowest step, Jonah nodded and climbed up. The straight vertical angle was odd, but he made it to the top without a problem.

He stood and turned in all directions, admiring the view. To the north, he could see the Embracing Valley building and the low hills beyond. Looking east, he could peek past the Asian-inspired pavilion roof to see the darkening sky. The south view featured the lake that reflected faint stars on the calm waters. Trueblood had faced to the west and the unobstructed view over that compound wall.

Facing that way, Jonah sat cross-legged, pulled the triptych out of his pocket, and connected the pieces. He'd discovered by reading the device at night that the Tales gave off a faint glow that made it readable in the dark. Jonah turned to the last page and the 2D drawing of the five smaller stars surrounding the central, animated, pulsing star. Pausing to glance into the darkening sky, he thought the barely visible stars above should aid his spark of inspiration tonight.

"Let's see," Jonah began, sounding out the plan to himself. "The five Protectors in the Tales were the brothers, but each one was different. The Deliverer talked about their personalities." Flipping through the pages, he found the entry for the Second Brother.

He winced as he read the page. "Selfish, prideful, and a desire for recognition." Of all his new friends, AJ was the only one outright jealous. *He hated the recognition I got.* Plus, AJ did like knowledge and having the answer. Gazing at the page and willing his suspicions correct, Jonah spread his fingers wide over the surface.

When that didn't produce a result, he resisted the sudden doubt and touched the word *prideful* with his forefinger. Still nothing. What would AJ say right now? Just wondering about that produced a flood of feelings—jealousy, longing, laughter, and enjoying each other's company.

A warm sensation flowed from his heart, down his arm, and through the finger still touching the triptych. To his surprise and relief, the word he touched turned red and pulsed. Was that it? Did he have to imagine how his new friends made him feel?

He recalled Bertonneau's emotion scale and the emphasis on how they felt at any given moment. And, Jonah realized, his ability to decipher a person's emotions with his Reaper stare had less to do with the color of their aura. He detected the subtle difference by the way he felt. His feelings were like a fine-tuned sensor!

Feelings. The feelings and emotions that Jonah's friends produced inside him made the difference! Eager with anticipation now, he touched the word recognition. It, too, turned red. He found five words the Deliverer used in describing the Second Brother's personality. Flipping to the last page of the Tales, he almost jumped with excitement because one of the stars was as bright as the center star.

"Finally," he said. Picking another of his new friends, he settled on Monisha. Recalling her actions on the Flint River, he decided she was brave and liked a challenge. But Monisha was also impulsive, resulting in Lisa's injury.

Reminded of the Eldest Brother, Jonah flipped to his section. Following the same steps, he read down and found the Deliverer's accusation of this Protector. Like Monisha, the brother proved impulsive and emotional but also a decisive person.

As before, Jonah focused on how Monisha's personality made him feel in all those moments. Again, he could sense her as if she sat beside him. Those words and other character-describing terms turned red at his touch, and he confirmed a second star on the last page pulsed with animated 2D light.

Caught up in the game, he decided to continue in order and review the Third Brother, who the Deliverer described as arrogant, disdainful, and scornful. He was also the strongest of the brothers, and Jonah could think of no one else but Darren. However, the boy was never outright disdainful like the Protector in the story.

Flipping the ethereal pages to the next section, Jonah scanned the page, and his eyes widened. "Wow, the Fourth Brother was filled with self-doubt, confusion, and nervousness." He scrunched up his face in thought. "Eddy?" Feeling a little guilty for thinking of his new friend that way, he nodded and touched all those words.

But Eddy also had his back, giving Jonah a sense of security. And Eddy also made sure to include Jonah in everything, so he felt accepted. The change in his mind's focus continued to astonish him.

The Fifth Brother, the last one, was extremely loyal. Of all the new kids he met, Lisa was the most faithful to the Alliance and to him, Jonah realized. His face warmed with embarrassment as he reconsidered her comments in a new light. Reminding himself to focus on how he truly felt, Jonah realized Lisa made him feel special. She had faith and belief in him as the Deliverer.

As a sense of gratitude overwhelmed him, Jonah flipped to the last page. All five stars pulsed in time to the center star that represented the Destiny Medallion. The sense of all his new friends washed over him, strengthening him.

What now?

Going on an inner prompt, Jonah placed his hand on the page. Closing his eyes, he recalled the first time he crossed over into the Afterworld. It was just after he had slipped on the Protector's Ring, and it transported him there so he could release the original Deliverer's Spirit.

The man had instructed Jonah to listen to the ring, and it would guide him. Likewise, in the Tales, the Deliverer told each of the brothers to do the same.

That must be it, Jonah thought. "Show me the way. Show me the Destiny Medallion."

Even with his eyes closed, he sensed the sudden illumination. Sure enough, when he opened his eyes, the triptych glowed as bright as a nova, casting a blinding beacon into the night air. Like an exploding firework, six shining symbols appeared and circled above his head before spiraling down and hitting the triptych.

Each collision shook the device and produced lines that spread across the surface, forming a land map. But instead of Destiny's mountain hideout, the final image was a meadow or marsh. Jonah stared in shocked recognition at the Underworld map and location. It was one of the places on the triptych's map!

He gulped because the last time he'd journeyed to the Underworld, he and his cousins had to fight his aunt, who was possessed by an ancient goddess's energy. And for good measure, a horde of Phantoms had also attacked them.

And phantoms attack us on the Flint River.

An unsettling sense of foreboding overcame Jonah's moment of accomplishment. Although thrilled to know the medallion's location, he had the feeling something big and probably awful was about to happen.

"Everything's fine," he whispered, feeling good that he completed the mission. He'd found the Destiny Medallion's location.

Should he run across to Mandara's office, or tell Kevin first and let him decide? Filled with the prospect of shocked expressions when he delivered this news, Jonah almost didn't catch the warning throb from his Death Sense.

He paused, looking around the courtyard below but not seeing anyone. While he had worked, dusk had come, and the shadows had lengthened, creating dark crevices between buildings. Scrambling down the rock's side, he turned for the main building when Jennifer stepped into view.

Her eyes narrowed as she searched him. "I saw the flare of light. Want to share?"

The mocking tone let Jonah know the devious mage understood why he came out here. He soon suspected her apparent show of talking with the other mages had been just that: a show. But how did she slip out without Kevin noticing?

"Nope." Jonah prepared himself by sliding his hands into his pockets to grip the blades.

Jennifer's hands curled, and he sensed the magic gathering. "You sure?" she said. "I heard the Council gave you a new toy. Let me see it. That's what team building is all about, isn't it?"

"You're not my partner."

When Jennifer laughed, Jonah wanted to groan. "Yeah, I guess I'm not your type, huh?" She hurled the hex without warning.

Keyed up, Jonah had his blades activated and out to deflect the spell. At the same time, he dived for cover behind the boulders to avoid a second hex. That's when another dark shape charged at him from the shadows between the rock display and the pavilion.

The person conjured a tendril of lightning, but Jonah ducked and rammed the newcomer in the stomach. He felt the person grab at his pockets, trying to get the Tales! Jonah whirled back and away. That's when he saw the person's face. *Vanay!* When the young mage lunged at him, Jonah blurred and came up behind the boy to kick him in the back. Vanay pinwheeled and slammed against the nearest rock.

By then, Jennifer had darted into view and attacked again. Jonah ducked, avoiding her conjured lightning. Realizing she cut off his escape between the buildings, he slipped by Vanay and headed for the compound exit. Jennifer paced him and hurled actual fire! Infuriated at the girl, Jonah whirled at the exit, called up the wind, and sent the roaring flame back at her.

The effectiveness of his counterattack shocked him when the flames ignited her head wrap. But just as he witnessed Deyanira do, she performed a quick spell that extinguished the flames before they did any real damage. Still, Jennifer flung the head wrap to the ground, revealing a closely shaved head.

Something dropped to the ground on the outside of the compound's wall.

Jonah feared Vanay had climbed over the wall to cut him off. He was about to blur out of their reach when a Phantom roared at him out of the darkness. The shock of seeing the powerful Wraith in the camp caused him to stumble. How had Jennifer and Vanay smuggled a Phantom through the camp's defenses?

Jonah's hands shook as he reacted on instinct and hurled his right blade at the dangerous creature. Phantoms were fierce, but Reaper blades could hurt and even kill the evil spirits. Yet when Jonah's weapon sliced through the Phantom's shield and disappeared, he knew something was wrong.

A startled grunt of pain erupted from the darkness, and then, the Phantom vanished. In its place, Vanay staggered and slumped onto its back. Jonah's quivering Reaper blade stuck out of the young mage's abdomen.

Jennifer shoved him aside, hurried to Vanay, and knelt beside him. She gripped her fellow mage's hand. "Don't move. Oh my God!"

Her concern sounded real to Jonah, who stood rooted on the spot. His mind finally put together the details and the fact Vanay had projected the fake Phantom.

"I didn't mean to do it. I didn't."

Jennifer whirled her right hand and shot something into the air. It was like a small bird and disappeared over the wall in a second. Already Jonah saw adults running along the bamboo path toward them.

Because of their mutual connection, Jonah sensed Kevin coming before the boy stepped into view and froze, taking in the scene. Trueblood appeared next and rushed to Vanay's side. Jonah let out a sigh of relief when the Healer also arrived and hurried over to help the downed mage.

Feeling a tug on his other blade, Jonah looked down to see Kevin pulling it free and deactivating it.

"I didn't mean to hurt him. Vanay used a projection on me."

Trueblood pulled Jennifer to the side as another adult stepped in to help the Healer.

The woman kneeling beside the Healer must have been a mage because she worked a spell that levitated Vanay. With the Healer by her side, they raced into the compound. "We should use the side entrance near my station," the Healer said.

Mandara finally appeared at the compound's entrance. "Wait in my office," he barked at Jennifer and Jonah. Then he turned to follow the others to the main building.

Jonah was so focused on the retreating huddle of people that he bumped into Alex, lurking just inside the walls. He was too stunned to give the young mage much thought.

Kevin was on point and said, "Get back inside, Alex." After a meaningful glance at Jonah, the Fallen Reaper followed Alex back to the main building.

As Jonah trailed Jennifer to the Campmaster's office, he tried to come to grips with how fast his moment of triumph had come crashing down in flames.

CHAPTER THIRTY-FIVE
CABIN DETENTION

The Campmaster's shelf of glittering timepieces and other objects usually drew Jonah's attention, but not tonight. He sat in front of the large desk, seething at Jennifer. Everything was her fault. She knew about the Tales and wanted to take them from him. And what was that fool Vanay thinking projecting a Phantom?

While his fury raged, beneath it was the terror that the boy wouldn't recover. For the first time in his life, Jonah had to face that he might have killed someone he knew. Rex's comment about the lethal blades became very real for him.

He peeked at Jennifer, but the girl kept her eyes closed. If not for her genuine shock, Jonah could believe Vanay's injury was part of her plan. How could she sit there when he wanted to pace back and forth or do something? Glancing at the shelf of timepieces again, Jonah rose to his feet as the office door banged open. Mandara entered, followed by Trueblood and another adult Jonah didn't know.

"Sit down, Blackstone," the Campmaster snapped as he swept around the desk and dropped into his leather chair.

Jonah obeyed.

Jennifer had opened her eyes, and she leaned forward. "Is Vanay well?"

"Vanay will recover," Trueblood said. "He'll have to stay in bed for another day and take it easy for another week."

Jonah slumped in relief, but his hands shook with pent-up fear.

"What the hell happened?" Mandara asked.

Trueblood winced but only crossed his arms, waiting.

"We were just messing around with Jonah," Jennifer began.

Jonah wanted to shout at her, but Mandara speared him with a warning glare, and he subsided.

Jennifer admitted that they had used hexes and even fire. "But he used the wind incantation to block the fire. Everything was fine until he used his blades."

"Vanay projected a Phantom!" Jonah finally said. "I didn't know it wasn't real."

"Is that true?" Mandara asked Jennifer.

She shrugged. "I was still in the compound and didn't see it."

"Given what happened to my Flint River group, that was a nasty thing to project in the dark," Trueblood accused. He raised an eyebrow. "I'm sure young Beraki and Marvin told the mages all about the river incident."

Jennifer didn't dare to try to deny it. Jonah wanted to smirk at her, if not for the seriousness of what he'd done.

"Even so," Mandara began, watching Jonah, "you should have sensed it wasn't real, Mr. Blackstone. You have Death Sense. Plus, blades are only allowed on the practice ranges and not in duels between campers." He stood and clasped his hands behind his back. "You'll have to surrender the weapons for the rest of camp."

"But my mom and dad made those!" Jonah protested.

Trueblood placed a hand on his shoulder. "You'll also need to surrender your back gate token."

"What about her?" Jonah asked, pointing at Jennifer. To his surprise, she handed over her token without comment. Outmaneuvered, he saw no choice but to unclip his wrist strap and surrender it to Trueblood.

"Mage Trueblood, escort Ms. Motombu back to the dorms. She's confined to her room until tomorrow."

"What about the overnight hikes?" Trueblood asked.

"They go forward," Mandara said. "I want things to remain as normal as possible."

"Are you sure?"

"Yes, I am. As far as the others are concerned, these two are on detention for another unsanctioned duel."

Not looking happy all, Trueblood nevertheless motioned for Jennifer to stand.

Mandara called out, "Have the kitchen staff send a meal to cabin number three."

With a final reassuring glance at Jonah, Trueblood led Jennifer out of the office.

Jonah expected Mandara to send him back or escort him to the main building. However, the Campmaster waited, keeping some internal schedule to himself.

The small device on the workbench began strobing a brilliant light, startling Jonah. That's when the Campmaster came around the desk and headed for the door. "Follow me, Blackstone."

Walking at a brutally brisk pace, the Campmaster headed away from the main building, across the courtyard, and out of the compound. Jonah jogged to keep up with the taller man's stride. He also began to fear the Campmaster had a nastier punishment in mind for him. Was Mandara planning to dunk him in the lake or something like that?

Okay, he thought to himself, that's a dumb idea.

Yet he didn't relax as the Campmaster led him into a section of the camp he'd never seen before. He took in the large circle of identical cabins, all done in a dark wood, he guessed. It was hard to tell at night. Each had an upper loft window in the slanted roof. Lights flared in the windows of most of the cabins, but Mandara led him to a dark one. Jonah made out the number three on the cabin's side and gulped.

Mandara unlocked the door and gestured him inside first. Jonah hesitated, testing his Death Sense, but it remained calm. Slowly, he entered the dark cabin. Mandara flicked on a light, revealing a cozy space with a kitchen, den, and bedroom and bathroom down a short hallway. The kitchen had a table and four chairs, and the den area contained a sofa and two sitting chairs grouped around a low coffee table.

After scanning the interior, Jonah turned a questioning expression on Mandara.

"I don't want you in the dorms tonight. You might stir up trouble."

Jonah thought that unfair because Jennifer and Vanay had attacked him. Plus, why did Jennifer get to hide out in her room, and he couldn't hide out in his? "How long do I stay here?"

"Until tomorrow morning. We'll see at that point." Mandara had crossed to the room's window and opened it.

Seeing the man standing there, Jonah had a sudden memory of his dad glancing out their dining room window after someone had smashed it with a brick. That night had been the first time Jonah saw his dad phase. Despite the uncertain situation, he'd felt protected with his father standing guard.

Without warning, the deep longing to speak to his parents, to ask them for help, to even hear his dad's deep voice telling him everything would be alright, overwhelmed Jonah. He flopped on the sofa as the tears fell unchecked down his cheeks.

"I wish my dad were here," he choked out, then stopped as more sobs came.

Mandara jerked straight, no doubt shocked. But he said nothing and did not move from the window for a long moment.

"Send me home! I don't care anymore!" Jonah shouted.

"No."

"Why not?" Jonah's voice shook the house. He leaped from the sofa, his hands glowing as if he could cast fire.

To his credit, Mandara eye's widened, but he didn't shrink back. Instead, he moved closer to Jonah, confronting him without backing down.

As the pain rolled through Jonah, the hurt, the loss, the hatred of being the alien burned inside.

Peering into Jonah's eyes, Mandara read his emotions with the Reaper stare. Finally, the man said, "I'm not sending you home, Jonah."

Hearing the Campmaster use his name shocked Jonah and cut through the agony and the desire to strike out. He sucked in a ragged breath and sat down again. His hands no longer glowed as the sudden power ebbed away.

Mandara watched him. "You deserve to be here, more than anyone else. And I promised your mother I'd help you."

Jonah raised his face to stare in disbelief at the Campmaster. "You hate me!"

"I don't hate you, Jonah. I'm challenging you the same way your father would have." When Jonah remained silent, Mandara checked his watch. "Don't leave." He moved to the door and opened it. "I'll send Kevin."

Perhaps that more than anything else convinced Jonah the Campmaster's words were genuine. Once Mandara left, Jonah lay out on the sofa. Exhaustion warred with the nervous energy and embarrassment at his outburst. The negative emotions had lessened, allowing him to think about the positives, like the unexpected friends he had made at camp.

Jonah lay there for the next ten minutes until he sensed a familiar presence.

He jumped from the sofa and opened the front door a second after the first knock came. Kevin stood outside, holding a covered tray of food. He stepped inside, closed the door, and slipped an arm around Jonah, pulling him close.

They held each other for a few minutes. Finally, Kevin whispered, "You need to eat something."

Jonah released his boyfriend and pulled out a kitchen chair. Kevin searched his expression while placing the food on the table and removing the cover. The enticing aroma of pasta in red meat sauce and garlic bread wafted across Jonah's nose, causing his stomach to grumble. He dived in while Kevin sat and watched.

He didn't expect the raw anger he sensed from Kevin and paused in eating. "I'm sorry about Vanay."

"It was his fault for trying that Phantom projection. Even Trueblood's pissed." Kevin stroked Jonah's forehead. "Didn't I warn you to give yourself a second to check your Death Sense?"

Jonah lowered his forked and grabbed a piece of bread as he nodded. Kevin had warned him to be ready for tests. At the time, Jonah figured he meant tests by the staff, not by other campers.

Kevin moved around the table to Jonah's side and leaned down to hug him, kissing his neck. "I have to get back before they finish picking the hikers."

Jonah wrapped his arms over Kevin's, keeping the boy from letting go. "Can't you stay?"

"You're in detention, not a hotel," Kevin whispered in Jonah's ear. "I'll let Eddy bring your clothes later."

When Jonah released his grip, Kevin moved for the door.

"Wait! What about the triptych?" Jonah asked.

"I hid it in my room. Oh, here." Kevin handed Jonah his shield bracelet.

"Why'd you bring this?"

"Because you don't have your blades. I'd feel better if you at least had the bracelet."

"You can always sneak me my blades—"

"Can't. Trueblood has them. Sorry." After hugging Jonah one last time, Kevin slipped out of the cabin.

All alone again, Jonah put on the bracelet, then tried finishing the dinner, but worrying about Vanay ruined his appetite. Instead, he crossed to the sofa to stretch out. Gazing up at the ceiling, he tried imagining what the other campers were doing.

No doubt, Eddy and AJ speculated on his whereabouts and concluded he got in trouble again. He didn't cause problems; trouble found him. Not wanting to rekindle his anger, Jonah sat up and crossed his legs. Placing his hands on his knees, palms up, he concentrated on his breathing and his heartbeat.

He had to admit he didn't do too badly, because after fifteen minutes of quiet meditation, he felt the lessening of the tension and anger. With another twenty minutes of total calm in the cabin, he had achieved a new level of focus until he heard the quiet knock on the door.

"Come in."

AJ peeked inside. "Hey." He held out a change of clothes.

Jonah hopped from the sofa and came over. "Can't you stay?"

Placing a hand on Jonah's chest, AJ pushed him inside and followed, closing the door. "Kevin said I could have ten minutes." Leaning close, and without removing his hand from Jonah's chest, he whispered, "Tell me what happened."

"Oh," Jonah said, thrown off by AJ's assertive behavior and his surprisingly warm hand. Was that because the boy conjured flame? Could he be like Kevin, with a higher-than-average body temperature?

"Jonah?" AJ whispered.

"Yeah. Okay." Jonah took the clothes and draped them over the back of a chair, then flopped on the sofa.

AJ took the nearest chair and sat all the way forward so their knees touched.

"Jennifer and Vanay attacked me," Jonah began and told him everything.

When Jonah finished, AJ leaned back, holding his hands over his face. "That's his fault," AJ mumbled behind his hands.

"I know. So," Jonah prompted, "who went out tonight?"

"Alex and Eddy." AJ sat forward with a scandalous expression. "There was a little drama when Alastor admitted he had checked everyone's packs. Trueblood got angry at the Campmaster for telling him to do it."

"Why check the hiking packs?"

"For blades. You know, I think they expected you to go out tonight."

Jonah sat back, considering this news. "That makes sense. They activated the net to keep me from phasing. And I'm the only one who would take blades since I don't have another power like all of you." He ruffled his picky hair. "Wow, I guess I messed up their plans."

"Well, Alex volunteered before they could choose another mage. And Eddy got picked to go out with him."

"Hold on," Jonah said. "Why would Alex volunteer? Why was it so important he go out tonight and not Beraki or Crosby?"

"Like we speculated, they expected you to go out. No offense, but Alex is a more experienced mage."

"That's true, but why Alex, unless… of course!" Jonah tapped AJ's leg, making his point. "Jennifer and Vanay tried to take the triptych, AJ. She knew I had solved the riddle!"

"You solved the riddle?" AJ sat forward. "Show it to me!"

"I can't. I gave it to Kevin." Jonah stood. "I've been stupid. The overnight hikes are a perfect way to hand off the triptych." He turned to AJ. "What if Vanay was supposed to do it? With him injured, Alex had to volunteer."

"Then we're okay. You and Jennifer were in the Campmaster's office and Vanay's injured."

"But Alex saw everything."

The idea shocked AJ. "You think he'd go inside a Mentor's room."

"Yeah, he would." Jonah snapped his fingers. "Remember, when the hikers are selected, they go upstairs to get ready. The mentors stay in the main room."

"He could have snuck into Kevin's room to look. That's bold, but—"

"Or Alastor could have done it. You told me he took all the hiking packs from the dorms.

"Jonah, that's scary." AJ sat on the edge of the sofa, staring across the darkened room with a worried expression.

"You have to warn Kevin and come back to tell me if Alex stole the triptych," Jonah insisted.

"They won't let me come back," AJ said, watching him. "Oh. By the way, you're on kitchen detail again."

The side statement caught Jonah by surprise. "Whatever. I don't care about that right now."

AJ stood.

The sudden doubt on his face worried Jonah. "If Alex has the Tales, that means he's gonna give it to the enemy—tonight."

AJ gulped at hearing that. "You think they'll hurt Eddy?"

Jonah didn't want to lie or take advantage of AJ's reasonable fear, but it was true that someone like Thera would probably kill Eddy.

"What will Eddy do when Alex tries to sneak away tonight?" Jonah asked.

The question caused AJ to let out a doubtful sigh. "He'll follow Alex." He hugged himself, considering the situation. "Fine. I'll tell Kevin." He moved for the door.

Jonah gripped AJ's wrist. "Eddy will be okay."

Glancing at Jonah's hand, AJ nodded and left the cabin.

Jonah slumped on the sofa for a fourth time, desperately thinking of a way to stop Alex from giving the triptych to his enemies.

CHAPTER THIRTY-SIX
POCKET REALITY

The next twenty minutes were the longest of Jonah's life. He couldn't calm himself, no matter how hard he tried. Giving up, he paced around the small living room and then the short hallway to the bedroom. He'd made his sixth circuit around the cabin when he felt Kevin approaching along with someone else.

Jonah winced seconds before Mandara pounded on the closed door. Opening it, he wasn't ready to see the Campmaster and Kevin in their long coats.

"Come with us, Blackstone," Mandara barked. He turned and strode down the pebble-covered lane.

Once again, Jonah found himself fast-walking to keep up with the Campmaster. He wanted to ask Kevin what happened, but his boyfriend was tense while watching everything around them.

Reaching into their shared connection, Jonah sensed the

burning anger and a little guilt? "It's not your fault," he whispered.

Mandara's footsteps faltered, but the man didn't slow down. "Kevin tells me you solved the riddle?" Mandara said over his shoulder as they rounded the lake and moved past the outbuildings.

"Yes, sir."

"Tell me about it."

Jonah recounted his inspiration and how he climbed the rock formation to sit and solve the riddle. Kevin snorted when he explained how each brother reminded him of his campmates. He even included his expanded theory about the young mages stealing the triptych when they reached the back gate.

"Jennifer's evil," Jonah blurted out in a rush.

Mandara grunted and didn't move to open the gate. Instead, he turned to face Jonah. "Ms. Motombu was reckless, but her shock was genuine. She's in her room and never went near Kevin's dorm." He drew in a deep breath as if trying to remain calm. "We confirmed Alex took your triptych, but we don't believe he's working with either her or Vanay." Jonah started to object, but Mandara held up a hand to stop his outburst. "You're correct. There is a conspiracy to take the triptych. That's why I put you in the cabin. We needed to know if anyone else was involved."

Jonah's jaw dropped. "You used me as bait?"

"We had Alliance people watching the cabin," Kevin explained. At Jonah's sour expression, he looked at him directly. "Yes, I knew, but we all had to take an oath, so hate me later."

Glancing at his wrist, Jonah got why Kevin gave him the bracelet. It was his boyfriend's way of letting him know something was going on without breaking his oath.

"You were never alone," Mandara continued. "The cabin's protected and we could have apprehended anyone who tried to attack."

Jonah nodded.

"Good," Mandara said. "Now, where's the Destiny Medallion?"

"It's in the Underworld," Jonah answered, still a little dazed.

Mandara hissed under his breath. "If we can't recover the triptych, can you recall the code?"

"Well, the location is on the…" Jonah trailed off, stumped because the image of the Underworld was on the triptych, which was gone. Then he remembered Omar's original painting. "I have another picture of the Underworld at home. It has the designation codes on it."

Mandara looked to Kevin. "Be ready to take Blackstone to Mount Vernon and retrieve the picture, if necessary."

"Yes, sir."

Kevin's prompt reply to Mandara worried Jonah even more. Why were they talking about not getting the triptych back? They knew Alex had it. All they had to do was go into the woods and stop the mage before he gave it to Thera.

"What's happened?"

Mandara didn't answer as he finally used his key to activate the gate and march through. Kevin gripped Jonah's shoulder and guided him through the ward.

"Kevin?" Jonah asked, not bothering to whisper, though he noted Kevin held him back, so the Campmaster pulled ahead.

"You'll see."

Remaining quiet took effort on Jonah's part, especially considering all the awful thoughts entering his mind. The walk also grated on his nerves. Why didn't they just phase? he wanted to ask until he remembered Rubio's net. A vindictive spike hit Jonah. It served them right for setting up a trap to keep him from using his powers.

But what about Eddy? The guilt overcame his moment of spiteful pleasure because his friend was out there, and the net hampered their ability to help.

Eventually, lights appeared among the trees up ahead. Jonah's pulse and anticipation increased. With the illumination spilling into the forest, he recognized they headed straight for the clearing Trueblood had showed them during their first nature session.

Tonight, supernatural flames flickered in black bowls atop totem-like poles. Jonah had a chilling memory of seeing something similar in his snatch of dream-walk about the Grim Reaper's Keep. He resisted shuddering as he followed Mandara into the midst of the activity.

An Alliance Guard patrolled the area. Trueblood, Rubio, Albrecht, and to Jonah's surprise, Mitchell huddled together. Albrecht had just lowered his hands, letting a spell dissipate. The small mage said something to Trueblood and Rubio that Jonah couldn't hear.

"Well?" Mandara asked.

Trueblood faced the Campmaster. "They're using the net as a power source to generate the pocket."

Jonah moved to the side so he could see into the clearing. There was nothing there. No tent, sleeping bags, nor signs of his friend.

"It never occurred to me someone could do this with my net." Rubio puffed out his barrel chest.

"Can't we take it down?" Mandara insisted.

Albrecht shook his head again. "The spell's source tree is inside the pocket. Only someone on the other side can stop the spell now."

"It's a serious piece of sorcery." Rubio's voice sounded a little awed and angry to Jonah.

"I've warned the Council many times," Mitchell began in his even tone, "that Thera Rasmussen is a talented sorceress. In many respects, she's more dangerous than Deyanira."

Goose bumps raced up Jonah's arms at hearing the evil Reaper's name. He couldn't hold back anymore. "What happened? Did Thera take Eddie and Alex?"

All the adults regarded Jonah as if unsure how to respond.

Finally, Trueblood answered, "No, Jonah. We don't think she took them, at least not yet."

"Then where are they?"

"Thera used the net to create a pocket of reality that's out of sync with the normal world."

"They are here," Mitchell added, adjusting his glasses as he glanced over the empty clearing. "But we can't see them. As long as the net remains operational, we can't save the campers or our colleagues sent to test them."

Jonah heard the Fallen Reaper's words, but he all he could think about was his promise to AJ that their friend would be okay. A burning determination to find a way through the net welled up inside him. No matter what he had to do, Jonah wouldn't let Thera hurt Eddy or anyone else.

Tendrils of magic cascaded through the air, outlining the limits of the altered net. *The Pocket*, Jonah thought to himself. Trueblood lowered his hands as the magic dissipated.

Jonah watched, feeling useless in this situation. Once again, the discussion among the Alliance adults resumed. At one point, Jonah had grown irritated because they talked as much about getting the triptych as they did about saving Eddy.

"Can't Eddy just walk out?" Jonah asked. "This clearing has to be near the edge."

"No, Jonah." Trueblood came over. "I suspect that once you enter, the hex's effect remains in place."

Mitchell's grave voice made the news sounds so much worse. "Young Eddy could walk back to camp, and no one would ever see him."

"All the more reason to break the hex." Rubio gestured uphill. "We should relocate to the hilltop, where I first conjured the net."

Jonah let out a sigh of relief at the idea of the adults leaving him alone to think about the problem. He should have known he wouldn't be that lucky.

Sure enough, Mandara motioned to Jonah. "Come along."

"I want to stay here a minute," Jonah blurted out. "Maybe I can think of something to help."

Rubio snorted. "What can you do that we can't, son?"

"Have you forgotten who and what Jonah represents?" Mitchell asked with a hint of anger.

Rubio caught the tone. "Luck won't solve this problem." With that, he marched off. Albrecht and Trueblood followed their fellow mage.

Mandara regarded Jonah for a long moment. "Don't linger too long. I want you at the hilltop."

"Yes, sir," Jonah answered.

The Campmaster disappeared into the darkness, taking Mitchell and the Alliance Guard with him.

Alone with Kevin now, Jonah paced around the perimeter of the clearing, putting Rubio's snide comment aside. Jonah knew the mage was just pissed that Thera had ruined his little trap. Taking a deep breath, he finally cleared his mind.

Kevin trailed behind, remaining quiet and letting him think. For some reason, Jonah wondered if Kevin was just doing his job rather than being helpful or protective. The suddenness of the bleak thought stopped Jonah in his tracks.

That was unworthy, Jonah told himself. He turned. "Sorry."

Kevin narrowed his eyes, confused. "For what?"

"Never mind." Jonah gazed at the empty clearing, trying to force his eyes to see the net.

"Whatcha thinking?" Kevin asked.

"The same thing you are. Blaming myself."

Kevin snorted and moved closer. "I should have kept the triptych with me." He waved at the air in front of them. "This net was a crazy idea from the start."

"Wow. Too bad *someone* didn't warn everyone." Jonah glared at his boyfriend, but he didn't blame Kevin. What if he had kept the triptych? Would Alex have come after it at the cabin? At least that way, the Alliance would have Alex, and Eddy would be safe.

Facing the clearing, Jonah noted signs of where the other campers had set up the tents, and the depression where they had set a fire. Thinking about that, he tried to imagine Eddy and Alex in the campsite and the triptych in the thief's hand. He didn't know how long he stood that way, but he got a brief impression, a familiar sensation.

"Did you see something?" Kevin's voice was soft, but it surprised Jonah anyway.

He concentrated, trying to put the sensation he experienced into words. "I was thinking about the triptych, and it was like I felt it."

"Sounds like what you did with the Protector's Ring," Kevin said. "Remember?"

Jonah's jaw dropped because he had forgotten about that moment. Back in Mount Vernon, on the night they found the Protector's Ring, it had been in Aunt Imma's sculpture. The problem was the art piece contained over two hundred and fifty rings. Wick had suggested Jonah could sense it because it had belonged to his father.

True enough, when Jonah thought about the device, and pictured his dad holding it, the Protector's Ring had lit up like a beacon, allowing them to find it. Kevin was right. The sensation he felt just now was the same. The triptych had been his mom's. Plus, Omar, his godfather's partner, had made the Underworld image on the device. And, Jonah realized, his best friend Mike had updated the triptych. More so than with the Protector's Ring, the triptych had been touched by multiple important people in his life.

"Stand back," Jonah said, extending his arm straight out, his fingers splayed, as if pushing against the visible reality-altering net.

"Ah," Kevin said, moving away. "I was right. You can sense it."

"Yeah." Jonah intended to do more. Closing his eyes, he concentrated again on the triptych, but instead of visualizing it in Alex's unworthy hands, he imagined his mom, Omar, and Mike, each holding a piece. In his mind's eye, the trio stood in the clearing, holding the pieces out to him, calling to him. Within seconds, an image of the real triptych blossomed in his mind.

Just as he did with the rip into the Underworld, Jonah thought of opening a path between the realities. "Open," he intoned, causing Kevin to stir.

He reached out to the triptych, willing it to show itself. Slowly, a faint haze appeared in midair. Then it grew and expanded in a vertical line. "Come on," he gritted out through clenched teeth as the edges of both realities resisted his interference. All at once, an opening blossomed, reminding Jonah of the vortex a mage could conjure.

"Oh my God," Kevin breathed. "Hold on. I'll get the others."

"I can't hold it," Jonah managed.

The opening pushed against his will to hold it open, giving him a new appreciation of what mages could do.

Kevin stopped at the other side of the clearing. "Then let it close. You can always open it again."

"Just tell them what I did." The opening contracted more. Jonah's arm shook with the effort. "Come for me."

"Jonah! No!" Kevin blurred into motion, but Jonah stepped through the rip.

His boyfriend's outstretched hands went through his arm as his body adjusted to the frequency of the pocket. The next moment, Kevin and all the lights around the clearing were gone. Jonah had made it through!

CHAPTER THIRTY-SEVEN
NIGHT OPERATION

The relative darkness of the clearing surprised Jonah. Dropping to his knees, he allowed his eyes time to adjust first. He lost precious minutes before seeing well enough to notice the slight waver in the air around him, like a weird dream.

One sure sign he was in the right place was the fresh firepit and the hiking tent. Eddy's aura remained inside, but Alex's was gone.

Using his Reaper sense, Jonah spotted Alex moving far off to his right in the woods. Light flared in the direction, and two people screamed. Jonah froze, but everything went deathly quiet.

Unexpectedly, Alex headed back toward the clearing. That didn't make any sense. Why not go to the meeting place, unless the boy had to wait *or* the meeting was at the clearing!

Rushing to the tent, Jonah flung open the flap and peered inside. Eddy lay in a heap, though Jonah couldn't tell if he was asleep or stunned. He crawled inside and shook Eddy. "Hey, wake up," he whispered.

Eddy's arms lolled, and that worried Jonah. "Come on, Eddy, wake up."

To Jonah's relief, Eddy's mouth moved, and he groaned. The boy's eyes opened, and he jerked away before recognizing Jonah in the dark.

"What? Jonah?" Eddy asked, rubbing his head. "Alex zapped me! That bastard!"

"He did? But the net's supposed to keep him from doing that." Jonah's mind raced. If Alex could do spells, whatever Thera did to create the pocket also nullified that part of the net incantation. "She doesn't want her power muted," Jonah said, more to himself than Eddy.

"Huh? What are you talking about?" Eddy asked.

"Nothing. We need to get out of here. Alex just attacked some Alliance people who came to test you."

A sound came from outside in the clearing just as Jonah's Death Sense spiked. He jumped out of the tent. Eddy followed just as the darkness lit up and a fork of lightning struck the tent.

Once the brightness faded, Eddy dived back inside the tent.

"Eddy, don't!" Jonah whispered.

Lightning hit the tent again, crisscrossed the surface, and zapped Eddy's leg before he pulled it free. When he tried to stand, the numbed leg buckled, and he collapsed to the ground. The retrieved hiking pack dropped beside him.

That was fortunate because a third fork of lightning whizzed right over his head. Jonah pulled his friend away from the tent, dragging the hiking pack with them. The boys huddled behind a boulder as another zip of lightning hit the top of the boulder.

Then the clearing went pitch black again and silent.

"Thanks," Eddy breathed. "Oh! Alex stole your triptych and—"

"Yeah, I know that. He's gonna give it to the enemy unless we stop him."

"He can't."

Alex hit their hiding place again. After the light show died, Eddy dug in the pack and pulled out Jonah's triptych. "When Alastor made a big deal about checking the packs, I figured Alex might smuggle something in his to help with the test. I found your triptych."

Jonah couldn't believe it! He grinned despite the constant painful throbbing from his Death Sense. He motioned to Eddy. "Keep the triptych in your pack. It'll be safer there."

Eddy put the pieces away. "Why didn't you bring Kevin or someone else?"

Jonah winced. "That's a long story, but the short version is, we're cut off from help because we're in a magical pocket of reality."

Even in the dark, Jonah could see Eddy's eyes widen. To his surprise, Eddy nodded rather quickly. "I knew something was off. Look around—the air's all wavy."

"Yeah. Help's coming, it'll just take a little longer."

Eddy subjected Jonah to a shrewd look. "So we stall for time. Got it." Without warning, he peeked around the boulder and called into the night, "Alex! What are you doing? I thought we were cool?" Eddy turned to wink at Jonah. "He's pissed that I took the triptych, huh?"

"That's why he came back to the clearing," Jonah said. In that case, Thera or whoever Alex would meet could already be in the forest. He closed his eyes and listened.

A rustle of leaves came from the left. Guessing that Alex had moved to get a better shot at them, Jonah motioned to Eddy, and they slipped around the rock to keep its bulk between them and their attacker. He didn't know why the young mage kept pausing his attack. When Deyanira had fought Agent Ramsey, the sorceress had poured it on until the Hunter fled for his life.

"Alex!" Jonah called out this time. "Talk to us."

Dead silence followed his shout. Alex was probably shocked, Jonah decided. What would the determined boy do now? Jonah had his answer when his Death Sense spiked. Reacting on instinct, he huddled lower behind the rock, pulling Eddy down with him.

Alex's bolt of lightning took a huge chunk out of the boulder. The explosion caused Jonah's ears to ring and filled the air with a choking, flinty smell. A tendril of lightning played over the entire surface, forcing them to scurry away from the temporary shelter.

One benefit of the light show was that they could see Alex's location. Eddy, feeling better, hurled lightning balls at Alex. When the young mage retaliated, Jonah and Eddy were already crashing down through the blackness. Despite the considerable racket they made, Alex didn't cast any spells, and Jonah began to suspect why.

"He's recharging," Eddy said, revealing he and Jonah were thinking the same thing.

When Jonah's Death Sense spiked, he said, "Down."

Lightning shot overhead, blasting a tree and scorching it. The falling branches caused Eddy to lose his footing and tumble. He came to a wrenching halt, slamming the hiking pack into a tree and absorbing the force of the collision.

Jonah rolled to a stop beside him. "You okay?" He had heard something break and feared Eddy had damaged the triptych.

Without answering, Eddy let out a growl, rose to his feet, and fired lightning uphill until his power fizzled. "Dang it," he said, dropping beside Jonah. "I think he's better than me." Eddy held up his hand. "I only have the one trick."

That was true, Jonah thought. Worse, he had no clue how long it would take the Alliance adults to break into the pocket, or if they could. And running from Alex all night wasn't a solution. What else could he do without his powers and Eddy running low on magic? Then again, Alex would eventually grow tired, but the young mage had his arsenal of other spells. There was also an unknown factor: the enemy could show up at any moment.

What would Kevin tell him to do? Well, he didn't dare blur in the darkened woods. That would most likely result in him ramming into a tree at full speed. The only other option was hand-to-hand. But Jonah didn't think he could get close enough to Alex for that—not unless he used Eddy to create a diversion. As the doubt increased, he wished he had the Reaper blades.

Wait! He might not have had his weapons, but the fighting techniques would still work. *I just need replacements.*

Taking a moment to orient himself, Jonah inched his way uphill, feeling in the darkness for fallen branches.

"Where're you going?" Eddy whispered.

"Shhhh," Jonah hissed. Searching with his hands among the wooden fragments, he found two likely candidates. When he broke them, the sound echoed in the sudden quiet and gave away his location.

Lightning sizzled in Jonah's direction. But the shot was off because Alex couldn't pinpoint the source from the echoes. Relieved that Eddy didn't return fire and reveal their true location, Jonah rejoined his friend and started stripping the shorter twigs off the branches.

His hands were raw and ached by the time he finished. On the positive side, the sap from the branches left his hands sticky, so the makeshift weapons wouldn't slip from his grasp.

"Cool," Eddy commented, peering at the branches in the darkness. "Those are like the practice batons."

"That's the idea. Now all we need is a diversion so I can get close to Alex."

"No problem." Eddy moved off to Jonah's right without making much noise. Jonah felt a bit of envy as he watched his quiet friend's shadowy shape slip through the surrounding darkness.

Eddy had learned more in Nature class than Jonah knew. His concern about his friend seemed a little clueless. Eddy was a capable campmate, and he would keep Alex from getting the triptych. When Eddy stopped, he produced a small ball of lightning in his palm, enough to show his face and his other hand. With slow, exaggerated motions, Eddy counted down from five.

The night lit up as Eddy fired lightning at Alex's last known position. As expected, Alex retaliated with lightning. As impressive as Alex's earlier attacks were, the final salvo was far weaker than the previous. Jonah had what he needed, and shifting a branch to each hand, he charged forward.

With the young mage's dark shape visible, Jonah risked blurring into motion and closed the distance in a second. Unable to keep quiet, Alex heard him and threw up his hands as Jonah came in, swinging the branches. But Alex was quick and dodged the first swipe while unslinging the pack. The boy used the bag to block Jonah.

Using the pack as an effective shield, Alex pressed forward. Fearing the mage would get close enough to knock him over, Jonah switched his focus and caught Alex on his unprotected legs.

Alex cursed as he went down, yet he wasn't out. A sizzle of real fire missed Jonah by a fraction of an inch, causing his skin to blister before he could roll aside. Alex regained his feet and continued casting spells in pure frustration, only to have Eddy zap him from the behind.

Roaring in anger, Alex let loose a spell that went off with a bang and knocked Jonah and Eddy away. Jonah found his branches and prepared to attack again when Eddy yanked on his arm.

"Come on," Eddy said, pulling Jonah with him. They dodged into the trees before the angry mage could hex them. A few terrifying moments later, they stopped and huddled as Alex spent his rage, mixing in hexes with the lightning. Eventually, the magical outburst died down.

The boys exchanged wide-eyed glances, and Jonah suspected Eddy thought the same thing. Alex was more powerful than they had anticipated. Or, it occurred to Jonah, maybe Jennifer and Thomas had shown the mage some new tricks. Whatever the reason, the boy was destructive. Several of the surrounding trees burned with green fire now, flooding the forest with flickering light and heat.

Jonah tapped Eddy's shoulder and motioned downhill. Staying low to the ground, they inched farther into the darkness.

"That was brilliant, don't you think?" Eddy asked in a low whisper. "At least now Alex knows we'll fight instead of run."

"Yep," Jonah muttered. All they had to do was survive long enough for help to arrive.

CHAPTER THIRTY-EIGHT
FRIENDLY FOE

"We need to get back to camp," Eddy said, keeping up with Jonah.

"That won't help us," Jonah answered. He explained everything Trueblood had told him.

"Dang, dude. This sucks."

Jonah stopped and tugged on Eddy's hiking pack strap. "Don't you have a map?"

"Oh yeah, right." Eddy slipped off the pack and opened it. When he pulled out the map, Jonah heard the soft click on glass from inside. "Oh, Dang!" Eddy took the busted flashlight from the pack next.

Jonah relaxed. "Where's my triptych?"

"In the side pocket. Don't worry. I guess we'll have to use matches to read the map. I need to save my lightning for the next fight." Eddy held up the small box of matches.

Huddling close, he ignited a match while Jonah held up the map.

"Why's Alex blocking the way to camp if he knows we're inside a pocket?" Eddy asked.

"I don't know." Jonah said. They were way off course from the back gate and moving farther away from the clearing. "I think we need to ambush Alex again."

"Okay. I can zap him first," Eddy suggested. "Then you come in with the branches."

"That may work," Jonah hedged.

A sound came from behind them. Eddy snuffed out the match while Jonah concentrated on a solution. He needed something defensive.

What about the wind? That would be something Alex wouldn't expect. Jonah hunkered down, closed his eyes, and focused inward. A twig snapped farther uphill and broke his concentration.

Eddy whispered, "He's coming."

Resisting the urge to move to a new position, Jonah applied his will and summoned the wind. In his haste and worry, he also opened himself to the magical energies around him.

Rubio's hex-augmented net made him shudder. It felt tainted, evil. Shrinking away, he focused on the well of energy inside himself. For a moment, it occurred to Jonah that summoning the wind wasn't a Reaper ability. It was magic.

Jonah pushed that revelation to the back of his mind and strengthened his intent to control the air. In response, the wind whipped up around him, rustling the leaves.

Another crack came from closer this time and Eddy stirred beside him.

"Be ready to hit him with lightning." Jonah's grip on the branches tightened and he waited. Anxious seconds ticked by until he heard Alex shift to the left and slightly away. "Now," he said.

Eddy's aim was true, but Alex reacted faster and produced a shield. As impressive as that was, the shield flared and disappeared after one solid hit.

With Alex focused on Eddy's attack, Jonah stood and called out, *"Sakoto!"*

The trees groaned as a sudden gust of wind rushed from Jonah's hand and slammed into Alex, knocking the boy off his feet.

Exhilarated with the power, Jonah shouted the invocation again as he made a grabbing motion.

Alex had just regained his feet when the second gust of wind whirled around his ankles and swept his feet off the ground. With a whoosh of escaping air, the young mage fell hard on his hiking pack a second time.

Jonah came at Alex, catching the boy across the left forearm.

"You maniac!" Alex screamed, cradling the injured arm.

Jumping on top of the boy, Jonah swung his branch, but Alex bucked and threw him off. When Alex tried to scramble to his feet, Eddy kicked the guy. Since Alex was bigger, he didn't budge much and Eddy stumbled backward, landing on his butt.

That was enough of a distraction for Jonah to hop on Alex's back and lock the branch under the boy's chin. Only when Alex began to choke and sag to the ground did Jonah grow nervous and let up.

Alex slumped to his knees, sucking in air. "You bastards." The words were little more than a croak.

Jonah let out a relieved breath that Alex was okay. Just as quickly, his anger returned, and he jabbed the mage in the chest with the branch. "You tried to kill us!"

"Yeah!" Eddy ran at the boy, ready to kick him until Jonah pulled him away.

"It was supposed to be a test, idiot."

Eddy waved a fist in the air. "Tell that to the rock you destroyed."

"We know you're lying." Jonah grabbed the front of Alex's blue shirt. "You had my triptych in your hiking pack and led Eddy into this pocket reality to cut him off from help.

"I thought it was the net Rubio created."

"Stop lying, Alex," Jonah shouted. "Thera augmented it with a hex to create this pocket."

"I didn't know about that."

Eddy snickered at the boy. "You know what, Jonah? Alex looks too dumb to be a part of the conspiracy."

Jonah waved off his friend's comment. "Who were you supposed to meet in the woods tonight? The Alliance Mole? Thera and Fabian?"

Alex shoved Jonah's hand away and scrambled into a sitting position. He slipped off his hiking pack while shaking his head. "I can't tell you that."

The boy's stubbornness irritated Jonah until he got the answer. "They made you take an oath. Wait." The Rasmussen twins couldn't touch Alex while he attended Camp Alliance. However, the mole was an Alliance member and could come and go whenever he wanted.

"The mole had you take an oath," Jonah stated in a whisper.

Alex's eyes widened and he nodded while massaging his neck.

Eddy let out a snort of disgust and ignited his hands, watching Alex.

Despite Jonah's mixed feelings about the Campmaster, they had to tell the man that the mole got to one of his campers. Maybe they could find a way around the oath.

Once again, Jonah's snide comment to Kevin that maybe Memory Charmers could pull information from Jennifer came back to him now. Since then, he'd learned the hard truth about that. Now, he faced another camper who had information the Alliance Council needed. What would they do? What could they do? Suddenly, Councilwoman Bertonneau's fears became real to Jonah. Was that part of the mole's plan? Did he want to push the Council into making dangerous mistakes, as Bertonneau feared?

Jonah recalled her dire warning.

"I'm afraid we're headin' down a dark path, young man, a very dark path. We become our enemies. Good people will suffer."

Staring at Alex, Jonah knew the boy had more, but what could he do? Guess? "You took over the mission when Vanay got hurt, didn't you?"

"Vanay was never supposed to deliver—" Alex broke off, unable to produce words for several horrible moments. "The others don't trust me." Alex looked away while nursing his injured arm.

"You mean Jennifer," Jonah stated, glad to confirm his suspicions.

"Yeah. I told you, Trueblood discovered me, not Rubio."

Jonah settled down in a squatting position, making sure to keep his distance and an eye on Eddy who looked ready to kick Alex. "Rubio doesn't like Trueblood."

"That's an understatement. Rubio's pissed with the mage and the other Council members who won't…" Alex's eyes widened, and his Adam's apple bobbed up and down as he swallowed. When he opened his mouth, he sucked in labored breaths.

"I… can't tell you," Alex finally managed and pounded his fist against the ground. "I hate this."

Alex's reaction to almost breaking the oath horrified Jonah. He stood, looking around the quiet forest to avoid the mage's intense stare.

"How did you do a wind incantation?" Alex asked, his voice sounding more normal. "You're not a mage."

Jonah shrugged. "My father could do it."

"I knew it!" Alex shouted. "You were the one making all that wind in Meditation class."

"Yeah."

Jonah heard a sound from behind him, and whirled just as Eddy zapped Alex, who had jumped to his feet to charge them. The mage fell back on the ground, twitching.

He met Eddy's gaze and nodded thanks. Since his Death Sense didn't spike, Alex didn't mean to attack them, Jonah decided.

"Give me the triptych. Please," the boy managed. "You don't understand."

"What'll happen if you don't meet your contact?"

Alex refused to answer as he pulled himself into a seated position.

"I'll zap him again," Eddy snarled at the mage. "Maybe we should tie his hands behind his back, just in case."

Jonah agreed and moved behind Eddy to pull a length of rope from the pack. One look at Eddy's eager expression was enough for Alex to let Jonah tie his hands behind his back.

As Jonah finished, his Death Sense twinged. Since Alex couldn't move, Jonah began to worry as he pulled on the boy's hiking pack. "Alex, can you make a vortex?"

Eddy and Alex stared at him in surprise.

"Only a small hole," Alex began, "barely big enough to stick my arm through. I'm better with offensive spells."

"Try it."

"You don't understand," Alex said. "If I make a vortex and can't keep it open…"

Jonah did understand because he had to struggle to open the rip into this pocket reality.

Alex's comment also said something about Jennifer's ability. He'd seen the stable vortex she used to escape from the boathouse fight.

He found it strange to wish the mage, who had just tried to fry them, was more skilled. "Then we need to get out of here," he said in a weary voice. Alex met his gaze and Jonah saw the mounting fear. The boy had missed his meeting. Whoever had arrived wouldn't be happy.

Eddy shook his head. "Jonah, I don't think a vortex would work anyway. You told me Trueblood said the hex would still keep us out of sync."

"Yeah, I know," Jonah replied. "I have a feeling that something else is going to happen." Remembering the stunned adults, he said, "We need to make sure the Alliance adults are okay. Bring Alex." Jonah ventured into the darkened woods while opening his senses in the general direction where Alex ambushed the others.

The sense of danger increased as they retraced their path back toward the ambush site. Several tense minutes later, Jonah's foot struck something that didn't move, almost tripping him.

Alex stumbled through the darkness to Jonah's position, with Eddy prodding him in the back. By then, Jonah had Alex's flashlight out, shining the light on Damian and another young mage on the ground.

"Oh my God!" Eddy said.

Jonah felt Damian and the other guy's necks. With a sigh of relief, he sat back. "They're alive."

"I wouldn't kill anyone," Alex protested.

"He did this?" Eddy zapped Alex again, causing the large boy to hit the ground and convulse.

"Eddy, stop!" Jonah waved his friend off while fighting the sinking feeling that had developed in the pit of his stomach. Reaching out with his mind, Jonah tried to find the source of the immediate danger.

Except for Alex and Eddy beside him, and Rubio's altered net, Jonah couldn't detect any other magic. Or, Jonah corrected himself, maybe the enemy could cloak their intentions until the last second.

Images of Thera Rasmussen flashed in Jonah's mind. She said she would come for him. With a growing sense of urgency, he asked Alex, "Can you wake these two?"

"Doubt it," he said in a pained voice. "I didn't make the hex bomb I used. The—" Alex broke off again.

At that moment, bloodcurdling howls sounded off in the distance, followed by snarls and barks.

Jonah shot to his feet, struggling with an odd feeling of inevitability at the attack. When Thera's warning echoed in his mind, Jonah pressed his hands flat against his head, trying to banish it.

Eddy spun toward the barking. "What the heck is that?" he asked, his voice full of fear. "Wolves?"

"No," Jonah said in a quiet tone as he lowered his hands. "Those are Grim Hounds."

CHAPTER THIRTY-NINE
TEAM WORK

"Grim Hounds?" Alex repeated as he turned on the spot, hands bound in front now. While Jonah still didn't trust the guy, he thought it better for Alex to at least have his hands useful. Watching the mage's agitated movements, Jonah reminded himself that not everyone had regular run-ins with the vicious, supernatural dogs.

"Yes, Grim Hounds. Come on," Jonah said, stopping Alex before the boy could repeat the question yet again. Eddy pulled the mage's good arm, tugging him downhill and away from the approaching beasts.

"But what about the mages?" Eddy asked.

Jonah gave it some thought. "The Grim Hounds were sent after you and me." His voice sounded confident. "We keep going."

"Who would send Grim Hounds after you?" Alex asked.

Jonah whirled, giving him a skeptical look. "Who do you think? Thera wants to stop me from finding the medallion."

"The what?"

"Keep moving!" Jonah snapped, ignoring Alex's question and moving through the trees as fast as he could.

Eddy remained quiet, but Alex wasn't satisfied. "They know I'm out here."

Jonah let out an exasperated breath. Didn't the idiot understand? "Why do you think the Grim Hounds are coming from the clearing's direction? You're learning what happens when you cross the KIN."

Alex didn't say anything for several minutes as they raced blindly away from the Grim Hounds. Running was useless, Jonah knew. The creatures had excellent night vision and could whip around trees and rocks quick as lightning. Even now, the occasional barks drew closer and closer. Soon, Jonah felt the vibrations of the beasts' heavy footfalls.

"This is so freakin' messed up," Eddy wailed.

Jonah heard the desperation and intense fear in his friend's voice. To be honest, he had to fight off the despair. With the Grim Hounds behind them, the group didn't have many options and very little time.

A noise rose above the racket of their passage, drawing Jonah's attention. "There's water ahead."

Moments later, he, Eddy, and Alex stumbled onto a shallow path. They followed it downhill, picking up speed. In the dimness, Jonah didn't see the sheer drop-off until it was too late. He dug in his heels, but still tumbled forward! At the last second, Eddy tugged on his pack. With a grunt, he and the mage heaved Jonah back and away from the edge.

"Thanks," Jonah breathed.

"Don't thank me. We're still trapped," Eddy complained, "and the Grim Hounds are close."

His friend was right about that, Jonah admitted. Plus, the eager growls of the beasts were louder than ever. The sounds grated on his nerves, causing spasms of fear to roll through his body. "Tune them out, or they'll cause you to give up."

"How do you know that?" Eddy shivered, rubbing his arms.

"Just listen to…" Jonah paused because an intense sensation, like many friends sending positive thoughts, washed over him. He spun around as a haze appeared for a millisecond in the air behind them.

The Grim Hounds must have sensed it too, because they let out questioning yelps. Peering up the trail, Jonah saw two huge shapes at the top of the hill. The beasts resumed their run.

"Stand beside me," Jonah told the others, knowing they had less than a minute.

Eddy obeyed without arguing.

"What are you gonna do?" Alex asked. "I can hear them, but I can't see them." He raised his bound hands that glowed with the buildup of magic energy.

"Don't." Jonah pressed down on the boy's arm. "Trust me." He held up his left hand.

Alex's eyes widened when he saw the shield bracelet. "Where did you get that?"

"My friend gave it to me."

"Is he a mage?"

"Yep." Closing his eyes, Jonah focused on the device and readied himself.

"Jonah, do it now," Eddy pressed.

"Be ready to shoot lightning when I tell you."

The vibrations of the Grim Hounds' feet shook them, and the snarls were terrifying. Jonah had no trouble imagining the double rows of sharp teeth bared and ready to rip them apart.

"Jonah…" Eddy's voice shook with terror.

At Jonah's mental nudge, the bracelet grew hot as a prickling sensation spread from it and along his arm. A blue bubble of distortion popped into existence around them.

The first Grim Hound flew out of the darkness, rammed into the shield, and produced visible distortions. Eddy yelled while Alex covered his head with his bound wrists, but the creature rolled over the protective bubble. Its startled yelps and growls grew faint as it tumbled over the cliff.

The second Grim Hound landed on the shield and snapped its massive jaws as flecks of saliva hit the barrier like raindrops and dribbled down the sides. The creature's growls vibrated Jonah's backbone, numbing him.

Struggling through the effect of seeing the creature up close, Jonah willed himself to move. Just before the shield gave out, he shoved outward with his left hand. The effect was to push the Grim Hound off to the right and into the trees. Unfortunately, the creature didn't tumble far enough to fall off the cliff.

Jonah pointed straight off to their left. "Alex, Eddy, there. Now!"

Eddy used lightning, but the young mage let loose with an impressive volley of supernatural fire in the direction Jonah indicated. The attack caught the Grim Hound in time, before it regained its feet. The beast roared in frustration.

Alex's eyes widened as the fire outlined the Grim Hound. Panicked now, he pushed more energy at it. "Take that!"

Jonah added his attack by calling up the wind to knock the Grim Hound off its feet and toward the cliff. But the creature dug its huge claws into the ground and stopped its fall.

Alex screamed as he ran toward the creature.

Jonah tried to stop him. "Alex, don't do that."

The mage twisted out of Jonah's grip. "I can see where it's digging into the dirt."

As Alex reached the Grim Hound, it opened its jaws, exposing the double rows of teeth.

Eddy hit the creature with a bolt of lightning.

Seeing that, Alex brought his bound fists up and shot the creature with lightning. The Grim Hound took the blows, whining in pain as its spasms tore the paws loose. The beast seemed to suspend in the air as currents played over its body. Then it plummeted out of sight. A loud splash reached them from far below.

Jonah collapsed into a kneeling position, and Eddy slumped down onto the ground beside him. Both boys took time to suck in ragged breaths.

When Jonah recovered, he stood and slugged Alex on the arm. "I told you to use lightning from the start."

"I didn't know fire wouldn't work."

"They're Grim Hounds," Jonah explained. When Alex gave him a weary shrug, Jonah grew impatient. "They're like the mythical Hell Hounds. Hell. Get it? Fire doesn't affect them."

"How do you know so much about these things?"

Jonah gave the boy a hard look. "Experience." He motioned to Eddy. "I don't know if the fall finished them, but we should get going."

Eddy took out his compass. Jonah fumbled with Alex's flashlight and shined it on the device. After getting their bearings, Eddy pulled a map out of a side pocket. "I know it won't make a difference, but can't we head toward camp? It will make me feel better than running around the woods."

"We can follow the stream. It goes right by the northern edge of the camp." Jonah turned the flashlight on his face so Alex could see his icy glare. "That okay with you, Alex?"

"Yeah," Alex mumbled, sounding miserable.

The boys set off in the direction they ran earlier, making sure to keep the water's sound on their right. As they went, Jonah drew in power and suspected Alex and Eddy of doing the same thing.

He thought that this night couldn't get any worse when new snarls came from behind them.

Alex smacked a nearby tree. "This isn't fair."

"Get over it." Jonah broke into a run, and the boys followed.

Thera wanted them dead and didn't care how many Grim Hounds she had to use.

After five more minutes of crashing through the trees, Jonah stopped running. "We can't keep going like this. They're gaining on us." He felt the tug on his pack as Eddy snatched Alex's flashlight to shine it in his face.

"Are you serious?" Eddy asked. "We barely got away from the first two Grim Hounds."

"Turn that off."

"This won't make a difference," Eddy said in a sour voice.

Jonah let out a frustrated groan as he blocked the light so he could look around. Eddy's fear was getting the better of the boy, and Jonah understood. He needed a plan and now.

Scanning the area, he noted the coverage was thinner, and the land had a slight incline. He'd see the Grim Hounds approaching in the weak starlight, but they had little cover. Jonah turned in the direction they came.

Alex grabbed his shoulder. "Where are you going?"

"Nowhere. We should stay here and fight the Grim Hounds off."

Eddy pointed at Jonah's wrist. "You plan to use your shield again?"

Jonah concentrated, and the shield flared into existence around him for a few seconds before sputtering and fizzling out.

"It's done."

"Wait! I saw him do a shield," Eddy pointed at Alex.

"It popped after one hit." Alex's shoulders slumped a little. "I told you, I'm not that good with defense spells. Now, Crosby's really good with shields."

Eddy let out a disgusted sound and whirled on Jonah. "Then what's your plan?"

Jonah held up his remaining branch. It had a slightly sharpened end. "First, we need to release Alex."

"Why?" Eddy shot back.

"He can light up the area with his blue fire." When his friend hesitated, Jonah grew testy. "Just do it, Eddy."

With a disgusted snort, Eddy undid Alex's hands. Without being told, the young mage fired off several balls of the pale blue fire, washing the immediate area in an eerie glow.

Jonah nodded to Eddy. "You two stun them with your lightning, and I'll rush in and stab them."

"That'll never work." Alex pointed at his eyes. "We can't see them."

"I'll tell you where to shoot, but you'll have to stand in the open." At Eddy's frown, Jonah added, "It'll work. Help me up into that tree."

Alex's large size came in handy as he lifted Jonah high enough to reach the bottom branch. Jonah hauled himself up and reached back for his makeshift weapon. Eddy tossed it to him.

"Make sure you stop them near the tree, guys."

"Whatever." The mage positioned himself several yards away. Eddy went in the opposite direction.

Crashing and muffled thuds drew nearer as the Grim Hounds crested a bump in the hill. Jonah's insides froze when he saw the creatures' silhouettes. They immediately slowed, sniffing the air. Jonah signaled Alex and Eddy, and the boys raised their hands, which already glowed with crackling lightning.

The Grim Hounds resumed their charge, but the creatures weren't dumb. Just as they reached the edge of the illumination, they dodged sideways to come at the guys from two directions.

"They split up," Jonah stage-whispered. "Quick! Eddy, you shoot lightning to your right. Alex, you shoot lightning to your left. Now!"

Eddy sent lightning flowing, catching a Grim Hound as it entered the illuminated area. The creature bucked and spasmed in pain. As soon as Eddy let up, Jonah dropped on the Grim Hound's back.

Off to his left, Alex caught the second beast with lightning. Jonah's attention snapped back to his Grim Hound because the creature's skin was harder and smoother than he anticipated. Slipping sideways, Jonah fumbled to get a firm grip. At the last second, he managed to grab hold of an ear.

The Grim Hound twisted its body around so that its red-within-red eye focused on him. Then the creature bucked and turned its head left and right. Rather than dislodge him, the movement enabled Jonah to hook the branch under the creature's jaw. That resulted in the Grim Hound going even wilder and rolling over.

The sudden, smothering pressure of the Grim Hound's body shocked Jonah, and he lost his hold on the stick as he used both hands to push the hound off. Thankfully, the creature continued its roll.

Desperation and terror propelled Jonah now as he scrambled for the stick. When he grabbed it, he whirled and lunged for the dark shape rising in front of him. The stick slid into the Grim Hound's chest, and dark blood gushed out.

Reminded of Mandara's move to draw him in close, Jonah let go. But the Grim Hound swiped and clawed Jonah across his forehead. Something wet splashed on his face, followed by intense pain.

He landed hard on the ground, dazed. Despite the injury, he scrambled away from the injured Grim Hound, which continued to roll around with death spasms.

"Help," Alex called. His reserve of energy dwindled fast so that the Grim Hound stalked forward through the weak lightning. When Alex fired his last bolt, the creature leaped and hit Alex's weak shield. As the mage said, the shield failed at once. The Grim Hound pounced again, knocking him to the ground.

Eddy rushed forward and brought his hiking pack around to smack the Grim Hound in the head. Jonah froze, shocked when the creature sank its double row of sharp teeth into the bag and yanked it free.

The triptych!

He winced when Eddy hit the creature with a weakened lightning bolt and then had to dodge back to avoid being ripped open by the Grim Hound's claws.

Jonah pulled himself to his feet and shouted, *"Sakoto!"* All he achieved was a bracing gust of wind that caused the

Grim Hound to pause. It turned its angry red eyes on him for a second and let out a challenging growl.

"Come get me!"

The Grim Hound roared, then turned back to Alex and raised its massive paw to rip him open. For his part, Alex let off a feeble burst of green fire, which did little more than outline the creature's head. In the middle of fighting for his life, Jonah felt the strong surge of friendly energy again. This time, he knew what it meant and whirled around. Seeing the thin line in midair, Jonah reached out for it and shouted, "Open!"

He detected the helping power from outside the bubble. A beautiful rip formed and he saw his friends. Just as quickly, he had to duck a ball of blue flame that struck the Grim Hound attacking Alex.

Along with Alex's supernatural fire, the attack helped outline the creature even more to the naked eye. A second later, something invisible hit the beast, knocking it away from Alex and Eddy and into a nearby tree with a loud whack.

Monisha, AJ, Lisa, and Darren charged into the battle. It was obvious Trueblood had found a way into the pocket reality. Jonah expected the mage or even Mandara to step through next, but the last person was Kevin.

AJ pulled a handful of glittering dust from a pouch and muttered under his breath. A second later, the special dust exploded from his hand in a concentric circle, shimmering in the air like a cloud of a thousand tiny fireflies.

Monisha let out a surprised grunt as sparkling dust coated and revealed the Grim Hound she held against the tree. AJ stood beside her, his hands glowing with blue fire.

Jonah started to whoop and congratulate his friends when someone tackled him around the waist. Instead of falling to the ground, Jonah and his attacker shot straight up into the air.

"Whoa! Lisa?" Jonah blurted out.

"Quiet! I'm concentrating," Lisa hissed in a strained voice.

"But why—"

Two more Grim Hounds, also covered in glitter, sped toward them, leaped, and nearly caught Jonah's foot with their massive paws. Lisa yelled and buried her face against Jonah's shoulder.

Kevin blurred into motion and body-checked one creature off to the side. Pulling out his blades, he attacked, forcing it back.

Because of the glitter coating the beasts' bodies, Eddy had no trouble hitting the other with a bolt of lightning. The Grim Hound writhed in pain under the assault.

Eddy's face was a mask of concentration as he poured on more power, and the creature's growl turned into a pitiful whine. "Take that!"

Another stream of lightning joined the first as Alex, battered but recharged, regained his feet. The Grim Hound's entire body glowed, and it dropped to the ground, dead.

"Adios!" Alex pumped his fist in the air, and Eddy did the same.

Meanwhile, Kevin came under the other Grim Hound's swiping paws and sliced the creature across the neck. It dropped to the ground, jerking and spasming for a few seconds before dying.

Lisa's concentration gave out, and she and Jonah dropped to the ground. The impact numbed his legs, yet he managed to stay on his feet. Lisa's leg buckled, and she let out a startled cry as she crumpled to the ground.

Jonah knelt beside her. "You alright?"

"Bad landing, that's all." She offered him a pained grin. "Sorry."

"Don't worry about it." Jonah helped her stand while noting that she favored her left foot.

"A little help," Monisha called out.

Darren let out a challenging yell as he crossed the fight area and came up to the struggling Grim Hound Monisha still held. He grabbed it on either side of its head and gave it a violent twist. The Grim Hound's neck broke with a sickening crack.

A sudden silence filled the area. Jonah glanced around at his campmates as pride and gratitude roared inside him. "Thanks for helping."

Darren's face sobered, and he traded serious looks with the others.

Kevin stepped forward, looking as grim. "We have to shut down the net. That's the only way to get out."

In an instant, Jonah's hope at his friends' arrival vanished. Hiking back to camp would have been dangerous. Taking down the net was suicidal.

CHAPTER FORTY
GRIM JOURNEY

"Reaching the hilltop is gonna be a problem." Jonah pointed at the nearest Grim Hound carcass. "Thera will send more."

"Grim Hounds?" Monisha asked, staring at the body.

"They're canine-like supernatural creatures of the Underworld," AJ answered, staring at a different body. "They take a dog shape when they cross into the mortal realm."

Almost on cue, the Grim Hound's body caved in on itself and dissolved. It was like watching a time-lapsed body of a dead animal decomposing. In less than a minute, all evidence of the body was gone.

Lisa scrunched up her face. "Whew! That's gross."

"At least it's dead," Eddy pointed out.

Without warning, Jonah's Death Sense throbbed, causing him to clutch his head as he scanned the surrounding forest.

"More Grim Hounds?" Eddy asked, watching Jonah's face.

"Yeah."

Darren whirled around, trying to see into the darkness. "Shouldn't we start running?"

"It won't help," Jonah insisted. "The Grim Hounds can catch us before we make it to the hilltop. We need to fight."

"But if we keep moving, we'll be a lot closer to the hex's source each time we fight off an attack," Darren countered.

"He's right," Kevin said.

Jonah bit down on his instant irritation when he noticed the way Kevin's gaze went to the injury on his head. Jonah knew his boyfriend wanted to make a fuss over him but wouldn't do that in front of the others. Still, he sensed Kevin's concern.

Plus, everyone glanced between him and Kevin, no doubt wondering if their mentor would take charge. In truth, Jonah wouldn't mind that at all. Yet Kevin knew him well enough and pointedly waited for Jonah to make the decision. His affection for Kevin only deepened as a result.

"Okay." Jonah nodded. "Let's do it."

His agreement seemed to jump-start Kevin, who pointed to Darren and Monisha. "You two cover our backs."

Darren nodded, looking just as eager to do something.

"We'll help Lisa." AJ offered the girl his arm to lean on. Eddy stood on her other side, with Alex behind.

That left Kevin and Jonah out front. He started walking, and Kevin matched his steps.

The Fallen Reaper pulled out two silver cylinders. "I thought you could use these."

"My blades!" As soon as Jonah took the cylinders, they activated, and he weaved them through the air. With the calming effect the blades produced, he was ready to finish their mission.

After a moment more, he deactivated the weapons and glanced behind at the others. "How did you all get through? Trueblood?" he whispered.

"Yeah, he made us all concentrate on you and Eddy," Kevin said. "I told him how you did the same thing to get inside the pocket. And he gave AJ the kufwa dust to use if we ran into Grim Hounds."

Jonah glanced back at Darren. "I'm surprised they didn't send Darren's dad."

"He's not at camp, but they gave Darren a baton to knock out the hex." Kevin smirked. "Mandara and Rubio wanted to come, and the Council argued, but Trueblood explained that only someone with a deep connection to you could get through the hex. That sealed it for Mandara. He didn't argue anymore."

The Campmaster's strange behavior that evening confused Jonah, but he sensed something else. He nudged his boyfriend's arm. "You mean a deep connection like being my soulmate? True love?" He smirked.

To Jonah's surprise, Kevin smiled. "Trueblood says you made a special connection with all the others, smart butt. That connection let him power the spell."

Of course, Jonah immediately thought of how he had solved the riddle. He had reflected on how all the other kids made him feel. That connection allowed him to activate the remaining stars! And Mitchell said he'd develop a group of friends, Protectors.

The possibilities sobered Jonah. "Maybe they were just worried about Eddy?" He offered, sensing that wasn't the case.

"Nope." Kevin laughed, bumping into Jonah. "Everyone likes you."

Though Kevin meant the idea as a compliment, it worried Jonah. His campmates had willingly run into the thick of danger, risking their lives when the adults couldn't help. He swallowed hard, moved by their bravery. With that came a sudden sense of responsibility.

"We're all going home," Jonah muttered.

"Yes, sir." Kevin smiled.

⁓

Even with a full crew of people, and Lisa's limp growing worse, the group covered a fair bit of ground in the precious minutes before the Grim Hounds drew too close to continue. Jonah held up an arm and stopped. He glanced at the others, noting the various levels of fear in their expressions.

"The Grim Hounds' barks sap your strength and make you want to give up," Jonah said. "I know it's hard, but try to block it out."

"That's perfect." Lisa frowned at the others. "What are we gonna do?"

Alex half raised his hand. "I think we should move closer together and watch each other's backs."

"Gather in a circle," Jonah said when they glanced at him. "Eddy and Alex, move together. You two can focus on one Grim Hound and take it out with your lightning."

Darren and Monisha standing together came in handy. Jonah gestured to Monisha. "I want you to grab a different Grim Hound and hold it so Darren can break its neck. Unless you want to use the baton?"

"No way. I'm saving it for that hex tree." Darren had tossed his backpack behind a tree and out of the way.

Not willing to argue with the boy's logic, Jonah continued his instructions. "I'll use the wind to pull the feet out from under another one and then take it down with my blades." He slid off the hiking pack, not wanting to fight while wearing it.

Lisa elbowed him. "What about me?"

"I want you and AJ to stand out as an easy target. When a Grim Hound comes at you, lift into the air."

"I can't keep two people floating for long," Lisa complained. "You know that."

"You won't have to. Eddy and Alex will finish their Grim Hound and help you out." Jonah pointed at himself and Kevin. "We'll do the same for any other hounds. That's the plan." He glanced around the group. "Got it?"

Everyone nodded. Only now did Jonah notice the approaching Grim Hounds had gone silent.

"I don't like this," Lisa said in a shaky voice.

"Just concentrate," Jonah encouraged.

At that moment, a howl went up from behind them. That was answered by three more from all around.

"They split up to attack." Darren smacked his hand against his fist. "That's smart."

Kevin called out to AJ, "Can you give us some lights?"

Without missing a beat, AJ cocked his hand like a gun and fired off balls of supernatural fire into the darkened forest. Alex helped, and in short order, they created two circles of blue flames, one farther out than the inner one.

"I should use the dust again," AJ suggested.

"I can help," Alex offered.

Splitting the dust between themselves, AJ and Alex worked the spell and filled the area with the sparkling dust. As before, the dust glittered around them like a cloud of fireflies.

Jonah smiled. "Cool! The circles and the dust will give us a few more seconds to attack."

Eddy snorted. "A few seconds before they rip us to pieces."

"Eddy!" Monisha punched the boy then straightened.

AJ pulled Lisa off to the east while the other teams moved away from each other. Alex and Eddy stayed close and faced the southern approach. Jonah turned to the west, and Darren and Monisha readied themselves to handle the Grim Hound coming from the north.

Lisa whimpered a little, and AJ patted her arm. "It'll be okay. You want to hold me, or should I hold you?" When Lisa hesitated, AJ slid his arms around her waist. He caught Jonah watching and winked before saying, "We're ready."

Of course, Kevin noticed. "What was that about?" he hissed.

"Nothing," Jonah whispered back.

The excited snarls of the Grim Hounds echoed through the trees and ended the argument. Within seconds, four shapes hurtled out of the shadows and into the first circle of bluish light at a frightening speed. Jonah heard the others react in various ways. Even he couldn't get used to how fast a Grim Hound could move. However, the supernatural creatures' charge faltered when they hit the dust cloud, and the particles adhered to their fur. The beasts tumbled around, trying to dislodge the dust.

Jonah couldn't believe it. Their updated preparations had worked. "Attack!" he yelled.

Lightning laced the air and struck a Grim Hound that had charged in from the south. A ball of lightning followed right behind and set the creature into uncontrolled spasms. Its agony seemed to galvanize the rest of the creatures, which were all visible now.

Monisha used her power to pick up a second creature and shoved it into a tree. Darren darted forward to grapple with it.

Jonah and Kevin rushed a couple of Grim Hounds. Jonah's creature reared up on its hind legs to swipe at him. Coming in low, his blades connected with the Grim Hound's paws, causing blood to flow. The creature howled in anger as it rolled to the side. Jonah summoned a gust of wind to knock the hound into a tree. That's when he heard Lisa scream.

She and AJ had to dive out of the way of their Grim Hound. But the creature was quick and spun around to rip them apart, except Kevin rammed into it and shoved it aside before turning back to the hound that had attacked him. AJ whispered to Lisa, and a moment later, they soared into the air. The boy was taller than Jonah, something Lisa hadn't anticipated.

Before AJ could draw up his feet, the Grim Hound had recovered, leaped, and smacked a paw against one of his shoes. The blow caused Lisa and AJ to spin in midair. Lisa screamed but maintained her concentration enough to keep them aloft.

Meanwhile, Darren's Grim Hound had him pinned to the ground. The powerful boy let loose with two punches to its throat, and a resounding crack echoed through the woods. The Grim Hound collapsed, dead.

Heaving the creature off his body, Darren rolled to his feet. "I'll help Lisa and AJ."

Monisha's eyes widened, and she pointed. "Look out!"

Darren had just enough time to turn before another Grim Hound plowed into him. They rolled through the trees struggling until the Grim Hound sank its teeth into Darren's arm. The boy screamed in anger and pain.

Jonah whirled and slid both his blades into the side of the Grim Hound he fought. The creature twisted, but Jonah pulled back, watching as it spasmed and died. Another leaped at him out of the darkness.

Not having time to move aside, he charged forward instead, bringing his blades across in a reckless move he copied from Kevin. Although the blades sliced through the creature's neck and separated the head, the body smacked into Jonah, knocking him to the ground. A stunned moment later, he heaved the body aside and scrambled free.

"Stop copying my style," Kevin shouted to Jonah as he finished off his hound.

Lisa let out a high-pitched scream from overhead as the Grim Hound ripped her pants. It was enough for her to begin losing her ability to levitate. AJ shot ball after ball of fire into the Grim Hound's mouth, causing it to gag and fall back several times. The Grim Hound recovered and prepared to spring for them.

That's when lightning sliced through the air and slammed into the hound from behind. The creature howled as the second ball of lightning from Eddy caught it in the mouth. The added attack succeeded, and the Grim Hound twitched as it died.

AJ and Lisa sprawled on the ground. Kevin hovered over them, searching the woods for more attackers.

Monisha ducked the determined attack of her second Grim Hound and reached out with her power. Instead of holding the beast against a tree, she let out a scream of pure frustration as she made a throwing motion with both hands. The Grim Hound swung around through the air and ricocheted off one tree before slamming into another. When the creature dropped to the ground, it didn't move.

"Darren!" she called out.

Caught in a deadly struggle with the last Grim Hound, Darren managed to get his hands inside the snout and grunted as he called on his extraordinary strength to rip the mouth open. He didn't stop there but continued to pull until the creature's jaws snapped and broke.

With a final anguished gurgle, the Grim Hound died. Darren clutched his bloodied arm and scrambled away from the creature to slump against a tree. Monisha was at his side in a second.

"I'm alright."

Jonah finally noticed the blood covering his shirt as he regained his feet. Besides his earlier cut on the forehead, he now had scratches on his arms. And the others didn't look any better as they gathered in a loose circle again. Eddy pulled the hiking pack's shoulder straps tighter, ensuring it was snug against his back.

Jonah gulped. The pack was ripped and filthy from the all the fighting tonight, but he was glad the triptych had some protection against all the bumps and bangs.

Pulling his attention away from the bag, Jonah realized that his head had stopped buzzing. He let out a breath. "That's it. For now."

"Darren needs help," Monisha gasped. "He's bleeding all over the place."

Darren pulled his arm free. "I told you I'm okay." He ripped his shirt off and used it to wrap his arm. The action exposed all the bleeding scratches on his torso. "The only way to get help is to take down the net."

"You're not okay," Jonah insisted. He was worried because Darren didn't have a healing ability, and Lisa had a sprained ankle. Taking in the rest, Jonah feared they would never take down the net before someone got hurt or, worse, died.

"We're going, Jonah," Eddy said.

"It's the only way to get Darren help," Kevin added, his arms crossed.

"I know. We keep going."

Everyone nodded and prepared to continue the climb uphill. With AJ helping Lisa, the group resumed their trek to the hex tree. The fact that no more Grim Hounds attacked unnerved Jonah. Thera had to know her previous attempts to kill them had failed. That could only mean one thing. She and her brother were waiting for them.

As his group drew closer to the net's center, the pressure on Jonah's senses increased until he perpetually squinted against the pain. He glanced at Kevin and noticed his boyfriend didn't look pleased either. While Rubio's net canceled his phasing ability, the hex caused the air to waver even more, creating a slight nauseous tingling in his gut.

"I hate this," Monisha grumbled, her arms wrapped around her stomach. Others muttered their agreement, but Jonah only saw the determination on their faces.

"Whoa!" Eddy hissed as they moved through the trees, approaching an area of blazing, reddish light.

The original tree that Rubio used to empower the net was ablaze with magical energy. The red haze came from the undulating currents of power that traveled up and down the tree's trunk. Rubio's original sigil had been updated to include more shapes.

Pulses of energy spiraled up to impact the net. They faded away, showing the augmented net was as strong as ever. What Jonah didn't understand was the absence of anyone else.

Darren set down his pack and reached inside for the baton. "Let's do this."

"It won't be that easy," Jonah warned.

A split second later, his Death Sense blossomed with pain, causing him to cry out. Despite the agony, Jonah sensed someone phase into the clearing. "Get behind me!" He squinted through the agony to raise his activated blades.

Thera and Fabian stood before them with hands raised to cast spells. Kevin charged the twins at once, but the sister moved faster, hurling a hex past the Fallen Reaper and right at Jonah.

He deflected the attack but still caught a bit of it, and his arms went numb for a few terrifying seconds. That's all it took for Fabian to blast him with a tendril of lightning.

CHAPTER FORTY-ONE
THE SORCERER TWINS

Pain! Jonah screamed in agony as Fabian's lightning attack sent him tumbling along the ground. His body spasmed with unbearable pain until he thought his head would explode.

"Jonah!" Kevin shouted.

Monisha yelled as she sent broken branches and rocks flying at the sorcerer. The attack forced Fabian to relent and protect himself. Thera blasted debris out of the air, but at least a few chunks hit her, causing the dangerous KIN to roar in anger.

Her brother tried to hex Monisha, but she had activated her blades and used them to deflect the first hex. Alex dodged between them, conjuring a counterspell. When the magical attacks collided, it was with a huge bang.

Eddy, who moved to stand over Jonah, added his attack to the mix, blasting at Fabian with lightning.

Jonah struggled to take breaths because his chest ached with residual pain each time he sucked in air.

"Are you alright?" Kevin asked after blocking a hex with a blade. He knelt down to press a hand to Jonah's chest.

"No," Jonah managed. He sensed Kevin's deep worry through their connection. "I'll get over it." He tried to crack a smile, but only grimaced. Kevin held out the blades, which Jonah had dropped while screaming.

Taking a second to scan the fighting, Jonah spotted Darren dashing around the twins to come at the tree from a different angle. Fabian sent a hex at the boy, who used the baton to block it. Even so, Darren tumbled back among the trees. Dropping the baton, the super strong boy uprooted the tree instead, and toppled it on the dangerous KIN.

Thera conjured a blast of wind to push the tree aside. Monisha reached out, snatched the tree, and whirled it back into Fabian's chest. The sorcerer let out a grunt as he tumbled out of sight.

"Take that!" Monisha yelled.

Thera's face radiated hate as she retaliated with a hex that caused the ground beneath Monisha's feet to buckle and heave upward.

Caught off guard, Monisha was thrown to the ground. Thera caught her with a follow-up blast of lightning. Monisha screamed in pain, reminding Jonah of Deyanira torturing Lynn. Before he could help, Lisa charged over, grabbed her friend, and shot into the air.

"Alex and Eddy, slap Thera with lightning!" Kevin ordered.

The boys did so.

"We need to pull together," Jonah said, on his feet and deflecting hexes.

Lisa had maneuvered herself and Monisha closer to the group before dropping back to the ground. When she used a blade to bate aside a stray hex, Jonah's jaw dropped. Protecting her friend had shot through Lisa's hesitance to use the weapons.

They were all together and could cover each other's back. That's when Jonah remembered Darren. He turned and spotted the brash guy dodging through the trees with the baton held high and going for the hex tree again.

Jonah hoped the renewed attack would distract Thera. No such luck. Perhaps Thera sensed the baton's antimagic power because she whirled and hit the nearby trees with a spell. Jonah didn't get that until the branches came alive and wrapped around Darren's arm.

Though Darren's impressive muscles bulged as he struggled, the animated branches wrapped around his arms, torso, and neck while lifting him in the air. The baton fell to the ground, useless. Darren began choking, and his attempts to get free became frantic.

"No!" Alex shouted. He stood and shot a hex at the moving branches. When it hit, the branches shuddered and withered. That was enough for Darren to burst free and drop to the ground.

Jonah produced a gust of wind and funneled it at Thera while Kevin blurred into motion, coming to Darren's aid. Eddy helped with more lightning, and AJ created green flames to burn the underbrush near the sorcerer. Kevin hauled Darren to his feet just as Fabian stepped into view. The sorcerer snuffed out the fire with a spell, then grinned at Kevin, who had stopped.

With a shove to get Darren moving toward the others, Kevin drew his blades and attacked. The sorcerer was a KIN and had blades. He fought, meeting Kevin head-on in a duel. Jonah worried for Kevin, but the boy was fast, even mixing in blurs but no phases.

That Kevin couldn't microphase at all infuriated Jonah, particularly since the hex had neutralized sigils that kept mages from using all sorts of spells and curses. The sorceress undoubtedly did that so they could create a vortex in the clearing.

Somehow, Fabian kept up with Kevin and scored hits on the Fallen Reaper's long coat. The garment protected Jonah's boyfriend, but that wouldn't last, Jonah knew. As if proving his fear correct, Thera emerged from the smoke, her garments smudged, but she was otherwise unhurt and pissed.

"Kevin!" Jonah shouted.

He saw the second sorcerer and blurred away from Fabian before the siblings could corner him. Even so, Fabian blasted the ground, sending Kevin into a rolling tumble. The Fallen Reaper managed to stand and propel himself toward Jonah's group. Alex used a shield to stop the KIN from hitting Kevin in the back with hexes.

"Enough!" Thera shouted. She and her brother paused in their assault. "Give us the Tales, young Blackstone, and we'll let all of you live."

Jonah caught Alex's sudden jerk and speared the boy with a warning glare before turning to meet Thera's almost amused expression. "I told you before. No deal."

In an instant, Thera's face morphed into a furious mask. Before the twins could curse them, a large tree slammed to the ground right in front of the group. Darren had pushed it down for cover, and everyone huddled behind it except for Monisha, who used her blades to protect Darren while he uprooted a second tree.

Then she summoned her power to pull anything loose and add it to their cover. For good measure, Alex erected a shield over the barricade. Jonah recalled how he helped Wick in their battle with Deyanira when the boy's barrier began to fail. Reaching out, Jonah drew in power and gripped Alex's shoulder. He felt the energy race into the young mage. In response, the shield solidified, holding off the attacks.

Alex turned a stunned gaze on Jonah. So did all the others.

"Whoa, dude," Eddy gushed.

Despite the help, the sorcerer twins hurled hex after hex. Each passing second, they destroyed more of the outlying sections of log until all that remained was the shield-protected portion right in front of the group.

Jonah knew his team had no hope of defeating trained members of the KIN.

"We need to do something to take them out," Kevin grunted.

"I know."

The other kids gazed at Kevin then Jonah, clearly hoping one of them had a way out. After all, he was the Deliverer. He had escaped from the Grim Reaper and Grand Oracle and defeated a goddess. Blah, blah, blah. And Kevin was an Alliance member. None of that helped right now. They'd always had more help.

For a moment, Jonah considered sacrificing himself to save the others. The twins would love to take his dead body to the Grim Reaper. Yet Thera would promise anything just to get the triptych. Then she'd kill the others after he was dead. What else could he do?

He could still make a last stand so his friends could escape. Jonah had pledged to fulfill his mission, even if it meant his death. Balling his hand into a fist, he ignored the constant barrage of spells chipping away at their hiding spot and summoned his power. His blades soon glowed.

Kevin placed a hand on Jonah's shoulder. "Don't even think about it."

The simple touch ignited something else in Jonah, an idea. Why hadn't he considered it before? "Can we do the sync thing? They won't expect that."

Kevin's eyes widened, and after a moment, he nodded and activated his blades. "Darren? Get ready to try for the hex tree again."

First AJ, Eddy, and the others stared at the glowing blades; then they stared at him.

"Why?" Darren asked.

"We're gonna distract them so you can get another chance." Jonah rose to a better position, ready to charge from hiding.

"You can't sacrifice yourselves!" Lisa moaned.

"Yeah. That's a stupid plan," AJ objected. "We stay together." Jonah met AJ's gaze and didn't back down.

"We have each other's back, remember?" Eddy said.

"We don't plan to sacrifice ourselves," Jonah said, awed by his friends' determination. "You remember my blur session with Kevin. We're gonna do that again. Okay?" Jonah almost smiled at the relieved understanding on their faces. "On my mark."

Without warning, Eddy jerked backward. Alex had an arm around the boy's neck, and his free hand crackled with magic.

"Alex, what the heck are you doing?" Jonah asked, furious that the idiot was ruining their plan.

"Stay back!" Alex yelled because Darren and Kevin moved for him. "And let go of Eddy's pack, Monisha. I can feel you tugging on it with your telekinesis." Alex stood from behind their makeshift cover, taking Eddy with him. "Stop! I have the triptych."

An eerie silence settled on the clearing.

"We can't let him go," Darren snarled. Even in his weakened state, the boy was ready to do some damage.

Jonah held up a hand to the others. "Don't do anything." He focused on Alex. "This is a bad idea." He waved at Thera and Fabian, who watched the drama with amused expressions. "They're gonna kill you as soon as they get the triptych. You have to know that."

Alex tugged Eddy farther away and turned so he could see the KIN and the others at the same time. "I'm doing this to save all of you."

Jonah winced inside because he had briefly considered sacrificing himself only moments before.

Eddy gaped at him. "Serious, dude? First Jonah, now you?"

"Shut up!" Alex shook Eddy, then met Jonah's gaze. "You lost your parents. I can't deal with something like that."

Jonah had no clue what the boy meant. When Alex moved to take the pack off Eddy's shoulders, Jonah started to step from cover.

"It's okay," Eddy said, waving Jonah back.

Once Alex tugged the pack free, he shoved Eddy toward the fallen trees while he moved to the waiting KIN.

"Good choice," Fabian sneered.

Thera held out her slender hand as Alex approached them with the hiking pack.

Meanwhile, Eddy huddled beside Jonah and nudged him with an elbow. Jonah flashed his friend a questioning look when Eddy nodded downward. Jonah saw the edge of the triptych pieces sticking out of his friend's pocket.

Relief flooded him, and he resisted grinning. Yet just as suddenly, he realized Alex would die for sure when Thera discovered the trick. He turned and whispered to Monisha, "Be ready to grab Alex."

She and Eddy gave him matching incredulous looks. "Why?" Monisha objected. "Let them kill him."

Jonah flashed her a frown. "Just be ready."

"What about the net?" Darren hissed.

"Wait."

By now, Thera had snatched the bag from Alex.

"I did what the mole asked me to do. Let the others go," Alex pleaded with the sorceress.

Thera paused in opening the pack to peer at the young mage. "They'll be fine once we have the triptych." She looked at Jonah.

That glare confirmed it for him. She would kill them all, starting with Alex. Why couldn't the young mage see that? Jonah made a small motion to Monisha. She huffed but shook her hands and flexed her fingers.

Thera rifled through the pack, pulling out all the contents and throwing them to the ground. "It's not here!" She tensed, and magic gathered around her fingers. Her brother copied her movements and advanced on Alex.

The young mage took the pack and turned it inside out. Alex's shoulders slumped moments later as he realized what Eddy had done.

Jonah's Death Sense screamed with pain as the twins raised their hands. "Now!" he shouted.

Monisha made a yanking motion toward her body with her hands. Alex let out a surprised grunt as he flew backward in time to avoid a double dose of lightning from the twins. But the KIN quickly recovered and shifted their attack on the boy's new position.

Alex's hastily erected shield exploded under the assault, allowing lightning to shock him.

"Monisha!" Jonah called.

She grunted with effort and yanked the young mage close enough for Darren to grab the mage and haul him behind cover. With a deep growl of rage, Alex produced another shield, and this time blocked the attack without failing or needing Jonah's help.

Eddy counterattacked with lightning. AJ propelled green flames at the duo. As expected, the offense didn't affect the twins.

That was Jonah's cue. He shot to his feet and charged the twins, his blades glowing. Kevin was right with him. Delving into their shared link, Kevin blurred into motion first, avoiding a hex from Fabian. Jonah followed and engaged Thera. He had the satisfaction of seeing her eyes widen in surprise. Soon, they were into the midst of the duels.

Jonah recalled Kevin's warning to learn microphase moves without the actual phase. He did so now, launching attacks but using his blur ability to replace a microphase. He sensed Kevin matching his actions. Together, they kept the twins off-balance and, most importantly, occupied.

Jonah didn't dare pause to call out to Darren. Otherwise, Thera would know his intentions. To his relief, he saw the boy take off running when Thera locked blades with him.

She was good, but her strikes weren't as powerful as Mandara's. In a way, he appreciated the duel with the Campmaster now. *Just a little longer*, he told himself.

Out of the corner of his eye, he saw Darren hurl the glowing baton with all his might. It shot through the air like a missile.

Thera must have seen his glance because once again, she whirled away from him and summoned a torrent of wind. The gale force hit the baton, taking the weapon off course!

"I got it," Monisha called out. She gripped it with her power and fought, causing the baton to jerk several times, coming closer until it slammed into the center tree with a final push.

Kevin drew back from dueling Fabian as a blue distortion wave raced away from the impact point. The symbols making up Thera's hex fractured and split apart. The red haze dissolved as the baton broke the spell. High overhead, cracks appeared in the net. The next moment, the center tree exploded.

Without warning, Kevin grabbed Jonah and used the long coat to shield them both from the outpouring of energy.

"Don't worry about me," he objected. "Protect my friends."

"They're okay," Kevin answered.

Jonah peeked from under the coat and relaxed. Alliance Guards had appeared and rushed in to shield his friends. In addition to the batons, the guard's uniforms also gave them limited protection from magic. Once the blast of dissipating magic cleared, the guards raised their batons and marched toward Thera and Fabian.

The twins weaved their hands in matching countermovements, conjuring a deadly hex. A red shimmer appeared and solidified. On cue, they released the spell at their enemies.

The Alliance Guards, including Darren's dad, Jonah noted, plunged the sharpened ends of their batons into the ground. When they did that, energy snapped and raced up each baton and then to the ones beside it.

The weapons affected the potency of the onrushing hex. When the guards stepped back, Albrecht and Rubio strode forward. Mimicking the twins, they weaved their hands in matching motions and conjured a beautiful shield barrier between everyone and the hex.

Nodding to each other, the mages made a shoving motion, and the shield moved forward. The collision of the magical forces canceled out each other with a bang. When it was over, Thera and Fabian had fled.

Mage Albrecht lowered his hands with a weary sigh and turned to the kids. "Thank goodness, you're all okay."

Alex rushed forward. "Darren's hurt!"

Darren's dad lumbered over, lifted his son into his arms, and marched to the still open vortex that Jonah finally noticed. Monisha and Alex hurried to follow. AJ, Lisa, and Eddy went next as the other Alliance Guards watched the perimeter, their glowing batons at the ready.

Rubio stared at the blasted pine stump, the only remains of the tree he used to create the net. He shifted, scanning all the other downed trees and debris. Finally, the mage faced Jonah. Sucking in a deep breath, he said, "Thank you. Deliverer."

Jonah nodded in response, watching the mage step through the vortex and disappear.

"That was progress," Albrecht said in a weary voice, coming over.

"Maybe," Jonah admitted. "Oh, Damian and another Alliance guy are in the woods. Alex zapped them."

Albrecht nodded. "Help was sent to them. Now, come along. It's not safe to stay here in the woods tonight."

"Tell me about it." Jonah started for the vortex when he remembered Alex's hiking pack. Hurrying over to grab it, he almost regretted when his body spasmed and ached. Fabian's attack lingered, but Jonah gritted through the pain.

Moving at a more cautious pace, he returned to Albrecht with the pack and stepped through the vortex.

CHAPTER FORTY-TWO
CONSPIRACY

Jonah's eyes took a moment to adjust to the dimness on the other side when he exited the vortex.

The others were already through the back gate. Darren's dad continued to support his son as they walked up the bamboo path. Serena and Monisha walked on either side. Not far behind, Lisa limped along, using AJ for support.

"Go on," Jonah said as he reached the gate where Eddy and Alex waited with Kevin.

The young mage nodded, and with a nervous jerk that Jonah guessed resulted from his guilty conscience, he followed Albrecht.

Eddy didn't move until the mages were well out of earshot; then he pulled the triptych from his pocket and handed it to Jonah. "No offense, but don't ask me to hold this again." He flashed his silvery smile and added, "I'll keep an eye on Alex and make sure he doesn't run for it." With that, he hurried to catch up with the others.

Jonah slipped the triptych into his pocket and pulled on Alex's ragged hiking pack.

Kevin helped, only to sniff in disgust at the pack. "This smells like Grim Hound." He turned to watch the others move onto the Long Corridor Bridge before he started walking. Without warning, he slid his fingers into Jonah's bushy hair. "I told you to wait for me."

"Sorry."

Tilting Jonah's head to the side, Kevin examined the partially healed gash on his forehead.

"I'm okay." Jonah squirmed because it felt strange echoing Darren's words, considering the big guy hadn't been okay.

Kevin lowered his hand, balled it into a fist, and tapped his leg as they walked along in silence. They remained close enough that they bumped each other every few steps. When they entered the near-pitch blackness of the Long Corridor Bridge, Kevin slipped an arm around Jonah's waist.

Jonah welcomed the embrace as he prepared himself for the coming arguments about this sorry night.

Except for Darren and Lisa, the rest of Jonah's friends stood off to the left of the walkway leading into the main building. All the young mages huddled on the right with Thomas. Alex stood slightly apart from his fellow mages.

Mandara, Trueblood, Bertonneau, and Sterne stood in a loose circle arguing but broke off as Jonah drew nearer.

"Jonah?" Marcus stepped out of the Pavilion and crossed to him. "Are you alright?"

Relief flooded Jonah at seeing his godfather. "Yeah, I am. When did you get here?"

Marcus ignored the question as he scrutinized every inch of Jonah. His gaze lingered on the forehead gash and the cuts on the arms. When his godfather subjected him to a Reaper's stare, Jonah didn't bother to hide his true feelings. He was exhausted and a little scared.

Marcus nodded in understanding before turning him to face the rest of the adults. With Kevin and his godfather beside him, Jonah had never felt safer in his life.

The Campmaster called to AJ and Monisha. "Thank you two for helping out tonight. Go get some rest."

Their shocked expressions mirrored Jonah's, but they nodded and headed inside.

Jonah started to ask Kevin a question when he glimpsed Alastor slipping around the pavilion corner. He suspected where the little man was headed.

Those Grim Hounds had homed in on them. While the twins knew about the clearing's location, the creatures found them even after he, Alex, and Eddy ran.

Jonah had been down this road before, during his first summer in Mount Vernon. Deyanira had tagged him with her business card. A short time later, a Grim Hound had used the card like a homing beacon. It was a sure bet Eddy, and maybe Alex, had been marked tonight. He needed the pack to prove it.

Mandara motioned to the mentors. "Please see to the campers under your charge."

As the others filed into the building, Mandara turned and led everyone else to his office.

⁓

"Tell us everything that happened," Mandara ordered, sitting behind his desk with his hands folded.

Jonah, Alex, and Eddy occupied three chairs crowded in front of the Campmaster's desk. Before Jonah or Eddy could begin, Alex started into the story. Listening to the boy, Jonah was relieved he told the truth, as far as he knew. Yet Eddy watched the young mage with a strange expression. After a moment, Jonah, too, thought there was something off about Alex's story. Then he realized the problem.

"You lied to us!" Jonah blurted out.

"Thank you," Eddy said. "I thought it was just me."

"Gentlemen, please," Mandara cut in. "You'll have a chance to talk."

"You don't understand, sir." Jonah speared Alex with a glare. "Alex said he couldn't tell us anything because they made him take an oath. If that's true, why's he telling us stuff now?"

"Yeah," Eddy agreed. "Even if we already know most of it, he shouldn't be able to do that."

"You two are correct," Trueblood said. He loomed over Alex. "Who told you to take Jonah's triptych?"

"I can't tell you," Alex said, his voice pleading and his entire body shaking as he hugged himself.

Jonah met Eddy's irritated gaze.

Eventually, Mandara said, "Mr. Martinez, did you actually take Mr. Blackstone's device? Or did someone give it to you?"

From the miserable look on Alex's face and his trembling lower lip, Jonah thought the boy was on the verge of crying. "I took it, but I didn't have a choice."

"Liar!" Eddy accused him.

"I'm not lying!" Alex roared back, half standing from his chair.

Trueblood gripped the boy's shoulder and pressed him back into the seat.

Like a trigger being released, Alex began crying, shocking everyone. "The mole threatened my parents, okay?" His voice was muffled because he had buried his face in his hands. Even so, the confession felt like someone had yanked it out of him.

In response, Trueblood gently patted the young mage's shoulders, reassuring him.

Marcus stepped forward. "Cedric, we have to—"

"I know." Mandara rose from his chair and crossed to the table of glittery objects. Jonah sucked in a breath when Mandara pulled a small portal-like device forward. It was just like the one Agent Ramsey had used to contact the Grand Oracle.

If Jonah's Death Sense hadn't been quiet, he would have called Mandara a traitor, but that wasn't the case. The Campmaster tapped the center of the device with his fingertips, and an irritating pulse filled the office, causing Jonah and Marcus to stir.

Mandara, seemingly unaffected or used to the pulse, spoke quietly into the device and ordered an Alliance Guard and mage to go to an address. Finished, he returned to his desk and stood there watching Alex, whose shoulders shook with quiet sobs.

"We'll get your parents to a safe location and protect them until the mole is caught."

Alex raised his head, revealing a face wet with shed tears. "They'll be okay?"

"No one will hurt your parents, son," Mandara assured him.

Jonah was impressed, not only with the promise but also that the Campmaster didn't even have to check to make sure of Alex's address.

"Can we assume you never saw his face?" Mandara asked Alex. When the mage nodded, the Campmaster returned to his chair.

"I think it's time for you to hear what Jonah has to say," Marcus suggested. Jonah wondered if his godfather did this so Alex could get himself under control.

The Campmaster agreed. "Go ahead, Mr. Blackstone. Begin with entering the pocket without waiting for help."

Jonah grimaced and launched into how he found Eddy after Alex had zapped him, their tense running battle with the mage, and then fighting the Grim Hounds. He was careful to mention how everyone worked together to defend themselves.

Mandara watched him with an intense stare through the entire tale. Yet Jonah recognized the shock in the man's expression when he looked past Jonah to the back of the room. Turning in the chair, Jonah saw Alastor had entered the office during their retelling of the escape. The little man's chest heaved, although he tried to hide it. *He's been running*, Jonah decided.

Trueblood spoke from behind him. "You and the others did a brilliant job, given the circumstances."

"Yes, they did," Mandara agreed.

"In your twisted way, Cedric, you got the campers to work together," Bertonneau began, speaking for the first time since entering the office. She made a disapproving sound and glared at Trueblood. "That being said, I'm disappointed in you, Symon, sending more children into a potentially dangerous situation like that."

Trueblood cast a troubled gaze at Marcus before saying, "It was their collective focus on their friends that allowed me to open that limited window. They had to go. And I had confidence in them."

Bertonneau stared at the Campmaster. "And what about that net in the forest the Rasmussen twin was able to hex? Why did you allow Rubio to create that?"

"To test the candidates." When Bertonneau's eyebrows shot up, Mandara grew testy. "We're at war."

"Oh, spare me the speeches, Cedric. That was supremely dangerous to leave these children vulnerable to Grim Hounds and KIN members."

"Well, I certainly didn't intend for any of this to happen in the forest tonight," Mandara countered. "And what they accomplished is encouraging."

"That may be, but we still have a conspiracy to unearth," Marcus observed in a raised voice. "Isaiah warned the

Council several years ago. Given what the young people showed us tonight, we must root out the traitors for their safety."

Bertonneau pressed a hand to her chest and closed her eyes. Mandara and Marcus met each other's gaze, apparently sharing the same thought.

"The mole knew Jonah had the Tales on the triptych and threatened Alex to pass that information to the KIN," Marcus continued. "Albrecht and Rubio confirmed the Rasmussen's presence. I'm afraid, Mr. Martinez, they planned to kill you after obtaining the triptych. Jonah was a bonus."

Though Jonah told Alex the same thing, he began to question whether Thera and Fabian got lucky. If he hadn't stabbed Vanay and been given detention by Mandara, he would have gone out tonight, and he knew why.

Jonah nudged Alex's foot. "So the plan was for you to volunteer and then pick me to go out with you?"

Alex's eyes widened, and he looked around at everyone like a caged animal before nodding.

"And because Jonah's your partner in Team Building," Trueblood concluded, turning to Jonah. "You would have gone."

"The Rasmussen twins." A wave of burning anger radiated from the Campmaster. "How did you get your orders?"

Pointing at the device Mandara used, Alex confessed, "I have one of those hidden my dorm. It's tricky using it without my roommate seeing, but I managed."

"I'll go and fetch the device," Alastor volunteered, drawing everyone's attention.

"No," Mandara called out. "Leave it there."

"That's a dangerous play," Marcus said, though he adopted a thoughtful expression.

"In other words, the usual practice tonight," Bertonneau uttered, still irritated.

Mandara ignored her comment and addressed Alex. "I want you to keep it. If the mole contacts you again, tell us immediately."

"Yes, sir."

Mandara shifted his gaze to Bertonneau. "If the Council agrees, of course."

"You're head of security," Bertonneau said, "but keep the children safe."

Jonah, Eddy, and Alex winced at being called children for a third time. Eddy caught Jonah's look and grinned.

Alastor didn't look happy, and Jonah didn't know why. He had a gut feeling that stopping the sneaky Fallen Reaper from touching the device in Alex's dorm was the right thing to do.

Meanwhile, Mandara met the tired boys' gazes. "Mr. Martinez's circumstances do not leave this room, understood?" Jonah and Eddy nodded. "Now, you three go and get cleaned up."

The boys shot to their feet. When Jonah hesitated, Marcus whispered, "I'll see you tomorrow if I can."

"Okay." Jonah turned for the door, expecting to confront Alastor, but, with the meeting over, the strange man was gone. Following the others out of Mandara's office, Jonah found Thomas and Kevin in the small entrance area. The mentors faced in opposite directions, and both looked angry. Jonah could sense the tension. Thomas motioned to Alex. After flashing them a miserable look, Alex followed his mentor from the building.

Kevin blocked the doorway to keep Jonah and Eddy inside. He rubbed his jaw in an agitated motion. "I told Thomas he was wrong for helping them set up that net."

It pleased Jonah that his boyfriend stuck up for him, but he remembered Thomas questioning the net. "I don't think he liked Rubio setting it up."

"Exactly. But to him, his personal feelings didn't count. He followed orders and said I should understand how the Alliance works. Total bull—" Kevin bit off the rest of the sentence, glanced at the Campmaster's door, and motioned them outside. "Come on."

Jonah trudged along beside Eddy in silence, replaying Jennifer's attempt to take the triptych. As AJ had suggested, they'd expected him to go out tonight. Had Jennifer messed up in trying to take the triptych herself?

Of course, the girl was still guilty, in Jonah's opinion. However, with Alex's confession, any claims against her were little more than conspiracy theories as far as the Council was concerned. That pissed off Jonah because he knew Jennifer worked for the mole, or she had.

He slowed when it occurred to him that maybe there were two different plans to get him. Marcus called it a conspiracy, and the idea of more than one scheme sent a chill down Jonah's back.

CHAPTER FORTY-THREE
PROTECTORS ASSEMBLE!

Steaming hot water sloshed over Jonah's head and shoulders, quieting the occasional shuddering. He took his time in the shower, confident that Kevin was just outside, watching over him.

The Healer had stopped him outside and given him a tonic. Just like his blade cut, magical injuries required longer to heal. As much as he loved the hot shower, the residual pain from Fabian's lightning attack would continue to make his body twitch until he recovered.

Hugging himself, Jonah sucked in deep breaths until his heart rate slowed. The attack reminded him that people wanted him dead and would get pleasure from making him suffer first. He was simply thankful all of his friends had survived.

Half an hour later, Jonah came out of the Lavatory Building. Eddy had already cleared out. Kevin leaned against the wall with his arms crossed and stared into the darkness.

"Don't trust Alex," Kevin said as Jonah came over.

"I don't trust him, but Alex helped us."

"To save his butt. He's part of whatever's going on."

"The mole threatened his parents."

Kevin scowled. "We don't know that for sure. He lied about the oath."

The sudden argument frustrated Jonah and destroyed the calmness the hot shower had produced in his mind. "The Alliance has to find the mole."

"We know that," Kevin grumbled as he set off toward the dorms.

They reached the branch in the path that led to the rear entrance of the main building in one direction or directly into the garden maze in the other direction. In the clear night air, the scent of the various flowers was a bit intoxicating. But Jonah's mind was on Kevin's hesitation, which revealed a lot about the boy's limits on helping.

That sad reality stung Jonah, and he stopped, catching Kevin by surprise. "I know you can't tell me things." His hand tightened around his bundle of dirty clothes as he searched Kevin's face. For the first time, he saw a drawback to their dating.

Most troubling was Kevin's confirming expression. The older boy shrugged. "It's not my choice. You know that, right?"

In his irritation, Jonah wanted to ask if Kevin was following orders now. At once, he knew better than to ask that, and settled on, "Yeah."

The first night they met, Kevin had said he wanted to tell Jonah everything but couldn't. He still meant it, but the Alliance was in the way. In the pit of Jonah's stomach, a growing dread began. Had Kevin been told to keep him away from certain subjects?

"I'm starting to think Rubio made the trap to keep you and Marcus from helping me."

Kevin let out an angry snort. "That bastard."

Reassured at the Fallen Reaper's genuine anger, Jonah nudged his boyfriend. "You worried so much about me that you never thought about yourself."

"Well, you think too much." Kevin poked Jonah in the forehead, smirking.

"Am I wrong?"

"No." Kevin let out a long breath. Instead of turning for the main building's side door, Kevin surprised Jonah and went toward the maze.

"I need to stick these dirty clothes in the bin," Jonah complained.

Ignoring Jonah's protest, Kevin led the way through the darkened maze and emerged on the inlet side.

Stopping halfway to the water, Kevin sat down and motioned for Jonah to join him. Slipping an arm around Jonah's waist, Kevin pulled him back into an embrace. They watched the darkened inlet and listened to the soothing sound of water lapping against the stones.

Jonah sensed Kevin's frustration. "I told you," he said, leaning back to see Kevin's face. "I'm okay."

"Once you went through the rip, I couldn't do anything to help."

Jonah stroked Kevin's arms as the two gently rocked back and forth. Of course, he wasn't okay. He was angry and scared and a lot of other things.

When his body began to shake, Kevin hugged him tighter.

That desire to protect him from harm touched Jonah, and he had to blink back tears.

"Don't hold back," Kevin whispered in his ear. "Let it out."

Jonah didn't cry, but it took him a while to let go of all the tension. Eventually, Kevin kissed him lightly on the neck.

"No one threatens my man."

At that moment, Jonah wanted to stay in Kevin's protective embrace forever. And he did, for a while longer at least, allowing the horror of tonight's events to recede.

Eddy awakened Jonah way too soon, and he felt sluggish as he got out of bed. After dressing, he left his dorm only to encounter Trueblood at the second-floor landing.

The mage had a cloth-covered box in his hands. "I have something for you, Jonah." He nodded toward the dorm room.

Unsure of what to expect, Jonah returned to his room. Trueblood followed and nudged the door partially closed.

"Now that we have the Destiny Medallion's location, the Council was concerned with the information remaining on your triptych. Mandara suggested we lock the device in HQ or even destroy it."

"You can't do that!" Jonah blurted out. He had the triptych stuffed inside his pocket. Even though things had settled down, he wanted to play it safe and keep the device with him.

"I told the Council that you'd want to keep it. After all, it belonged to your mom." He tapped the box in his arms again. "This is the compromise."

"What's in there?" Jonah couldn't fathom what Trueblood had.

The mage opened the cloth pouch to reveal a golden-colored box with symbols etched into the surface.

Jonah's eyes widened. "A Seeker's Box!" Unlike Robert's Seeker's Box, which was tall and thin, this one was low and wide. Jonah guessed the top lifted open.

Trueblood withdrew the box. "I suggest we install this in one of your drawers."

Jonah hurried to the closet and removed his clothes from the bottom drawer. Trueblood sat the box in the back corner, stood up, and pulled out his wand. A spark shot out, hit the box, and a line of illumination spread around the bottom edge.

"There you go," Trueblood announced, putting his wand away. "No one can remove the box, not unless I perform the counterspell."

"Huh, what happens when I go home?" Jonah thought to point out. He couldn't take the entire drawer with him.

"I suggest you lock the triptych in Robert's archive box."

Jonah hadn't considered that. His mind was still a little tired this morning. "Good point."

Trueblood smiled. "You know how to activate the archive box, right?"

"Yeah. I do." When Jonah hesitated, Trueblood held up a safety pin. Jonah took it. "Thanks."

With that, the mage left.

Being careful to place the three triptych pieces in the box first, Jonah closed it. Screwing up his courage, he pricked a finger. A small bead of deep red blood formed. Bending low, he touched it to the archive box's lock. As soon as he did, the box absorbed the blood, and the real locks slid into view and clicked shut.

He stood, wiping the rest of the blood off his finger as he headed down to the common room for breakfast. With his mind focused on the Seeker's Box, he hadn't noticed that his friends milled around in a loose group near their usual table. Shrugging to himself, Jonah picked up his typical breakfast items and sat down to eat.

Considering AJ and Eddy weren't on their second helpings, Jonah should have known something was up. Before he could ask AJ or Eddy what was happening, the mages trooped into the room.

Thrusting a fist in the air, Darren shouted, "Protectors Assemble!"

As one, Monisha, Lisa, AJ, and Eddy formed a tight circle around Jonah and struck ridiculous superhero poses. The mages stared at the group in shock. Jonah's own heart raced, and all vestiges of tiredness disappeared. The best part was the priceless look on Jennifer's face. She had prepared herself for a real attack.

When Darren laughed, she sneered and continued to her table. The rest of the mages reacted similarly, and of course, didn't say a word. Alex wouldn't meet Jonah's eyes, even when he could do it without the other mages noticing.

Jonah poked Darren in the shoulder. "That was cool."

Darren glanced at the mages and raised his voice so they could hear. "We're sending a message that we stand together."

Jennifer glared back at him. Monisha returned the favor.

At the staff table, Jonah noticed Trueblood hiding a grin, while Albrecht was hard to read with his busy mustache and perpetual shades. The reaction he wanted to see was Mandara's, but neither the Campmaster nor Bertonneau were at the table.

Wide awake now, Jonah's mind was on fire with the fantastic show of solidarity and the knowledge that he had a new team, something he never expected to happen when he first arrived at Camp Alliance.

⁓

Jonah solved the mystery of the Campmaster's whereabouts when he stepped outside after breakfast. Mandara and Bertonneau stood outside, talking with Marcus, who wore a dark suit, perfect for the office.

Jonah paused, causing the rest of his group to hesitate and look around.

"I'll catch up," Jonah told them.

"You sure?" AJ asked.

The mages exited the main building, and at Darren's signal, Jonah's friends dropped into their superhero poses again. The commotion drew the Campmaster's attention. Too bad they were Fallen Reapers, Jonah thought, when Marcus and Mandara hid their real reactions.

Bertonneau waved an impatient hand and excused herself from the conversation. By now, the mages had marched on to class mumbling to each other. Marvin flashed Darren a thumbs-up as he passed. That caused Monisha and him to burst out laughing until the Meditation teacher turned and beckoned them all to session.

When Marcus held Jonah back, it occurred to Jonah his godfather and the Campmaster were going somewhere together. "Going to HQ?"

"Yes, we are," Marcus said, "but I wanted to talk to you first." He gestured toward the entrance. They exited the compound and started down the bamboo pathway at a leisurely pace. Marcus watched the kids, Bertonneau and Mandara, walking along the path ahead of them.

A smile tweaked the corner of Marcus's mouth. "Given your friend's display, I'd say you've made a space for yourself at camp."

"It wasn't my idea," Jonah said.

"But you enjoyed it." Marcus smiled. "I'm glad to see you made friends, Jonah. By the way, I know about the activities of your Mount Vernon club."

"You want us to stop, don't you?"

Marcus raised an eyebrow. "Not at all. I'm impressed. You and your friends are keeping mortals safe. And now, you've led another group of young people." He took a breath and glanced at Jonah. "The quiet, shy boy I took under my charge two years ago would have hated the attention."

"Yeah," Jonah admitted, thinking back to his first days in Mount Vernon. "Is that a bad thing?"

"It means you're growing beyond your fear of being the center of attention."

"Oh. I mean, I didn't think about that at the time. All I knew is we had to help and protect each other."

Marcus nodded. "Exactly. You're becoming a leader like your mother and father. They would have been proud of you."

Jonah sucked in a breath as he imagined his parents here congratulating him. "My dad would have argued with Mandara, wouldn't he?"

"Certainly," Marcus said with a grin. "Your father never backed down from a fight and the Campmaster never intimidated him."

"Or you," Jonah said. Watching his godfather's reaction, he recalled something he had just learned. "You made a blood oath with my parents when you became my godfather. How is that different from a regular oath?"

"A blood oath is like a life debt."

Jonah's godfather shocked him by allowing the emotions to radiate out. It was the most open Marcus had ever been, and Jonah swallowed hard. A life debt? Now he understood Trueblood's statement about Marcus's fury.

"Does a blood oath really last a lifetime?"

"Oh, no. This blood oath only lasts until you're eighteen." Marcus regarded the array of plants along the smaller compound's western wall. "But I'll always be here to help you."

His godfather's sincerity made Jonah gulp. Listening to the rest of the kids on the other side of the wall going inside for class, he made up his mind. "I need some advice on personal stuff. Dating."

Marcus let out a quiet, "Oh." And his shoulders slumped a little. "Do you know about protection?"

Jonah's insides squirmed. "Yeah, I know about that."

"Really?"

"Yeah. The Teen Center had a class for the older kids." Jonah's face warmed, remembering the advocate groups' samples on the table. The volunteers had taken the girls into one meeting room and the guys into a separate one. "They told us… everything."

"Well, that's good." Marcus blinked. "Not that I wouldn't tell you what I know."

"I need to talk about relationships. It's about Kevin and me."

"Ah. I see." To his surprise, Marcus smiled again. "Well, why don't you come to DC after camp? If your aunt and uncle agree, you can stay with Omar and me for a few days and talk."

The relief that flooded Jonah shocked him. Why had he been afraid to talk to his godfather? "Yeah. That'll be cool."

As they hovered in the courtyard's entrance, Marcus said, "Like any parent, there comes a time when you have to let the child make their own decisions and hope that everything you tried to teach will hold."

He gestured at their surroundings. "That's why you and the others are here. This camp is the last phase of training for all of you."

"Playtime is over," Jonah said, repeating Mandara's words from the first night.

Marcus peered at him with an earnest expression. "I have one last question for you, Jonah. If it were still possible to join your relatives in Florida, would you go?"

The question startled Jonah, and he blinked hard, wondering about it. "Why ask me that?"

"Considering what's happened, I would give my blessing if you wanted to leave now and go home."

"Seriously?" Jonah closed his mouth, thinking. He was sure his cousins would want to do something special if he came home early. And he missed Mike, Danita, and the other Club members.

But picturing all the new friends he'd made at camp and thinking about their teamwork in the forest, Jonah realized he couldn't leave them. Not yet. He shook his head. "No. I still have things to do here. Besides, my cousins and friends are home now. They'll be there when I get back."

"Ah, you couldn't know this. Your family is vacationing an extra week at a beachside home on the Florida panhandle," Marcus explained.

"They are?" Jonah didn't know what else to say.

"The property is owned and used by Monarch Associates' families," Marcus continued. "Symon suggested we make the offer to smooth over things with your aunt and uncle."

"Yeah, that was smart," Jonah agreed. Despite the new information, he still felt the same about his decision.

Besides, he'd given the Protector's Ring to the Alliance and was fine with Mandara and the others fetching the Destiny Medallion. "There's still a lot for me to learn at camp and," Jonah hesitated, not wanting to sound weak. "I just want to spend time with my new friends."

"Excellent." Marcus smiled and checked his watch. "I'm sure the Campmaster's grown restless. I'd better go."

"Wait." Jonah moved closer while lowering his voice. "So what happens next?"

Marcus gazed down the pathway. "The Council will decide the next move now that we have the Destiny Medallion's location."

Jonah's eyes widened, and for a split second he almost asked if he could attend the meeting. After his previous experience at Headquarters, though, he changed his mind. "You'll let me know what the Council decides, right?"

Marcus nodded. "Of course. You deserve to know." He held Jonah's gaze. "No matter what you think, the Campmaster and the Alliance Council are impressed with you and the others."

"Thanks," Jonah said. When his godfather checked his watch, Jonah held out a hand.

Instead of shaking hands, Marcus pulled Jonah into a one-armed hug. "Omar would kill me if I left you with just a goodbye handshake." He released Jonah. "Enjoy the rest of camp."

"I will." Happy and satisfied, Jonah watched his godfather stride down the path. As he hurried to class, one truth dominated his thoughts.

My parents would have been proud of me.

CHAPTER FORTY-THREE
IMPROMPTU COUNCIL MEETING

Am I in trouble? Jonah wondered.

He accompanied Thomas to the top level of Alliance HQ. The lack of information bothered Jonah as much as the Council summons, interrupting his evening free time.

The only consolation was Kevin had also received a summons. Yet as soon as they had arrived at HQ, Kevin went off with Mitchell to a confidential meeting. Jonah had enough experience to know the Fallen Reapers were on a mission. Was his summons connected to that?

Exiting the elevator on the Alliance Council's level, he followed the young mage to the opposite side of the floor and the entrance. A sign with the words *Alliance Council Offices* in large silver letters stretched along the curved faux-stone wall.

No sooner had they stepped inside the department, than the receptionist motioned them to a couple of seats. "Wait there." The woman went back to her work.

As they waited, Jonah became aware this was his first time alone with Thomas. A burning question surfaced, one that had irritated him since meeting Jennifer.

"Can I ask you a question?"

Thomas stirred. "Sure."

"Why does everyone let Jennifer get away with attacking me and breaking the rules?" His face warmed, remembering his detentions.

Jonah thought he saw a ghost of a smile on Thomas's face. But it was gone in seconds, replaced by the mage's apparent struggle to find an answer.

Though Thomas never turned to Jonah, his eyes darted back and forth as if he sifted through data only he could see. Finally, the young mage said, "You don't know everything that's happening, Jonah."

"I get that." Jonah leaned forward, wringing his hands. He knew the limits of an oath when he heard it. "Did I ever say thank you for saving us?"

"You don't have to thank me for doing my job." Thomas seemed embarrassed. He blew out a breath and stood to address the receptionist. "We'll be in the conference room. Please, let me know when the Council's ready." The woman nodded and watched them as Thomas led a confused Jonah to a side room.

The room was a regular conference room with a long table and chairs. The normality surprised Jonah, given they were in the Alliance HQ. The door sealed itself with an audible hiss, letting him know the place was soundproof. Even so, Thomas lifted his right hand and muttered a spell. A slight distortion appeared in the air, creating a translucent dome around them.

The spell's effect—cutting out sounds within the room—awed Jonah, and his jaw dropped. He'd never seen the mages do anything like this, revealing Thomas's skills.

The young mage lowered his head as if preparing to meditate. "What do you know about the search for Protectors?"

The change of subject surprised Jonah. He stood straighter. "Nothing. My godfather doesn't tell me anything about Council business."

"Did Mandara give you the assignment to solve the Tales?" When Jonah nodded, Thomas grunted. "Then I can tell you this without violating the oath. Mandara and Mitchell tested all your new friends with the ring, and all of them could activate it."

"What?" Jonah stammered. "Did they know? Why wouldn't anyone tell me?"

"Well, in most cases, Mandara tested the interns in ways they wouldn't notice. And all your friends were given an oath not to talk about certain things revealed to them. Although I think AJ might have figured it out."

Jonah couldn't believe it. "Wait. Did Kevin know?" Jonah asked, fearing his boyfriend had hidden something so important.

"No. Neither does your godfather." Thomas had lowered his voice. "I only know because a couple of mages also passed the test."

Jonah's jaw dropped. "Who?"

"Alex and Jennifer," Thomas whispered.

Jonah's perception of everything tilted sideways. His first emotion was anger. How could the Alliance let Jennifer touch the ring? But as he thought about the Protectors in the Tales, the devices chose the person, not the other way around. That meant Jennifer could be a Protector! Still, his annoyance with the girl persisted.

"But, Jennifer's a—"

"Jonah," Thomas warned. A little impatience had entered the mage's voice. "Haven't you noticed Jennifer came to camp when she didn't have to attend? She's learning and developing like everyone else. Someday, she may be part of the Alliance. So Mandara felt I should know about her ring test."

"And nobody thinks Jennifer figured it out anyway?" Jonah sucked in a breath. "Maybe Deyanira knows, and that's why she worked with her!"

The idea didn't seem to bother Thomas. "All the more reason for Jennifer to attend the camp where we can monitor her."

Though shocked, Jonah got it, and a calm certainty replaced his feeling of unfairness. It made sense the Alliance wanted to keep Jennifer close.

Thomas must have sensed Jonah finally understood and nodded.

The new revelation prompted Jonah to review every word and encounter with Jennifer. Her taunts and jealousy made a certain sense now. It was a lot to process, so he paced back and forth, remaining quiet until a rap came at the door. Thomas removed his spell and opened the door to reveal the receptionist outside.

"The Council's ready. They're in the Hearing Room."

Thomas escorted Jonah out of the office and down an inner hallway. When they reached two large wooden doors at the end of the passage, Thomas opened one and stood back for Jonah to enter first.

The room had a long, curved table on a raised section of the floor at the front. Facing the table were at least ten rows of tiered seats.

"Stand in the center," Thomas whispered.

Not only was the center area the lowest spot in the Hearing Room, but that put Jonah under a literal spotlight. He followed instructions and moved into the hot seat as he saw it. Thomas chose a spot where he could stand in the shadows at the far-left end of the room.

Jonah stood alone, facing nine adults, all with serious expressions. The three mages sat on his far right in their royal blue tunics. Marcus, who nodded to Jonah, Mandara with a perpetual frown, and a short woman with large, curious eyes were on the far left. Jonah blinked and focused on the center three chairs where Sterne, Bertonneau, and Thomas's mom sat.

Sterne's rich voice carried an air of command as he spoke. "Fallen Reaper Mandara told us you solved the location of the Destiny Medallion. On behalf of the Alliance Council, I want to thank you for all of your hard work."

Jonah met his godfather's eyes, and Marcus smiled briefly.

Mandara leaned forward in his chair and steepled his hands under his chin. His stare was as penetrating as ever. "We called you to hear the Council's decision on the Destiny Medallion."

At Mandara's words, Jonah's intimidation disappeared. Was the Council really going to share information with him?

"So I guess the Alliance is going after it, right?" Jonah feared they hesitated to respond because he had talked without permission. Again, he felt bolder, maybe because he and Mike had achieved something their archivists couldn't do. "That's why you wanted me to find the medallion. It's important."

Trueblood, who had been quiet, finally spoke. "We agree with you, Jonah. The Destiny Medallion is important."

"And yes, we will mount a mission to retrieve it," Mage Rubio interjected, "even though the device is in the Underworld."

"Given our enemy's recent activities and certain security concerns," Mandara continued, "some of us argued that we should hold off." An edge had entered his voice as he finished.

Jonah couldn't believe it. "But you'll need the medallion, just like the Protector's Ring."

Trueblood's mouth twitched. "That's the issue, Jonah. You don't know this, but our efforts to find an individual, besides yourself, who can wield the ring hasn't been a total success."

"It's been a failure," Thomas's mom blurted out. Her eyes narrowed at Jonah as if she blamed him. "If the individuals aren't allowed to use the rings, what good are they to the Alliance?"

Although Jonah knew his friends had passed the Protector's Ring test, he was on the verge of saying he would wear it again and the Destiny Medallion if it came to that; but he caught his godfather's expression and bit back his response.

Now, Jonah began to see the other side of the problem. "So you'll send a team in a month or a year?"

"No," Trueblood said, grinning. "We're sending a team this evening."

"Oh. Good." He met Mandara's gaze. "I'm glad." Everyone watched him as if they expected him to say something else. When Jonah remained quiet, a stir went around the room.

Rubio stroked his chin while appraising Jonah. Marcus's expression went thoughtful, letting Jonah know he'd surprised his godfather with his answer.

"Interesting," Trueblood said. "I told everyone you'd want to go with the team."

"And, as I told the Council, that will never happen," Marcus added, regarding Jonah with a bemused expression now.

Jonah smiled. "I'm okay with staying behind. I did what I had to do and discovered the location of the medallion." Jonah breathed, genuinely relaxing for the first time since entering the room. "I just want to hang out with my new friends and enjoy camp." When Thomas's mom looked away, and Rubio frowned, Jonah added, "Of course, I want to learn everything I can while at camp. That's why I'm here." He turned to his godfather and nodded. "I'm cool. Honest."

Rubio sat forward. "In that case, Mr. Blackstone will have to take an oath not to reveal anything discussed in this meeting." He glanced down the table at Marcus, who returned a nod.

"Very well," Sterne said.

"Wait." Jonah raised his hands. "Who's going on the mission? Kevin and Mitchell?"

The Council members exchanged glances before Mandara answered, "We'd prefer to keep the team's composition confidential and ask you not to speculate about it with your friends."

While Jonah didn't like this, he knew inside that Kevin and Mitchell were going to the Underworld. He'd have to let AJ and Eddy speculate on their own, he guessed. "Alright," he muttered.

Thomas left his perch against the sidewall like someone had sent a silent signal. All the adults regarded Jonah with matching, somber expressions.

"Mr. Blackstone," Sterne said, "hold out your hand."

Jonah hesitated but followed the order as Thomas gripped him by the forearm.

"Do you promise to keep your solving the Tales and the mission details secret?"

"I do," Jonah said.

Faint lines of Angel script flared on their hands and forearms. After a few moments, the glowing symbols faded.

—

Despite a persistent concern for Kevin's mission, Jonah looked forward to an easy day until he spotted Trueblood in the main room.

The mage greeted everyone as usual, then motioned to Jonah. "I need a word with you." He headed down the east hallway to a conference room.

A knot formed in Jonah's stomach, and he couldn't avoid a gnawing dread as he followed the mage. Once inside the room, Trueblood performed the same spell Thomas had used in the conference room at HQ. The significance of the protection wasn't lost on Jonah and he prepared himself.

"That should keep our conversation private," Trueblood said. "Hold out your arm. I want to remove the oath so we can talk freely." Jonah stuck out his arm, which Trueblood gripped and began muttering under his breath. Thin lines flared for a second, then disappeared.

The mage sucked in a breath. "I'm sure you realized we used the Deliverer's Seal to send the team to the Underworld?"

"Yeah, I do," Jonah answered with a little apprehension. "What happened?"

"Well, we reopened it at the scheduled time this morning," Trueblood continued, "but the team didn't show or send a signal. I'm sorry to tell you this, but Mitchell and Kevin were part of the team."

Even with his suspicions about Kevin's absence, the mage's words still shocked Jonah. He sat hard in a chair, trying to get his mind around losing Kevin. "Maybe they're okay," Jonah weakly offered.

"The Alliance Guards on the team would have checked in if they were able," Trueblood countered. "Their batons can send a signal to another baton. The idea is similar to mages using the Alliance Symbol to signal each other."

Jonah whirled to gaze out the nearest window, trying to calm his racing heart. "What if they were pinned down and couldn't send the signal?"

"That's possible, Jonah, but the Council's prepared to assume the worst without the return signal. We believe the mole compromised our security to warn his Underworld allies, and they attacked our team."

"You make it sound like a suicide mission," Jonah accused, turning to peer at Trueblood. "Let me go to the Deliverer's Seal," he said. "Maybe I can sense Kevin or the others."

"We've had Fallen Reapers try that, Jonah." Trueblood's voice was firm and unlike his normal hopeful tone. "I said the Council is prepared to assume the worst, but they haven't given up yet. Like you, some believe the team is waiting for the enemy to give up and leave the doorway free. If something happened, we had an emergency plan. We'll open the doorway two more times, six hours apart."

"When's the next attempt?" Jonah asked.

"Late this afternoon," Trueblood said. "The final attempt will occur this evening. After that…" The mage didn't finish the comment.

"That sucks." Jonah shook his head. "How will the missing team know what time to show up? Time doesn't flow the same way there."

Trueblood lowered his voice despite the dome of silence in which they stood. "The Alliance created timepieces that can keep track of mortal time when taken into the Underworld or Afterworld."

Glancing down at his watch, Jonah asked, "So my watch can do the same thing?" When Trueblood nodded, Jonah held up his timepiece, amazed that his initial suspicion, that the extra dials could track other time rates, was correct. He just never imagined that involved the other realms. This news strengthened his desire to do something.

"I understand your willingness to help," Trueblood said, still watching his expression, "but we can't risk sending anyone else, particularly you."

Jonah couldn't accept the Council had given up on Kevin, Mitchell, and their team. "What about the Destiny Medallion? What if the Wraith King or Grim Reaper has it?"

Trueblood studied Jonah's face, searching his reaction. "You've shown us, Jonah, that only another Deliverer can fetch these devices. So it may be that Thera and her brother weren't able to get the medallion, even though they know the location."

"So," Jonah said, his worry making his answers terse. "We're gonna leave the medallion where it is?"

"The Destiny Medallion's been hidden for two thousand years," Trueblood continued. "It'll be safe for another day."

"That disrespects Kevin and Mitchell's sacrifice." Jonah realized he'd just assumed his boyfriend was dead.

"Jonah, please understand the problem. The mole found out the details of a protected Council decision."

The urgency in Trueblood's voice troubled Jonah. He paused, forcing his mind to focus on the matter instead of only stressing about Kevin. When he did so, the answer became obvious. "The Council members are worried about each other. They don't know who to trust."

"Not quite, but the matter's more serious than ever. Until we find the mole and arrange new security protocols, we don't dare send anyone else." He peered at Jonah. "That's the Council's final decision. I pray that Kevin and Mitchell respond. Believe me, I do, but everyone in the Alliance accepts the risks. I'm sorry."

With a wave of his hand, Trueblood released the spell. "Let the Council try its plan first." With that, he left the library.

Jonah slumped back in the chair with his mind in deep turmoil. *Kevin dead? Mitchell dead?* He wouldn't accept that!

When the conference room door opened, he expected Trueblood had returned and prepared to continue his argument. Instead, Darren, Monisha, Eddy, AJ, and Lisa all stepped into the room and closed the door.

They spread out in a semicircle facing him.

Darren crossed his muscular arms and glared down at Jonah. "What's going on?"

Thankful that Trueblood had removed the oath, Jonah didn't hesitate to tell the others what had happened. He needed to tell someone, or he'd go lose it.

He finished with, "I'm going to the Underworld, saving Kevin and the others, and getting the medallion."

No one even blinked in surprise.

Eddy seemed to speak for everyone when he said, "You're not going alone."

Darren tapped his chest. "Dang straight, you're not going alone. We're all Protectors."

"This is gonna be different from the fight in the woods," Jonah explained. "We're talking about the Wraiths' realm, a place that's a lot stranger than our world." Despite his impulse to argue, Jonah's voice grew sure and confident as the daring plan developed in his mind. "And just so you know, only your soul can cross into the Underworld."

"We get that," AJ said. "And we want to go anyway."

Rising to his feet, Jonah searched each face, seeing determination in some and a little uncertainty in others.

Regardless of their personal feelings, they had all agreed, as Protectors, even without knowing it, to offer their help to save others. Plus, they had fought the KIN and survived. They were Protectors and they were ready. It was time they did something bold.

John Darr is a native of the state of Georgia. As a graduate of Columbus State University with a B.A. in Communications, and with work on his M.F.A. degree at Howard University in Washington, D.C., John has over twenty years of experience as an author, screenwriter, independent filmmaker, an educational television producer, screenwriter teacher, and technology specialist. His current projects include two YA Urban Fantasy book series; The Jonah Blackstone and Forest Heights series. He's currently working on a third adult Fantasy/Science Fiction series, Omega Quest Chronicles, as well as completing the screenplay adaption of the first Jonah Blackstone book, The Protector's Ring. Visit him online at www.johndarrbooks. com.

GLOSSARY OF CHARACTERS

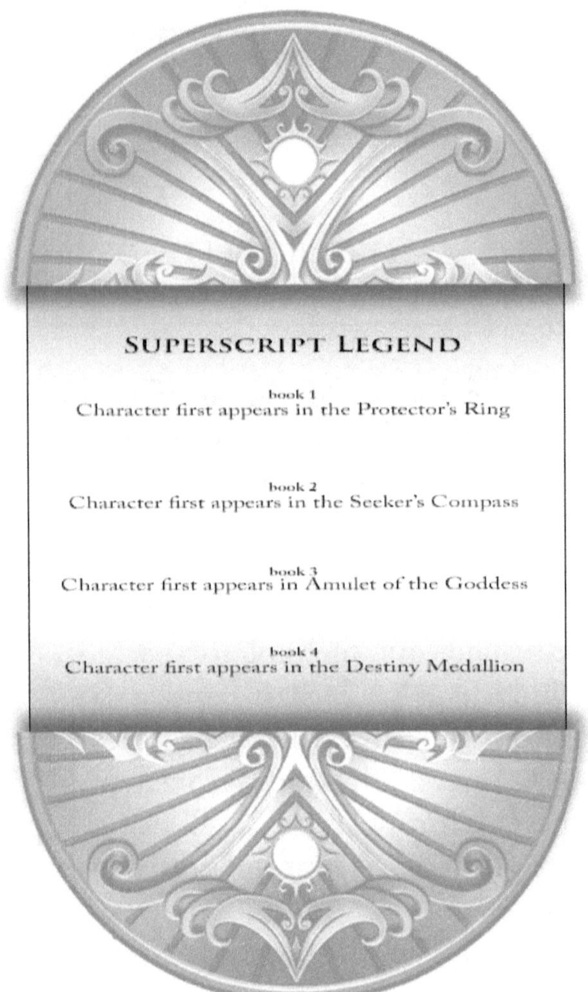

GLOSSARY OF CHARACTERS

MAIN CHARACTERS

Jonah Blackstone (Deliverer) is a half-Reaper born from the union of a fallen Reaper (Isiah Blackstone) and gifted mortal (Janice Blackstone.)[book 1]

Lynn Hightower (Gifted Mortal) is Jonah's cousin, Robert's twin. Her Sight grants her powerful intuition. Naturally proficient with a Reaper weapon. [book 1]

Robert Hightower (Gifted Mortal) is Jonah's other cousin and twin of Lynn. The twins keep their unique mental link a secret. His clairvoyance is displayed through his artwork. [book 1]

Wick Jean-Baptiste (Mage) is the twins' best friend. He's a gifted Firecaster earning him his nickname. Amazed by his abilities, the Alliance envisions him becoming a full mage. [book 1]

Mike Littleton (Seeker) is Jonah's best friend and all-around nerd. Mike serves as Jonah's Seeker after a mind boost. They're the only two who can activate the Compass. [book 1]

Kevin Brown (Fallen Reaper) is an Alliance member initially assigned to protect Jonah. However, after becoming connected to Jonah and sharing a deepening, mutual affection for one another, his assignment changed. [book 1]

Marcus Armstrong (Fallen Reaper) is an Alliance Council member and Jonah's godfather. After taking the blood oath his allegiance is to protect Jonah at all costs. [book 1]

Symon Trueblood (Mage) is an Alliance Council member serving as a camp counselor and mentor. He was best friend to Jonah's mom and is an energetic free spirit. However, beneath his eccentric exterior is a powerful and keen mage who only uses his power as a last resort. [book 2]

Deyanira (Reaper) in the mortal realm, she's Nira Bledsole, a bookstore owner and clever sorceress. However, in the Reaper World, she is Grim's most loyal subordinate. [book 1]

SECONDARY CHARACTERS

Cedric "Blackstone" Mandara (Fallen Reaper) serves as Camp Master and is an Alliance Council Member. He believes a Fallen Reaper's first job is to attack the enemy and that they shouldn't engage in distracting mortal pursuits. [book 4]

Mitchell Hama (Fallen Reaper) works for the Alliance as an expert in occult studies, history and practices. [book 4]

Alastor (Fallen Reaper) is an Alliance member and Mandara's assistant. [book 3]

Thera Rasmussen (Reaper – Twin) is a member of the Grim Reaper's inner circle. She is an occult expert. [book 4]

Fabian Rasmussen (Reaper – Twin) is a member of the Grim Reaper's inner circle. [book 1]

Serena (Memory Charmer) – Camp Mentor & Alliance member. [book 3]

Aunt Ruby (Gifted Human) is Jonah's aunt on his mother's side. Always jealous of her sister, Janice Blackstone, Ruby sought a deal with the Wraiths to become a powerful Seer. [book 1]

Omar (Gifted Human) is Marcus' partner and a Memory Charmer. He was a close friend to Jonah's mom. [book 1]

Brandon Warner (Mortal) is the local rich kid and bully. He is secretly jealous of Jonah. [book 1]

Antwan Motombu (Mortal) is Brandon's buddy and a fellow bully. [book 1]

Eleanor Trueblood (Mage) is a Native American Mage and Symon's sister. [book 1]

MOUNT VERNON SOCIAL CLUB MEMBERS

Danita Jackson (Mortal.) With everything she experiences after joining Jonah's club, she remain skeptical of the supernatural world. [book 2]

Lorraine (Mortal) is Danita's best friend and club member. Unlike Danita, she believes in the supernatural realm and truly supports Jonah. [book 1]

Anthony (Mortal.) Even though he spends far too much time trying to impress Jonah, he's become a trusted friend to Jonah after joining the club. He's also Danita's boyfriend. [book 1]

Rodney (Mortal) is a musician and a member of the club. Like Lorraine (his girlfriend), Rodney believes in the supernatural and likes helping Jonah. [book 1]

Margaret Bertonneau (Gifted Mortal, Memory Charmer) is Council CoChair and a Moderate. She comes from a long line of Creole Memory Charmers and developed the training protocols for all memory charmers. book 4

Ambrose Sterne (Mortal) is Council CoChair and a Centrist. As a former Judge, Sterne is the voice of reason on the council. He is also a self-taught supernatural historian. book 4

Daniel Rubio (Mage) represents the Council Hardliners. His military background underscores his desire to take the offensive to the enemy. book 2

Albrecht (Mage) is a Council Centrist, but often supports Marcus. Field work is a chore for Albrecht because he prefers the comfort of a classroom and the solitude of the his magical potions. book 2

Stella Pledge (Mortal) is a Council Hardliner and Thomas' mother. She passionately believes that gifted or magical individuals have a responsibility to use their gifts to overthrow the villains. book 4

Cynthia Ramirez (Fallen Reaper) considers herslef a Council Centrist. She works hard to be fair on the Council because she believes blind loyalty to one view leads to tragedy. book 4

Darren (Gifted Mortal.) His muscular density and extraordinary strength often overshadow his high level of creativity. With a love for the arts such as, painting, sculpting, casting and molding, he fears that others see him physically as nothing more than another Alliance Guard like his father. book 4

Lisa (Gifted Mortal) has control over levitation and gravity fields. Lisa's loyal to the Alliance and is fascinated with fallen reapers. She's also skilled at getting others to work together and is often the voice of reason with the other kids. book 4

AJ (Gifted Mortal) is a talented musician and Pyromancer. His insatiable desire to learn is only matched by his love of reading. Jonah has become his greatest mystery and new found source of knowledge. book 4

Eddy (Gifted Mortal.) Primarily responsible for bringing Jonah into the group, Eddy can manifest lightning. His demeanor is easygoing. He's always open to meeting new people and is a team player. book 4

Monisha (Gifted Mortal.) Whatever Monisha puts her mind to, she gives nothing less than a 100%, whether in sports, music, academics, or her telekinesis. Even though she has readily accepted the supernatural world, her expectations push Jonah to prove himself continually. book 4

Thomas Pledge (Mage & Memory Charmer) is an Alliance member and mage mentor. He's one of the youngest people ever to obtain rank as a full mage and a memory charmer. [book 2]

Jennifer (Mage – Sorceress in training) is Antwan's cousin. She comes from a long line of women who had magic and mystic abilities. She's stronger at charms and hexes than the other young mages. [book 3]

Alex (Mage) a young mage with a strong talent for powerful casts like lightning or fire. However, subtle spells still elude him. [book 4]

Vanay (Mage) is an graceful and talented young Indian mage. He excels at casting magical projections. [book 4]

Marvin (Mage) is a talkative, friendly young mage. He comes from a large southern family who don't know anything about his magical abilities. [book 4]

Beraki (Mage) is Crosby's best friend and a confident mage. Unlike the out-going Crosby, Beraki doesn't want to be noticed. [book 4]

Crosby (Mage) is a smart, nerdy, and confident kid, particularly when it comes to magic. [book 4]

ADDITIONAL CHARACTERS

James Hightowers (Gifted) is Jonah's Uncle. He's Janice Blackstone's older brother and has a bit of the Sight, though not as strong as his sister. He knows about Jonah's power and Robert and Lynn's abilities but keeps it from his wife. [book 1]

Imma (Imogene) Hightowers (Mortal) is Jonah's Aunt. She's a creative woman and becomes a second mom to Jonah. Little did she know that her art piece would become the center of attention of the Supernatural world. [book 1]

Rex Montgomery (Fallen Reaper) is an Alliance member. He's loyal to Marcus and believes Jonah is the Deliverer and will restore the balance. [book 2]

Rico (Mortal) is Lynn's boyfriend. He joined the Practice Club to score points with Lynn, but it turned out he had natural ability with defensive weapons. [book 1]

Tamara (Mortal) is Wick's girlfriend. She's used to magic and the supernatural because her grandmother is a priestess from Barbados. She's also has the potential to wear a medallion. [book 1]

Mr. Hackett (Mortal) is Mike's uncle. Hackett has experience with the supernatural world and has written books on the subject. He also owns Hackett's Book Emporium where Mike sometimes work. [book 1]

OTHER BOOKS BY JOHN DARR

Jonah Blackstone Series
Book One: The Protector's Ring
Book Two: The Seeker's Compass
Book Three: Amulet of the Goddess

Forest Heights Series
Book One: My Prince, My Boy
Book Two: Satyr's Melody